FLARE

SCORCHED EARTH SERIES: BOOK TWO

FLARE

SANDRA MACEK

TURNER, OREGON

To Parker and Rebecca, the best of my creations.

THE RECKONING CALL

January 4, 2108
Earth

In the darkest hour, when human destruction of the natural world reached its zenith and all the mistakes of the past became irreversible, the Creator spoke. The Divine's voice reached into the mind of every soul upon Old Earth. To them the Creator said,

This land you have destroyed, I made for you.
Face now the great cleansing of your greed.
All children conceived yesterday will be my New Order.
They will lead this world as I reshape it.
Females all, they shall be revered and protected.
I have touched their minds, and they shall bear my mark.
They will hear my voice while you cannot.
Keep them safe, for they shall be the last human-born for forty years.
No other human conception shall occur, natural or through science.
Humankind shall shrink to near extinction for my hand to remake.
From these chosen few, a new race shall emerge, join with you, and flourish.
They will be legion.

This is the Call. Blessed be the words of our Creator.

1
EDDIE

Current year: 2701
Monday, 7:30 AM
New Juneau

Sometimes it feels like time is repeating itself—a melodic dal segno in the song of my life. Edelweiss's Requiem in D minor…. Eh, what a drama queen I am. But the repetition isn't my imagination.

I stood on these very steps not long ago, with these same people, expecting this same train. That was at the very beginning of our first mission, when Mercy still wanted to bury her head in books, before we knew SciCorps had kidnapped her parents and were targeting other leaders, before we knew anything at all about the Spheran civilization in Chileru, or about the possibility of civil war.

How could so much have changed and yet still seem the same? I'm not the same person I was a few months ago, but I *look* the same. I think I was even wearing the same skirt. Is it like that? Same on the surface, but really not beneath?

"I'm having déjà vu."

My best friend Mercy shifts next to me. "No, this is totally different than last time."

"What do you mean? It's exactly like last time."

"No, this time there are no Terrans."

I search the crowd and realize that she's right. This isn't a protest with two opposing sides, ours and theirs…this is a Pilgrim *rally*. We're the only Terrans here.

"There's us." Mercy's husband Van echoes my thoughts as he pounds a fist against his Terran insignia—a round pin in the shape of a perfect Earth. I realize for the first time how much he stands out. He's not just a gigantic sapiens among a crowd of petite praenex humans, he's also in uniform. His Terran Army Corps tans might offer camouflage on the dry flats of Scorch, but at a Pilgrim rally where most of the citizens are dressed overwhelmingly in SciCorps black, not so much.

"Right!" Mercy agrees.

They haven't been married long, but they're already doing that united-front thing. I peer around the low hood of my solar jacket to see if she's joking, but instead she's wearing her determined face.

She nods to me. "At least this time we have Van."

A fresh chant goes up on the far side of the crowd. *"Birthright, take flight…True sight, take flight…Our fight, take flight…Take flight!"*

I sigh. "That's getting old."

"I like the rhyme," Mercy says.

"Aye, this is bushels of fun. I especially like the part where all the glarin' Pilgrims are blockin' our way into the station." Van motions to the rally crowd clogging the steps above us.

"Don't worry about them." I raise my hand to the shoulder of Mercy's father, Councilmember Dr. Parker Adams.

Dr. Adams squints into the sun; his eyes are lavender slits as he scans the crowd of demonstrators. Even he seems surprised.

I wish I'd spent an extra hour in prayer this morning; I think I'm going to need my faith. "Well, Councilmember, should we play it like last time?"

He nods. "Just like last time. Friends!" Dr. Adams spreads his arms wide as he strides toward the Pilgrims clustered to our left.

"It's Councilmember Adams!" someone shouts. The crowd's attention swings our way.

"God's grace on you all!" Dr. Adams steps to the side, drawing them slightly away from me, Mercy, and Van. "Come and tell me your concerns. Or perhaps we can talk about the promise of my ozone replenishment research. I always have time for a chat with you good citizens."

I'm glad I'm incognito, but the stiff hood of my jacket limits my field of vision. It captures the scene around me like images on a domed video screen, so I use my telepathic skills to listen as well. So far, no one's really interested in us, they're focused on Dr. Adams now. That's good. Since our last mission to rescue him from SciCorps, we've had much more attention than I'd like.

"Dr. Adams!" A tall Pilgrim with a microphone pushes through the crowd. "Dr. Adams, why aren't you rebutting the social media post suggesting that your visit to the Hub was a kidnapping?"

Mercy's father puffs up his chest and waits a moment before answering and I know he's using his unique mental gift to sense the correct path forward. "Information about those events is still being processed within our legal system. As a Councilmember, it would be inappropriate for me to discuss it, but I will say that a serious crime was committed by SciCorps and is being investigated."

The crowd reacts with grumbles and a few shouts. I sense escalating hostility.

"But you're here, and you look fine," the Pilgrim with the microphone continues. "If the information is secret, why allow your daughter and her friends to spin these lies about Pilgrims?"

Mercy's father opens his hands in front of him, a gesture of patience like he's going to try to explain. "I—"

"Traitorous daughter!" someone shouts, cutting off his reply.

"Liars!" Another demonstrator screams. Others shout and raise their fists.

Close around us, the attention shifts to Van and Mercy.

"That's Mercy Adams, there!" a Pilgrim nearby says.

"Out of the way!" someone shouts behind me.

People start to jostle us and I pull on Dr. Adams's sleeve. "We need to leave now."

His brows are furrowed in confusion, but he nods.

The jostling eases a bit as a group of SciCorps soldiers in their crisp black uniforms cross in front of us, approaching the Pilgrim with the microphone. I'm about to start toward the station when a familiar figure follows their group. The soldier stops abruptly and slowly turns to face me. All the little bells inside my head ring *danger*.

"Naveen." Van's voice is a dangerous rumble at my side.

I stare at Caesar Naveen, our old friend-turned-enemy.

A black bruise along one cheekbone mars their deep mocha skin and they hold their arm in a sling across their chest, but their purple irises show no sign of fear, no pain. Their eyes flit to Van— the enormous sapiens who gave them those wounds—and quickly back to me.

I raise my chin and squeeze my eyes to slits, daring them to take us on. Maybe it wasn't extra prayer time I should've been wishing for; maybe what I needed today was an extra hour of martial arts practice.

"Commander!" their friend calls.

Naveen holds my gaze. They wait a second and then, without any change in expression, turn to follow their friend.

"That was close," Mercy says.

"We're not done yet, Cricket. Van, we need to get her out of here." Even though Mercy is tiny, I know she can defend herself. But she hates confrontation, and I don't want to see her harassed.

"Aye, let's move." Van pulls Mercy into the shelter of his arms.

I focus my energy on the noisy crowd blocking the steps to the train station. Some people are still concentrating intently on Mercy and I don't like the tone of their thoughts. I use my training to conjure what I need deep within my mind and then I mentally hold it, mold it, and push it out through my nova gem and into the crowd.

Separate.

It's like a whisper that carries the strength of a shout. It rasps through my mind, compressing into a sharp command squeezed through the funnel connecting my novitas lobe to the black gem of skin on my forehead. It explodes out of me like a gush of thought, searing the praenex around me with my will.

Separate.

Mercy draws a quick breath and starts to back away. Van catches her.

"Nah, not you now, Cricket." Van's lilting Irish voice is soothing and I know he'll keep her close. "A wee bit of warnin' would be nice, princess."

Sapiens. How nice it would be if I could influence them too. I ignore him.

Separate. I repeat my command.

The people nearby fall silent. They move confusedly away from me and each other. A path begins to open, and I think we're going to be fine, just when a loud shout comes from the crowd.

"Witch!"

I barely have time to turn before something hard hits my head.

"Hey!" Van shouts.

"Witch! She's controlling you! All of you," a soldier shouts at the startled crowd. "Resist! Don't be her puppets!"

I brush my hood, causing it to fall back from my head. There's a collective gasp from the onlookers, but I'm focused on something else. My hand comes away from my hood sticky and slimy with…egg. I grimace and try to shake it off.

"It's Bozan LeRoux!"

"Bozan!"

I look up just as another egg connects with my head, this time, smashing my temple and ear. "Agh!" I brush at the mess, but all I manage to do is free half of my hair from the elastic band holding it. I'm standing in the full Alaskan sun now with my albino skin and lilac eyes gleaming in contrast against the field of darkly garbed Pilgrims all around me, several long tendrils of my white hair whip through the air like smoke. Just the kind of attention I was hoping to avoid. Already a barrage of thoughts accosts my mind.

I throw up my mental shield, growl, and grit my teeth. I'm so embarrassed and I'm getting mad too. Egg? No one has ever disrespected me like this. Ever. I'm a bozan of the Legion. I'm the daughter of two of the most powerful diplomats on the planet. I'm Eddie LeRoux, for God's grace, don't they realize what that means?

An eerie quiet has settled over the crowd as they stare at me, yellow yolk running down my neck, onto my collar, and across my own insignia—a pin depicting my neutrality. I look down to see the image of the rocket ship superimposed over the planet as it's smeared by sticky egg. My gem is humming, so I'm sure anger is rolling off me in waves now, but I don't really care. I turn my attention to the egg thrower and see the soldier with their arm pulled back, ready for another throw.

"No!" Naveen grabs the man with their good hand. "Put that down now, private. That's an order."

The soldier pauses, then lowers their arm.

The crowd takes a collective breath.

"Witch!" The soldier shouts again, before whipping their arm around and sending the egg flying toward my friend.

I act on reflex, jumping in front of Mercy to take the hit square in the chest. The egg splatters on everyone in range.

Van roars. "Oh, aye, ye're gonna pay for that one now. Ye almost hit my wife!" He takes a menacing stride forward.

"Van, stop!" Dr. Adams raises his arms. "That's enough."

Everyone's focused on them now. No one seems to notice that I'm quaking where I stand. I've completely lost the grip on my temper. The fury running through me pushes my blood like a screaming crescendo up my neck and onto my cheeks. I'm no albino now; I'm a red-hot brand. The thought takes shape deep in my mind. I mold it into a weapon fueled by my rage and expel it out through my gem.

Danger! Run! Run away now!

No one resists. In seconds, people are screaming and running away in all directions.

"I gotcha, lass. You, too, Papa Adams." Van has an arm around Mercy's waist and Dr. Adams's hand in his. He looks over his shoulder at me. "Aye, this is craic, but I'd say that's enough now, Eddie, if ye don't mind."

I ignore him.

"Eddie!" Van elbows me.

Mercy claws frantically at his arm around her waist, trying hard to run away. Dr. Adams has stretched as far away from me as Van's tight grasp will allow.

"Oh." I shake myself and let the command fade away like an echoing note in the wind. "I'm sorry."

"It's fine now." Van hugs Mercy to him and nods to Dr. Adams. They're both wide-eyed and quiet.

"I'm okay." Mercy steps away from Van's protective arms. "Are you okay, Papa?"

"Of course." Dr. Adams shakes himself and stands taller. "Of course. Good work," he tells me, nodding. "Let's go."

I know this stunt is going to get me in trouble, but right now, I can't seem to care about anything except my friends.

Van turns Mercy and Dr. Adams up the steps. I'm glad they recover quickly; they're getting used to my unusual talent. It helps assuage my guilt over catching them in the crossfire.

I brush a large gob of egg off my chest and I follow my friends, gingerly holding my skirts so as not to cover them with more goo. A shell crunches under my shoe and I glance over my shoulder at the deserted street.

Caesar Naveen stands alone where the Pilgrims had been. They lift their chin and straighten when I meet their eyes. Again, I have the sensation of déjà vu. For the second time, they alone resisted my command. They are the *caesura* in my requiem—the abrupt stop before the music resumes—and I wonder when next our paths will cross.

Then another idea strikes me—this might be *their* gift. How odd that in all the time we spent together in the years that they were friends with my brother—my friend too, if I'm being honest—I never noticed it before. If they were an acolyte in the Legion, I could help them explore it, develop it. But no, our paths are very different now.

"Come on then, Eddie," Van shouts at me.

I race to catch up. "Mercy." I clutch my friend's hand. "Dr. Adams. I'm so sorry!"

"Oh, hush. We're fine, and that was really something to experience." Mercy's father brushes bits of eggshell from his sleeve. "You're getting stronger all the time. It's very impressive."

"Well, now, I wouldn't go that far." Van puffs out his chest as we step inside the station. "Yer mind control still doesn't work on me."

"And it never will, sapiens. You don't have a novitas lobe for me to influence."

"Oh, but I agree with Papa," Mercy says. "You were truly

impressive. And your skin was terrifyingly pink, like you might burst into flames. You would have looked even more fierce if…"

"If what, Cricket?" We're inside the station now, and I nod to a passing acquaintance.

They hesitate before nodding back and scurrying away.

I'm starting to feel more myself again. I take a slow breath as my composure returns.

"Oh, um, never mind," Mercy stutters.

"I don't want to be fierce anyway."

"Well that's good then because…" Mercy stops again.

We're at the platform now. I wave to a child sitting on the old bench that Mercy and I used to frequent.

They gaze back at me transfixed and slowly point a tiny finger at me. Their parent whispers something to them and gently reaches out to fold down the pointing finger.

I'm starting to get an odd feeling that something isn't right. I open my shields a sliver and hear confusing thoughts directed at me. "What, Cricket? What were you saying?"

"Oh, nothing."

"Good, because I don't want anyone to fear me, not really."

She shrugs. "I don't think there's any worry about that right now."

A laugh escapes me. "Because I'm no longer bright pink?"

"No, because you have half of an egg stuck to your ear."

Rill O'Brien

In the past...
Feb. 4, 2637, 64 years ago
Subterranean Severe Weather Research Station 21A, North
America

Rill clung to the metal door jamb and tried again to look away from the broken, sobbing figure of his mam as his da shushed her and guided her into their basement room. His da whispered something and then shut the door, which shook the flimsy wall he'd erected to give them privacy. The cement ceiling was an open mess of duct work, conduits, and technology so Rill could still hear the horrible keening sound his mam made. It made all the hair on Rill's arms stand on end.

His da turned and hurried over to Rill, motioning him back into his bedroom. "Mam's just having a good cry."

Rill knew what crying was, and it didn't sound at all like what his mam was doing. Rill cried when he got hurt, but that didn't count cuz he couldn't help it. Sometimes he cried when he was angry. He even secretly cried when he couldn't do something he wanted to do. He hid that kind of crying, burrowing deep into some cold crevice of their subterranean compound, cuz that kind of crying was for babies.

He peeked around the door jamb one more time before his da pulled him into his room and shut the door. "That's not cryin', Da."

"Sure 'tis. Now let's just give yer mam a few minutes to herself."

"When's she gonna finish?"

"In a wee bit, Skipper." His da sat on the bunk next to him and wrapped an arm around him. Rill felt better right away. His da's arm was big and strong. Rill shifted to lean into his da's side, closing his eyes a minute to block out the overhead light. His da smelled of engine oil and dust. The scent soothed him.

His da sighed. "She just needs some time to come to grips is all."

"With what?"

"Well, ye know that communications array we've all been workin' on? The one in the west side junction?"

Rill nodded. "Sherman says west side's a goner. Fixin' anything west side's like pissin' into the storm."

His da strangled a laugh. "Yeah, well, it's true, but don't let yer mam hear ye talkin' like that. Anyway, Sherman went out to try to fix that array…."

Rill looked up at his da when he stopped talking. His da's face was all scrunched up and his Adam's apple was moving like crazy. "Did he fix it, Da?"

His da shook his head. "Eh…storm caught him, best we can tell, with the junction box open. Storm took everything, Rill. Every damn thing."

Rill tried to rub away the awful pressure in his neck. He thought about Sherman, about the way his eyes changed when Rill made him laugh, or how his voice got higher when he and Jameson fixed something really hard. Sherman was teaching Jameson, and Rill too, everything he knew about tunnels. Everybody in the station was a scientist, but Rill's da said Sherman was a special kind. What his da meant exactly, Rill didn't know; all the grown-ups seemed special. But he knew for sure he'd miss Sherman—his science lessons, his funny way of humming when he worked, his happy eyes.

"Sherman always said we'd get outta here one day, that we just needed to science the piss outta it."

His da laughed, but it sounded like choking. "Aye, he did say that, Skipper. He did."

Sherman's quarters were right next to theirs. Sometimes Rill could hear him playing the harmonica or cursing at a piece of tech he was fixing. Would Sherman's room be empty now like the room on the other side? Cold and still, another dead place in their buried world below the great storm?

Rill didn't want to cry. He focused on the flashing lights and gentle hum of the air purifier over his bunk. When it cycled off, he heard a familiar squeak and looked down at his feet. There was Sweets, his little white mouse with the black foot. He picked him up gently and stroked his soft back.

"Why'd he go out there, Da, when he said only an eejit would? Why'd Sherman go out there and get swept up?"

"Well now, Rill, it's been over six years since we last had a transmission from outside. We finished the software upgrade, but it didn't help. The hardware on the array was our last hope."

"Yeah, but why'd *Sherman* have to go? He didn't want anybody goin' topside. He said we had everythin' we needed down here to get out once and for all. Why'd *he* have to go if he didn't wanna?"

His da patted his shoulder. "Cuz it was his duty, son. Just like it would've been my duty if it'd been my turn on the roster. We gotta share everything here, right? Like we share the food and the chores. We gotta share the hard things, too. The risks. Ye understand?"

Rill nodded. "Nothin's mine, nothin's yers, everythin's ours, good or bad."

"Right. That's our code—*our troubles and our joys.*"

"Then how come I don't have hard things to do?"

His da laughed again. "Ye will. Sooner than ye think probably. Ye just need more schoolin'."

"More people would make the work easier, right Da? Mam says many hands make light work."

"Sure and that's the truth."

"Then how come you and Mam don't have more babies? I heard ye talkin'. If had some brothers, we could all help."

"Ye sneakin' in on grown-up time?" His da gave him a stern look.

"No, sir. You were in the kitchen. I heard Mam say…" Rill swallowed hard, unsure whether he would get himself in trouble for telling what he heard.

"What did ye hear her say, Rill?"

Rill lifted his hand and rubbed noses with Sweets before sliding the mouse back into his shirt pocket. He was afraid that if he said what he'd heard it would make it true. "I heard Mam say she wished I'd never been born."

His da went very still. It seemed like a million years before Rill felt his da slouch next to him and take a deep breath. "She didn't mean that like ye think, Rill. We love ye to the moon and back, ye know that. She only meant that now we can't know if anyone will ever come for us here…that you'll be alone some time long from now, after yer mam and I pass on. If no one comes to find us."

"If I had a baby brother, I wouldn't have to be alone. Even a baby sister would be fine."

His da reached over and pet Sweets's little head where it stuck out of Rill's pocket. "I'll try to explain it, Skipper, but it ain't easy. Let's see…. If ye knew that ye could do something to make yerself happy, but it would hurt yer mam or me, could ye do it?"

Rill thought for a long time. "I don't think I could even do it if it hurt Sweets." He looked up into his da's face. "I don't wanna hurt nobody."

His da nodded. "We don't either. Ye see, if we had another baby, it'd make us happy, and it'd make you happy, but it'd mean another person may be stuck here alone…never being able to leave here. See, we didn't know this would happen when we had you, Rill. Yer mam and I, we knew the Farms had plans for three more expeditions after ours. Those folks were already in trainin'. Yer mam and I came here after the last crew never reported back. We'd assumed that they made it but had issues with communications."

"Sherman's crew, Da?"

"No." His da shook his head. "The crew after Sherman's, Rill. We dunno what happened to the lot of 'em, but after yer mam and

I got here, we realized they'd been lost."

"What happened to the crews after ye?"

His da stood but left a hand resting on his shoulder. "We dunno what happened to them either, Skipper. Some think the storm took 'em. Yer mam and I hope they never came—that they figured out the danger after they didn't hear from us either."

Rill sat quietly for a minute, thinking about what his da had told him. He thought about the crew that no one knew and the ones they planned, and about Sherman. "Are we gonna have a funeral, Da?"

"We are, son. We are."

"I'm gonna have to be at all of 'em, aren't I?"

"What d'ye mean?"

"All the funerals. Yers and Mam's…the others'. I'm gonna be at all of 'em cuz I'm the youngest."

His da didn't say anything. When Rill looked up at him, he saw his da's Adam's apple jumping around again.

Finally, his da just squeezed Rill's shoulder. "I best see to Mam, now. Ye stay here with Sweets."

When his da opened the door, Rill could hear the strangled keening noise still coming from his parents' room. He wondered how long his mam would cry and wondered if it was okay for him to cry too.

2
Eddie

Current year: 2701
Monday, 8:00 AM
The Legion Enclave, New Juneau

I never really thought about sitting at this judicial bench; Councilmember Edelweiss LeRoux was never the title I aspired to. *Orchestrator*, maybe. *Concertmaster*, definitely. Yet here I am, viewing this chamber not as a performer, my true talent, but as one of thirteen politicos. Of all the labels our society wants to pin on me, *politician* may be my least favorite. I'm a public servant now thanks to the fluid and sometimes fickle social media election process of Scorch.

More surprising though, are the two empty chairs to my left—normally filled by my parents. I always thought that I'd be happier as an adult—more recognition, more freedom, more music—but as it turns out, it's just a lot more work. A lot more roles. The empty chairs are part of that.

My mother, SciCorps Fleet Admiral Pèlerine Reine LeRoux, refused to attend the hearing. Today my father, Admiral Yuri LeRoux, sits in the chair across the room reserved for the accused.

Add to that that I have bits of dried egg in my hair.

You could say I've had better days.

My mind wanders into the chords of my latest composition and I startle when Sibling Rumesa rings the bell calling us to order. "I hereby open this Council session." They set the bell aside and steeple their fingers in front of them. "As our first order of business today, I call a vote on the measure to make this a closed hearing. All those in favor?"

I flinch at the chorus of "ayes" from the councilmembers around me. It's not the kind of chorus I'm used to, not perfect blends of soprano, alto, tenor, and bass, but rather the flat and guttural sound of democracy.

Rumesa waits only a moment. "All those opposed?"

"Nay." My father and I answer in perfect unison. A chill passes across my flesh as I look at him—his voice, distanced from the council bench, is a disembodied sound. His silver-lilac eyes stare back at me, unmoved.

Rumesa clears their throat. "Let the record show that the measure passes with seven votes in favor, four abstaining, and two against."

That's two *LeRouxs* against—me and my father, and one LeRoux abstaining, my mother. Though my reasons to vote against a secret hearing are opposite of theirs, it clearly looks like a family alliance. As with everything in my life, I'll have to fight to set myself apart from my parents' powerful politics. Being a *LeRoux* is a label I can't avoid.

"In accordance with a closed hearing, citizens assigned roles in today's proceedings may remain, along with any Advisory

Committee members present; however, I must ask all others to please leave the chamber. We hereby secure and seal all recordings."

People start to leave—some reluctantly. A few stop at my father's chair, touch his shoulder, or speak quietly to him. He nods and whispers responses. I'm not the only one watching. The enigmatic Ambassador Cairo Varela focuses on my father. I've seen that look in the Ambassador's eyes before, and I'm pretty sure it means he's reading minds. As if to confirm my suspicion, he cuts his gaze to me.

Over the last weeks of our acquaintance, I've begun to suspect that he too wants something from me. His scrutiny is uncomfortable and he seems confused at times, like I've surprised him in some way, which makes no sense at all because I'm nothing to him. Still, I sometimes get the feeling that he wants to label me in some very unusual and very specific ways.

I look away. My anxiety is rising, and with it, I know that my albino skin will be leaning toward translucent. My friends will worry when they see me sitting here with blue veins popping out all over my face, winding up into my white-blonde hair. I focus on my training, try to control my stress through a meditation. As I reach for the Creator, my mind expands. *I am more than the gray matter inside my skull. I am a bright light, a little piece of the Divine, and I am not defined by this moment.* I reach and reach. I settle into reaching and eventually a sense of calm returns.

In a few moments, the audience has dwindled to a few dozen members of the Advisory Council—the top-rated citizens of Scorch. Most are politicians and scientists, but a few military officers and several Couvies, the archaic praenex from Vancouver

Colony, also remain.

Rumesa waves at the soldiers guarding the doors, and they immediately key in the locking codes. "Let the record show that the room and communications are secure, and the closed session of the Council is ready to begin—"

"—the *first* closed session," I interrupt.

Rumesa looks at me. For a second, it's a battle of wills, and then their expression changes from frustration to resignation. "As you say, *Bozan* LeRoux."

I understand their emphasis on my title—their role as acting *Gran* Bozan is my doing. That title and all the power that goes with it is mine whenever I have the courage to take it. Gran Bozan Li passed the title to me recently in the last, fraught moments of her life. Moments that I fear history will one day say were the prelude to a civil war. A war with victims like Mercy's parents. A war with many preludes, like the anticipation of the Nina's return after nearly six hundred years on a secret deep space mission. Or the discovery of a secret society in Chileru in South America. Secrets, secrets. This hearing today, my title, my parents' maneuvering—it all seems insignificant in comparison.

"Dr. Mercy Adams, please proceed," Rumesa motions to my best friend.

Only weeks ago I never would have imagined Mercy fitting in here with this group of leaders, and while I can still picture her with her long straight hair hanging loose over a pile of books in some library cubicle, she's also confident and alert here. Though tiny in stature, she's gained a sense of presence and embraced her position among the most influential people on the planet. As a bona fide hero, she didn't have much choice, I suppose.

Standing up from her chair in the front row, Mercy clears her throat and approaches the makeshift witness booth.

I don't envy her job facilitating today, but in a society devoid of crime, attorneys are hard to come by. And as it turns out, her transition from historian to diplomat seems to fit. It might not be what she wants to do, but we've all made sacrifices, stretched our limits. At least we're surrounded by friends—this ramshackle bunch of us forged in the fire of civil war. We may be an incongruous group, but we're a team.

Mercy clears her throat again, then takes a breath. "Ambassador Varela, how would you characterize the time you spent in the Hub after your abduction from New Juneau Station?"

Ambassador Cairo Varela—Cai, as he wants to be called—seems to be searching for the right words. Having only recently adopted the English language, I suspect he's reading the minds around him to find just the right nuance. God knows he's read mine enough. As the recently arrived representative of a secret society, he's more than a little mysterious, even after our numerous interactions.

Mysterious? I grimace at my own ridiculousness. I don't find him mysterious. Those dark purple eyes are just eyes, after all. His curly brown hair and olive skin are probably commonplace in his homeland. The black gem glistening between his eyes, the nova that connects to his brain's novitas lobe, is like mine or any other praenex's. For all I know, his appearance could take hours in front of a mirror. Perhaps that's it, perhaps that's why he stands out in this room of normal, pragmatic people. Perhaps—

Too late, I realize that I'm staring right at him.

The corner of his mouth turns up and I know he's fighting a grin. I quickly glance away, knowing he heard my speculations. My teeth grind as I fight a blush that would turn my albino face a clownish pink. I'll never learn to live with other telepaths. I liked it better when we were few. These Spherans will change everything by knowing too much. I already feel like he's maneuvering me, probably in more ways than I realize.

"Ambassador?" Mercy sways sideways to temporarily interrupt my line of sight to Cai. Smart friend.

"Apologies, can you repeat the question, please?"

"I asked how you would characterize the time you spent in the Hub after your abduction from New Juneau Station?"

Cai sniffs, then looks around the room. "It was *captivity*, largely peaceful, but captivity all the same." His eyes settle on my father, who looks away.

"Were you mistreated?"

Cai inhales deeply through his nose. His piercing gaze, unwaveringly fixed on my father, seems to sharpen even more. "We were drugged with some kind of depressant meant to keep us calm and manageable."

Mercy makes a note on her tablet. "They injected you?"

Cai shakes his head. "No, it was in the food or the water, maybe both. I realized this after the first meal because your father, Dr. Parker Adams, began acting strangely."

"Strange how?"

"Friendly, content, increasingly happy. I noticed then that my own anxiety had decreased as well. Not as much as Parker's, but I felt different. Less angry. I realized that they had tampered with the meal. I hadn't eaten much—your food is still strange to me."

Mercy opens her mouth to speak, but Cai waves her aside, reading the next question in her mind before she asks it.

I huff out a breath and he smirks. Mind reading is very rude.

"Then they brought us work. Parker was only too happy to comply with their fascinating scientific puzzles, and I saw no reason to alert them to my less than controlled state. We continued like that until the rescue team arrived."

Mercy nods. "Did you see Admiral LeRoux during your captivity?"

"No." Cai shakes his head and looks again at my father. "I didn't see him until the rescue, but I knew he was there, that he was in charge of the operation."

"How did you know that?"

Cai refocuses on Mercy, and I sense her discomfort, know the unsettling feeling his dark purple irises evoke. "Our keepers constantly repeated his name in their minds. They, all of them, were almost obsessively focused on the name LeRoux." He slants a quick glance at me, then turns back to Mercy. "It seems a name of some power in your world."

A chill runs down my spine. I glance at my father—his white hair and sharp nose a perfect mold for my brother, his younger version—but he locks his gaze straight ahead. I let my eyes scan the small audience. When I find my twin TJ among them, his eyes meet mine and I know he understands how much we have at stake, we LeRouxs.

Cai suddenly stands. His eyes are on me again, but I resist the urge to meet them.

Mercy takes a step back, surprised. "I have no further questions at this time."

Cai steps away from the stool and gives her a short bow.

Mercy hesitates, then bows back. "Thank you, Ambassador."

Cai strides away and sits in a nearby chair.

Mercy watches him. "You can have a seat…." She turns back to the bench. "If it pleases the Council, I would like to call Admiral Yuri LeRoux to the stand."

Sibling Rumesa nods. "Proceed."

My father stands, tugs his uniform jacket into place, and glides past me toward the booth. He's graceful in an aloof, condescending sort of way. He's tall for a praenex and, like me, just shy of skinny. The severity of his features only adds to his aura of authority, but I begin to see the years pressing on him in the sinking skin of his cheeks and the dark shadows around his eyes.

Sheriff Arson Henderson, my father's self-appointed guard, untangles his long limbs and stands to follow him across the room. Arson's sauntering gait reminds me of a cat, smooth and strong. He's older than the rest of us, mid-thirties maybe. He's a character out of time, the closest thing to a cowboy the Verge could produce. Since Mercy's obsession with history recently extended to the Old West, we've all been subjected to anecdotes from that period, down to the hat she procured for Arson—a wide-brimmed, cream-colored creation he seems never to be without. He chooses a place near the booth to lean back and watch, ready to act, but seemingly at rest. He doesn't fool me.

My father pretends not to notice his new, somewhat-menacing

shadow, as he rounds the booth and shifts onto the stool. Once seated, he crosses his legs and scans the crowd, pausing on my brother's face, and then pausing even longer on mine.

What I see in his expression surprises me—frustration, impatience, yes, but also pride and vindication—as if I'm exactly where I should be. Where everyone expects me to be. But I've always been more interested in independence than power, or more specifically, the kind of power that would allow me to set my own path, build my own destiny. I thought joining the Legion a few years ago, against my parents' wishes, would do that for me, but it only took weeks before the same old path opened wide before me. The path here…the path to the Council.

I look down at the desk and realize I've mangled my temporary name card into a curled paper mess. I quickly scrape up the bits and shove them into one of my many skirt pockets. Hands in my lap, I close my eyes and take a deep breath. A familiar thread of anger flares inside me and I tamp it down. I'm tempted to play out a melody in my mind, my fingers itch for a keyboard or a flute, but I know I'll fall too deeply into musical meditation to stay engaged here. I can't risk that kind of relief.

The click of a finger snap to my right startles me. I turn my head toward the sound and meet General Dixie Henderson's intense stare. She nods toward the floor where she's extended her hand toward me out of sight of any others. I hesitate, then reach for it.

Large, rough, and wrinkled with age, her hand closes firmly around mine. Her tan skin contrasts with my albino fingers—we're so different, our friendship so new. Only weeks ago I wouldn't have trusted her—to touch her would've been out of the question—but now the pulse of energy infuses me with comfort. Her Terran insignia of the Earth glints in the overhead light, sparking like fire.

I look into her eyes, brave and sure, the gem between them blending perfectly with her skin like any Couvie—and hear her voice clearly in my mind.

This is but a moment in time. By divine grace, this too will pass.

I try to smile, but I'm pretty sure it looks more like a grimace. As I pull my hand away, Mercy clears her throat and moves toward the booth where my father now sits.

Before she can swear him in, he turns to the bench and addresses all of us. "I have no intention of answering any questions today, regardless of how innocently you couch them."

What follows, I can only describe as painful. Poor Mercy. No matter how nicely she asks, no matter how simple the question, my father maintains his stony silence.

Finally, Sibling Rumesa stirs. "Admiral?" They lean toward him.

He slowly turns his angry eyes to them. "Bozan?" he replies, mimicking their exasperated tone. He should have called them *Gran Bozan*. His failure to use their new title is deliberate, like every other move he makes.

Sibling Rumesa inhales through their nose. I wait to see what tack they'll take. "You realize that by refusing to answer, you give us cause to retain you here while we arrange a formal trial. Is that what you want?"

One corner of my father's mouth quirks up, but he quickly pulls his bland expression back into place. Glancing down he brushes a bit of imaginary fuzz from the sleeve of his dark uniform, adjusts his Pilgrim's rocket ship insignia. The silence is just becoming awkward when he looks up, directly at me.

"Hold me, send me home—no matter to the cause."

Staring back into his sharp eyes, it suddenly hits me. I suck in a breath and straighten. I'm not the only one. I lurch to my feet. TJ and Cai have the same reaction.

The name LeRoux… Cai said *the name LeRoux* was constantly on the soldiers' minds. *Mother! Of course she's pulling the strings! Why didn't I see it before?*

I break away from my father's stare to look at TJ. My brother shakes his head just enough for me to understand—we'll keep this revelation a secret for now. The silence in the room finally reaches me. I look around to see that everyone is staring at me, holding their breath.

I clear my throat. "Excuse me." I pass a shaky hand behind my legs to smooth my skirts and sit. Looking down at my lap, I realize I've completely shredded the trim on my jacket. I smooth out my hem with both hands and search for calm. I've been so focused on the stand I hadn't noticed the other thoughts clamoring at my mind, the looks directed my way, the doubts, the expectation that I'm going to explode. When I open my mind further, the thoughts of the people around me hit me in a full-on rush. I brace my hands flat on the desk and struggle to suppress them as an officer leads my father from the stand.

He pauses directly in front of me, our faces level, and then he closes an icy hand over mine. I jump, and barely stifle my gasp.

Arson slides up right behind him and curls a hand around my

father's forearm, ready to pull him away if I give the word. "Easy now," Arson drawls.

I shake my head. "It's fine." I look into my father's eyes, so familiar and yet so new, like I'm finally seeing the real him. The gem between his eyes gleams dark and healthy against pale skin. No creeping outline of white to indicate the onset of disease. I shift my hand around to grasp his like I've done a thousand times. But I'm no child now. I hold his hand and wait.

My father's chin lifts. "You belong in that chair." He nods toward the seat occupied by Sibling Rumesa. He pitches his voice low. "You are a LeRoux, made to rule, not to waffle. Be who you are or don't be. Be Gran Bozan or don't be. But end this ridiculous indecision." He squeezes my hand, then walks on, back straight, steps sure.

"Mayor." He nods to Dixie as he passes. He calls her by her civilian title, not General, her Terran Army Corps title. He hesitates, and then turns back to her. "I must say I enjoyed your little…*comment dirais-je…sédition* a few weeks ago. A lovely speech. And the loom! *Bon!*" He gives one sharp clap that has half the room jumping. "What an achievement for your ragtag little settlement. Quite a crowd of followers. You know how to inspire your troops. 'We are Terrans!'" His grin is predatory as he raises a fist in mock enthusiasm. "As if anyone could mistake what you and your *classe populaire* really are. "

I wait for her reaction, but she simply straightens. "*Monsieur LeRoux.*" She greets him in perfectly accented French before switching back to English. "You must give my regards to your wife when you next see her, your *Pèlerine Reine*. She lives up to her name, I believe."

He smiles, all teeth. "Of course."

"I do hope that she is handling your…*separation* well. These kinds of situations can put such stress on a family, a marriage. *D'accord, Amiral?*"

My father sniffs. "My wife and I always support one another, the family, though we do occasionally disagree on…minor points."

"I'm glad to hear your commitment to family, especially since my granddaughter's betrothal to your son will soon make our families much closer."

He turns back to me then. "I haven't had a proper introduction to your future sister-in-law, my dear. What do you think of this Couvie woman who's caught your brother's eye?"

I lift my chin. "She's the best of us, by far, sir. My brother…our family…has the better half of the bargain."

His eyes narrow and he presses his lips together, and I realize that he was counting on me not liking Mayhem Forge.

He sniffs and nods toward Rumesa's seat again. "As I said, that seat is yours; you need only sit in it." He arches a brow before stepping away.

Arson tugs the brim of his hat as he passes, first to me, then to his mother, Dixie, as he leads my father out of the council chamber.

I mumble something, but my thoughts are on my father's words. It's been weeks since the Gran Bozan named me her successor. Weeks since I watched them carry her cold, bloody corpse from the tether carriage where she'd shielded my friends from the deadly bullets of my father's troops. Weeks since the red sash, smeared with the blood of people I love, came to rest in my pocket. Weeks passed, but I can't force myself to sit in her chair, can't take the role she bestowed upon me. Not yet. Maybe not ever. But the pressure is always there, pressing…pressing…

"Wait!" Mercy scrambles up beside us. "My mother?" She's asking Sibling Rumesa, but her focus is on me. The weight she carries echoes across the room, doubled by her father. They are incomplete, desperate.

I turn again to my father, but the door is closing on Arson's back as he leads my father back to his room. I turn to Rumesa. "Your Grace, please. Where is Mercy's mother, and why haven't they released her?"

A loud thrumming noise outside interrupts my question. It sounds like rolling thunder. It's getting louder by the second and has captured everyone's attention now. It's far too close to the council chamber deep within the enclave. Something must be going on. I stand, vaguely note that others have as well.

The room is completely still as the percussive sound of helicopter blades buffet the ceiling. Bright lights stream through the skylights overhead. My brother TJ leaps out from his row in the audience. "Everybody out, now!"

But it's too late. A massive explosion rocks the foundation of our building. People scream and scramble away from the sound.

Through the madness, soldiers struggle against the crowd, trying to push in the direction of the explosion—the corridor down which my father just disappeared.

In a few long strides, I find myself among them—soldiers, police, Dixie, my brother and Mercy's husband, Van Elder—we all rush toward the sounds of battle. Before we can reach the door concealing the passageway, it's thrown open by Sheriff Arson. He looks at us in surprise, his chest heaving, his face covered in blood and dust. A line of blood trails down his arm and over his drawn stun gun. We pull up short.

"He's gone." Arson scans our faces, and then holsters his stunner. He takes a second to run a hand through his hair before reseating his hat. He shakes his head and utters a curse before turning to Dixie. "I'm sorry, *Maman.* The Admiral got away."

Rill O'Brien

In the past...
June 19, 2641, 60 years ago
Subterranean Severe Weather Research Station 21A, North
America

Rill burst through the door into the canteen, knowing that if he was too late, he'd get nothing but a ration bar. Hunger was like his shadow these days, always there and always growing. Sometimes he thought he could eat nonstop and never get full. Mam said it was just another growth spurt, but whatever it was, it was darn annoying.

"Sorry I'm late, Da. Are there any scrambled eggs left?" He wiped his hands on a rag hanging from the toolbelt Jameson'd given him for his last birthday.

"To the sink!" His da pointed across the big lab they'd converted to a dining room. "Wash those hands with soap before ye touch a thing."

Old Patrick looked up from his plate and thumped a fist on the stainless-steel table. "You comin' in from the farm, lad?"

"Aye. I was just spendin' some time with Galadriel." Rill put his basket of eggs down next to the sink while he washed up. "Then

I got to thinkin' about her unusual feathers and just meant to look it up quick in the database, ye know."

His da paused with a fork on the way to his mouth. "Time run away with ye?"

"Like a racehorse." Rill rushed to the food counter to fill a plate, proudly kicking aside the small stool he used to need to reach the platters.

"What were ye lookin' up then?" his da asked when he slid onto the stool next to him at the table.

"I'm tryin' to figure out why Galadriel has black and white mixed in her tail feathers. It's different than the other hens."

Old Patrick shifted back in his chair. "She's part Wyandottes, like Earp, that bugger of a rooster."

His da nodded. "She's mostly Easter Egger—you can tell by those pretty blue eggs—"

Old Patrick raised his fork. "And the fact she lets ye fuss over her. We had more Wyandottes years back…mean birds, ye ask me. I know Aoife would agree with me—smart woman of yers."

"Sure as she would, my Aoife. Anyhow, all our birds are mixed Heritage birds now, Rill. That'll make 'em live a lot longer, and be happier, too. Nicer."

Old Patrick huffed. "I remember chicken dinners for my birthday back in the Farms. We should raise more chickens for meat instead of eggs."

"I don't like chicken meat. It's tough," Rill complained.

His da laughed. "That's cuz you've only ever eaten old birds that stopped layin'." He gave a sideways glance at Old Patrick. "Better for the environment to eat the eggs instead of the birds anyhow.”

"You sound just like them praenex now, Seamus, but back on the Farms we ate meat, and not just chicken. Aye, what I wouldn't give for a wee bit of real beef steak." Old Patrick squeezed his eyes shut, and Rill almost giggled at the funny, wrinkled face he made. "I guess I won't be waitin' long now. Gertie's gettin' older."

Rill frowned. Gertie was one of his favorite milking cows. Before Rill could ask what Old Patrick meant, Rill's da spoke up.

"Wish we could get more time outta her."

Old Patrick huffed. "Ten years is a long time for milkin'. Ye should be thankin' the Almighty for the meds that stretched it that long."

"Still, we only got about five more heifers in our future. Never expected to need an endless breeding program here."

"Oh, fine. Ye done the math then. I'm a meteorologist, not a farmer. Never meant to spend my life down here learnin' every damn thing about, well, every damn thing." Old Patrick grumbled something under his breath and went back to eating.

Rill cleared his throat. "What's he talkin' about Da? What's Gertie gettin' old have to do with eatin' beef steak?"

His da looked at him like he did sometimes when he wasn't sure if Rill could handle the truth.

"Ye can tell me. I'm not a baby."

"No, Skipper, ye're not. Well, when a cow stops givin' milk, she goes to slaughter just like the chickens who stop layin'. Last time ye were too wee to remember, but it's the best thing for our resources."

Rill thought about Gertie's big gentle eyes and how careful she was when she took a treat out of Rill's hand, her soft lips kissing his palm. "I don't think I can eat Gertie, Da."

His da closed his eyes and blew a breath slowly out of his nose. When he opened his eyes, Rill didn't like what he saw. It wasn't often that his da lost his temper, but when he did, Rill didn't want to be around.

Instead of speaking to Rill, his da turned to Old Patrick. "Does everything have to be so damn mean here?"

"Now Seamus—"

"Don't ye *now Seamus* me! Can't my boy be a boy for awhile? Does every damn thing need to be about survival?"

Old Patrick pushed back his stool. "Shelterin' him won't help a damn thing. Everything *is* about survival, and he'll have to be better at it than the rest of us."

Rill's da slammed his fists on the table making all the dishes jump. "Ye shut yer mouth now old man—"

"Hey, hey!"

Rill turned to the voice behind him and sighed with relief.

Jameson stood just inside the door wiping his hands on a rag hanging from his own elaborate toolbelt. "What's this all about then?"

"Nothin'," Old Patrick said.

"Everything!" Rill's da shouted at the same time.

Jameson looked at the two men for a long moment. "Well, that explains it."

He pulled his loupe down out of his hair and let it hang around his neck. "Mornin' young Rill."

"Mornin', Jam." It was a nickname only Rill was allowed to

use. He'd been calling his idol "Jam" since he was a toddler and couldn't say the whole long name.

"How'd you like to come on back to the hangar and take a juke at the schematics I've been working on today?"

Rill looked from his da to Old Patrick where they stared at each other over the table, then up to Jameson. "The plans for our escape ship?"

"Yes, that's the one."

Rill's da sank back down to his stool and rested his head in his hands. "Boy's gonna get whiplash goin' from harsh realities to hopeless fantasies that fast like."

Jameson walked over to Rill's da and put a hand on his shoulder. "How's the AI unit coming along, my friend? Did the parts I fashioned work out?"

"I'm still workin' on it."

Jameson picked a small potato off Rill's da's plate and popped it in his mouth. "Well, even if they don't, sure feels good creating something folks need, you know?"

Rill's da took a deep breath, picked up his fork and went back to eating. "Course ye're right," he said around a mouthful of food. "He can take an hour, but then it's back to chores."

Jameson smiled and snatched one more potato.

Rill's da slapped at his hand. "Get yer own plate, ye eejit."

"Ye wanna eat first, Jam?" Rill asked before quickly shoving more food in his mouth.

"To eat, perchance to dream," Jameson sing-songed as he filled a plate.

Old Patrick got up and bussed his empty dish to the sink. "Ye can keep yer Shakespeare. I still wanna a steak, I tell ye."

Rill relaxed. "Do the praenex eat meat, Da?"

"No, but some of them are pescatarians."

Old Patrick came back to the table with tea. "They swim like fish, too, those praenex. Greater lung capacity…"

Rill turned back to his da. "Mam says that if Old Earth'd switched to mostly vegetarian a long time ago, then maybe we wouldn't have ruined the planet so fast. Maybe we would've been able to save it instead of the Creator sending the praenex to the rescue."

"It sure woulda helped, son. It sure woulda helped."

Rill thought about it. "I can live without meat, but I think I'd like to meet a praenex someday, Da. I think we'd have a lot to talk about."

"Oh,   yeah?"

"Yeah. I think they'd like the station. I think they'd like what we do to make our environment better. Do ye think so, Jam?"

Jameson pulled up a stool and set down his plate. His toolbelt jangled and settled around him like a noisy skirt. "I think you're right, kid. I think they would."

"I have a feelin' they'll come here someday. I really do."

"I hope ye're right, son, cuz if anyone can figure a way out of here, it's those praenex."

"Well, now," Jameson pointed his fork at Rill's da. "There's plenty I can teach our young engineer here. He won't have to wait for the praenex to save us. Besides, when I play mechanic, I like to have more interesting company than my old self."

Rill nodded and hurried to shove the last of his meal into his mouth. He liked reading and watching vids, but the learning he liked the most was from his friends and family.

He liked people more than any other thing, even more than his mouse Sweets. And if he focused really hard and didn't worry about the future, he could pretend that he made Jameson and his mam and da proud by building an escape ship one day. And when he did, they'd all meet the praenex and he'd never be alone.

3
Cai

Current year: 2701
Monday, 10:30 AM
The Legion Enclave, New Juneau

It's been a trying morning. When I close my eyes and sink into this familiar pilot's seat, I can almost smell the spicy dust of El Misti, of home. I allow myself a single moment to indulge in the memory of the view from my apartment high above the desert. I miss my city. I miss my steady and disciplined telepathic people, and I'm grateful, as I send a prayer to the Creator, for the relative silence that the Agulha 3 brings me.

Ping…ping.

I think a command to Fofa before I remember that my trusty robot is not with me. I squeeze the bridge of my nose and sit up.

"Identify caller."

"Secretary Ilorin is calling on a secure channel."

"Accept call."

My friend's image hovers in the air in front of me. I clear my throat. "Divine grace—"

"Are you hiding in your plane?" she laughs.

"How could you possibly know that?" Blue-rimmed sunglasses cover Ilorin's blind eyes today. Fine gold swirls decorate the temples before they disappear into her mass of dark hair.

"The computer shared your location. What are you doing there? Why aren't you in the Enclave?"

I exhale slowly. "I like the quiet here."

"Did you not say the Legionnaires were more careful with their thoughts than other citizens?"

"Careful, yes, but still not very controlled. It's like listening to a hiss of gas constantly leaking from a faulty valve. I should be grateful, I suppose, that they're used to being around empaths. At least they keep most of their emotions in check. But their lack of discipline… Anyway, it's been a difficult morning, so here I am." I spread my arms to encompass the cockpit of the Agulha 3, my pride and joy.

"I heard about the admiral, I'm sorry."

"Me too. More than sorry. It's frustrating. Given time, I'm sure he would have leaked some useful information about their plans— the location of Mercy Adams's mother even, but now we'll never know." I tap a fist on the arm of my chair.

"Don't you think you're overreacting? You've said it before: their internal disputes have nothing to do with us."

"I know that, but this means a lot to her—"

"To her? To Mercy Adams you mean?"

I catch myself before I correct my friend. That's who I *should* mean. "Yes, of course. Who else could I mean?"

Ilorin cocks her head to the side. "I thought perhaps you meant Bozan LeRoux. Are you sure about her?"

"Am I sure that she's the *Tesouro Branco* of our legends? Yes, or the closest thing to it we'll ever see. It makes everything more complicated."

"How so?"

I push a hand back through my hair, unsure how to describe Eddie in a way that Ilorin will understand. "She's, I don't know…stubborn, willful, commanding of attention, yet not wanting it. She bristles at labels; I'm afraid to assign another one to her. Afraid she'll resist just to avoid raising expectations. I have to tread lightly."

"Hmmm. Are you still feeling that odd connection with her?"

Sometimes I don't know why I tell my friend everything. "I don't want to talk about that, Ilorin. Hold on…"

I watch a group of guards exit the hangar building. Their leader points in several directions, sending people everywhere except toward my area of the tarmac. I'm glad Gran Bozan Rumesa Kahinu agreed to keep the existence of my cloaked jet a secret. The cordoned-off section of concrete that separates my plane from the rest of the area has worked to deter prying eyes, providing me with a welcome haven these last few days. I owe the GB for that.

"Is everything alright?"

"Yes, fine." I relax back in my seat. "But I still don't want to talk about Bozan LeRoux."

My friend hesitates and I'm relieved when she doesn't press me.

"Okay, but then explain to me why helping them find Mercy Adams's mother is suddenly so important to you?"

"They saved my life, Ilorin."

"Well." Ilorin shrugs. "I don't agree with SciCorps' methods, of course, but did you really feel that your *life* was in danger?"

I sigh. "No, but they drugged me, if you recall. My perspective may have been somewhat skewed. Aside from the rescue, we're going to be asking a lot of them, as you know. I would've liked to have something more to offer in return."

"Speaking of asking, when are you meeting with the Council?"

I check the time. "Ugh, right now actually. I have to hurry, especially if I want to speak with Bozan LeRoux first." I lever myself out of my seat.

"You need to hurry in more ways than one, I'm afraid."

"Why?"

Ilorin's mouth pinches into a flat line. "I'm sorry, Cai, but Giza's taken a turn for the worse."

"No." My knees bend as if struck from behind and I sit down hard in my chair. "How much time do I have?"

Ilorin shakes her head. "The doctors can't say for sure…a few weeks, a month or so? They're keeping her comfortable and she's not alone. I'll visit her myself as often as I can, I promise."

"Thank you."

"We'll be here for her. All of us. Focus on your mission, but…do hurry if you can."

Ilorin takes off her glasses and I stare into her familiar violet eyes. I let her confidence and calm wash over me for just a moment, before standing again. "Thank you, my friend. May the Creator bless you."

"The Creator's hand in yours, Ambassador."

I end the call and look out the canopy dome to the stark gray stone of the Enclave. Mt. Juneau looms so tall overhead, it almost seems to lean protectively forward. The colors here are deep and alive—green of every shade surrounded by blue skies and cerulean sea. I long for the rusty soil and red-black shadows of the desert, for the rugged vista that spreads south of my home, for the ancient arms of El Misti where she rises at my back to embrace my city.

A life is ending there, far away in Chileru. Brilliant Giza, on whom my every childhood memory centers. Beautiful Giza, my life's partner—*former* partner, though I still struggle to think of her that way. Gentle Giza, my best friend always.

There's nothing I can do to save her, but my mission could save many others. So many others. I roll my shoulders and reach within for my resolve, my determination. It's waiting there like a banked fire. I think of my people, let their trusting faces wash through my mind, and then straighten my spine and turn back to my sacred path.

As if hearing my silent call, Eddie LeRoux steps out of a nearby door, her white skirts whipping like sails in the hot wind.

I scramble out of my plane and stride across the tarmac.

She turns sharply, suddenly aware of my approach from a seemingly empty patch of concrete. Her eyes narrow.

"God's grace, Bozan." I bow slightly.

"Ambassador." She scans my face. "Did you… Did you want to speak with me?"

I nod, not entirely surprised that she knew. Our odd connection continues to grow. I gently reach out with my thoughts, and for an instant I think she'll allow me in, but then her shields fly up and I pull back.

She humphs. "Did you want to *speak*, or are you simply going to pull my thoughts from my head without permission?"

"I apologize. Habit." I shrug. "I'm addressing the Council soon to ask for aid. While I have things I can offer in exchange for Terran assistance, there's one reason that we came here that I need to review with you personally."

"With me?"

"Yes."

She sighs. "Well, let's have it?"

I consider how to broach the subject of the unique defenses her blood has against the Trade, the disease killing my people in droves, but we're not even supposed to be aware of their research. At the same time, I can't surprise her with this, it's too big.

"You know that my people suffer from the Trade as well?"

She nods.

"I wonder… Can I show you?" I tap a finger to my temple.

Her eyes narrow and I think she's going to refuse, but then she lifts her shoulder. "Fine."

I close my eyes and conjure a memory of one of my hospital visits. Once I have it firmly in place, I reach out to her mind and find her shields parted just enough to allow me in. I progress slowly, sharing the image of the children gathered around me, some in wheelchairs, others sitting on cushions on the floor with oxygen tubing dangling from their noses to pool in their laps, each with only a tiny dot of black pigment remaining in their diseased gems. Their eyes are sad but attentive as I read to them.

I let the sorrow of the memory spread through our link—the hopelessness, the desperation I feel as a healer, a doctor, a leader. I can't save them, any of them.

When I open my eyes, Eddie's are wet and shiny. I track a fat tear as it rolls down her cheek.

"That—" I clear my throat. "That is how extinction begins. Fewer and fewer of our youth reach maturity. Regardless of an aggressive genetics approach, our generations shrink, our neighborhoods empty."

She swallows hard. "I'm so sorry."

"We know about your resistance to the Trade. It's why we came."

"You know?" She inhales sharply through her nose. "We are a sovereign state. You have no right to spy—"

"Rights?" I take a step forward. "You speak of rights, of secrets when you know what my people face, my friends?" I struggle to keep my temper. The connection between us pulls tight. We stare at each other for a moment.

Finally, she lifts her chin and steps back. "Forgive me. Of course you're right. If I were in your shoes, there's no limit... When will you talk to the Council?"

I roll my neck to release some of the tension gripping me. "Now, actually."

"I'm sure they'll share the research that you want."

I laugh. "It's not the *research* that we want."

"But you said..."

I shake my head. "We don't want data, we want you."

Vengeance Forge

Current year: 2701
Monday, 11:00 AM
Subterranean Severe Weather Research Station, North America

Vengeance Forge rolls his shoulders and settles more comfortably into his lab chair inside the Virtual Reality Theatre, his elaborate tool belt coiled within reach. He taps behind his ear to turn on the interlink before taking a deep breath. The lab smells of hot wires and cleaning chemicals, with an underlying scent of sweaty praenex. He's been working too long without a break.

"Computer, activate Paris simulation alpha ten."

After a short delay, the lights in the surrounding computer banks start to blink and fire to life. The projections begin from the outer edges of the glass VRT box in which he sits and work their way in, so that Vengi feels as if he's being swallowed by the emerging train car. The heavy plastic seats with their dingy rainbow fabric and steel supports surround him. The color-coded map rises above them and the familiar buzz sounds as the doors slide shut.

He is there, on the Paris Metro Line 1 traveling toward La

Défense. He inhales the fragrant oils and dust of the train, the human scents of cologne and sweat and coffee, and just a trace of garbage nearby. It's morning in Paris, and the car is filling up. Yet all around him the sapiens are silent, except for an occasional "*pardon*" as they jostle for position. Everyone dresses in black, the women with an occasional splash of color, the men with more subtle coordinating shades. No one makes eye contact, and no one looks his way.

Across from him sits one of his favorite Parisians. The man is not young or old, but somewhere in between. A few gray hairs blend from his temples back into a head of neatly styled dark brown hair. The skin between his dark eyebrows is smooth—no gleaming gem above his long, bony nose—and his eyes, when he looks to the side, are a mix of green and brown, like the forest. He wears a multicolored, jewel-toned scarf of soft, woven wool in a loop around his neck and he's reading a book—a real book, made from paper and ink. In fact, almost everyone is reading on the train. The people are calm, but purposeful, as if they do this every day and know that very little variation will occur from the time they leave their door, until they reach the office.

"*Charles de Gaulle - Étoile.*" Vengi settles back and smiles to himself as the familiar female voice announces the stop and the train slows. With a lurch, the doors open. A few people step off, but many more enter, moving confidently, but not hurriedly, as far into the car as possible. Vengi pulls in his feet and sits up straighter to let them pass. A group of teenagers enters last, and this is the part that Vengi loves.

They're louder than the adults, speaking in whispers

punctuated by an occasional laugh. And they're dressed in layers of clothing that look well-worn but have a put-together quality. They don't match each other, and yet they belong together. He listens to their heavily accented French, loving the way they lose half their consonants, yet understand each other so easily. These are Parisian teenagers on a school trip, and he feels his own excitement rising along with theirs.

The boy with the flirty lock of hair across their eyes slides into the empty seat next to him. Their lean muscles flex under fabric pulled tight across their thighs, and Vengi feels the warmth of their hip where it presses against his own. They continue their quiet discussion with their friends as the buzz sounds and the doors shut. Vengi closes his eyes and pretends, just for a minute, that he knows them, that he knows *anyone* his age, but when he opens his eyes, he feels the sadness looming just beyond this moment and knows he must stop.

"Computer, switch to simulation Finland beta 12."

Vengi watches as the projections change, bleeding in from the outside again.

Just before the new scene takes over completely, the man across the aisle looks up and meets Vengi's eyes. He raises one eyebrow. "*Ça va?*"

Vengi sucks in a breath, just as a set of glass doors replaces the image of the man. He's in the glass igloo now, in Finland, gazing out at a wide-open world of white. The new smell is crisp and clean and cool. He can feel his rem coming fast, so he bends down out of his chair, reaches for his sleeping bag and rolls onto his back. Above him, the stars of the northern sky compete for dominance against the green swirling fingers of the aurora borealis.

He knows he'll be in trouble for sleeping in the VRT—a wanton waste of energy—but he can't find a reason to care anymore. Old Rill will be mad, but he forgives easily. *Maman* won't mind either; she knows he needs a break. Besides, soon the station will be empty, they can afford a few extra watts.

Yawning, he carefully removes his father's old Couvie rings, smiling at the coils of yarn he uses to make them fit his smaller fingers. The rings aren't safe to sleep in, and they're also not very comfortable. Setting them aside, he rubs a hand up over his face, across the rough skin of his gem and pushes back his hair. Staring heavenward, he says a prayer and starts to count the stars—the only ones he's ever seen—before closing his eyes to dream.

It's only a matter of days now before his life will have purpose…meaning. The sleds are ready, all the rescue gear prepped for quick execution. His bags are packed, his mother's and the others', too. And he can feel them coming, whoever they are, just as clearly as he can feel the Creator's warmth inside his soul. They're coming, and they will change everything.

4
Eddie

"This feels ominous." I squeeze Mercy's hand as we move deeper into the Gran Bozan's office.

"I agree. I think we're living history at this point. Maybe even something as big as the Call." She returns my hand squeeze before holding up one finger to Van where he waits across the room.

"What do you remember learning about the Call?"

Mercy tips her head to the side. "Well, 600 years ago, when the devastation of the planet reached a tipping point, the Creator spoke to every human on Earth. It lasted one full day, repeating every hour."

"Homo sapiens lost their future."

She nods. "For forty years they'd have no children while a new sub-species took over their world—us, the praenex."

"It must have been terrifying."

"By all accounts, it was chaos. There were over a million suicides. Wars broke out everywhere. By the time that day ended, sapiens knew their days were numbered."

"They knew more than that; they knew God was real." I turn to face her. "Mercy, whatever happens next is going to get dangerous, even more than the mission to SATO Space Station to save your father. People could die."

"I know." Her eyes are glassy with unshed tears. "Violence can be devastating. In the first month after the Call, more than 400 million sapiens died violent deaths."

"God's grace, that's terrible." I glance around the room at all the motivated, angry leaders gathered together. My father's escape from custody has everyone questioning our strength against a force like SciCorps. "I can imagine it, here in this room with all the people of the Enclave around me. I hear their thoughts—frightened, but vengeful too."

Mercy nods. "I can still hear the chaos in the council chamber even here in Bozan Kahinu's office—the *GB's* office, I mean."

"My office, you mean to say."

She shakes her head. "Sorry. It *is* your office, but only if you want it. No pressure."

My office. I let the idea roll around in my head like a refrain. Since my recent promotion to Bozan, all my responsibilities here have changed; my apprentices have new mentors and my few music pupils have new teachers. I'm waiting for new duties, but the Legion can't seem to decide what to do with me yet. Could this be part of the Creator's design? To empty my hands just when Cai needs to fill them?

"In the meantime," Mercy continues, "There's this portent of a great culmination. We need to figure out what's next."

"Yeah, big portent, but few tactics." I want to say more, to tell her what Cai revealed to a few minutes ago, but Van waves at us again. "Speaking of which…"

"I should join them. Do you want to come along?"

"No thanks. I've had enough attention for today. I'm just going to stand here looking stern and try not to do anything for a few minutes."

She laughs and winks at me, before rushing over to join her husband.

I'm not particularly good at doing nothing, as it turns out. My impatience feeds the anger that's been growing inside me since Mercy's parents were abducted by my own. I cross my arms and lean against the wall, projecting as much calm as I can while I wait for the group to settle. I fight my constant thread of anger and push it down so far that I must focus to find it.

And now I have this new weight. I have no idea how to feel about yet another label being forced upon me by Cai's desperate people. *Savior* is a heavy word.

I close my eyes. *I am a bright light, a little piece of the Divine, and I am not defined by this moment.* I open my eyes and look around.

The room is spacious, cool, and comfortable in a functional kind of way. Artificial lighting illuminates panels set into the natural rock wall to my left, giving the impression of windows. A simple, large conference table stands along that wall, directly opposite the large desk and surrounding chairs to my right. Deep skylights along one end pour soft pools of hazy sunlight into what truly is more cave than structure, reminding us that outside these walls, the world still turns, the sun still hangs over our heads, this mountain exists in the real world.

Everything within this space is white or gray, sleek and crisp or natural stone. I know from experience that it has excellent acoustics. If I concentrate, I can hear the sound of my violin as I played it here just a few days ago—the sweet, sad notes rising to crescendo. Maybe I'll come back with my flute later, although I can easily find a more comfortable place to play. Somewhere warmer, less sterile. It occurs to me that my albino skin and white-blonde hair blends in with the decor. Today I even wore white. I'm a fixture. Maybe I can disappear—just shrink into the rock, like a camouflaged moth.

Sibling Rumesa strides toward me, a knowing look on their face. I smooth my many-layered skirt.

"God's grace with you, Bozan. We missed you at training this morning." They raise one eyebrow in question.

"Good morning. I…had to meet the Adamses right after prayer. I'm sorry."

"Hmm. Tea?"

I try to see into their thoughts, but they're holding their emotions carefully beyond my reach. All I can sense is the pressure of leadership that surrounds them, that surrounds me, and permeates this powerful place.

"Sure." I push away from the wall to help as they gather cups and pour from a waiting pot. I fuss with the sweeteners. "Honey?"

"Two please. Perhaps General Henderson and I can join you later for a few songs."

I hand them two straws of golden honey, raising an eyebrow in response as I squeeze my own straw into a cup. The sticky syrup clings to my finger. I shrug and hastily suck the sweetness from my thumb.

"I hear she plays quite well."

"Thank you, but I prefer to play alone."

Rumesa sighs. "Yes, well, more than the music, I was hoping for a private word. We need to talk about the scene outside the station."

I hang my head and squeeze my eyes shut, before rolling my shoulders and looking them straight in the eye. "I'm sorry about that, Ru. I let my temper get away from me. It won't happen again."

Rumesa tips their head to the side. "It *was* a regrettable display. I appreciate your apology, but I think we both know that it *will* happen again if you don't practice more control. Will you promise to continue the meditation and prayer that we discussed?"

"Yes, I will. We can practice together—tomorrow if you're free?"

They're about to answer when a hiss sounds behind us. I jump a little, surprised. Few people can sneak up on me and I find it annoying when they do. I know before I meet his eyes who it is.

Cai Varela's face shows thinly veiled impatience. Tension rolls off him in waves. He's holding his indrawn breath and staring at me. I set my tea aside and straighten to my full height, but at the same time I find it hard to catch my breath.

Rumesa clears their throat in the awkward silence. "Ambassador Varela, tea?"

Cai's eyes shift to them, and finally I can breathe. "No, thank you. If we may, Your Grace, I've just come from the aviation office. The information you requested is complete. There are urgent issues we've still to discuss. Can we call the rest of the Council here?"

So it begins. The thread of anger rises higher in me—he's maneuvering us, even now. I understand his motivation, but I don't have to like this. I pick up my tea again and force myself to take a slow sip.

Rumesa looks around. "No, they'll be busy helping with the triage, as we are, but we have several members here. What did you want to discuss?"

Cai looks around the room. Dixie, Mercy, and Van stand off to one side in deep discussion. TJ is at the conference table typing furiously into the virtual keyboard he's called up on its surface. Several images project in the space around him while General Elder, Van's father and my fellow Councilmember, points at the displays and issues quiet commands.

Cai gestures to the table. "Can we sit?"

"Of course." Rumesa motions for me to collect Dixie.

I settle my teacup in the saucer, allowing it to clack a little harder than is proper.

Dixie, Van, and Mercy look up as I join them. "Cai—" I purse my lips and blink slowly. "I mean *Ambassador Varela,* would like a word with us."

Van stiffens. "Well that's craic. SciCorps just attacked the council chamber. King Cai can't wait?"

In the weeks we've spent together, Van's nickname for Cai has stuck. Whether it's meant sarcastically or endearingly seems to change day to day. But right now, it sets just the right tone.

"Let's just see what he wants." I don't wait but walk over to the table and sit near TJ, leaving the chair between us at the center of the table for Rumesa.

My brother raises a brow, but shifts his attention when Cai sits in the chair directly opposite. TJ shuts off his displays and the others quietly sink into chairs around the table.

Rumesa sits between us. "Do you want to run this?"

I roll my eyes in answer.

"Dr. Varela," they begin, "I'm sure you understand that the Council is very busy at the moment. While it's clear that this attack was an isolated extraction aimed solely at recovering Admiral LeRoux, we have a lot of damage to control. And we still don't know where Dr. Coral Adams is being held. So please forgive my bluntness, but what can we do for you?"

Cai waits for a moment, letting the silence draw everyone's attention. His piercing dark gaze rests a second on each face before he inhales deeply and speaks. "There are four of 13 Councilmembers present. I wish to go forward with my briefing and Terra Faire's...*request*...as originally planned for after the hearing today. I sense that I can do so, and you have a mechanism for sharing this information and calling a vote. Is this correct?"

He looks at me, but I shift my eyes down. I don't want to lead, especially not in this.

General Elder stirs. "Aye. I think, my friend, that we can listen and convey yer request to the rest of the Council, whatever that constitutes at this point. Please begin."

"Excellent." Cai smiles. "You see, the Creator has spoken to me, and I'd like to share the Creator's plan with all of you."

5
Cai

Finally I have their attention—their thoughts settle, their curiosity rises, and suddenly I'm unsure how to begin.

Please God, let me convince them. And give me the strength to hold back what I must. I can't help but smirk as I send this prayer heavenward, because I know that the Creator would have me conceal nothing, would have me surrender all. And maybe someday I'll have to, but not today.

I glance at the faces around me and appreciate again the control this group of leaders keeps over their own emotions. The Legion Enclave, with its trained order, has been a slight reprieve from the general cacophony of thoughts in New Juneau and the Verge.

General Dixie Henderson catches my gaze. She raises one eyebrow in question, and I take a deep breath and begin.

"As you know, the Creator's plans are multi-layered. Divine vision is not limited to a single path, but multidimensional and complex." Some people nod in agreement. "Terra Faire may have many purposes, many roles in the greater plan, but Spheran society has long known that we build toward one great purpose, this *culmination*—to come to the aid of humanity when again humanity finds itself conflicted."

There's a press now, from several directions, several minds trying to probe for a better understanding of my words. I rub my gem to let them know that I'm aware of their feeble attempts to read my mind. As I do, I notice that the warm pressure of Eddie's mind is not among them. She's either starting to trust me or knows it's pointless to try to read my thoughts when I don't want them read.

I clear my throat. "We have advanced technology—robotics, genetics, defenses, and others—that we are prepared to share openly. Our goal is to even the scales against SciCorps while the evaluation of your population studies and negotiations for peace take place. Given the recent discovery of the Nina's return from deep space, our plans should be put into place immediately and I recommend departure for Terra Faire beginning within the next 12 hours. I have a full proposal, including workforce and flight plans, ready for your review."

The room is quiet when I finish. Several people exchange astonished looks. A few chairs squeak as their occupants shift.

I wait.

General Elder exhales loudly, but it's his son, Van, who says what several people have been thinking.

"Aye, but that's a very kind offer, surely, and fortuitous in its timing, ye might say…." He leans back in his chair.

While his lyrical voice is polite, underneath it I sense mistrust and await his acerbic response.

"But how do we know it isn't just a load of manure that ye hope will divide our resources while SciCorps moves in for the kill?"

"Van!" His father shakes his head.

"Captain!" Bozan Kahinu says at the same time.

Everyone starts talking at once, the control I appreciated earlier is abruptly gone. They're arguing amongst themselves now, like so many other meetings. Disorganized. Undisciplined. I relax back in my seat and wait for the inevitable moment when someone—

"Shhhweee-eee!" A piercing whistle sounds from the end of the table. Everyone stops talking and stares at General Henderson.

"That's better. Now if you all are done acting like a bunch of civilians debating a weather report, we can get back to a serious discussion." She stretches her thick arms out in front of her and folds her hands, their wrinkles and age spots reminding me that she earned the wisdom in her dull lilac eyes through years of leadership.

"The Verge has had a fruitful, if hesitant, association with Terra Faire for a few decades now. We know their shielding technique works and have benefitted directly from it. We've no reason to doubt Ambassador Varela's good intentions. But Captain Elder raises a fair, albeit rude, question. I think we need to understand what exactly you have that ensures the scales are balanced? And I'll add a question myself…what do you want in return?"

It's now or never. What I share and what I withhold will change my people's future. "Our scientists have monitored Dr. Parker Adam's research and development on the loom technology.

We have several teams ready to collaborate with him to accelerate the program. We offer to help you with your loom technology and thereby provide a means for you to begin major planetary environmental restoration."

Bozan Kahinu leans in. "How much acceleration?"

"Several months, perhaps more, if they have any luck."

This news gets nods and whispers around the room.

"And in return?" General Henderson asks.

"In return we need your help with some of our domestic programs. Our genetics department would appreciate an evaluation of their projections and research by your own physicians. Our educational curriculum has some issues we cannot identify, but which seem to be creating problems for our children as they take on adult roles and occupations."

"Education?" Mercy Adams perks up. "I'm already working with one of your teams remotely. You say your education system has additional problems?"

"Yes, and though we've tried, we cannot determine root cause."

"That's intriguing. I'd be willing to volunteer for that."

I smile at her, understanding that her youth and small stature are no reflection of her effectiveness. As Eddie's best friend, she's also an ally I'm glad to have on my side.

General Henderson holds up a hand. "Let's not get ahead of ourselves. Go on, Doctor."

"As a general condition, I want to make it clear that Terra Faire is not interested in integrating with your cultures. We recently held a referendum and agreed; we will remain separate."

More murmurs and some frustration flow around the room.

"We're not interested in forcing ye to be our friends." Van Elder leans back in his chair again, distrust emanating from him in waves. "What else?"

How to put it… "Some additional medical research." I wait a moment and lean back in my seat too, watching the faces around me, absorbing their scrutiny.

"That's it?" General Elder asks. "Collaboration on some scientific and social programs and assured independence?"

"And some medical research."

Bozan Kahinu waves a hand. "Forgive me, Ambassador, but we'd have agreed to this with very little else at stake. Why wait until now, what are we missing?"

"Perhaps I should more fully explain another of our technology projects. Though we've come to the point where our robotics and our own crew can no longer…shall I say, *progress* the project, it is a promising one, and could be pertinent to answering the Nina's call for help. With your workforce, and technical skills from the Verge and New Juneau, we believe we could complete our project in a matter of weeks."

"What project, exactly?" Van Elder's patience is strung tight. Though I rarely sense anything from him, his impatience is a tripwire in my mind.

"We have a prototype virtual tether."

The room is temporarily frozen, and then everyone talks at once. Van stares at me, then abruptly shoves his fists in the air. "Yes!"

Eddie's brother TJ smiles and nods at Van before he joins the others in a barrage of questions.

"What do you mean prototype? Will it work?"

"How like our tether is it?"

"Why virtual? Have you ever used it?"

I answer their questions as best as I can. "Yes, it will work.… Very like your tether; the same basic principles with some changes to meet its intended use as a stationary rail to the exosphere.…" And on and on.

"Does SciCorps know about it?" General Henderson's question has everyone quieting.

"No, we don't believe so. We've activated it only a few times, and not within the last few months as tensions here arose."

The excitement in the room is still palpable, but they're starting to wind down. I look over at Bozan Kahinu. With their ebony skin and bold features, they remind me of a regal queen from days of old. Their expression is open and sincere. They're formidable but seem willing to trust me. As I open my mouth to answer their last question, my gaze shifts to their right and a finger of ice trails up my spine.

Eddie is staring daggers at me; her normally pale albino skin is vibrant pink. When I reach for her thoughts, all I get before she shuts me out is "*I am a bright light.*" I don't know what that means.

Her eyes are wide. Their color is a lighter purple than mine, more lilac, and their depths…so deep I sometimes get vertigo when I stare too long. I remember the first time I saw her—my people's fabled savior, *Tesouro Branco*—across the mayhem of the train terminal in New Juneau. I'd been expecting an elder because of the *branco* part, but I'd known instinctively that I was wrong. There was to be no *ancient* white-haired soul to gently guide my people;

this woman was a tempest, white-hot as a burning ember and as easy to grasp as smoke. The pull was immediate and visceral, just like it is now. I swear there's a *snap* as our fates align.

It takes me a moment to draw my thoughts back to the present, to this room and its audience, and when I do, I realize that Eddie's actually glaring. Her emotions are so high that the people around her are starting to squirm. She's furious. At me.

Bozan Kahinu lays a hand on Eddie's arm, breaking the spell. "Sister, what is it?"

Eddie breathes in deeply and looks at her friend, seeming to just as suddenly remember that we are not alone in this room. She shakes her head slightly and rolls her shoulders before addressing me. "These people—these friends and comrades—have risked their lives and the lives of those they love to save you and bring you to this moment. They deserve your honesty and transparency. Tell them what you really want, or you will surely lose it."

Now it's my turn to squirm. It's not a feeling I'm accustomed to, being told what to do. I instantly rebel against it until I hit a wall in my mind. This is what the Creator wants. It's what I need from Eddie—her threat isn't veiled. I have to do as she wishes, or lose what I want, too. My reluctance evaporates.

"The medical research I mentioned is very specific. It involves the greatest threat to Spheran society, to our continued existence. We want to take the lead on the cure for the disease you call the Trade. And to do that, we need Bozan LeRoux…in Terra Faire. Indefinitely."

You would think that the earlier helicopter assault had returned. Most everyone is out of their chairs. Voices explode from every direction. Van Elder makes it halfway around the table before his father catches his sleeve and, together with Mercy, drags him into a corner. I'm also getting a surprisingly close look at Eddie's brother's face for the first time. Except for the deeper skin tone, TJ LeRoux looks much like his sister. I can see his father in him too, in the longer features and more razor-edged jaw. The vein pulsing in his temple is a little worrying, though. Now standing, his torso stretches halfway across the table as he leans toward me. I'm sure I should be grateful for the way that Bozan Kahinu keeps pressing him back so that they can better see General Henderson.

Tink, tink, tink! The general taps her spoon against her teacup. "Alright, settle down, settle down!"

"Everyone, please…" Bozan Kahinu spreads their arms and motions for the group to take their chairs.

I risk a look at Eddie. She's composed again. Nothing I said surprised her in the least of course. If nothing else, I'm glad I told her first.

Others settle back into the chairs they'd pushed aside—Van rather noisily.

"Ambassador." Bozan Kahinu takes a moment to gather their thoughts. "Do you understand what you're asking? Do you understand the role that Bozan LeRoux stands to play in our government, in our society?"

"I do, Your Grace."

This quiets the last bit of restlessness.

"Do you?"

Their attempt to read my mind is like gentle fingers nudging at my thoughts, attempting to find an opening. I conjure in my memory the power and strength I felt from Gran Bozan Li in the short moments I spent in her company just before her death. What it means to be Gran Bozan. What will one day be expected of Eddie if she accepts the sash. I hold this aura, this weight, present in my mind as I let Bozan Kahinu in, just a small breach into my thoughts.

They sit up straight, appraising me before they pull back their mental fingers. "Yes, I believe you do." They look at Eddie, and then back at me. "Well, regardless of what any of us believes or wants, it really comes down to one thing. This is a democracy, and Bozan LeRoux is a free citizen, it is up to her where she will go, with whom and when." Bozan Kahinu turns in their seat to face Eddie. "What have you decided, Sister?"

Rill O'Brien

In the past…
March 28, 2656, 45 years ago
Subterranean Severe Weather Research Station 21A, North America

Rill respected Jameson's sense of humor almost as much as his engineering skills. His mentor was the only survivor now, besides Rill's own family. They'd buried so many friends that Rill had seriously begun to dread every difficult or risky task. This one had his heart hammering and his bravery ready to bolt.

"The hinge is completely shot." Jameson spoke calmly, but with authority. "Aoife, I tell you, if we don't move the fan now, it's going to tear free on its own and get smashed beyond repair."

"I dunno…we can repair a whole lot, as ye well ken." Rill's mam chewed the inside of her cheek. "Goin' into the tunnel right now with the storm as it is, we might lose somethin' more important than the blessed blower." She exchanged a knowing glance with Rill's da.

Jameson didn't say anything at first. He pulled a cloth from his toolbelt and cleaned the lenses of the loupe that he wore like a necklace while he waited patiently for all of them to think it through one last time before they started the operation. A few years older than Rill's da, Jameson had been the only scientist not from the Farms. He had an engineering degree from the university in New Juneau and, before getting stranded in the SS Worse over 30 years ago, he'd had a family and a career. Rill sometimes wondered what that had been like—he would've been about Rill's age when he married and started a family. He really couldn't imagine it—a life so different from his own.

"Now, Mam, we all know the consequence of losin' that blower." Rill rested a hand on his mam's shoulder, the corded muscles reminding him just how much of a load she still carried. "Losin' the blower means losin' the tunnel. I know we can live here without the tunnel, but if we ever hope to be rescued, 'tis the only feasible way. Without a functional access tunnel, they won't even be able to reach us, or us them."

Rill's da pounded a fist on the workbench behind him. "Damn foolish! We shoulda moved that fan months ago, before it came to this."

"Aye, Seamus, but we didn't know." Rill's mam reached over and patted his da's fist. In her late fifties now, Mam bore all the signs that the years of hard labor and isolation were taking their toll. Her movements had grown slower; her face often grimaced in pain. "I think we have to do it. Jameson's right, we have to try for—"

She caught herself, but Rill knew what she was going to say. *For Rill's sake.*

He closed his eyes and took a deep breath. So many of their decisions these last few years had been for his sake, for the sake of the last person expected to be alive in this God-forsaken place.

Well, he wasn't about to cancel out the bravery and hard work that went into all those other decisions just because he was afraid now. "Aye, I agree, let's go."

They went through the plan one more time, fastened their helmets and checked their dust gear, and then mounted their modified sleds. Rill counted the wind breaks as they ascended the tunnel. Three days ago, an F4 tornado had separated from the constant storm that swirled over the SS Worse and blown open the door at the surface. A large piece of debris had smashed into the blower and broken one of the huge hinges, preventing them from using the blower to clear the tunnel and close the door. Yesterday they'd managed to remove two of the hinges, providing the fallback position for the massive blower that kept the tunnel clear to the outside, their only exit.

"Almost there." Jameson's calm voice came through Rill's headset. "Rill, get ready to activate the robots and fall back."

Rill was physically the strongest of them now. It would be his job to maneuver the heavy hinge into place. He leaned lower over his sled, surprised by the force of the wind as they passed the last wind break. He watched the others pull ahead to the big blower attached to one side of the tunnel wall. As soon as they were in place, he spun his sled around, jumped off and released the robots that would detach the fan from the wall.

The robots worked fast, and soon the fan was loose and resting on its massive casters. They followed Rill back to the new blower position while the others controlled the fan's descent. With their help, Rill wrestled the huge hinge into position. "Hinge installed. We're ready."

As he said it, a huge gust of wind knocked him back against the wall. He heard his mam scream.

"Look out!" His da's voice sounded panicked.

Rill struggled to his feet and jumped on his sled. He rounded the curve just in time to see a wave of sand encroaching on the others. His folks were using their sleds to control the leading end of the fan. Jameson had attached his tether to the trailing end, trying to keep it centered in the tunnel.

As Rill watched, the wave covered Jameson's sled. "Jam!"

For a moment, they all stared in silence, and then breathed a sigh of relief as Jameson crawled out near the exposed rear of his sled.

"I'm okay, I'm off, but I can't get to the controls. Did we lose the robots?"

Rill spun around. The clever robots had sunk their pincers into the wall like anchors. "No! They're okay."

"We need ye to let the winch out, or the sand will take everything," Rill's da shouted over the deafening wind whipping through the tunnel.

"Stand by and I'll release it manually," Jameson called back.

"I'm coming to help!" Rill pulled his sled alongside the fan just as another gust of wind pushed it toward him, trapping him against the wall.

"Stop! It's too risky. If I can just release the winch—"

With a shriek of metal against cement, the big blower lurched away from the wall and started back down the tunnel.

"You did it!" Rill shouted. "I'm coming to get ye! Walk toward me." He saw Jameson struggle to his feet and take a step. The next thing he knew, his friend was flying through the air toward him, and then he too was off the ground, the gust of wind tossing him several meters like a dry leaf. He looked up just in time to see Jameson crash into the ceiling of the tunnel and drop down a few feet from him.

"Jam!" Rill scrabbled along the pavement trying to reach him.

"Jameson! Rill!" His mam called to him in his headset. "Rill! Come back!"

Rill pushed against the wind, reaching out blindly for Jameson. He felt something—an arm! He wrapped his hand around his friend's wrist and pulled him along back down the tunnel. "Help me!"

One of the robots arrived and unceremoniously gripped both men in its pincers and pulled them the rest of the way back down the tunnel behind the fan, which his da was working frantically with the other robot to attach to the hinge.

"Almost there!" He heard his da say.

The robot dumped Rill near his da's sled and lifted Jameson onto the back.

"Jam! Oh God!" Rill pulled at his friend's neckerchief to search for a pulse. "Come on, Jam. Come on, buddy. Please God." He felt a faint pulse.

"That's it! Let's go!" His mam pushed him aside and began strapping Jameson down. "Get the bots and get on yer sled, Rill! We've gotta go!"

Rill pulled himself up. The pain in his back was excruciating, but he pushed through it, locked the robots in place and climbed onto his sled. What would he do if Jam died? His friend, his mentor. Rill loved and respected his parents. They were brilliant in their fields, but Jam was something else entirely. Jam was a genius engineer. They'd never escape without him, because no matter how hard he studied, Rill still didn't know enough. But then, what would it even matter if Jam were gone?

"Let's go!" His mam called as she took the lead, followed by Rill with his da bringing up the rear.

The trip back seemed so much faster. Soon they were back in the garage. His da went to the blower controls while he and his mam carefully moved Jameson's unresponsive body to a nearby workbench.

Something was wrong with Rill's chest; he couldn't get enough air. He ripped off his helmet and gasped for breath. He tried to breathe normally, but his lungs pumped in short chuffing breaths.

"Easy now." One of his mam's hands settled on the back of Rill's head, the other on his chest. "Slow it down. Jam needs us, son. He's not gone yet and he needs us. Aye, that's it. Just slow it down."

Rill closed his eyes and bent over so his head was lower than his heart. He reached out a hand and gripped the table. Jameson's boot brushed his fingers and he found the will to push through, to help his friend.

"Aye, I'm fine now. Let's do what we can." Rill pulled his way along the table.

"Easy does it." His mam held Jameson's head and neck while Rill removed his helmet.

"Oh, God." Rill's throat closed painfully. "Mam, look." Rill held up the helmet to show her the massive web of cracks that sank into the back.

She sagged and looked down at Jameson. "I feel a pulse. It's faint, but he's still alive."

Jameson's lashes fluttered and he opened his eyes.

"Jam?" Rill took the man's hand gently. "Can ye hear me?"

Jameson moved his lips as if to speak, but a trickle of blood ran out instead. He coughed then, causing more blood to flow down the side of his mouth and pool on the table.

"The blower's operatin'!" Rill's da yelled and gave a loud whoop. "The tunnel's clearin'. The door should be free in…about two hours. We did it!"

Rill sighed and closed his eyes before looking down at his friend. "Mam, what can we do?"

Rill's mam was slowly examining Jameson for injuries. Her face was white, the wrinkles around her eyes already wet with tears when she shook her head and took Jameson's other hand. His da joined them at Jameson's side, the joy on his face quickly changing to horror when he saw his son's face.

Jameson moved his eyes to look at each one of them, before resting his eyes on Rill. "Worth it," he said. "You're worth it. Up to you now."

"No. Jam, no. Stay with us." Rill bent his head over his friend's hand and cried. He didn't know how this sacrifice would *ever* be worth it.

6
Eddie

I've been alone for over two hours, according to the screen on my wall, though I would have guessed only minutes. I tried praying but couldn't settle. As usual, music centered me. Music is my praenex gift. Well, music and a few other things. The final, haunting notes of my flute still drift in the air as my door chimes.

"Come in." I stand and straighten my skirts, then wipe the dampness from my face as Mercy quietly steps into the room. The fact that she wasn't here already means they're all trying to give me space.

She smiles at me tentatively. "Hi."

I blow a long breath through rounded lips and roll my eyes. "Drew the short straw, did you?"

She laughs. "Worse. I volunteered."

"Ever the hero these days."

I hold my hands up and Mercy responds, folding her fingers through mine. We lean together and touch foreheads, gem to gem.

Her assurance pushes into me, a strength that has only grown since her ascension into adulthood and recent marriage to Van. I briefly take what she offers, and then draw back.

I move to the bed and begin disassembling and cleaning my flute—a process so automatic I could do it in my rem. *I am more than the gray matter inside my skull. I am a bright light, a little piece of the Divine, and I am not confined to this moment, to this task.*

Snapping the case shut, I turn and place it in my instrument cabinet with the others—violin, oboe, guitar, and more—before reluctantly shutting both doors.

"What have you decided?" she asks.

I turn and consider my best friend—my sister by all but birth, and then bend to reach under my bed and pull out my suitcase.

Mercy gives a little squeal and bounces on her toes. I can't help my eye roll when she rushes over and squeezes my shoulders. "This is going to be great. *You're* going to be great! It's the right thing to help these people. I feel it!"

"I didn't really have a choice, did I? Oh, let me see, should I help you literally save your civilization, or stay here and pout about being made queen? Hmmm…" I stare at the ceiling as I tap my cheek in thought.

"Stop it." Mercy gives my shoulder a little shove. "Gran Bozan is not queen."

"Pope, then."

"Come on, GB isn't that either."

"I wonder," I tap my finger on my cheek again, "are *you* going to 'Your Grace' me when I take the job? Hmmm?"

"Oh! You said *when* not *if.* Have you decided—"

"No!" I unzip my bag. "I'm still not sure, and now we have this mission."

"Well, you wanted more time to think things through. This will give you that time while you help the Spherans. Tell me honestly, does it feel wrong to you? Does it feel like you're acting against the Creator's plan to go there?"

I search my feelings, opening my heart to divine purpose, to *my* purpose, and feel only a settled warmth and rightness, not my usual indecision. Still, there is that thread of anger—that sense of being manipulated, controlled—but it feels like the right decision. Leave it to Mercy to point out the obvious. I'd been so caught up in mourning my music that I forgot to simply *feel* the decision.

"No, it doesn't feel wrong. It feels just right."

Her smile falters. "I agree, it feels right, but it also feels dangerous. Every bit as dangerous as the last mission to rescue my father."

"And that was the devil you know."

She thinks for a moment. "True. I think part of it is knowing we'll miss what's happening here."

"The leaders here can handle Scorch politics. What we're going into is something entirely new. We don't know anything about Terra Faire or the Spherans really. But we'll face it together, and that's a comfort. I'm glad you'll be with me, all of you."

She hugs me. "Me too. Okay, I have to go and pack. Van's almost done—he was so sure you'd go—but I didn't want to jinx it. I've gotta run. Send me the departure time when you know it."

The door chimes again just as Mercy reaches it. She looks back over her shoulder in question.

I shrug. She presses the release and Cai Varela stands in the opening. He seems a little surprised as he looks from me to Mercy.

"Excuse me, Ambassador, I was just leaving."

He steps back to let Mercy out, and then moves forward again. "May I?"

"Yes, please, come in." I move away toward another cabinet and the door hisses shut behind him. The nervousness I usually feel in his presence immediately returns, only heightened by our being alone. In my room. And the thread of anger, the knowledge that he has masterfully maneuvered me *again*, hums a little closer to the surface of my mind before I tamp it down.

When I turn back around, I gasp in surprise at how close he is and step back to avoid colliding with him.

"Sorry. I, ah, came to see if you…" Cai looks at the suitcase lying open on my bed, and then down at the clothes I hold clenched to my chest. He freezes. Slowly his gaze returns to my face.

I brace myself for his push against my thoughts, but he doesn't.

"You…you're coming?"

Gathering my bravery, I look directly into his eyes. For a moment I'm struck by my reflection captured in the prism of his violet eyes. With the lamp light behind me, it's almost as if I'm looking through the mirror of his mind at a tiny, inked version of myself.

Then he raises his hands to wrap around my biceps, strong but warm. He squeezes.

Panic rises within me and heat crawls up my neck.

"You're really coming?" His voice is a whisper of warmth on

my upturned face.

I nod. "Of…of course."

Suddenly I find myself crushed against his chest, which is rising and falling in huffs.

He burrows his chin into the space between my jaw and neck and whispers in my ear. "Thank the Creator. Thank you, *minha flor*."

I hold myself stiffly—so surprised by every sensation I experience. Goosebumps flare on my arms, while heat swarms from my belly straight to my cheeks. I'm sure that I'm going to lose control, but to my amazement, nothing terrible happens. I don't erupt. I don't feel trapped. It's a novel and strange sensation to be held like this, by him, but I realize I don't hate it. Just as I begin to relax, he abruptly pulls away.

"Oh, I'm sorry. Forgive me. I'm just so…relieved."

"Of course." *Of course?* Can't I say anything else? I shake my head to clear it, to push down the rush of blood heating my cheeks. "I mean, here I'm considered a problem for many. In Terra Faire…perhaps I can do some good, help your people. We have one stop to make first, however."

"Ah, yes, your brother's nuptials in Vancouver Colony. I will follow you there and then we can all leave together."

"You're welcome to attend. I mean…it would be a good chance for you to meet his fiancée Mayhem Forge. Since she'll be coming with us, I mean, not because she'll be my new sister-in-law. Not that that's important. Oh, um…" I shake my head as heat rushes to my cheeks.

Cai smiles. "Well, thank you. That will be nice. Eddie?" He

moves closer again, lifting his hand to my face as if unsure what to do or say. Just as his fingers slide along the edge of my jaw and into my hair, the door chimes again. Cai steps back quickly.

Of all the interruptions, I like this one the least. "Come!"

I move around Cai toward the door, immediately regretting my sharpness when I see my colleagues and children waiting outside. "Oh, forgive me. Divine grace to you all. Won't you come in?" The clothes I'm still clutching I hastily dump into my suitcase.

The group moves into my room noisily, responding to my greeting, but looking unsure once they see Cai.

"We're interrupting you, Bozan. I'm sorry. We'll come back later," one of caregivers says.

"Not at all." I reach for the toddler in their arms, pulling the chubby albino girl into my embrace. "I always have time for my fellow LeRouxs." I giggle as the girl's short arms twine around my neck and she presses her cheek to mine. My biological daughter, one of many.

Two years ago, once we were sure of my immunity to the Trade, my egg donation began. Willing surrogates signed up to be parents. I'm only 18, but I have 29 offspring so far, with nearly that many more on the way. Crazy? Maybe. But it's necessary for our survival—they're all immune. I won't parent them, but I do love them, each and every one.

I bend and try to touch them all in greeting—a few more toddlers, but mostly babies still too small to walk on their own. I try to see them often, whenever I'm in the Enclave. I won't raise them, but their parents understand the importance of their heritage; all these children share the surname LeRoux. Someday,

I'll bear a child of my own—perhaps through the *aeterna-sui rituali,* a clone—but for now, these children are my contribution to my people.

I don't notice that I've sunk to the floor in the gaggle of toddlers until a masculine pair of boots comes into view. "Oh, God's grace."

I try to get up, but several children have ahold of my skirts, some sitting in the pools of fabric. I struggle for a few seconds, before giving up and sitting back down.

"Don't get up. I…" Cai's voice trails off.

"Everyone, let me introduce Ambassador Cairo Varela, of Terra Faire. Mr. Ambassador, my friends and offspring."

"*Maman,*" a small voice says.

I turn my head and find one of the albino toddlers using my shoulder for balance staring back at me. I smile.

The toddler smiles too, then lets go of my shoulder and reaches out to gently smack my cheeks with tiny hands. "*Maman,*" they say again, their smile revealing four funny little white teeth that make me think of a bunny.

"Yes, sweetheart. Now give us a kiss."

I pucker my lips and strain my neck forward.

The toddler presses my cheeks and carefully bends to smack my lips in a wet, sticky kiss.

We both laugh.

When I look up, Cai has a strange, almost-pained expression on his face. He's pressing his fingers into his chest, just above his heart, as his eyes dart around the group.

"Are you alright? Your chest…are you in pain?"

"My chest?" He stares at me blankly.

Is he having a heart attack or something?

"You're rubbing your chest. Are you alright? Sibling, call a doctor. The ambassador's not well." I struggle harder to move the children, but they seem as entranced as Cai now and stare at him rather than me.

"No!" Cai drops his hand and waves to the caregiver. "I'm fine, really. I just…" He spreads his arm to encompass me and my children. "It's a lot…it's nothing…I'm sorry. I need to go and announce our departure. Make preparations. I'll send you the time." Cai shakes his head and steps toward the door.

"Ambassador? Are you sure?"

He straightens as he focuses on me. "Yes, I'm sure. I'm sorry. I must go. I'll see you in the Verge tonight." His face relaxes, and with one last indecipherable look at the children, he leaves.

"I really *am* sorry," the caregiver says again.

I shake my head, confused. "It's no matter. Thank you for bringing the children to see me."

"It'll be the last time for a while, I take it?"

"Yes. For a while." I pull the closest boy into my lap and inhale the scent of his curly black hair, trying to commit the sensation to memory. "For a while."

Giving into temptation, I raise my mental shields slightly to let them in. Instantly, my mind is awash with a sense of sadness, of concern for me and, surprisingly, for Cai. I take a deep breath and focus on my happiness here with them. I let them feel my love and just like that, their minds shift to replace earlier sadness with eager joy, former concern with sweetness. They love me, they love everyone, and they know we love them.

My cheeks begin to hurt from grinning, and this thought makes them giggle and squirm. "Shall I play for you?" A resounding *yes* fills my mind as the children let go of my dress so I can stand.

"Which instrument will it be today?" I look around the group and my eyes land on the little girl I first held.

"Violin, please." Her voice is high and light. She pushes an image of me playing the violin into my mind.

"The violin it is. Your speech is so lovely, sweetheart. Soon you'll be big enough to start learning your instruments too." Her broad smile is my reward.

I stride to the cabinet that I just closed up and withdraw my violin from its case. I adjust my grip on the bow, find my finger placement and close my eyes. The ballad that comes is uplifting and joyful, with just a touch of goodbye.

Rill O'Brien

In the past...
September 14, 2676, 24 years ago
Subterranean Severe Weather Research Station 21A, North America

"Is it workin'?" His mam bent and squinted at the recording unit as Rill adjusted the settings.

He could see tiny versions of themselves and the surrounding lab in the preview window of the app. They were recording; it had worked.

"Aye, Mam, it's workin'. Just ignore it and go about normal-like."

"Not sure why ye'd want a vid of us workin' in this dusty old workshop." The way she straightened her vest and ran a hand along her graying hair told him that, despite her words to the contrary, he'd flattered her.

"Never mind." Rill pulled a tool from Jameson's old toolbelt, now his, and moved next to her at the workbench. "Let's see if we can finish this kit, then, alright?"

His mam nodded and sniffed. "Jameson or yer da woulda had it done in half the time. I'm sorry ye're left with a scientist instead of a technician."

Rill sighed. She was having one of her melancholy days, and he'd hoped working on the AI kit would cheer her up. Maybe he'd been wrong. Since his da had died of cancer two years earlier, his mam seemed to have lost some of her will to keep on. "None of that talk now. I'll be the technician, and ye can supervise. Please hand me that hemostat."

She handed him the small scissor-like tool. "When I'm gone, these AI will be yer only company. I'm sorry, Rill. Sorry to leave ye here alone. Sorry ye won't know the love of a wife and children of yer own. Sorry—"

"Sorry I was born?"

His mam jumped like he'd slapped her. She gripped his hand. "No! Never!" For a moment she stared at him, her expression too aghast not to be true. Then she took a deep breath, squeezed his hand one more time and let go. "I've always been glad to be yer mam, always. Should I tell ye about the night you were born then? The storm was so fierce that week, it shook the earth at times, but yer da—"

"Computer, end program." Rill stepped back from the holographic workbench as the images died away. He'd replayed that one-and-only station recording hundreds of times over the last three years since his mam had died, and it always left him bereft anew.

Stepping out of the Virtual Reality Theatre, he moved over to the counter and washed his hands in the sink. Once they were clean, he pushed Jameson's loupe up into his hair. At 45, Rill figured he had another 30 years of nothing ahead of him, if the systems lasted, if the AI could help him keep the station running, if he survived his own self.

Crossing to the medical chest, he looked down at the prepped syringe. How often did he do this now? Once a week? Every other day? Time had little meaning in a place where nothing changed.

It would be so easy—painless, really, just the prick of the needle and then the drowsy lull of morphine. He ran a finger along the cylinder, causing the tiny bubble in the syringe to wobble like the bubble of air in a level. It was an apt comparison—which way led to balance? Staying the course day to day in this God-forsaken place, alone except for one last cow and a few chickens, and his fickle friend the mouse, whom he always named Sweets, no matter how many generations removed from the original. How many more mouse-lives could he endure? How many more artificial nights with artificial company, with all-too-real emptiness?

He glanced over at the robot steadfastly vacuuming dust from the walls at the end of the lab. His mam's old apron swayed on its metal midsection as it moved its mechanical arms. What a joke he'd become, trying to make companions for himself.

Perhaps the morphine *was* the balance. Half his life was gone by now. Could he say it was enough? Could he just close his eyes and let the morphine do its magic?

He lifted the needle and thought of all the others. 20 souls. Good people, his mam, his da, Jameson, Sherman, Old Patrick, so many others—all of them had kept going, through pain, through illness and injury. None of them had taken the easy way out. And why? When it came down to it, he knew why. They lived for each other, and for him. In the long run, it was for him that they'd endured.

Rill took a deep breath, slid the needle back into the tiny glass vial and depressed the plunger. With the morphine stowed away, he looked up and reviewed the titles of the books he'd brought to the Holographic Lab. Religion, philosophy, and poetry mostly— words to feed the soul. He ran a finger across the spines and tried to imagine a world in which such diversity existed. He paused a moment on the Christian Bible, and then its neighbors: the Quran and the Dao De Jing, but they weren't what he sought today.

Sweets scurried along the tops of the books, stopping on one and rising up onto his rear legs to squeak at Rill.

"Did ye find one, Sweets?"

Reaching out, he picked up Sweets and slid him into his shirt pocket before pulling down the short volume of Seamus Heaney poems. He leafed through the volume as he stepped back into the glass VRT and sat.

"Computer, activate program *Downpatrick Head, County Mayo beta two*."

Rill was sure he could smell the salty surf even before the expanse of blue sky and angry gray ocean appeared before him. From his seat on the giant letter "R" of the *Eire 64* signal paved into the green grass at the cliff's edge, he could see Dun Briste, the ancient sea stack blooming with white flowers. The same flowers bloomed pink at his feet. He inhaled and imagined their perfume in the wind. He was home in the verdant fields of Ireland, a place he'd never really been to, but always seemed to know. He opened his book and read *When Human Beings Found Out About Death*.

He imagined himself as the dog sent to Chukwu, knocking on the Almighty's door, saying "let me back into the house of life."

There were many days now that he felt lost forever like the Irishmen in the poem. He himself was ash disappearing into the dust of the Great Storm—processed through air filters and blown out into the tempest that kept him trapped beneath the surface.

He let the book sag in his hands. It caught on something on this toolbelt and he watched the paper tear as he tugged it free. "Dust it! God damn-it." He set the book aside and grasped the offending tool. It came loose smoothly, as it should—a small ball peen hammer. Rill rolled it over in his hand to reveal the familiar pyrographed name *Jameson.* He remembered the pride he'd felt as a child giving this gift to his idol.

"Jam. What am I goin' to do?"

Sweets climbed out of his pocket and scurried along Rill's arm all the way to the head of the hammer. His whiskers twitched as he sniffed the new object, and then he sat up to stare at Rill as he cleaned his snout with tiny pink paws.

"Aye, back to work. Computer, end simulation."

Rill tucked Sweets in his pocket. "What should we focus on today, friend? Propulsion design or cooling systems?" He'd kept up on his old friend's designs for an escape vessel, if for no other reason than to distract himself.

A crash across the lab startled him. The robot paused in vacuuming and swiveled toward the pile of boxes it had knocked to the floor when its apron had snagged on the edge of a shelf.

Rill blew out a breath and crossed to the robot. He carefully disentangled his mam's apron and folded it gently into his pocket.

"Rosy, restack these cartons. Make sure they're in the right order."

"Right away, Skipper."

Rill closed his eyes and took a deep breath. The robot's use of his nickname always caused a pinch in his chest. Anger flared. He wanted to break something—just smash something to smithereens.

He breathed again and recognized his need to create, to build something hopeful. Working on the temperamental cooling systems was not going to cut it. "Okay." He turned on his heel. "Propulsion design it is."

7
Eddie

Current year: 2701
Monday, 8:00 PM
The Verge, Vancouver Colony

I'm not the only one in our group who prefers to stay busy. It's my brother's wedding day, but he's still managed to post several very controversial articles about recent events on his anonymous blog.

"It's not illegal." TJ paces back and forth in the small waiting room in the Verge's City Hall. His dog, Cousteau, prances at his heels.

I sigh and find a perch on an ugly sofa along the wall. "I agree it's *mostly* not illegal, but the information about what happened at the closed hearing…that could be illegal."

"It's not. I checked." TJ waves a hand dismissively as he turns and paces back across the room. "The rules of the closed hearing are so new and so brief that they don't cover the responsibilities or limitations of witnesses at the hearing."

I slump back in my seat, a little surprised that I find this information comforting. Only weeks ago, I wouldn't have cared about breaking the rules, but now I'm a Councilmember and GB-apparent, or whatever. "It *is* controversial though."

TJ stops abruptly and stares at me. "Since when does that bother you?"

"You're right. But when our parents and all the pilgrims everywhere find out it's you…"

My brother spreads his arms wide and raises both brows. Cousteau perks his ears at me.

"Okay, okay! *Us*…when they find out it's *us*, they're going to respond. Maybe we don't know how, but I'm betting bombs in the worst case, and pursuit, bare minimum. I liked it better when their target was broader, less specific, less…us. Don't look at me like that," I tell the dog.

Cousteau whines and shifts his attention to TJ.

"I've only made the posts under a pseudonym to keep the heat off a little while longer. Normally I'd welcome the discussion, but I really don't need any more attention right now. I have enough to worry about."

"Huh." I tip my head to the side and watch TJ pace some more. "I'm not sure I've ever heard you say that before. I always wondered what 'enough attention' would look like for you, brother. Anyway, they're going to figure out it's you…*us!* Only so many people were there for the events you posted about…the GB's death, father's hearing and escape. Even General Henderson's annoyed with the information you included about praenex abilities among the Couvies. Now that Scorch knows that Couvies aren't null, the Legion is pressuring her to register their talents. Couvies don't like that kind of attention."

"Well, maybe it'll at least end that infuriating derogative, 'nulls.' Ridiculous for anyone to think that just because their gems aren't black, that they're any less praenex."

"Sapiens cultures held prejudices based on skin pigmentation for millennia."

"Yeah, and we praenex reveal ourselves to be no less ignorant."

"So, the blog has some good and some bad, but all of it's risky when it comes to our parents' roles."

TJ looks at the ceiling, hands on his hips. "It's worth the risk. I'm running a program to analyze all the subsequent posts by anyone who reads our anonymous content. Within a few weeks we'll have a real idea of how allegiances are split. Whether they call father's dramatic exit from the hearing an *escape* or a *liberation*. We need to know how people feel about what SciCorps is doing."

"About what all of us are doing." I stretch and slouch back on the sofa, lazily picking at fuzz on the upholstery.

"Right." TJ picks up his pace, striding back and forth until I expect him to start jogging. The tension rolls off him. In just a few minutes, he'll be a married man.

As often happens when my brother's kinetic energy kicks in, I have the opposite response. It's as if our twinness needs constant balance. So, he's pacing back and forth, putting wrinkles into his khaki green TAC dress uniform, and I'm calm and settled in a way I haven't been since before the mission a few weeks ago to rescue Mercy's father.

"Maybe we should try meditating. Repeat after me, *I am a bright light—*"

The look he gives me almost makes me laugh. My brother jabs a hand in the air. "Let the Council be angry. We'll deal with that then. For now, it's important that the citizens of Scorch understand what's really happening. Everyone needs to understand the events of these last weeks. They need to understand that the Nina returning after nearly 600 years sent SciCorps into a tailspin. We are an open society; secrets will destroy us."

I agree, but instead of commenting, I continue to watch him. I'm not sure I ever understood the expression "wringing of hands" before, but I do now. I wonder how long it will take for Cousteau to accept this anxiety as the new normal and curl up in the corner. "I think your comm rings are going to start removing skin if you keep rubbing them that way. Why don't you sit down?" I motion to the seat next to me.

TJ sits for a split second before bouncing back up as if he'd been burned. He crosses to look out the window. Cousteau jumps onto the seat instead, tucking his nose into his paws and blowing out a restful huff.

I run my fingers through Cousteau's wiry hair and rest my head back on the cushion. "It's night…there's nothing to see out that window." My free hand twirls the silky ribbon on my dress. Despite its many primitive customs, the Verge can really make a nice dress. What will Cai wear? If he comes at all.

"Are you even listening to me?"

"What? Oh, um…" I sit up to check if something's changed, but TJ's still pacing. The dog whines and follows him with his eyes.

I realize that I'd better do something before he makes a mess of this for May. I wasn't sure at first, but I've come to admire my soon-to-be-sister-in-law. As an orphan—she was an only child when her parents were lost in a scavenging run when she was little—she told me how much she's looked forward to having a sibling. Me. That was pretty much all it took to win me over in the end. I want the day to be perfect for her, and I know just the tack to take to get my brother's focus on what really matters. It's time for a little reverse psychology.

"Are you sure you want to go through with this now?"

He barely glances at me.

I heave a dramatic sigh. "With everything else going on, what's the hurry?"

He turns to look at me, and then at Cousteau. The dog cocks his head at an angle as if to say, *yes, what's the hurry?* TJ blows out a long breath. "Maybe you're right."

"After all, there'll always be time later. If we survive the trips between here and Chileru. Oh, and I guess there's the issue of Mercy's vision of an attack on the Verge. But I mean, besides those things, it's really only half the unmarried men in the Verge who want to steal her from you. Though I guess some of the women might too—ow!"

I try not to giggle because his kick to my shin really did hurt. "Those boots are hard!"

"You're insane, do you know that."

I ignore him. "I mean, maybe you haven't *really* been in love with her all these years. Maybe if you wait six months, you'll fall in love with someone else. There are a lot of single men and women in the Verge. Just because things went terribly wrong with Naveen doesn't mean you should rule out guys completely—"

"Will you shut up?" TJ stops pacing. I finally have his attention.

Someone taps on the door and Van sticks his head in. "Safe to come in?"

"Ha ha." TJ waggles his head.

Van smiles and pushes through the door, his bulk making the small room seem even smaller. "Well now, it's tradition for the best man to help with the groomin'." Pleasure clear in his voice, Van gives Cousteau a hello scratch, and then opens up a small shaving kit set on a nearby table. Picking up a small towel, he moves toward TJ. "Not that ye have much of a beard."

"Do we have to do this?"

"Yes." Van and I say at the same time.

I watch as my brother and his best friend go through the ritual of shaving the groom. They bicker at first, like usual, but by the time Van finishes the final stroke and the sound of the shaver goes silent, both men look as near to tears as I've ever seen them. I blink and brush a tear from my cheek.

I blow out a breath. "Right, then. Ready to get married?" I watch the color drain from my brother's face. Cousteau jumps down to sit at his feet as I stand and straighten my skirts, doing my best to wipe my tears without drawing their attention.

Van clears his throat and squeezes TJ's shoulder. "Aye, good luck, brother. May's…well, all and sure ye don't deserve her. I wish ye both long years of making each other crazy while making each other better."

TJ laughs. "Guess I don't need the luck—"

Another tap sounds at the door, and Ava Henderson, May's aunt, joins us. "Divine grace."

"Peace with you." We chorus the response.

She smiles and extends a small plate to TJ. "It's tradition for the groom's future mother-in-law to feed the bride and groom nuts and honey before the wedding. I know I'm not her birth mother but May has always been like a daughter to me." She lifts the plate higher. "Anyway, she told me to tell you she left the almonds for you."

I laugh outright and TJ's smile splits into a toothy grin.

Ava raises and eyebrow. "What?"

I look over the plate and chose a nut. "TJ hates almonds." The taste of honey explodes on my tongue.

Everyone takes a nut, even TJ.

"Well then, I guess it's best to start as she plans to go on." Ava smiles.

TJ holds up a finger telling us to wait, then he picks the nut out of his mouth sucked clean of honey. "I can't have you thinking ill of my bride. You see, while *I* hate almonds, Cousteau loves them." TJ shows Cousteau the almond. The dog twirls one circle then sits neatly and holds up a paw. "Good boy." TJ tosses the almond in the air and Cousteau catches it in his mouth.

"Bravo! Clever boy." Ava rubs the dog's head before turning back to TJ. "Are you ready?"

He hesitates and I rest my hand on his shoulder. "All set, right, bro?"

"I want to marry her." He looks me straight in the eye. "I want to marry May. I love her, and that will never change."

I smile and nod. "Then let's go do it."

It still takes a little pulling to get him out of the room, but once we're in the hall and we can see her at the other end, it's my turn to try to keep up. Soon we're at the front of the room with the rest of the group. May is glorious in her elaborate gown and ornate jewelry. She's left her usual gloves behind, and I see her bare hands for the first time that I can remember. The many rings on her fingers sparkle in the light. Even her dog, Piper, looks brushed up for the occasion with her white hair crowning around bright blue eyes. May's twisted her amber coils and braids atop her head in a complicated structure laced with glittering bands. Her tan skin and strong arms look graceful and capable as she reaches for my brother.

Mercy steps up beside me and together we gather the long lasso of fresh green leaves and scented white flowers and twine them over the bride and groom's shoulders to form an infinity loop.

"Thank you." TJ leans to touch his forehead to mine. "Will you play for us now?"

I nod and move to the side where my cello waits. With a nod to the oboist, I settle my endpin and prepare my mind for the piece I selected, the achingly deep and surprisingly short Movement No. 4 from Eugène Bozza's Contrastes II. I know the song will take me away, and I let it. The music lifts me up and draws me out, filling my mind and soul with the Divine. As the last note resonates through the hall, I wait for my audience's response. They're silent and that is how I know I reached them. It's not the kind of music for which you want applause. With a deep breath, I rise and bow to my partner, and then return to my brother's side.

He nods to me, and his joy and gratitude is like a warm embrace.

"That was beautiful, Bozan." General Dixie Henderson steps

up and places her hands on both TJ's shoulders and mine. "I know it's the thing unsaid, but I want you both to know that everyone wishes your parents could be here today. There's nothing that makes it right, nothing that fills that void, but we will try to be a family to you both, as you have been to May and to all of us. We are truly blessed to be a part of this." She swallows hard and for a moment I think she might cry, then she straightens her back. "God's grace with you."

"Divine peace with you," TJ and I both reply.

Dixie wipes at her eyes and turns to Sibling Rumesa. "Well, I don't know how you do things in that fancy Enclave of yours, Your Grace, but I think you better get things started."

The group laughs, and everyone relaxes a little as Rumesa begins.

"Love is a gift from the Creator that comes in many forms…."

Their voice is a satiny song. I let it wash over and through me. I lift my mental shields just enough to allow the surface emotions of those around me to slide into my mind. So much love and care, it fills me with a kind of warmth I've only experienced with my closest friends. The timbre of one mind rises above the others, warmer, more direct.

I turn my gaze and meet Cai's where he stands behind Sheriff Arson. There's no lingering sign of his strange behavior from earlier. I checked the database—he didn't seek any medical care or complain of any more chest pains. Still, I'm wary. As May and TJ exchange vows, I let myself look at him looking at me. I know I invited him, but now I wish he hadn't come. It's uncomfortable.

As I stare back at him, a familiar *snap* ripples through my mind, like a latch catching—a sensation I always feel in moments like this with him. My lack of control makes me angry at myself. I'm now stewing when I want to be celebrating. It's not until May's uncle, Arson, steps forward and blocks our view of each other, that I realize the ceremony is almost over.

Arson clears his throat. "I woulda been happy being the only man in your life for the rest of my days, girl." He clears his throat again as the laughter fades. "But I can see now that there's a certain amount of sense in your marrying a LeRoux."

"Like knows like!" Someone jeers from behind us.

"I suppose that's the short of it, yeah. Still, I would give damn near anything for my best friend, Aro—my big sister's husband—to be here holding these rings for you, with her by his side. I hope to God that they can see us now."

"Amen." Dixie nods. "You're doing fine, son. Aro and Lucy would both be proud."

Arson blows out a breath. "Let these rings be eternal symbols of the love you share—an unbreakable bond under God and blessed by this family—for all the years you live."

Arson holds up his hand cradling the two wedding rings.

May makes a little sound, like exasperation.

"It's alright," TJ whispers.

I study the way they stare at each other, as if some silent conversation is occurring. My brother shifts slightly, and shrugs one shoulder. I watch May decide—her shoulders relax and she smiles, just a little, as she and TJ place their hands atop Arson's. All the guests within reach place their hands on top of TJ and May's and all the rest place their hands on nearby shoulders so that all of us are connected.

I feel something new—a strong and steady power emanating from the group, something more than I expected. I try to focus on it, but when I do it shifts away, like when you think you see someone from the corner of your eye but when you look, there's no one there. The power is captivating; it draws me in. I reach, and reach.

"Let be," Dixie whispers. I look up at Rumesa and they are looking at us too, a wrinkle creasing their brow.

The group pulls back and the feeling dissipates as May and TJ take turns exchanging rings. They kiss. The group erupts into loud whoops, cheers, and applause—the dogs barking and jumping at our sides—and it's over. My brother is married.

I notice Cai then, staring at May with a look of astonishment. Dixie calls his name to ask a question, and it takes him a moment to focus on her.

When I turn back, it's my turn to congratulate the happy couple. "Those rings are stunning." I reach to turn their hands to get a better look at the intricate, swirling silver filigree, but May drops hers to her side and I'm left with only TJ's to admire. She doesn't want me to touch her. I'm too confused to be offended. I'm about to ask why when Arson leans into our trio.

"Beautiful, huh? Took the best craftsman in the colony two weeks to make them. They'll outlast all of us. Just don't get them too close to an open current." Arson grins.

TJ's eyes widen in terror.

May gives her uncle a chastising look. "Don't worry. I'll make sure he knows how to use it safely before we leave."

I exchange a glance with my brother. We've both recently learned that the Couvies' gaudy rings are tools and weapons in disguise.

"Use it?" he mouths to me, and then we're both laughing.

"I may need a ring like that." Cai's breath rushes across my neck as he looks over my shoulder.

I'm instantly irritated, even if I can't say exactly why.

"You may need a wedding ring?" Mercy asks him.

"Uh, well no…I mean…"

I can feel the blood rushing to my face now. Even in this shadowy room, I know I'll be fiery red if I stay near him another minute. My anger rises—what is he trying to maneuver now? I'm just about to ask him when Mercy squeezes past me.

"I would be very interested to learn more about the wedding customs in Terra Faire." She takes Cai's elbow and draws him away.

It's got to be the wedding; I've never had problems being around attractive men before. It's got to be the romance and emotions getting all mixed up in my head. With a little distance, I'm sure I'll have this under control.

I sigh and grit my teeth. *Distance* is what I'm about to lose. In a few hours we'll be traveling together with all my friends and their dogs in a small invisible jet to *his* city.

"Right," I say under my breath. Then I straighten my spine and prepare to rejoin the celebration. "Let's just get through the night and see what tomorrow brings."

8
Cai

Current year: 2701
Tuesday, 10:30 AM
The Verge, Vancouver Colony

I'm losing my patience. First a wedding and now this. While I'm here dealing with Terran bureaucracy, my people are dying from a disease that Eddie's blood could cure. Giza…my God, Giza is dying and I'm not there.

I take another deep breath and try not to explode. I'm not used to waiting, but at least that odd pinch in my chest is gone. I know that if allow myself to conjure the image of Eddie surrounded by her children, it'll come right back. Watching her, I could almost feel the weight of my baby boy in my arms—so small, so sick. Eddie is nothing like Giza, but when I saw her holding that child…. No! I can't think about it. I have to stop thinking about it, so I focus on my frustration instead.

"I don't understand your insistence on sending domestic law enforcement. I told you, we have no crime in Terra Faire." I watch as Sheriff Arson Henderson and Commander Vi Garcia help the rest of the passengers aboard one of the transports leaving the Verge for my home in Chileru. They're capable police officers, but I don't need them. I don't want them.

General Dixie Henderson, also mayor of this place and a relation to just about everyone, stands quietly beside me—a matriarch overseeing her flock. The warm air gusts across the tarmac and we watch another jet take off before she responds. "We have very little crime here, too—"

"I didn't say 'very little.' I said 'none.' When you live in a society of telepaths all racing against the clock to survive, crime becomes irrelevant. We don't prize our possessions, we prize each other. All we want is to live long enough to see our children grow up, and that brings me back around to the time we're wasting here."

Dixie continues to gaze out over the busy scene before us. "No crime, huh? Maybe. Or, respectfully, that may mean none that you *know* of. People are people. Besides, you're about to add over 50 non-Spherans to your mix—the smartest, most adventurous, cocky, and forthright people we have. They think it's a holiday, something they won, and based on how many people applied to go and how few we can afford to send, they're not altogether wrong."

Another plane taxis to the runway and we watch as the sheriff turns from his now-full plane and gives a final salute. The general salutes back and he jumps aboard the final transport.

"Besides, they're not just domestic law enforcement. They're Terran Army Corps. I think you'll be happy to have some TAC in the mix. You'll have those farmers from Alberta Farms who managed to fit just what you needed for your tether labor. They'll teach you and your people more about sapiens behavior than you can possibly imagine, plus challenge you in all sorts of ways that big people do in a praenex environment."

She smirks, and I have to admit, it had already occurred to me that our living quarters are going to feel miniature to the sapiens men, and some of the women, too.

"And then you'll have your New Juneau-variety of praenex. Scientists, doctors, teachers—even a few with Pilgrim political views—and a few lofty, serious-minded clerics from the enclave to keep you busy. Most days they'll make you feel like an idiot just for sayin' the sky is blue, but then a little humbling never hurt anyone, don't you agree, Ambassador?"

Her eyes are on me as I consider her words. It's only been a day since we left the Legion Enclave in New Juneau. At first, I admired the Legionnaires' discipline, but now I'm relieved to be away from their critical, probing minds. To my surprise, I can finally take a deep breath here among the busy, capable minds of the Verge, regardless of how disorganized and noisy their thoughts can be, how annoying the delays. "I do appreciate your hospitality, and for letting us stage our departure here instead of..."

The general chuckles. "Yes, I can imagine. I'm not telepathic, myself, but I bet it's been a trying few weeks keeping the Legion out of your head."

"They lack…. I don't know how to express it."

"Tact?"

I smile tightly and turn to face her again. I can see now that there's no rushing this departure; I'll make up time in the air. "Perhaps that's it. I wanted to say 'manners,' but they're so outwardly formal that's not quite right. Mental prevarication is unpleasant, but I'd been forced to use it over and over again to keep the simplest privacy in that place."

She nods. "I understand, but I don't think they mean any harm—they're as curious as any praenex and not used to telepaths outside their own." She glances past me and grimaces. "And as luck would have it, you're not free of 'em yet."

I turn and see she's right. My traveling group—Mercy, Van, TJ, May and Eddie— are making their way toward us with Gran Bozan Rumesa Kahinu in the lead. The GB stops and motions to the luggage truck waiting nearby, and the group turns off to load their bags. The GB continues toward us. Their slender form, encased in a fitted gray top and flowing skirts, makes them look like smoke drifting across the tarmac.

"Peace with you." They raise their gentle hands first to the general and then to me. We go through the customary greeting, touching hands, saying the right words, and then their focus shifts entirely to me.

"You cannot imagine, I think, the profound discomfort we feel in seeing this group of young people—all priceless treasures— depart into your keeping."

The general shrugs one shoulder and dips her chin in glum agreement. "What they said."

Gran Bozan Kahinu continues. "I see many things in the future. As a group, they have many roles to fill—many victories, many tragedies to know."

"I'll take good care of them."

They cock their head to the side. "Sometimes I walk in the great forest to the north. It took many years, but now I can discern which sprigs of green will become undergrowth on the forest floor and which will become towering Sequoias adding to the canopy overhead." They turn to look at my group.

Dixie and I follow her eyes to the group of young praenex.

I tamp down my impatience and let the GB's words settle into my heart as we watch the normal things happening around us. A few meters away TJ and May are trying to settle TJ's dog, Cousteau. He's showing off for May's dog, who looks thoroughly disinterested where she sits contently at May's feet.

I'm reminded of the strange energy I felt during the recent wedding ceremony. "May LeRoux—"

"No," Dixie interrupts me, "May Forge. She's keeping her name to honor her father."

I nod. "Very well. May Forge—she's something more."

The GB gives Dixie a curious look.

"I've always thought so, but then she's my granddaughter, so I'm biased."

I sense Dixie's immediate ill ease and turn to face her. "That prevarication we spoke of, it's not absent in Vancouver Colony either, I believe."

She blows out a breath and speaks over me. "Well, ready then?"

I turn and see that my team—I pause for a mental check. My *team*? When did I start to think of them as my team? The *group* is joining us. It's time to go.

"General." Van and TJ salute her.

"Captain. Commander. Ready to go?"

"Well, sure as it would be easier if we had an airplane." Van motions to the empty tarmac.

General Henderson laughs and waves to a technician standing by.

The man approaches and hands me a tablet. I type in my command code as General Henderson directs the group to look at the cordoned off area to our left.

She straightens. "A small demonstration of Spheran tech."

With my final code entered, I send the command, and hear the familiar buzz of electricity as my plane's cloak falls. I don't gasp, like some of them, but the sight of my exquisite jet fills me with pride for my people and our creativity.

"We're flying in that?" Mercy takes a small step back and reaches for Van's hand.

"Excellent!" Van punches the sky with his free fist. "Come on, Cricket." Then he grabs Eddie by the elbow. "You, too, princess."

"Wait." The GB steps after Eddie. "I have something for you." They reach into a pocket concealed in their long skirt and pull out a narrow black case about the size of my forearm. "This is for you. For your journey, and to remind you of home."

Eddie reaches out slowly and opens the case the GB is holding. "Ottavino! Oh, Ru, I love it."

The GB smiles. "A piccolo—the perfect size for traveling, although I suspect you've other diversions in your bag already. It's one octave higher than your flute, and so it fits someone whom we esteem so highly."

"Oh." Eddie runs a finger over the keys, picks up the instrument and raises the mouthpiece to her lips. A lyrical birdsong trills into the air around us and ends on an abrupt, stunted note. They laugh, and the lightness of Eddie's expression makes my chest ache again.

What is this pain? Is it regret? Longing? Or something else? Is it possible that I'm developing feelings for a woman while my best friend, my partner—former partner! —counts her last days in a hospital bed on the other side of the world?

Eddie gently returns the piccolo to its case, as if it could break. "It's beautiful, but it's not really a solo instrument—it's for orchestra, or marching."

The GB closes the case and hands it to her. "I know. If you don't find an assemblage where you're going, remember you'll always have one here. Divine grace with you, Bozan LeRoux." They hold up their right hand for Eddie to clasp. "May your soul feel the glory."

"Peace with you, Sibling." They touch foreheads, and without another look, Eddie tucks the piccolo into her pocket, and follows the others to the plane.

I take a deep breath and realize I'm rubbing my chest again. I turn to make my farewells and see that TJ has stayed behind. I'm not sure why.

His gaze darts down to my chest. "What's wrong?"

I put my hand down, annoyed with myself. "What?"

Instead of speaking, he narrows his eyes and attempts to read my mind. It's only a moment before he shrugs and tips his head toward my plane. "What do you call her?"

"She's Terra Faire Agulha 3."

"Agulha…hmm." TJ concentrates for a moment. "*Wand?*"

"Close, *needle*. I didn't know you spoke Portuguese."

"May and I learned last night."

"Last night?" At first, I think he's joking, but he shrugs it off, so I guess not.

"What's her top velocity? How high have you to taken her? How's her glide ratio?"

It's a barrage of questions as we walk toward my sleek silver jet. His eyes are still pinned to it. I answer what I can, as quickly as I can, but the questions are endless.

"TJ?" I stop, forcing him to stop, too. Finally, he takes a breath and meets my eyes. "I could use a co-pilot, if you're interested?"

"Ha!" He breaks into a grin and thumps me on the back before jogging the rest of the way to the plane. "May! May!"

She sticks her head out of the door as TJ bounds up the stairs. "I'm flying this jet, can you believe it?"

As they disappear into the plane, I stop and take one last look around. The gray peak of Mount Strachan shows through low hanging clouds in the north, like a bearded old man looking down on us. I close my eyes and try to imagine it topped with crisp white snow. One day…once our joint project with the ozone loom has done its work.

When I open my eyes, a dappled sunlight streams onto the runway spreading out before me like steppingstones. Finally, it's time to go.

"Verge Ground, this is TF Agulha 3 requesting takeoff." With the engines humming around us, and all my passengers secured and settled, two big dogs included, I prepare for departure.

TJ acclimated to the unfamiliar controls with the ease of a born pilot. "This is impressive tech." He adjusts the level of the virtual control panel on his right.

"Roger, Agulha 3, this is Verge Ground. Taxi via alpha charlie and hold short at delta."

"Roger, Ground. Taxiing via alpha charlie to hold at delta." I check over the commands TJ has entered and begin our taxi.

"Cross winds look mild today." TJ continues checking readings as we pause at taxiway D.

I glance back into the quiet cabin. Eddie sits in 1B, directly in my line of sight. I'm relieved that she's not looking at me—it gives me the rare opportunity to watch her. She's turned her pale face to the window. A slant of sunlight warms her skin, transforming her lilac purple eyes to points of blue fire. She looks determined, but a little sad. The corners of my mouth pull down, too. I don't want her to be unhappy. Does this mean that maybe, just maybe, it's okay to have feelings for her? I let her ethereal beauty penetrate my thoughts. It's instinctive when I reach out with my mind to touch hers—

"Agulha 3, this is Verge Ground. Taxi to runway two seven left. You are cleared to cross runway two seven right and wait for Tower instructions."

Reluctantly I turn back to the controls. "Roger, Verge Ground."

"Sometimes I wish things were different for her, for both of us." TJ's voice is quiet now. He looks over at me and I notice the sense of serenity that's come over him since he sat in the co-pilot seat. "But in the end, we're just where we're needed. Where the

Creator wants us to be. Anyway, I wanted you to know that I appreciate you giving her the space to decide on her own about this trip. I know that you could have been more…persuasive if you'd wanted to."

I meet his eyes and see a degree of understanding, one man to another, and know that, while many people may not see it, the connection that Eddie and I share hasn't eluded her brother. "Has she spoken to you? About me, I mean?"

"Agulha 3, this is Verge Tower. You are cleared for takeoff on runway two seven left, direct to Terra Faire."

"Roger, Verge Tower. This is TF Agulha 3 ready for takeoff."

Our attention immediately shifts to piloting, and the exhilaration of speed and liftoff.

"She's amazing." TJ's voice is wistful, and I'm not sure if he's talking about the Agulha or his sister.

"She is. Verge Tower, this is TF Agulha 3 beginning our journey direct to Terra Faire."

"Roger, Agulha 3. Radar contact. God speed."

"Roger, Tower, and thank you. Divine grace with you."

"And peace with you, Ambassador."

Vengeance Forge

Current year: 2701
Tuesday, 11:00 AM
Subterranean Severe Weather Research Station 21A, North America

"I'm so confused." The voice is faint and male. "Are you going to help me?"

Vengi stirs in the dream, fighting to focus on the voice. "Yes, I'll help you—"

"How can you, when you're still asleep?"

"I'll wake up, and then I'll help—"

"You're only saying that, but you won't come. You're not a traveler like them." The voice is defeated.

"No, I am! I...I built the ship and everything."

"Then why're you sleeping?"

"I'm waiting."

Hands grab Vengi's shoulders and he opens his eyes to see a familiar face...the face of his dreams. The young man's skin is a deep brown. His almond-shaped eyes are brilliant violet and his gem is black—not a Couvie, then. Vengi hadn't registered this fact before.

"Why are you sleeping?" the man demands again.

"I'm waiting…I'm waiting for them."

"They're coming." The man turns to look behind him. "You won't be ready! Wake up, Vengeance! Wake up!"

"They're coming!" Vengi jolts upright, pain immediately radiating down his neck from where he'd slept on the interlink. He pulls it off, instantly muting the sounds and snuffing out the foreign smells in the VRT. Only the images remain. The black and green Finnish sky swirls silently above him, stars winking. "Computer, end simulation!"

Vengi scrambles out of his sleeping bag and races for the door of the glass simulation box. "Damn!" He turns and runs back to get his rings, carefully sliding each onto the proper finger, including his two comm rings. Then he fastens Jameson's old toolbelt back around his hips.

Snapping his comm rings together, he voices the command. "Call *Maman*." Outside the box, he shoves his feet into ancient sneakers.

His comm rings crackle. "Did you sleep in the sim again?"

Vengi opens his palm as he races through the lab, his mother's image appearing on the virtual screen hovering there. "*Maman*, they're coming!"

"What? When?"

"Now!" Vengi grabs the hover bike leaning against the wall outside the lab, powering up the bike with one hand while he climbs aboard. "Get everyone, get to the garage! I'll meet you there!"

"Vengi, slow down! Even if they come soon, we can't go out right now. We have to wait for a lull."

"Just get everyone, okay?" He closes his palm and switches to audio only so he can steer with both hands. The hover bike takes off down the long underground corridor, reaching 32 kph in just seconds. His tools flail around him. "Is everyone up?"

"We're all awake, thank the Creator. Why do you think they're coming now?"

"God told me, in the dream."

His mother is silent for a moment. "Vengi, dreams can be—"

"Trust me! We've got to be ready."

"I'll get them. We'll meet you there."

Several turns later, Vengi can finally see the blast doors leading to the garage up ahead. When he jumps off the bike, letting it clatter gracelessly against the wall, he hears Robb's voice behind him.

"Wait up there!"

"No time!" Vengi pushes through the heavy doors to find the inner room coming to life. Their two robots have already arrived to start up the computer equipment spread around the perimeter. "Rosy, how's the range?"

Rosy swivels, facing its audio port—a metal circle outlined with faded red marker for lips—toward Vengi. "Radar coming online in 50 seconds."

Vengi pushes a chair out of the way, pulls back a chalky dust cover and begins pounding on an old-fashioned keyboard. "Do we have line of sight? Can you ping the receiver? What's the state of the storm?"

His mother's voice answers from behind him. "We're waiting for a lull; it'll probably be early tomorrow morning before we can go out. The eye is 450 kilometers due east, circling back in approximately twenty hours, but we're still in the tail of the last cycle."

Vengi glances over his shoulder as his mother closes her palm display and switches to a nearby terminal. "That's not good!"

His mother sighs.

He swivels to watch Robb limp from keyboard to keyboard nearby. "Telemetry coming online now."

Po rides through the doors in a small electric golf cart. Old Man Rill, the only sapiens among them, sits on the backward facing bench, one hand gripping the roll bar, the other gripping his cane.

"What in God's name is the ruckus?" Rill swivels to stand heavily on his cane.

"They're coming!" Vengi waves to the screens.

"I know that youngin'…they've been 'coming' for months." Rill holds a hand to his back as he shuffles over to Robb's display.

"I mean they're coming *now*." Vengi moves to join them as they all huddle around Robb's virtual display, where radar will show their immediate airspace…if conditions are right, and if the equipment hasn't been damaged…again.

Tinker, the other robot, hovers behind Robb. "A stool for Robb," it says, holding out the metal seat in its pincers.

"Let me help." Vengi grabs the stool and holds it while Robb shifts a hip onto the stool, taking the weight off his bad leg. *He should have got the stool*, Vengi realizes as he feels the usual pang of guilt at his friend's injury—any injury he caused, albeit by accident.

"Thank you. Here it comes." Robb points to the flickering lines that begin to fill the screen.

Everyone concentrates on the west side of the screen. Nothing lives to the east.

"We need to get suited up!" Vengi tells them. They all keep looking at the screens. "We need to get suited and onto the sleds, hurry!"

His mother waves a hand back at him.

Vengi blows out a huge breath. "Why isn't anyone listening to me?"

"We've listened, lad." Rill turns and lifts his free hand to Vengi's shoulder. "That's why we're pushing watts to get a reading. Now find some patience and watch." Rill turns back to the screen.

"It's up." Robb types into his keyboard, then slumps back in the chair. "No contact."

Everyone sighs and slouches.

"That's impossible!"

His mother holds up her hand. "Okay, Vengi. We'll figure it out. Robb, what's the range?"

"That's it!" Vengi nods. "I bet the range is lousy. They'll be on top of us before we know it."

"Range is…400 kilometers, almost our maximum." Robb looks over his shoulder. "I'll keep watch, kid. As soon as they're on the grid, we'll start getting ready for the mission."

Vengi feels like a deflated balloon. "More waiting?"

Po moves off to another bank of computers. "Once they appear on the radar, we'll still have hours before we need to stage the outer tunnel. Can't go out in the middle of the night with those winds."

"This is so unfair." Vengi slides off his stool, tools thumping against his legs. "Why would I have such a specific dream if it isn't true?"

"Dreams can be tricky, maybe even more so when they're messages from the Creator," his mother says.

"I guess."

"Come on." His mother reaches for a small plastic bin. "You just woke up, you need to eat."

"You brought me food?"

She nods. Vengi looks at her face—amber hair and violet eyes like his, a long, raised scar along one cheek and a rough gem poised neatly between her brows, perfectly matching her light brown skin. He wonders for a second if tomorrow he'll meet another woman—his mother is the only one he's ever known. Are all women so caring? Are they all a strange mixture of soft and stern? Are they all so tireless, so demanding, and yet so forgiving?

"*Merci, Maman.*" He opens the lid of the container and grabs a square of rough brown bread.

She rubs his arm. "When you're done, you might want to think about combing your hair and brushing your teeth."

Vengi rolls his eyes.

She laughs. "If you're right and if today's the day, you don't want the first new people you meet to be impressed by your breath."

"Good point." Vengi finishes chewing. He points into the lunchbox. "There's grit in the container."

His mother laughs again. "There's grit in everything, Vengi. And if today's the day we prepare a rescue mission, there's going to be a lot more grit in everything before it's over."

Vengi looks across the garage to the retrofitted snowmobiles ready to take them out into the sandstorm. They're ready. When the new people arrive, a gritty sandwich is the last thing he'll be thinking about.

9
Cai

Current year: 2701
Tuesday, 12:45 PM
Over the Albuquerque ruins, North America

"Beep, beep, beep…beeeep, beeeep, beeeep…beep, beep, beep."

In the moment it takes me to understand what I'm hearing, TJ has already started trying to locate the signal. "We have a distress signal. Bearing…on screen."

"What's going on?" Van Elder's bulk fills the remaining space in the cockpit. For a large man, he moves incredibly fast. I wonder if that's true of all sapiens, or just him.

I look at the screen. "That can't be right. Check your inputs."

It only takes a heartbeat for TJ to answer. "Confirmed. Signal originates approximately 804 kilometers due east."

I shake my head. "That's impossible. We've never picked up any kind of signal before. Maybe it's a sensor glitch."

Van snorts. "A sensor glitch that sounds out S-O-S? Where are we?"

I check our heading. "About 520 kilometers east of the Humphrey's Peak. Best to ignore it—"

"Aye, that puts us over Old New Mexico—near the Albuquerque ruins." Van crouches down so he's level with our screens. "Are we off course then? Why're we so far east?"

"We adjusted course to avoid a thunderstorm," I tell him. "That's the only adjustment we're making."

TJ turns to Van. "They closed Albuquerque to scavenging years ago. No one flies here anymore."

"Let's not get distracted—"

"Sure as that would explain why no one else has intercepted the signal." Van interrupts, ignoring me again. "So then, what are we waitin' for?"

I can't believe his question. "What do you mean, what are we waiting for? We can't afford this distraction; we've got to get to Terra Faire. We can't go 800 kilometers off course after some unidentified signal."

Van tips his head to the side. "It's not unidentified, it's an SOS. That's quare specific. I dunno about yer little city, but in the Farms, when someone sends up a flare, we run toward it, not away."

"Even if we had the power reserves, we can't do it. It would lead us directly toward the eye of the Great Storm. The Agulha's sturdy, but even *she* can't withstand those winds."

"We can't do nothing."

TJ checks the readings again. "Look at these figures on storm activity. The storm's almost in a lull—these are nearly the best conditions we could hope for, and that's probably why we heard the signal."

I shake my head. "No, no, no. We've got to stay on course." A warmth that I know well is spreading through my limbs. If I were to check my moral compass right now, I know I'd find myself a bit off course myself. But I'm more stubborn than that, I *will* stay focused on the goal of reaching Terra Faire, of seeing Giza before it's too late.

"What's going on?" Eddie's muffled voice comes from behind Van. "What's that noise? What's the problem?"

I blow out a breath. "Do you have the controls?"

TJ nods.

I've got to control this whole situation or I'm going to lose everything. "Okay, let's go."

I motion Van back into the main cabin and unbuckle my harness to follow him. Bending slightly under the overhead compartments, I look at the concerned faces of my passengers. I can do this. I can. I've convinced a tougher audience than this to see my way of things. I can do this.

Van tucks himself into the area surrounding his seat. "We've encountered a distress signal due east, near the eye."

This announcement meets with silence as the women absorb the information.

I clear my throat. "There's no way of knowing whose signal or how long it's been active. We need to stay on course or risk running out of power."

"What? We can't ignore it!" Mercy tries to stand, but her seatbelt holds her down.

"We know nothing. Where would we land? How would we take off again?"

"Hey!" May points her hand toward the floor. She's a woman

of few words, and I've learned that when she speaks, others listen. "The Creator put this in our path."

I turn to Eddie in frustration, hoping that she'll see reason, but her face is turned away from me, her eyes closed in deep concentration. When her eyes fly open and pin mine, I know she's made some kind of decision. "We have to go. We have to see what's at the end of that signal."

"What? No!" No, no, no! I want to scream at them. I've got to get control of this! Everything is at risk. If we somehow survive the landing and get stranded, my people continue to die. If by some miracle we only get delayed, Giza dies alone. If, God forbid, Eddie is lost to the world completely, how much longer will our world have to wait for a cure? "No, nuh, nuh, no!"

Mercy raises a hand. "This is a democracy—"

"I vote yes!" TJ shouts from the cockpit.

"Yes," Eddie says.

"Yes!" Mercy and May shout.

"I'm sorry, yer highness." Van clamps his beefy hand on my shoulder. "Majority rule."

Immediately the plane banks east and accelerates. TJ shouts from the cockpit. "I've got it, I'm locked on the signal! New heading, on course."

These people! So frustrating, so unfocused! I close my eyes and push down the anger rising in me. I *don't* have control of this. Because they're like children at times, chasing after a shiny red balloon! But what are my options? They already understand this mission, that my people are suffering from the Trade at a far more aggressive rate than theirs. I could tell them about Giza.... No, that's like emotional blackmail. Eddie'd never forgive me or herself if I told her and then she chose to follow the signal anyway. She's already straining against the many labels her people have tried to put on her. How would she react to so blatantly adding *savior* to the list?

Van drops back into his seat. "Don't worry, princess, we'll get ye back to yer adoring masses somehow."

"Don't call me that!" The heat in Eddie's eyes as she stares across the aisle at Van tells me I'm right about labels.

She shifts her attention to me. "Well? I'd really rather not die today so maybe you could help TJ fly your plane?"

I grit my teeth and stride back to the pilot seat to strap in. The sky ahead of us is menacing. It's a permanent storm so large it can be seen from outer space, turning part of our once blue-green planet into an orb with a big splotch of swirling red and brown. The Great Storm may be nearing a lull, as TJ called it, but it's still a sight I never imagined I'd intentionally fly into. It matches my mood perfectly.

Both of the dogs start whining in the back. I know how they feel.

"If we're doing this," I say, "here's how it's going to go—"

Beep, beep, beep.

"Now what?" I check the new warning blinking on my virtual display. "Proximity alarm!"

"Proximity?" Eddie asks.

"Everybody buckle up."

TJ swivels between controls. "I've got signals coming in from the west. Approximately…God's grace! Twenty aircraft flying in formation."

"Have they seen us?"

"I don't think so, not yet. They're staying on course heading south of our new course east."

"I'm tracin' 'em," Van calls from behind me.

"What are you doing? Get back in your seat!"

He's crouched in the aisle, his TAC combat communication kit open on the floor. A tiny virtual screen projects a map of blinking lights over his controls. "Holy hell! It's SciCorps. Twenty class three unmanned drones on course to…has to be South America."

I turn to TJ. "They must have gone around the storm like us. What are they doing?"

He shakes his head. "The only thing that fits is that they're looking for us, and maybe trying to find Terra Faire."

"Aye, fits fine I'd say." Van settles on the floor with his tech spread around him.

I take a deep breath. It makes sense. "I agree."

"Yer shielding technology, is it on?" Van asks.

"No, I turned it off shortly after departure to save energy."

Eddie leans forward. "If those drones see us, they'll follow us, now or later after we reach that distress signal. Mother won't just lose interest once she realizes they've found their target."

TJ nods. "I agree, she'll sink her teeth in."

"Mother?" I ask.

Eddie sighs. "We discussed it. The name on everyone's minds while you were captive on SATO Station? That *LeRoux* wasn't our father; it was our *mother*, Fleet Admiral LeRoux. She's pulling the strings."

TJ swears under his breath. "We should cloak."

I tap in the commands. "Cloaking now." The interior lights dim as my jet diverts energy to the technology that shields it from both sight and radar. Now we should be safely invisible.

"God's grace!" Van's big hands run over the controls.

"What?"

"They've found us. The drone at the tail end of the convoy just changed course to intercept us." He pounds a fist on the wall. "We're bloody eejits!"

"Why? What happened?"

TJ banks left. "Still following?"

The dogs are barking now; May tries settling them but without much luck. We wait for Van's reply.

"Aye, course adjusted. Eejits, like I said."

"It's chance, has to be." I turn to TJ. "It picked us up right before we cloaked."

TJ shakes his head. "More like right after. SciCorps's smart. They must've found a way to identify the energy signature of your cloaking tech. The second we cloaked we lit up like a beacon."

"Bollocks." Van taps furiously into his control board. "Confirming, drone is unmanned. I'd bet good credits those drones don't have independent operators yet, but that won't last long."

"We need to put distance between us and that drone. It doesn't matter now if they see us. Dropping cloak. Prepare for acceleration," I warn them.

"Go, now!" Van shouts. "Drone accelerating. That little

gobshite just got a pilot."

"Get in your seat!" I can't wait for Van to comply; I increase speed, the jolt pressing me back. I hear the dogs yip and May's answering gasp.

"Van!" Mercy cries.

Van's kit crashes against the wall with a loud thud, knocking Van down with it.

The wind picks up and TJ and I fight for control. We're flying fast, the tempest buffets us from all directions, reducing visibility to less than a kilometer.

"There it is!" TJ points to starboard just as a flash of light passes in front of the windshield. A new alarm blares.

"What was that? Quiet those dogs!" I shake my head. "Are they shooting at us?"

"Tracker!" Van shouts.

I risk a glance back to see he's juggling his kit again, trying to operate his combat tech.

"Get in your seat!"

"Nah, got better things to do. That one missed us, but they'll try again. Stand by to bank left on my mark."

The plane shakes violently. Turbulence pushes us up and down within dusty clouds of pale orange. The dogs are absolutely crazed now.

"I see it! There!" TJ points ahead of us.

The drone is a black shadow in the haze. I catch the flash of light and bank hard left even before Van gives the command.

"Left! Gah!" Van groans as his head smacks Eddie's seat.

"Missed!" My joy is fleeting. Like a surreal image from a nature vid, I watch the drone swirl past us again caught in the funnel of a small tornado. One of its wings rips away before it's sucked into the core.

"The drone is down!" TJ shouts.

"Brace for impact!" I don't even have time to pray before the edge of the funnel catches our nose and tosses us like a skipping stone toward the ground. "Creator, help us all."

Eddie murmurs a prayer. Her words lace through the cacophony of noise—gusting wind, barking dogs, screaming engines. TJ's hands fly over the controls as fast as mine. Somehow we manage to correct our descent. We're losing altitude too quickly, but at least our nose is forward.

It comes down to just me and the yoke. The Agulha takes the bumps better than I expected at first, and then we hit the *real* wind.

"We need more control!" TJ has to shout now to be heard over the screaming wind of the storm.

"I'm doing the best that I can!" But he's right. The jet is bouncing on the turbulence like a boat crashing through an ocean gale. Up and down, then listing sideways. Sweat trickles down my temple and my fingers have gone numb.

"Two-thousand feet!" TJ shouts. "No obstacles. Close to zero grade."

"Everyone hang on!" I fight to keep the jet's nose up while the craft continues to jump around on bursts of wind.

"Van!" Eddie screams this time. "Van's not buckled."

"Oof! I'm tryin'!"

Van's combat kit smashes into TJ's footwell. "Ignore it!" he shouts.

"Five-hundred feet!" I call out. "Here we go!" For a moment the landing feels almost normal as our wheels tap the ground, then a cross wind hits the plane and tosses us back up, only for another gust to slam us back down again. My teeth snap in my jaws, my bones jar against the force of the landing. The swirling storm outside the canopy is uninterrupted brown, and I know we're on the ground, sliding, only because the readings tell me so. I'm conscious of one positive thing: we are not being torn in half in a ball of flame. I start to hope. We're decreasing speed, the noise still a deafening roar. The dogs sound a little less wild. We're slowing down. Just as I think it might work, the power of the sinking sand overcomes the power of velocity and catches our landing gear in an abrupt and jarring halt.

Slam!

I'm too disoriented to understand why I feel weightless—to comprehend that the nose of my amazing jet is buried headfirst in sand and I'm hanging nearly upside down in my seat. All motion has stopped. For one breathless moment we're still, then with a hideous screech, the Agulha tips to the side and crashes down on her back.

For a moment we sit in stunned silence, just the sound of the storm reminding us we're alive.

"Is everyone alright?" May shouts. The dogs begin to bark again—two distinct sounds. May shushes them.

I look over at TJ, hanging next to me. He nods.

"We're unharmed. How are the rest of you?"

"Van is hurt!"

TJ curses before gracefully releasing his harness and flipping over to stand. "I've got him."

I twist to see Eddie. Her long white hair hangs loose, dragging on the roof of the plane. Her feet and slender bare legs are kicking in the air while her many-layered skirts obstruct her body and head from my view.

She grunts. "God's grace! Somebody get me out of this thing!" Her clothes muffle her voice while her arms flail and her hands try to find the straps.

Suddenly Mercy appears, picking her way carefully along the roof of the plane, wincing with each movement. It's a strange juxtaposition to see her walking in the upside-down cabin. "Van! God's grace, you're bleeding."

"Just a bump on the head, lass. Don't worry."

TJ helps Van into a seated position on the floor and covers his bleeding forehead with one hand. "What else hurts? Can you move your arms and legs?"

"Can I…" Van pushes TJ away. "Of course I can move. Get off me now. I'm fine I said." He stands as much as he can in the tight space.

TJ shakes his head. "You get hurt a lot, brother."

"Oh, Van." Mercy cuddles into his side. "You need to be more careful. You were bouncing around like a rag doll."

"'Tis just a scratch."

"Will somebody get me out of this seat please?" One of Eddie's feet nearly kicks Mercy in the head.

She deflects it, instinctively covering her gem with her free hand, and then crouches down next to Eddie's face while TJ tries to find the seatbelt release. "Really, Eddie. I keep telling you that pants are much more practical for travel. Maybe when we get to Terra Faire, we can see one of their tailors."

"Ouch, TJ!" Eddie smacks his leg. "You stepped on my hair."

"And maybe get a haircut too," May adds, propping both elbows on the upside-down seats behind TJ. "The dogs want out."

"Don't let them out!" Eddie insists.

"Let them out," TJ says at the same time.

"Get me down first. This is ridiculous." Eddie tries to cover her bare legs, but every movement exposes a different area.

TJ swats her hand. "Hold still. Why do you wear so many layers?"

"Here, let me help." Mercy raises an arm, then drops it again. "Ow, that seatbelt hurt my shoulder.

"Let me see, Cricket…"

Their childish bickering fills my ears. I take a few more breaths while I figure out the best way out of my seat. Slowly the giddy sense of having survived begins to penetrate past the adrenaline. I recognize their banter and silliness for what it is now…joy to be alive. I take one last deep breath of relief before maneuvering free from my seat. I'm alive, they're alive, but what will become of us now? And what will happen to Giza while we wait to find out?

Rill O'Brien

In the past...
October 30, 2682, 19 years ago
Subterranean Severe Weather Research Station 21A, North America

"Tinker, try it again!" Rill shouted, hoping his voice would carry through the carbon monoxide mask to the robot at the central controls.

"Leak reduced by 50 percent," the robot responded.

"Alright, ye bugger." Rill tapped the pipe before moving on to repair the next crack. He'd been waiting to see what yesterday's earthquake would bring, and the screech of the carbon monoxide alarm had roused him from a fitful sleep. If the gas reached the farm, he was in real trouble.

"How 'bout now?"

"Stand by…stand by." Tiny lights flickered on Tinker's control board.

"Oh, come on, ye metal eejit! Is it out or not?" He took one step down his ladder.

"Confirmed. No leak detected. Level four ventilation recommended for another 30 minutes."

"What's that gonna do to power consumption?" He finished his descent and transferred his tools from his belt back into his toolbox.

"Estimating—"

A new alarm started blaring—one Rill had never heard before. "Now what?" He rushed to the control panel, trying to unbuckle his mask as he went. "Computer, identify alarm."

"A radar proximity alarm is sounding," the computer answered.

Rill straightened. Tinker mirrored his movement. For a moment they just stood there.

"Go!" Rill shouted and took off toward the door, the robot by his side. As soon as they reached the long open corridor leading back to the garage, the robot took off at a speed Rill couldn't hope to match. "All AI report to the garage and monitor incoming radar signal!"

He ran like a man possessed, at first trying to struggle with his gas mask, and then giving up so he could use both arms to pump his sprint. With his heart galloping—he was over 50 now—he burst through the huge doors to the garage and rushed to the radar control center. On the screen, overlaying an image of the SSWRS, he could see a tiny red blip. "They're just outside! Any contact?"

"Negative," a robot answered, "but the computer has detected unauthorized access to the west lateral turbine shaft."

"The shaft? Gads, they'll be shredded to pieces. Shut it down! Shut down the turbine!" Panicked, Rill turned on his heel and raced back through the door to reach another corridor that led to the turbine control room. Almost to the door, still struggling with his mask, he saw a familiar shape scurrying toward him along the wall.

"Sweets!" His mask muffled his voice as he scooped up the mouse and tucked him into his shirt pocket. "Where have ye been? We've company. Please God, let it be people."

He stumbled into the maintenance room and crashed into something soft. Something that wasn't supposed to be there. Something that moved.

"Oof!" Rill flailed his arms to try to keep from falling, but tripped and went down hard on his butt.

"Divine grace!" A man's voice said.

Rill looked up to see two people dressed in what he assumed must be flight uniforms. They were covered in dust, one leaning heavily on the other, leg bent to keep the weight off it. Rill stared at them; their purple eyes stared back. Between those eyes Rill could see diamond-shaped nova gems, dusty for sure, but matching their skin tones.

"Yer gem's supposed to be black."

"Is it human?" They spoke at the same time.

"What?" Rill asked.

The uninjured person pointed a finger at Rill's face and circled their finger. "Is the air not safe in here?"

"What?" Rill asked again. "Oh!" He finished unfastening his gas mask and pulled it off. "No, I was just—"

"There's a mouse in their pocket," the injured one slurred, before slumping even more.

"Easy there." The uninjured intruder lurched over to a stool and lowered their friend down onto the seat. Rill could see they were shorter than him, by a lot, but otherwise looked mostly like normal young people.

"We're Couvies," one said without turning around. "Our gems aren't black anymore, haven't been for generations."

"Couvies?"

"Yeah, we're scavies from Vancouver Colony, the Verge."

"You're not from the Farms?"

"The Farms?" The uninjured one turned to look at him, and then held out a hand. They'd covered their fingers in ornate rings. "Do you need help up, friend?"

"What? Oh!" Rill scrambled up from the floor, trying hard to remember what you're supposed to do when you meet people. "Jesus, Mary and Joseph, my manners! I'm Rill. Rill Ban O'Brien, *pronoms mascu*. This is my place." He held out a hand to shake, sapiens-style, then remembered his mistake and raised it instead. "Welcome to the SS Worse."

The intruder cocked their head to the side before reaching out a hand to shake. "We Couvies shake hands." They thrust theirs further toward Rill, and Rill gripped it. "I'm Poacher, and this is my brother, Robbery, *pronoms mascu*, but you can call us Po and Robb."

"Uh…nice to meet ye." Rill shook the outstretched hand.

"What's the SS Worse?" asked the injured man, Robb.

"Oh, um…" Sweets squeaked and Rill took him out of his pocket to sit on his shoulder. "Subterranean Severe Weather Research Station 21A. We call it the SS Worse for short, because 'no matter how bad things get, they can always get worse.'"

Robb huffed a laugh that turned into a cough, and Po shook

his head.

"How many people live here?" Po asked.

"Just me, and Sweets here. A few eejit robots. And some chickens, a cow. We used to have a goat, but she—"

"You're alone here?" Robb interrupted.

"Well, I mean, I was…"

The two men exchanged a meaningful look.

Rill took a deep breath. He must look like an old fool. He stepped forward to put one hand on each of the men's shoulders. "I'm bungling this like an eejit, it's just that I've waited so long. Don't worry, now. Ye're strong if ye survived out there. This place is safe. Ye're safe. I can treat yer injuries and answer all yer questions, give ye a warm meal. I'm mighty glad to meet ye, Couvies Po and Robb. You're the answer to a million prayers, and I can't wait to hear all about yer world."

10
Cai

Current year: 2701
Tuesday, 6:00 PM
34.6036° N, 98.3959° W

I always imagined sapiens were sturdy, rugged people—their size certainly gives that impression—but as I suture a wound on Van Elder for the second time in only a few months, I'm really starting to wonder. He's got some bad bruises too, but the head wound was the worst.

"I don't have ointment, but if you leave the bandage alone it should stay clean."

"Aye, thank ye, doc. Much obliged to ye for sewin' me up again." He turns to Mercy. "Alright now, wife. I did as ye asked, though 'twas just a scratch, now it's yer turn."

She sighs and winces.

I've been watching her wince for the last half hour. "Mercy."

She finally looks at me.

"Just let me see it." I lay a gentle hand on her injured shoulder. "I'm sure you're right, that it's just a bruise, but if we're going to get out of here and find the source of that distress signal, we need to know all the facts, including any injuries among our team, understand?"

She chews her lip, but nods.

Eddie squeezes in and gently elbows Van to move him aside. "Let me help with her shirt."

"No." I shake my head. "If her ribs are injured, then shifting them to remove her shirt will be risky. I'll have to cut it off. I'm sorry."

Eddie and Van both grimace.

"What?"

Mercy sighs. "Favorite shirt. Doesn't matter. Just go ahead."

"Uh…" Eddie touches my hand before the scissors reach fabric. "Will you let me?"

I shrug and hand them over. Van and I move back so that Eddie can get in a better position next to Mercy on the ceiling-turned-floor. I watch her gentle hands as she removes Mercy's neutral insignia and hands the pin to Van. She starts to cut Mercy's shirt at the vertical seam all the way at the bottom by Mercy's waist. She murmurs quiet words to Mercy as the scissors cut, feather light, through the fabric. Mercy whispers in reply. When Eddie gets near the armpit, she shifts to snip with just the tip, careful to avoid touching Mercy's skin. When the final cut from shoulder to neck is finished, she pulls the fabric around Mercy's back, helps her remove her uninjured arm, and finally slips the remaining sleeve off Mercy's immobile hand.

I'm moved by her gentleness. She's usually either fully engaged in whatever action is happening or entirely reserved and aloof. Seeing her in softer moments like this one, and the moments with her offspring, I'm struck by how little I really know her.

"What?" Eddie stares at me. "Are you hurt?"

Her frank question brings me back to the present. "Hurt? No, why?"

"You're rubbing your chest again."

"I am?" I look down and quickly drop my hand. The stinging pressure in my chest eases. "Oh, it's nothing. Good work. Thank you."

She holds up the shirt to show her handiwork. "This way we can mend it along the seams."

I nod. "Very considerate." I clear my throat.

"Oh, Cricket!"

At Van's concerned voice, I grip Eddie by the upper arms and shift her out of the way so I can reach my patient. Mercy sits in her bra, staring down at the angry red bruise running diagonally across her chest from shoulder to sternum.

"I really didn't think it was this bad."

"Okay, let's take a look."

After a few minutes of careful examination, I'm sure there are no fractures. "It looks worse than it is. The seatbelt did its job, it just had a bit too much give in it. No broken bones, but you're going to be sore for several days. We'll immobilize the arm with a sling to keep you from moving the shoulder too much. And I want to check every twelve hours to see how you're healing. If you start experiencing any shortness of breath, or any other symptoms, no matter how disconnected they seem, I want to know right away, no hedging. Understood?"

"Of course. But don't we need to pack up and go? How can I

help with my arm in a sling?"

May leans in over us and hands Mercy a button-down shirt. "We're not going anywhere right now. Storm's too strong."

"How do you know?" I ask her. This is exactly what I was afraid of, more delays.

"TJ got Van's kit working again. Well, sort of. It's estimating windspeed well beyond what we can navigate on foot."

Heart sinking, I grit my teeth. "How long before we can move?"

She looks over her shoulder toward TJ.

"Winds should die down overnight, but then we have the problem of darkness," TJ says. "I say we move at first light."

At his announcement, the anxiety emanating from our group escalates and I'm forced to raise my mental shield higher to keep from giving in to their fear. I prefer my own frustration and anger to theirs.

Everyone takes a moment and then, by silent agreement, we start setting up places to rest along the fuselage. My temper is getting the better of me. I shove a pillow and my inflight bag into the space I've selected for myself near the flight deck. When Eddie hands me a blanket, I tug it away instead of gently taking it from her. Closing my eyes, I take a deep breath.

"I'm sorry. Thank you for the blanket."

She nods, and I'm surprised when I drop down into my makeshift cubby to find her following me. She scoots out of the aisle and sits cross-legged facing me. Our knees touch and I feel a jolt of that odd electricity again, but when I brace my arms to move over, she waves it off.

"I'm fine." She chews her bottom lip before making eye contact with me. "I want to ask you something. A bit ago, after I helped Mercy with her shirt? That look on your face…the way you rubbed your chest? You did the same thing back in my apartment when the children were there. I know it's probably none of my business, but what is it? What's wrong?"

How much can I tell her without making it *about* her? Without adding too much pressure, but at the same time, sharing some of my motivation.

"Your gentleness, it reminded me of something…*someone* from my past. My friend and I had just become adults, though we were very young. We had so many plans for the future. Big plans, and small. She wanted nothing more than to be a mother. I watched her joy during the months of her pregnancy and was so excited to be there when she gave birth. Everything seemed normal—I'm not an obstetrician, but as a medical student, I'd attended other births. I was holding her hand when the baby was born. I was focused on her, on her face. We were both surprised when we heard a sob and watched the young nurse run out of the room."

I swallow hard against the lump in my throat. I haven't replayed this memory in such detail in many years, and I've never told anyone else out loud. I'm not sure I can continue.

Then Eddie slides her hand into mine. It's soft and warm. She squeezes my hand with the same strong, slender fingers I've seen expertly guide the bow of her violin and stroke the soft hair of her offspring. I lace my fingers through hers and draw on her strength.

She grips hard. "You don't have to—"

"No, I want to tell you." I roll my shoulders. "The doctor's expression was grim. My friend asked what was wrong, but the doctor just shook her head. When she handed the infant into my friend's arms…it was like the end of the world."

I squeeze her hand. She squeezes back just as hard, just a strong.

"The boy—it was a boy—he was gorgeous, absolutely beautiful. But his gem... There was only a tiny speck of black pigment left. The disease was so far advanced; he lived only a few days."

"I'm so sorry."

"Thank you. It was a long time ago, and we have measures now to prevent such a thing from happening. But it was a difficult time. It changed so many things. But I remember her in those short days—the way she held him, the gentle way she touched him and cared for him, with such single-minded focus. As if nothing else existed in the world." I sniff and run a hand through my hair. "I haven't allowed myself to think about that for a long time. When something reminds me of that time, I get a kind of pinch in my chest. It's nothing. I don't mean to worry anyone."

"I'm not worried." Eddie says before squeezing my hand and slowly unwinding our fingers. "Thank you for telling me. Your friend, is she—? I mean, will I meet her when we arrive in Terra Faire?"

My head whips up to meet her eyes. It's such a simple question, but I hadn't thought of it before. Would Eddie meet Giza? "I don't know. I hope so."

She cocks her head to the side. "So do I." She shakes herself and looks around. "Well, I'll leave you to rest."

I nod and watch her half walk, half crawl over to her own space on the other side of the plane.

The wind howls outside, occasionally rocking the plane slightly and causing the dogs to whine. I listen as the people around me settle in to wait it out. The air is warm, but a coolness seeps into my bones as I contemplate our situation. I let my mind drift and, in that place just before sleep, I see an image of myself from a great height. I'm curled into the side of my plane. Nearby a blinking red beacon flashes in the sand. Another faint light shines far to the south, its luminance ebbing and flowing in a cloudy pattern over my home in Chileru.

"Giza," I whisper her name. "Giza, what am I going to do?" I fall asleep waiting for an answer that doesn't come.

Vengeance Forge

Current year: 2701
Wednesday, 5:40 AM
Subterranean Severe Weather Research Station 21A, North America

"They're nearly on top of us." Robb zooms in on the radar and tightens the image of the SSWRS schematics overplayed on the grid. "Only half a kilometer." Robb looks at the others. "They're practically outside the tunnel entrance."

Vengi snaps the strap holding his goggles to his helmet. "Good, let's go get them."

His mother stifles a yawn and swivels to check another screen. "Wind conditions consistent with F0 gale tornado, but I see gusts coming in at…God's grace!" She sits back in her chair. "Gusts up to 210 kph!"

Old Rill chuckles. "Aye, that'll test ye. I hope ye ate yer breakfast, lad."

Vengi leans back. "We've traveled in worse. Let's go."

His mother waves a hand. "Hold on."

"We gotta go!"

"Vengi, one second for a prayer." His mother holds out her

hand to him, and he takes it, knowing that arguing will only take longer.

When they've all linked hands, his mother looks at each one of them in turn. "Remember, the people are the mission, everything else is secondary."

"Secondary, but really important," Vengi adds.

His mother blows out a breath. "Okay, let's pray." When they sink to their knees for a moment of silent prayer, Old Rill bends over and leans on their shoulders instead of his cane. As soon as the prayer is over, they jog for the outer garage. Rill follows with one of the robots.

Vengi checks over the trailers attached to the three sleds, slapping the side of his helmet impatiently.

His mother joins him. "What's wrong?"

"I feel like I've forgotten something, but I don't know what."

His mother, Po, and Robb all quickly check the trailers and sleds. Rill runs through the punch list the robot shares with him.

"Looks okay." Robb says.

His mother nods. "It'll be fine."

Po twirls his hand in the air. "*Allons-y!* Let's go!"

Vengi checks Po's helmet and dust suit, making sure his neckerchief's securely tucked in. Po does the same for him and they climb aboard the modified snowmobile. They clip their tethers together, and then to the sled.

"Ready?" His mother's voice is tinny in his headset.

Vengi looks over to where she and Robb wait on their sleds. He gives a thumbs up. "*Allons-y!*"

The sleds are the noisiest of their electric vehicles, not because of a poor retrofit, but because Vengi redesigned them that way. He watched old vids, so he knew what they were supposed to sound like. The others were angry about the noise at first, but after the initial ride, everyone agreed the sound was helpful for keeping track of each other out in the storm.

Vengi enjoys the hum and grind as they pass over the concrete and through the first dust curtain. The pavement is dusty here, but largely clear. The ceilings and walls are high and wide, large enough for trucks to drive side by side, but as they twist and turn upward through the snaking tunnel, the grade increases and sand begins to cover the pavement and gather along the walls. As the minutes pass and Vengi counts down the dust curtains they've passed, the sand gets thicker and debris begins to appear. As it accumulates, the tunnel seems to get smaller and smaller until they're forced to ride single file. He knows they're near the exit when a gust of wind buffets his sled and he has to compensate quickly to avoid crashing into a small dune that's formed along the wall.

"Here we go!" His mother shouts into her microphone. With a burst of speed, her sled darts forward through the last curtain and into the storm.

He grips Po's waist tighter just as their sled shoots forward.

"Brace for the barrier!" Robb shouts into the microphone.

Vengi tightens expectantly as they explode through the artificial wall of forced air that serves as the tunnel's final door. Outside, the world is the same as ever—brown, brutal, and loud. They navigate largely by the maps and data displayed on the inner faces of their riding helmets.

Looking out past Po's shoulder, Vengi sees his mother's sled appearing and then disappearing in the dusty wind ahead of them.

"Almost there," his mother announces.

"Debris!" Po shouts, and Vengi watches in horror as his mother narrowly misses running headlong into a giant tumbling piece of metal. Po takes a hard right into the wind, avoiding the obstacle that screeches as it slams into a dune and stops. Vengi stares in disbelief as they pass it—a shiny metal airplane wing.

"Where's the fuselage?"

"There, to the south!" Robb shouts through the comm.

Vengi stares at the sleek plane on its back ahead of them. It's so much larger than he was expecting, and then he remembers what he forgot. "God's grace! I remember now."

"What?" his mother asks.

"The heavy duty clamps I fabricated to hold the equipment we're taking. I, uh… left them in the garage."

"I didn't see them," Po says.

"Yeah, um…they're in the paint dryer," Vengi admits.

"What?" Robb's sled pulls alongside his.

"I just thought they'd look better painted."

"God's grace!" Po shouts. "What does color matter?"

"Details matter!"

"Okay, forget it," his mother shouts. "We'll figure it out. Right now we've got to get to that door and get on with this mission."

Po pulls their sled to a stop next to his mother's sled, and Robb joins them. Directly ahead, the long silver plane rests on its back— silver belly to the sky like a dead fish. It's already half covered in sand and debris.

"No fire detected," Po says, "but that wing back there is a lost cause."

"Okay, I see the door." His mother motions toward the plane. "Robb and Vengi, you're with me."

"This is going to be great!" Vengi thumps the side of the sled. "They're bound to have the tech we need. Look at how sophisticated that fuselage is! It's a treasure trove, for sure."

"*Vengi*." His mother's voice is thick with disapproval.

"Oh, and I'm sure the people are going to be nice, too."

"Let's get prepped. It's going to take a few minutes. Before we get tethered for the walk, I want the med kit, just in case. Leave the sleds running, we might need to navigate by sound."

11
Eddie

After a fitful night tensing with every groan of the fuselage around me, it's finally morning. Not that much light is coming in through the windows; most of them are buried in sand now. Fortunately the plane's door faces away from the wind, the windows on that side show a dusty brown world slowly brightening to a sickly tan.

Cai clears his throat. "Everyone finish what you're doing and let's go through the plan again."

With a lot of argument all around, we'd decided we're all going, no one stays behind. So we sorted the debris and packed our bags. I filled my pockets with my most precious belongings, wanting to keep them close, almost as if I'm expecting to find myself once again hanging upside down over a scattering of cargo and junk very soon. It's as orderly here as we can make it.

I wish I could say the same about my inner state, but between the seriousness of our situation and the story Cai shared with me yesterday, I'm good and truly scared. How can I save anyone if I die here?

I am more than the gray matter inside my skull. I am a bright light, a little piece of the Divine, and I am safe in my next breath, and the next. I am not confined to this small space, this moment. I reach and reach.

"Eddie?" Mercy touches my shoulder.

When I turn, she's still wincing from the movement. "Cricket, are you sure about this? We can scout it out and come back for you—"

"No! We stay together. I'm fine. I'm coming along."

"Of all the stupid ideas—"

We turn toward Van's raised voice.

"Ye two are bigger eejits than I thought if ye're gonna argue with me about this now."

"They're our dogs, we get to decide." May stands with hands on hips, two leashes fisted in her grip. Both dogs shift anxiously around her legs.

"And ye're my friends!" Van shouts. "Do ye really think I'm gonna let ye get blown to kingdom come just because ye're too daft to let me take those leashes? I weigh nearly twice as much as the two of ye eejits bundled together."

"That's an exaggeration." TJ shakes his head. "Besides, May and I have skills you don't have when it comes to keeping our dogs safe."

"We don't have time for this." Cai steps between them and hands out ration bars. "We'll put the dogs in the kennels and carry them. Hurry up and eat."

He waves Mercy and I to join them, handing each of us a bar.

I take Mercy's from her and tear open the wrapper before handing it back.

"Who put you in charge?" TJ asks Cai.

He cocks his head to the side and I can see by his pinched expression that he's barely controlling his impatience. "Well, I'm the oldest, it's my plane, and technically I'm the only one here who's literally been elected, so, um…God? God put me in charge."

It's probably the worst thing he could have said. Everyone starts arguing at once. The men are all competing for dominance. May looks like she might strike them all down with magical lightning bolts or something. And Mercy keeps trying to reach out to people with her bad arm, wincing and cringing with every new insult they throw at each other.

I close my eyes and block out their voices. I focus on the world around me, on our purpose here. It only takes a moment for me to feel the pull of the signal we intercepted: I'm sure there's life nearby. I center first my mind and then my talents on the lifeforce outside in the storm.

I am a bright light, a little piece of the Divine. I am not confined to this small space, this moment. I reach and reach.

When I feel them—people! —I'm sure we were right to come here, to risk everything. I step into the fray and take Cai's hand.

He stops talking abruptly and searches my face.

I smile into his eyes. I allow the feeling of purpose and serenity to flow through my mind and out through my gem like a gentle wave. I reach for May next and tense at the jolt of power that connects to me through her gloved hand.

She swallows hard and heaves a sigh.

I give Mercy a meaningful look and she joins hands with Van. "What?" Van asks. "What's going on?"

"Let's take a moment for prayer." I raise my eyebrows at TJ.

He straightens and hesitates but doesn't argue when May takes his hand and points for him to take Van's.

Cai is the final link. With a sigh, he gently reaches his free hand around Mercy's back to her uninjured shoulder.

I sense the moment my praenex friends connect with the Creator. It's a moment of peace and affirmation. The serenity winds its way through my scattered thoughts like a familiar melody. I share my certainty about our purpose here; I connect them to the lifeforce outside. My voice weaves words of love, of affirmation and entreaty. We worship the Creator, the spark woven in us, between us, and around us in the form of the world we long to save. The music of prayer soothes us, or most of us, anyway. Cai's impatience is like a wild thing, barely contained. It's the best I can do to show him what I sense. As the prayer ends, I release the hands I hold and open my eyes.

The dogs whine in the relative silence.

"Amen," Van says.

"That was…helpful." Cai clears his throat and looks around nervously.

I'm sorry that we got him into this mess. I try to remind myself that this trip was his idea, his manipulation, but between surviving a plane crash and learning more about his people, his past, I can't muster the same degree of inner angst I felt when we set out yesterday.

I touch his sleeve. "It's going to be alright. We've been in worse situations than this."

He stares at me for a moment, his mouth slightly open. "Worse than crashed in the middle of nowhere without a means to communicate with the outside world?"

I grimace and glance at my brother.

TJ shrugs and bends to pet his dog. "I hate to point out the obvious, but has it occurred to anyone else that the tracker implants we were so recently happy to turn off would come in very handy about now?"

"Lost is lost." May stands, hands on hips, in the aisle. "And I never had a tracker anyway."

"Aye, we've been banjaxed before…maybe not this exact situation with the comm, but at least no one's gushing blood."

Someone says "Amen," and we all huddle around the virtual screen that TJ erects in the open space by the door.

I glance at Cai. The mental *click* is immediate, surprising us both. The more time we spend in each other's company, the more unpredictable that connection's become. I still don't know what it means. It's a small consolation that Cai doesn't seem any wiser.

"I know it's not easy for you—taking on so many strong…*personalities*, I guess. Listening to us when making decisions. I can't say we'll change, but maybe it'll get easier the more you know us, the more you learn to trust us."

"Aye, and when ye get used to TJ's quare annoyin' habits," Van adds, trying to squeeze into the small space next to TJ.

"Oh, my habits, huh?" TJ replies in a mild voice, free of lingering anger.

Cai tips up his chin. "It's not a matter of trust really. It's about my mission and the risks I'm willing to take weighed against the needs of the entire Spheran society." He looks around at the surreal upside-down scene. "So far, siding with the majority has not worked out so well."

I can't help the smirk that lifts one corner of my mouth. "And yet, it still feels right to me. This is all going to work out, we just have to trust in the Creator and see how."

Van waves a hand. "So now, here's what we want to do next. We'll suit up and follow the signal—"

His explanation is cut off by May. "Shhhh. Do you hear that?"

I listen, but the raging wind mutes everything else. "All I hear is the storm." I try harder to tune my ears to whatever has May— and the two dogs now that I care to notice—straining their ears to hear.

"Yes." TJ stops navigating on his screen. "It sounds like a motor."

"More than one, I think." Cai closes his eyes.

I do the same to help me focus, but the sound is clear now that I can separate it from the wind.

Van steps toward the door and instinctively places a hand on his belt where his stunner would normally be. "Whoever they are, it must have been their signal we were tracking."

Mercy takes his hand. "Why are you worried? This is why we came, right? Those have to be the people we're here to help."

TJ also focuses on the door. The dogs mimic his concentration.

"Everyone stay calm." I say it to myself as much as them.

"This is better," Cai comments. "It saves us having to look for them. If they have vehicles, maybe they can help us get to Terra

Faire."

The engine noise continues. Mercy takes a step back toward me as May makes room for us. We arrange ourselves in a straight line down the makeshift aisle with Van and TJ flanking the door and Cai pressing back into the cockpit. We wait for what seems a ridiculously long time.

"Bang, bang, bang!" We all jump. Before we can react, the sound comes again. *"Bang, bang, bang!"*

I come unfrozen first. "Open it!"

Van looks unsure, but then the mechanism starts to turn from the outside. He reaches over and helps, but instead of gliding gracefully out and away, the initial push sends a rush of sand through the crack.

"Wait!" The wind distorts the disembodied feminine voice outside.

I glance at Mercy, and then at May, whose eyes are wide as saucers, as if she's seeing something different than the rest of us.

"A woman," Cai says. "And two…no, three men. One is very young, almost a child."

TJ takes a step closer to Cai. "How do they feel?"

Cai's brows furrow, creasing around his gem. "They feel…hopeful, excited, and a little…concerned for us, and themselves." He blinks and looks at us. "We're hardly safe here."

"Let's see what the dogs think." TJ unleashes both dogs.

Outside the *scritch, scritch* sound of digging stops and Van pushes again on the door as it begins to glide out. Two pairs of gloved hands curl around the edge of the door as the gap widens. The dogs squeeze through the gap barking excitedly. Wind and dust fly in from outside. I cover my face.

We hear raised voices outside before both dogs jump back into the plane.

TJ signals them back. "They're excited and a little confused, but they don't sense any danger."

"How do you—" Cai's question is interrupted by the activity at the door.

The wind dies down as someone blocks the opening and steps inside. A dusty black environmental suit covers our visitor head to toe. The dogs greet them with sniffs and nudges before May whistles them to her. We all push back to make room as two more people, similarly clad, enter the plane. We wait and watch silently as the last person limps back a step and helps the person remaining outside close the door.

"Po, keep that sand clear or we'll never get out of here!" The woman speaks into her helmet. The man outside taps once on the door to confirm, and all three visitors swivel to face us. We stand motionless for a moment, and then the woman raises her hands to remove her helmet. Van helps her with the fastenings, while TJ helps the man behind her.

As the helmet lifts off her head, a ponytail of glossy amber hair falls over her shoulder. Her face is light brown, with a matching gem. A long, raised scar runs from her temple to her neck before disappearing into her collar. She reminds me of someone, but I can't say who. She's staring up at Van now, and I watch as she reaches up and rubs the smooth blank space of skin where his gem would be if he were praenex.

"Sapiens." She pulls her hand back abruptly and offers it to

Van in the sapiens custom. "Hello. I'm Lucy."

Van looks lost for a moment, then he reaches out and shakes her hand. "Van Elder, ma'am. And it's sure I'm glad to meet ye."

She smiles and turns to greet Cai with a raised hand. It's when she turns fully to face TJ that the explosive, nearly crippling wave of emotion hits me from behind. I throw up my mental shields. Cai grunts and takes a step back and even Mercy gasps as we all whip around to face May.

She stands, feet planted, arms limp at her sides, her face filled with disbelief and joy and fear all mixed up together and emanating from her in waves. Her jaw moves, but all that comes out is a hoarse squeak. She clears her throat and tries again. "*Maman?*"

I turn back to look at the woman, Lucy, who stands staring past me at May. "Mayhem?"

The next thing I know I'm nearly knocked to the floor as May shoves past me, the dogs at her heels. Mercy squeals and jumps out of the way. The two women embrace in a fierce hug. The stranger, Lucy, kisses May's face and hair. Both of their faces are wet now as their tears mix and their exclamations turn into fits of joyous laughter.

A lump rises in my throat as I watch them and I know I'm not alone. Mercy reaches out between the seats to take Van's hand. Her smiling face is already striped with tears. TJ too is now laughing as he struggles to keep the excited dogs from knocking people over. His hand cradles the back of May's head when she reaches over and pulls him in.

"I can't believe this."

"Is it really you?"

"*Maman*, this is TJ, my husband."

Her mother blinks, stunned. "Husband?" She pulls back to look at TJ. "Has it really been that long then? You were just a girl…."

"What the dust, *Maman*!" We all turn our attention to the young man—or boy, really—behind Lucy.

"Oh." She wipes tears from her face with the back of one chalky hand. "Oh, God's grace. Come here!" She doesn't wait but pulls the boy to her. "Vengi, this is May…your sister."

"His *sister*?" May whispers. We all stare at the boy, his features are a softer, younger version of May's. She turns to her mother. "I have a brother?"

Her mother nods.

"*Papa*?"

Lucy's face falls. "He passed, a long time ago. I'm sorry, baby." They hug again, then the boy, Vengi, clears his throat. He holds his hand up to May, his Couvie rings sparking in the light. "God's hand in yours, sister."

May smiles, but a look of uncertainty passes between her and her mother. Lucy nods, so slightly that I would have missed it, had I not been watching so closely. May hastily peels off her gloves and tucks them in a pocket. She reaches her hands up and folds her ringed fingers through Vengi's. "Divine peace with you, little brother."

I'm so caught up in their contagious joy, I'm surprised by the burst of frustration that breaks through the atmosphere in the cabin. It's emanating from the man behind Lucy. I inch forward as the others sense it too and fall silent.

Lucy cocks her head at him. "Robb, what is it? What's wrong?"

"There are six of them." The man shuffles to take weight off one leg.

Lucy and Vengi whip around to look at us. Immediately their shoulders fall.

"Oh." Lucy sighs.

"No, that can't be right—" Vengi stops when his mother touches his arm.

"We'll figure it out." She faces Robb. "We'll figure it out. What's important right now is getting everyone safely out of here. We don't have much time."

"If she's right, we've really got to move. Let's grab what we need." I point to my satchel and Mercy pushes it across the floor to me.

Lucy, the leader of our rescue team, has explained that the lull we saw in the storm is a weather pattern that they know won't last another hour. Outside, three snowmobiles, which Vengi explained have been modified to run on sand instead of snow, wait with small trailers ready for us to load. Mercy, May and I have covered our clothing with the safety suits we found stashed in Cai's emergency supplies. TJ and Cai have geared up in spare environmental suits Lucy's team brought with them.

"I'm sorry, Van," she says as I secure the last closure on my face shield. "We don't have anything that'll fit you. But we can make this mouth covering work, and your own jacket should protect your skin well enough. I'd remove that pin though; the wind will probably take it." She runs a finger over Van's Terran insignia. "You're all wearing these pins, but yours is different—there's no rocket ship."

"Aye, my pin indicates a purely Terran alliance. I want everyone to stay here and heal the planet. The others are neutral—they think we can do both, evacuate *and* save Scorch."

"Huh," she tilts her head to the side, "a lot of things have changed since I've been away, but we'll have time to talk about that later. Let's get ready."

I reach over and help unroll the concealed hood in Van's jacket while he removes his pin. I flip up his collar when he's done.

"Thanks," he mumbles.

"You're welcome. What's that all about?" I nod my head toward the heated argument taking place near the cockpit between Cai, Vengi, and the other man, Robb.

Lucy finishes adjusting Van's hood. "I think they're trying to convince the ambassador to give up his fuel cell converter and motherboard, equipment we desperately need for a project." Lucy chews her lip.

I can tell that she's serious; it's not a trivial thing. I get the impression that nothing in these peoples' lives is trivial.

"We made that board and the converter specifically for this jet." Cai runs a hand through his dark, wiry hair and clenches his jaw. "Whatever you have in mind for them, it won't work."

"It will work, I know it will." Vengi's voice has the whiny tone that younger siblings master so well.

"I can't let you dissect my plane. How can we expect to fly her out of here without power?"

Lucy shakes her head and speaks to her son. "You didn't tell him?"

Vengi shrugs. "I don't like to focus on the bad stuff. It should be enough that he trusts what we need."

Lucy grunts and places a hand on Cai's shoulder. "Ambassador, I'm very sorry, but your port wing is completely severed. We had to navigate around it to reach the plane. It's about fifty meters away, consumed by the sand by now. There's no way your plane will fly again."

Cai lowers his head but says nothing.

When I reach out to him with my mind, to comfort, to commiserate, he welcomes me in so swiftly that I physically stumble. Pulling back, I meet his eyes. "This is not how our story ends."

"That's what I've been trying to tell him." Vengi throws up in his hands in frustration and marches off toward the door.

Robb limps forward again. His demeanor is gentler now that he's had time to process his surprise about our numbers. Lucy's promised to explain later why finding six of us so upset him, but for now we're focused on leaving.

"I'm sorry about your plane," he says, "but we really do need those components for an important project, one that's sure to benefit your group. With your permission, we'll remove them and load them on the sled?"

Cai nods and reaches for his helmet. "I'll help you."

I move next to him as he fastens his helmet, and then brace myself for the gust of wind that blows in as the three men leave the plane. "Okay, what's next?" It seems like I have to shout to be heard through my face covering.

Lucy clears her throat. "We're going to form a bucket brigade from just inside the door to the sleds. Po and I will work at the end of the line and load the sleds. May, leash the dogs. They're going to have to ride in the hardcase we have on the middle sled. It'll be tight, but as long as they get along, they'll be safe."

"How far is your base?" I'm still confused by their earlier explanation that they live in some kind of subterranean weather station from days of old.

"Not far. About half a kilometer east. With this load, it'll take us about twelve minutes, if nothing goes wrong."

Without meaning to, I hear her thought then…*but something always goes wrong.*

"What about the passengers? How are we riding?" I ask.

"We must distribute weight and size. We're ten people across three sleds. It's going to be cozy, but we'll manage. I'll lead with May and TJ on my sled. We'll take the dogs. Vengi will take Mercy and Van in the middle. Po and Robb will take you, Eddie."

"What about Cai?"

"Cai volunteered to ride on the trailer with the tech. It's important that someone keeps an eye on the straps because that's the heaviest load, and the most crucial to all our futures. When we finish loading the cargo, we'll immediately proceed to our assigned sleds and leave. It's important that you stay tethered to each other and your driver. The driver will be tethered to the sled so that if anything goes wrong, you can't lose the sled. Any questions?"

I look around and everyone nods. Van and TJ enter and wait by the door. "Okay, let's get into the right order."

Soon we're passing our bags and the emergency supplies from Cai's plane along our line and out the door. I'm starting to feel uneasy about Cai riding on the trailer tethered only to the sled, instead of being tethered together like the others will be, but there's no time to dwell on it. TJ passes me a tether line and we move toward the door.

"Clip one of the calipers on the metal loop at your waist." He points to my side.

I grab the loop and snap the hook through it as I shuffle along. By the time I finish, I'm at the door.

Robb is there. He takes the tether line from me and snaps the next caliper onto his own suit, then reaches out and attaches the last to Po. Po stands just outside the door, using his body to block the wind. Robb motions me ahead and together, we maneuver out the door. I turn back to watch as Po closes the door behind us, then I accept Robb's arm as we shuffle toward the empty third sled.

It's my first view of the dusty terrain, and there's almost nothing beyond our three heavily loaded sleds. They're lined up end to end, and I can make out the profiles of my friends and their drivers already waiting to go. At the end of the line sits Cai, his arms hugging the tarp under which we stored the converter and parts from his plane. He's hunkered down behind the tallest item, using it to block the wind, but it's coming from every direction. There's a hand at my back and we're at the sled now.

Po sits in front of the controls. The front skis of our vehicle are already gathering drifts of sand. I notice that the rest of the sled appears to be attached to a long, articulated tread.

Robb swings a leg over the seat and motions for me to do the same. As I straddle the seat, a short, raised edge behind my back holds me in place. Robb gathers up the loose length of line between us and hands me the coil. He pats his sides and I see fabric loops sewn into his suit. I grab on and almost immediately, the engines roar to life. With a jolt, we're off.

With one last bit of regret, I glance back at the jet. It lies spread wide, its shiny silver belly bared to the sky like a dead whale, giving itself over to the wild. Though I know it's silly to pray for an inanimate thing, I say a blessing in my mind and send my thanks skyward. She was a good plane and I know that Cai loved her.

As we move out, I strain to see anything through the dusty wind, and though it's daylight, all I can make out are vague shapes and occasional hills. One such shape gains detail as we get closer and I recognize the exposed silver metal of the Agulha's wing, almost completely consumed by sand now. I close my eyes and pull my body closer to Robb's. The hum of the engine thrums through my limbs and into my body like a sedative. I'm glad to be alive. The minutes pass and we start to slow down. With a jolt, the sled hits a bank of sand, and for a moment I think we're going to capsize.

"Lean!" Robb shouts and bends hard to the left, trying to counterbalance the sled. I lean with him and with a hard thump, the sled levels out and we're on our way again. A few more minutes pass and we slow down. Larger shapes appear ahead and I realize we must be close to the station. The sled turns and the air changes. Suddenly we're inside a dark space with a ceiling dotted with small yellow path lights. The walls are concrete, as is the low ceiling that rises as our angle descends.

The other sleds and trailers come into view ahead of us and I whoop in happiness. "Yay!"

I turn around to share my joy with Cai and can't understand what I see. The trailer is there, but no Cai. The tower of tech has shifted and is listing to one side, barely staying on the trailer but for one strap attached at an odd angle across it. I shout and tap wildly on Robb's shoulder. He looks back, then quickly taps Po to stop.

We jump off the sled awkwardly trying to untether from each other as we scramble back to the trailer. No Cai. I look down at the tether line in my gloved hand and notice it's the same as the strap holding the tech in place. It's Cai's tether. He used it to secure the load when it would have fallen off.

I drop the line and start running up the concrete tunnel from the direction that we came. "Cai! Cai!" The suit is awkward. It covers my shoes and I can barely run with my skirts gathered in a bunch between my legs. I only make it a few meters before TJ's arms clamp around me.

"No, Eddie! No!"

He picks me up and I fight for all I'm worth, but he won't let me go. His arms are steel bands around my middle, trapping my arms and keeping my feet off the ground. "Stop! You can't go out there alone!"

All the fight drains from me. Panic clenches like ice inside my stomach and I go limp in my brother's arms. "Cai fell, TJ. What're we going to do? He's out there."

"Don't worry, we'll find him. We will."

I take one last look up the tunnel as Mercy and Van join us.

They take my hands and lead me down the tunnel into the earth, into a stillness that feels like death.

Rill O'Brien

In the past...
October 10, 2684, 17 years ago
Subterranean Severe Weather Research Station 21A, North America

Rill pushed aside the design schematics, tucked his flat pencil in his toolbelt and picked up his tea. "Aye, those changes look promising, but where are we gonna to get the parts?"

Po leaned back in his chair with a sigh. "There's really only one option. We're going to have to upcycle one of the helicopter engines and probably the last truck."

"Oh, now—"

"I know you don't like it, Rill, but we don't need either of those vehicles. The old west hangar bay will never be operational again—you said you don't remember a time it ever was. Even if we could replace the rotor, that heli would never fly. And the truck is too big to be much good for anything."

"We'll need it just to move the parts!"

Po nodded. "True, but we can pull the stripped-down chassis with one of the carts, use it like a trailer. Most of what we need is under the hood anyway."

Rill shook his head. He hated giving up engines that worked for something that might never, but what choice did they have? "I'm just not sure."

"We've got to keep building until we *are* sure, isn't that what you always say? We keep moving forward and bit by bit all the problems work themselves out."

Rill hated having his own words thrown back at him, but Po was right. Rill'd been working on different engine designs for years, even knowing that he wouldn't be able to build an aircraft himself, let alone figure out how to fly it.

"That's all well and true, but ye're forgettin' that we don't even know how to launch a craft if by some miracle we figure out how to build it."

At that moment they heard Robb call from the corridor. "All aboard!'

Po slapped the table. "Perfect timing, that brother of mine. Come on. We've got something to show you."

Rill eased his chair back and stretched his legs before slowly following after Po. It took a few minutes these days for his knees and hips to get moving after he'd sat for a while. "Thank ye." He pushed past the shop door that Po held for him and climbed aboard the golf cart Robb had pulled up.

"God's grace with you, Rill." Robb nodded his head respectfully. "How're your old bones treating you today, my friend?"

Rill waved a hand in dismissal. "Fine, fine." He gripped the seat rail as the cart shifted with Po's weight in the back. "And how's yer knee, then? Is it tellin' ye we'll be gettin' rain tonight?"

Robb rubbed his bad knee absently. "Likely." They'd done their best to help him heal after the injury he sustained during their crash, but none of them had much medical training.

All seated in the golf cart and ready to go, they sped down the long gray corridor as if watts were no issue.

"Easy there, what's the rush?"

The brothers just grinned at each other.

"Now ye're making me nervous."

"You should've brought Sweets along for courage," Po joked.

"Oh, ha ha. I get by just fine without that—"

Robb held out his cupped hand and smiled. Sweets twitched his whiskers as Rill silently reached over and took him. Rill petted the creature's smooth white head before carefully tucking the mouse in his shirt pocket.

"Here we are," Robb announced, pulling up short next to the giant doors that separated the vehicle garage from the old missile silo at the south end of the station.

"What's this then?" Rill asked.

Po jumped out of the back and held out a hand for Rill. "Come and see."

Rill narrowed his eyes at the younger man, but accepted his arm and climbed out of his seat.

Robb rushed ahead and hit the controls that caused the big bay doors to slide open. "Go on!"

Rill let Po guide him along into the dark circular space at the bottom of the huge silo. The lights blinked on as soon as they entered the cavernous space. "Aye, it's a silo. Have ye two lost yer minds? There's nothing to see here."

"Just wait." Po twisted around and gave his brother a thumbs up.

"Happy Birthday, old man." Robb shouted, and just as he said it, Rill heard the sound of a motor hum to life.

"Look, up there!" Po pointed up the silo.

In the darkness, a tiny spot of light appeared. To Rill's amazement, it got larger and larger until finally he could see the brown sky high overhead.

"I don't believe it. Ye fixed it! Ye fixed the aperture controls!"

Robb joined them on Rill's other side. The two brothers slung their arms around Rill's shoulders and smiled at each other. Rill felt Robb shift to take pressure off his knee.

"Maybe one day we'll have a night clear enough to glimpse the stars," Robb said, giving Rill's shoulder a squeeze.

Rill's throat constricted painfully. "That'd be a first. Never thought I'd…" He cleared his throat, but couldn't find any words.

"We've got a way out now, Rill," Po said. "All we have to do is build an aircraft that can make it up this silo—"

"And survive the storm," Robb added. "Well, how do you like it?"

"'Tis the best birthday present I ever had." Rill reached into his pocket and pulled out his mouse. "Hear that Sweets? We're one step closer." He nodded and lifted the mouse to his shoulder.

"*Joyeux anniversaire. Heureux anniversaire. Tous nos vœux sont sincères….*"

The brothers sang to Rill on his birthday, and later, when they produced a rare, sweet cake with a blazing candle, Rill had a hard time knowing what to wish for. It seemed his lonely days were over.

Not only did he have real human friends again, but they were friends wholly committed to his goal to escape to a world he'd only dreamed of—a world filled with people.

12
Eddie

Current year: 2701
Wednesday, 7:20 AM
Subterranean Severe Weather Research Station 21A, North America

*I am…*what am I again? Oh, yeah…*more than the gray matter inside my skull. I am a bright light, a little piece of…I am not confined…I'm gray….* No, that's not right.

I reach for Cai, but I can't find him. I'm not sure how much time has passed—ten minutes, maybe less—when I notice the cold of the concrete seeping into my crossed legs as I sit on the floor.

I stand and find myself in a ring of people all talking at once. "What's happening?"

Mercy grabs my hand. "It's okay, we're working out a plan."

I look around the circle, and my gaze stops on an old sapiens man I've never seen before. I open my mouth to speak, but he raises a hand.

"Quiet now." He doesn't shout, but his voice has a natural command. Everyone is quiet. "Yer friend is…*awake* now, so let's fill her in and get to it fast."

"Eddie." Van grips my shoulder. "This is Rill. This is his place. He knows what he's doin'—they have good rescue plans."

Van takes me through the plan. Three sleds, five riders. We'll retrace our travel path, which was recorded by the sleds and the station. They have an idea, within a ten-meter range of where it happened…of where we lost Cai.

"You're riding with Po."

Mercy tugs my hand. "Eddie, can you sense him? Telepathically, I mean."

I close my eyes and try one more time before answering. "No. I've been trying, but I can't." A wave of frustration rises up in me. Why can't I feel him? Is he dead?

May and TJ are in a serious conversation. I catch whispers in French. "*C'est sûr…Fais-leur confiance.…*" My brother seems to be both trying to convince her of something and soothe her at the same time.

May shakes her head. "*Impossible a faire marche arrière…*"

"*Ça suffit!*" Rill motions them to join the circle. "*Il n'y a pas une minute a perdre…* the man could be dying."

May straightens and steps forward. She shoots TJ a serious look before speaking. "I should drive Eddie's sled." When the men start to protest, she raises a hand. "I'm trained in search and rescue— I'm a cop. I know how to handle the sled. And I have…something more…a connection that can help Eddie find Cai." She moves to stand in front of me now and pulls off one of her gloves. Shyly, she reaches for my hand.

When I touch her skin, there's that unfamiliar power again, the same as at the wedding only stronger. It charges up through my arm and my whole body is alive, my mind infused with clarity and precision. My gem tingles. With a rush, all the thoughts and emotions of the people around me surge in before I can throw up my barriers.

"Oh!" I drop her hand like I've been burned.

May doesn't flinch. "Do you trust me…sister?"

I look into her glittering eyes, fierce with resolution now that she's made her choice. "I do… *impossible a faire marche arrière*. No turning back."

She nods.

Rill clears his throat. "Then get goin'! Every minute is one more yer friend must survive the storm."

Everyone rushes to the sleds. TJ throws me my helmet as we follow May.

I throw my leg over the seat as soon as May is settled. I grab her jacket, searching for the loop to hold, but she shakes her head.

"That won't work!" TJ shouts over the sound of the sleds.

I throw my hands up. "What?"

"You have to touch skin." He grabs May's jacket where she's already trying to raise it so that I can reach her waist. It seems strange to touch her so intimately and I hesitate.

"*Allons-y!* Let's go!" May shouts.

Robb's lead sled has already left and waits at the start of the tunnel. I take a breath and slide my hands under her jacket to grab her waist. The power surge is even stronger, but I grip hard, clench my jaw and take it. "My God!"

TJ laughs and thumps me on the back. "Don't worry. The sensation dissipates. In a few minutes it'll feel almost normal." He jumps on the sled next to us and attaches his tether to Po, taking my assigned spot.

"It's up to you now." May gives me a thumbs up. "So do your thing and when you feel something, just squeeze twice in the right direction." Without another word, we jolt forward and head up out of the tunnel and back into the storm.

At first, I can't focus on anything except the energy surging through me and the wind. My helmet covers my face, but it's not airtight. My eyes are already gritty and I taste dust. I close my eyes, giving up on sight. I trust the drivers and the computers to take us where we need to go. I settle my thoughts, focus on Cai—on the unique cadence of his thoughts—and begin to pray. As I reach for the Creator, my mind expands. *I am more than the gray matter inside my skull. I am a bright light, a little piece of the Divine, and I am not confined by distance. I am light, reaching beyond. I am a creator of shadows and I own what I create.*

I reach and reach. I settle into reaching.

When the thread of anger rises, I don't try to block it. I allow myself to recall Cai's manipulations, his determination to use anything and anyone to save his people. It's a strong emotion, and that strength is part of him and me.

I force myself to think too of that uncomfortable *snap* I feel when we really open our minds to each other. I don't understand it, don't know what it means, but I know that it's important and I don't want to lose it. I keep stretching out with my thoughts in search of Cai. Letting my need to save him ride on waves of prayers, I listen hard for a response.

Our speed decreases. The odd sensation of May's energy is

becoming more comfortable now, less overwhelming. The lead sled blows its musical horn as we approach the perimeter of the search area. We begin to creep through. The lead sled blasts its signal again. May answers with our own, and Po makes the same sound behind us. A fourth horn sounds faintly like an echo. That can't be right.

"Did you hear that?" I shout.

May shakes her head.

The lead sled honks again and the series repeats. As Po's horn dies, the fourth sounds again, louder this time and discernibly to our right. I don't understand it, but I trust it. I squeeze May's right side twice.

Before the lead sled can repeat the horn, May sounds ours and we turn right, taking the lead. The first sled sounds, then the third. They're following us. Straight ahead the fourth horn repeats through my mind like a beacon and I reach for it. *Cai!* I throw his name out into the world, into the wind and sand and diffused light of the rising sun.

"Cai!" I shout it now, too. I wait for what seems like an eon, and then without warning, he fills my mind with the white heat and steady strength that I would know anywhere.

Eddie, minha flor. You found me. Thank the Creator.

My eyes pinch with tears of relief. I squeeze both sides of May's waist and jump off the sled even before she stops. I'm lurching through the sand.

I'm coming! I can barely move against the strength of the deep sand, but the jolt of the tether still surprises me. For a moment, I can't move forward, then the tether eases as May climbs off the sled, and I take a few more steps. Just ahead I make out what looks like a small hill. As I crouch down, I hear him.

I'm here! The black material of one gloved hand punches through the base of the hill. "Help me!"

I grab his hand and squeeze it. A wave of joy and relief surges through my mind and I'm not sure if it's mine or his or everyone's.

TJ and Robb join us and begin digging.

We're here! You're safe! I repeat it over and over in my mind as I let go of his hand to help remove the drift that has covered his crouching form. When we finally clear it enough for Cai to stand, he needs help. TJ and Robb pull his arms across their shoulders, one on each side as he hobbles toward Robb's sled. I reach with my feelings and intense pain buffets through me. Gritting my teeth, I search for the source…Cai's knee is injured. He's in agony.

"It's his knee!" I shout at Robb. "Right side!"

Robb nods. They carefully set Cai on the sled and help him get his left leg over the seat while I hold the right steady. Robb climbs aboard and points to his right boot, indicating that he'll use it to hold Cai's leg against the body of the sled.

"Your leg?" I ask Robb. I'm not sure how bad it is, but I've noticed he walks with a limp.

"This one's fine!" He gives me a thumbs up.

"I'm sorry," I shout at Cai. I know it'll hurt as I ease his leg in behind Robb's. I watch as Robb presses into Cai's ankle to secure it. I tether Cai to Robb.

I tap May's shoulder to get her attention. "I'm going with them!" She nods and removes my tether to clip herself to TJ's harness. He climbs on behind her as I scramble onto the seat behind Cai and tether myself to him. Reaching with all my strength I manage to get my left arm all the way around him so I can grip Robb's jacket loop. I snug my body as tightly as possible against Cai's. "This time," I shout into his ear, "you're not getting away!"

His chuckle resonates through my helmet as I rest my head on his shoulder.

The sleds start the tricky task of turning around and soon we're zipping along again, back toward the bunker.

Closing my mind to everyone else, I search my feelings. The hot buzz of adrenaline is there, flowing beneath everything. But I also feel the freedom of shedding away worry like old skin. Somehow, I think it's more than just this recent drama that I'm letting go of. An oddly grown-up kind of contentment eases into place as I use my training to restore my calm. As my prayers drift upward on fits of joy, the Creator's hand is like a gentle presence releasing its grip on my shoulder.

13
Cai

The pain in my leg is so extreme that it feels as if some giant creature has me in its jaws. Beyond this world lies a fitful but pain-free plane of unconsciousness. It pulls at me. Makes promises so tempting I almost give in again. But besides the stabs of agony in my knee, there's the pressure of a fine-boned hand in mine. Graceful fingers that I've seen caress the keys of a piano with the same adoration they showed to the white hair on a child's head.

Eddie is here. I thought I would die out there in the sand, but by some miracle I'm here with her. Relief rushes through me in a wave. I'm with Eddie, thank the Creator. I hadn't realized how much she's come to mean to me, but now she's here and I will not waste a single precious minute of my time unconscious.

"I think he's awake."

Her voice is like music. I try to open my eyes, but the light is blinding. "Agh!" The sound that escapes my mouth when I try to speak is so completely undignified, I'm embarrassed that she's here to hear it.

"Are ye sure ye can't give him somethin' for the pain, ma'am?"

I recognize Van Elder's voice, but not the woman who answers him.

"I can't risk it. If Eddie's right and he can heal himself, I don't know what effects pain medication might have on his abilities."

It's the new woman, May's mother. It's all starting to come back to me now. The crash. The people who came to save us…Lucy and Vengi! That's right. May's family and two other Couvie men. We left on strange vehicles they called sleds. I had my equipment…my precious technology and then we hit something. All I had was my tether so I used it to secure the load, and then I couldn't hold on….

"My equipment…safe?" I can barely speak past the dusty muck in my mouth.

Eddie squeezes my hand. "Yes, everything's safe. Yourself included."

"What time is it?"

Eddie hesitates. "It's around ten…Wednesday morning."

"Ten!" I try to sit up. My torso shifts, my leg moves and pain explodes like I've been struck with something…no, worse than that—like my leg is clenched in the jaws of the wild animal again. The animal with razor sharp teeth.

"Agh!" I arch back into my pillow, which only makes my agony worse. I'm huffing and straining now as I wait for the pain to recede. Then Eddie's hands frame my face. Her fingers stroke. The animal still has my leg in its jaws, but the feather light touch of her lips on my forehead helps me focus. It's a sensation I've been dreaming of for weeks, gentle and warm. I can't believe she's touching me like this.

I try to look at her, but the light is painful. "Too bright. Thirsty."

Her delicate fingers slide behind my neck and I lift my head. Cool metal touches my lips and a trickle of water enters my mouth. For a moment, my thirst is everything. I drink and drink and when the cup is dry my frustration spikes. We have to get going. I've got to get home. I've got to get Eddie back to my people. I need to see Giza before…I sigh and try to settle my panic.

I open my eyes and find that the lights have dimmed and I can see now without straining. Eddie leans back, but I squeeze her hand and she stays close. Her pale features are twisted into a mask of worry. I ignore the tiny strain in my chest and look around. Van's giant form is on my other side. The rest of the people are the Couvies who rescued us, and also an old man I've never seen before. Sapiens. And ancient. His eyes are sharp as they look back at me.

"Here now, this is Rill O'Brien." Van motions to the old man. "He runs this place. Ye're in the infirmary."

I nod to the man. "Thank you for saving my team."

He nods back. "My pleasure, or at least my habit. Folks fall outta the heavens and I gather 'em up." He leans against the foot of my bed. "But what're we to do with ye, lad?" His voice is strong, his expression lyrical, and I recognize a distant touch of Irish in his accent, so similar to Van's.

Lucy steps forward and activates a virtual image over my bed.

"How much do you remember?" She taps through various data and images as she speaks.

I close my eyes to concentrate. "I remember everything up to the point I lost the sled. We hit something, a berm perhaps. The pack slid and I was losing it. The only thing I had was my tether, so I disconnected and strapped it over the pack. I tried to hold on, but the speed, the wind…. I remember falling—a sense of weightlessness—slamming down on my knee, and then nothing. I tried to call to you."

I squeeze Eddie's hand and turn to look at her. Tears run down her face and I want so much to wipe them away. "There was nothing out there. None of God's creatures even. I…I think I passed out. Then I heard a sound, like strange music. I thought maybe I was dying and my mind had conjured up the horns of heaven."

A tickle in my throat turns into a coughing laugh, which I cut off quickly when the movement reaches my knee. I take another offered drink. "I heard the sound again. When I was sure I wasn't dead—the pain helped with that—I concentrated on the sound and repeated it in my mind, and it came again, and again. I sang back to the sound in my mind. I don't know how many times. And then suddenly I wasn't alone…."

My throat is burning again and I can't speak past the lump that's formed there.

"Shhh."

Eddie traces her fingers over my cheeks and I taste the salt of my own tears.

"More water?"

I nod and she helps me again, discreetly wiping my tears away while I drink.

"What's the damage?" I finally ask.

Lucy turns the virtual display to face me. "No fractures, and that's the good news. The patella's displaced, but that's the least of your trouble. Torn ACL and meniscus. You need surgery."

I look at the images. "You're a doctor?"

"No, I'm just a tech, but I have basic scavie emergency training and since joining this group, I've handled my share of emergency procedures."

"Aye, she's a capable nurse." Rill stumps his cane on the floor. "But hear tell, ye're the physician, if we understand rightly?"

"Yes, but I've never healed myself before. Or at least, nothing like this."

Lucy pulls up the knee image and highlights the tears. "Eddie and Van have told us about the surgery you performed on Van's gunshot wound."

"I don't remember much." Van lifts a shoulder. "But I watched the vid after and read Eddie's analysis. She included it in her interviews with the other folks who were there."

"I…" Eddie's blush rises from her neck to her cheeks when I look back at her. "It was for my report to the Legion. I had to be thorough."

"I'm sure ye did well, lass." Rill shuffles closer to the image Lucy has highlighted. He studies the image, and then turns to me. "Right then, we understand ye need yer special tools like…." He waves to Vengi, and the boy places my wound kit at the foot of my bed. "And that ye need us—a group of willin' souls—to help ye.

We're willin'. So, can ye do it? Can ye heal yerself?"

I look around at the serious faces and realize for the first time that some are missing. My adrenaline immediately spikes. "Where are Mercy, May, and TJ? Are they hurt?"

"No." Eddie touches my cheek again and Lucy presses my shoulder back into the bed. "They're fine. They just needed their rem."

"Walkin' zombies." Rill chuckles. "This big lad here," he hooks a thumb toward Van, "had to carry that tiny wife of his off to bed, so exhausted she was."

"They're safe and sleeping comfortably," Lucy assures me.

I look up at Eddie. "You?"

"No, I have several hours yet, though I might start early. And we're lucky we caught the people here between cycles. We can all help you."

Lucy pulls the display closer. "Can you do it?"

I look back at the image. My knee's a mess. I don't see that I have a choice. "Yes, I'll have to try."

"Can you have any pain medication?"

I shake my head. "No, that will slow everything down, and we need to start right away. I'm going to need to sit up enough to reach my knee—not for manipulation, just to lay-on hands. And you'll all need to be within reach—"

"I've explained it to them," Eddie assures me.

It takes a lot of fussing, and I almost faint twice, but finally I'm sitting up with my kit arranged beside me. I slide the long silver case out of its sleeve and press the button. The top slides neatly back revealing the syringe.

"Wow! That is one mean looking—"

"Vengi!" Lucy interrupts him. "Not helpful."

"Sorry." The boy shrinks back and one of the Couvie men talks to him in French in a low, reassuring voice.

"It's alright." I pull the syringe from the case. "It is quite nasty looking, but it's the best way to deliver the MRTs."

Lucy leans in for a closer look. "MRTs?"

"Microscopic Robotic Tools. The *bots* will do the work from within. I'll use my mind to direct their work. And you…" I look around the room at the eager faces. "You'll help."

Lucy points around the room, directing people to touch the bits of skin exposed to them—my ankles and feet, my back and shoulders. "Eddie explained it to us."

Eddie rubs my shoulder before taking a firmer grip. "Focus your prayers on Cai. Send him everything good and strong. See him whole and healthy and vital."

"I'm ready. Lucy?" She looks at me and I hand her the syringe. "You'll need to do the injection, here." I point to the location closest to both tears. "Penetrate to four centimeters—the needle is marked—and then depress the plunger slowly as you draw back counting one, two, three, four. Understood?"

She nods and sets the syringe down on the surgical tray while she swabs the injection site. "Local anesthetic?"

I shake my head and begin rubbing my hands together. The friction warms my skin and my fingers start to tingle. I reach down to curl my hands around my kneecap, careful not to touch the injection site. I focus all my thoughts on the images of the tears, and then I imagine them whole and healthy. This is where I'll start when the bots are in place. "Let's do it."

Rill O'Brien

In the past...
August 14, 2688, 13 years ago
Subterranean Severe Weather Research Station 21A, North America

"I just don't have the parts." Rill huffed out a breath and took off his loupe glasses. He gazed down at the face he'd drawn on Rosy long ago. Its smiling red lips and huge, childish eyes had faded through the years, just like Rill's face had wrinkled. He thought of the many years in which this face and those of the other robots had been the only faces he'd seen. If he lost this robot, it wouldn't just be the technology he'd miss. "We need this robot, we really do."

His mouse, Sweets, sniffed at the loupe and stood on his hind legs expectantly.

"Ye just want a crumb, I know, lad." Rill opened his lunchbox and broke off a piece of the dense brown bread Po had made fresh that morning. He appreciated all the skills his new friends brought with them, but Po's ability to bake decent bread was at the top of the list. He watched Sweets devour the treat while he gathered up his tools. "It's great, right? Worth the time to mill the grain. So, any ideas how we can get more computer components? Hmmm?"

The mouse squeaked and climbed onto his hand. "Pray? Aye, that's about all I can—"

He was interrupted by a shrill alarm—an alarm he'd only heard one other time, six years ago when Po and his brother, Robb, stumbled into the station through a turbine shaft. Excitement-near-panic froze in his gut. "Computer, confirm alarm."

"A radar proximity alarm is sounding," the computer answered.

"Again?"

Rill scooped Sweets into his pocket and moved out into the hall. He grabbed the electric bike he'd left parked outside the AI lab and wrangled his toolbelt out of the way so he could mount. He snapped his communicator rings together. "Po?…Computer locate Po."

"Po is in corridor 10 heading to the residential wing."

They'd been working on boosting the signal in that area, but it still had blackout spots. "Computer, continue trying to reach Po. Let 'im know I'm on my way to the garage."

As he rode down the long corridor from the lab, pushing the bike to its top speed of forty KPH, he thought through the possibilities and all the drills they'd run over the years. If someone was coming, they'd be ready. For all their oddities—preferring French to English, those bizarre and dangerous rings, gems that matched their skin, and their disproportionate strength—the brothers were resourceful. They'd thought up technical solutions Rill barely understood, let alone envisioned. From all he'd learned about the Couvies at the Verge, they seemed to value innovation and hard work above all else.

"Rill, this is Po. Come in?"

"Po! I'm one minute out from the garage. Where are ye, lad?"

"I had to wake Robb, but we're here now, in the garage. I've confirmed the signal on radar. It's small, but it's real."

"Ye're sure it's not just debris caught in the storm?" The computer had never made the mistake before, but that didn't mean it couldn't happen.

"It's not debris. They're navigating under power against the wind."

"Okay, I'm here." Rill jumped off the bike, wincing slightly at a twinge in his back. The years of labor and light rations had kept him fit, but he wasn't getting any younger. Bursting through the fire doors into the garage, he jogged over to the radar screen Po was studying. "How far?"

"They're headed right to the tunnel. It's remarkable! If they stay on course, I put ETA to the front door at about seven minutes."

The *front door* was what the brothers had affectionately termed the door to the access tunnel—the easy way in and out of the station. They often joked that their own escape into the station would have been a lot easier if only they'd been "front-door people."

"Okay, let's get ready." Rill glanced at the other brother for the first time.

Robb stood with his back to the screen, resting against the table, with his head bowed and his hands curled around a steaming mug.

"Aye, what's the matter with ye?"

Robb cringed. "Shhh! Still waking up."

"Eh? What's wrong with 'im?" Rill nudged Po.

Po and Robb exchanged a few hurried words in French. Po nodded. "He was only halfway through his rem. Let's give him a minute while we prep the sleds."

"If he can't manage a sled, we shouldn't risk takin' 'im."

Robb waved a hand. "I'll be fine. Twice as strong as you when I'm full asleep, old man. Don't fret."

"Oh, fine, that's craic. Why don't ye wind yer head in some, lad." Rill pushed away from the table and headed for the modified snowmobiles waiting on the other side of the large underground garage. "Ye comin', Po?"

Po jogged past him. "We blew out the tunnel only two days ago. It should be clear."

"That's a bit a luck then."

"Let's take a trailer each, just in case."

Robb joined them, limping slightly on his bad leg, and they lined up the sleds and trailers along the bay doors and got into their gear. By the time Rill helped Robb with his helmet and neckerchief, the man seemed fully awake. "Are ye ready for this?"

"God willing, we'll find survivors." Robb helped Rill next. "The signal stopped about a hundred meters from the exit. With the storm in a lull, they should be easy to find."

"Let's go!" Rill mounted his sled and waited for Po to lead them out. He counted the curtains they passed through, and his thoughts drifted back to disturbing memories of the cost of saving this tunnel. *Jam.* What loneliness Rill had felt after losing his idol, then his da, and finally his mam, too. He gave thanks to the Creator for sending Po and Robb, and he wondered who the Creator had sent to him now.

He fought to maintain control as his sled cleared the outer door. They had to hurry now. Po's sled was visible ahead moving in and out of gusts of sand, but he could barely hear the quiet engines. Checking his gage, he watched as the three lights representing their sleds approached the red light that was the crashed aircraft.

"There it is!" Po's voice came over Rill's headset.

As Rill followed, he saw what Po had seen. The wind had downed the aircraft—a helicopter, not a plane—into the sand on their left, shattering the canopy. A dune of sand had already formed along this side—it would be impossible to get in from here. Rill followed Po around the tail and then back along the other side of the large dual prop helicopter.

"It's a Chinook! It's got to be scavies." Robb's excitement came through the headset clearly.

"Easy now, lads," Rill reminded them. "Let's see what we have before we make any assumptions." The helicopter was badly damaged. He could see several gashes where the prop had bent back into the body of the aircraft. And while he couldn't see any open flames, he smelled smoke in the wind.

They pulled their sleds into the shelter of the helicopter, grabbed med kits and scrambled off to reach the door. It slid open easily, but only about a meter before jamming into bent metal. Po vaulted in; Rob followed more carefully. Rill found a foothold and heaved himself up.

Inside they found a woman kneeling on the floor—a real

woman, God's truth! They were bleeding badly from a cut on their face. A man lay stretched on the floor in front of them. They stroked the man's hair methodically and their eyes held the dazed look of someone far away. Nearby, another man lay unconscious.

"Uh…divine grace with ye," Rill stuttered.

At his voice, they glanced up. "The others are dead."

"Okay…ye're okay. We're here now. We're goin' to help ye." Rill pushed past Po and knelt.

"Take a look around." He motioned for Po to check the back.

He pointed Robb to the unconscious man. "Check them out."

"Let's see if we can stop that bleedin'." He pulled supplies from his kit and examined the wound on the woman's face—a face so beautifully different than any he'd seen that he had to fight the urge to simply stare. The gushing blood helped him focus. The gash was deep and long. He could stitch it later, but for now he needed to slow the bleeding. Digging through a kit, he found what he needed and started on a field dressing.

"How'd ye find us here?"

They turned their eyes to him again—vibrant purple irises and a gem matching their tan skin tone. His friends had been right— more Couvies. They were young, maybe late twenties, with amber hair unlike any Rill had ever seen in person. He wondered what it felt like.

They raised a slender hand to touch his where it rested cupping their jaw. Their fingers were so slender, even with all their rings.

He wondered if all women were so different from men, so graceful.

"What?" she whispered.

"What?" Rill echoed.

"Don't mind him," Robb said, breaking Rill out of the moment. "You're only the second woman he's ever seen."

Rill felt heat spreading across his face…a blush! He'd read about it, but he'd never blushed before. He cleared his throat. "S'cuse me, lass. I asked, how did ye find us here—the station?"

The woman scrunched their brows in concentration, then grimaced at the pain. "I…Aro felt it. He said to follow…." They looked down at the man they held.

Rill checked the man's pulse and saw him wince before he opened his eyes. "What hurts?" Rill couldn't find any obvious wounds.

"My head."

Rill carefully reexamined the man's head to see if he'd missed something. "What about yer chest? Does yer chest hurt? Yer back?"

"No…I can't feel anything else. I can't feel my legs, or my hands."

Dread spread through Rill. He picked up the man's limp hand. "Squeeze my hand."

"I…I can't."

"Okay, that's enough for now. Not to worry. Robb, how are they?" Rill nodded toward the other man.

"Pulse is weak, but steady. No visible wounds that I can find, no blood, but I suspect internal injuries. They're still unconscious."

"Po?" He looked over his shoulder.

"Another dead back here."

"Our pilot's dead, too." The woman closed their eyes and tears spilled down their cheeks. "Cece…she's dead."

"There now." Rill patted their shoulder. "Don't think of it. We'll get ye outta here. We'll help ye. I'm Rill, and that's Po and Robb, there. Our station's nearby, we'll get ye there."

"It's your place?" The man Aro asked, his voice weak from the effort. "It's your place I could feel. Cece, the pilot, she trusted me. Once the twister had us…I could feel…life, like a string pulling me here." He grimaced in pain.

"Shhh! You got us here, quiet now, Aro. Let these men help." The woman whispered a few words in French, and then looked back up at Rill. "I'm Jealousy, Jealousy Forge, but you can call me Lucy, *pronoms fem*. This is my husband, Arrogance. And this is my unit. We're scavies. We were working the ruins in Albuquerque and…stayed too long. It's my fault that we stayed too long—"

"No!" Aro hissed. "It's not your fault, we all agreed. It was worth the risk to get the tech."

"Tech?" A pins-and-needles sensation started at the back of Rill's neck and spread all the way down his arms.

Lucy nodded, absently stroking Aro's hair. "High tech parts, AI components, some heavy metals, chips, power cells. Things the Verge could really use."

Suddenly Rill's heart was hammering in his ears. "Did ye get it, lass? The tech, did ye get it?"

Lucy cocked her head to the side and stared at him, and then she nodded and waved to the back of the chopper. "Red plastic cases, near the front. Why?"

Rill motioned to Po. "Get it! Get all of it."

Po hesitated. "We've got to move fast. The storm's in a lull, but even so we'll be buried soon."

"Aye! So let's not waste time arguin' about it, ye eejit! Go!"

Robb had already moved toward to door with the other man in a fireman's carry, wincing as he took the weight on his bad knee. He called over his shoulder. "Sleds are clear, but barely. Five minutes max!" He scrambled out, juggling his heavy load, and vanished into the dusty air outside.

Rill helped Lucy stand, and then bent to pick up Aro.

"What about the bodies?" she asked him, pressing a hand to her bandaged face.

Rill opened his mouth to answer, but Po beat him to it. "It's a tomb. The storm will bury them."

"What? We can't leave them!"

Rill shook his head. "I'm sorry, but we won't be comin' back here, there's no way." He turned away, but she caught his shoulder.

"Wait!" She limped a few steps to a panel in the wall and opened a small door. Inside were several switches. She flipped one and a small red beacon light started flashing in a slow, rhythmic pattern. Below the switches, she pulled out a small data drive and pocketed it.

Rill shook his head again. "That beacon won't last long—"

"We can rig a power cell. Something this small…it'll last for years."

Rill shook his head, Aro's weight feeling heavier and heavier in his arms the longer he stood there. "Nah, we can't spare one."

"Please?" Lucy closed her eyes, and when she opened them, Rill got that pins-and-needles sensation again. "It's important, I can feel it…I can see it. It's more than just a beacon. It's a necessary step in a brave and valiant future. It's needed, even more than what you need the tech for in your station."

Rill swallowed dry grit and coughed to clear his throat. Had she entranced him? Po and Robb told stories of praenex humans with special gifts. It wasn't often someone convinced him to do something he didn't want to do; maybe this woman could control his mind. But no, when he focused on her, all he saw was a confident, desperate woman with a badly injured face. "One unit."

Lucy nodded and rushed over to the cases Po had pulled from the cargo. "You won't regret this, I promise."

By the time Rill and Po had the men and crates secured on trailers, Lucy was jumping down from the helicopter. She pushed the door shut behind her, braced both hands on the steel for a moment of silent prayer, and then turned and took the helmet Rill held out to her.

"Let's get yer people home, now. We've much to do."

14
Eddie

Current year: 2701
Wednesday, 9:20 PM
Subterranean Severe Weather Research Station 21A, North America

I'm shoulder to shoulder with the Creator, reaching for peace. *I am a bright light, a little piece of the Divine, and I am safe in my next breath. The people around me are safe too. We are not confined to this moment, to this event. I reach and—*

I'm startled by a gritty, shuffling noise coming from the door to the infirmary. It's the old man, the one they call Rill.

"Is he dead?"

I can't tell if he's joking or serious. "No, just sleeping."

"Looks dead." Rill winks before joining me at the head of Cai's bed. "And ye, lass? How are ye holding up?"

"I'm…I'm managing."

"Aye." Even as he agrees, the serious consideration in his wise green eyes tells me he understands more than a stranger should. He's an insightful sapiens, I can already tell.

"This one," he nods toward Cai, "he called ye all his *team*, but

I think really they're yers, aren't they?"

I blow out a breath. "Yes."

Rill nods. "I suspect maybe ye two eejits get along best when one of ye's either in trouble or unconscious, do I have the right of it?"

"Yes," I laugh. "In fact, this may be the only time we've been this close and this…civil."

Lucy glances over her shoulder at me, one eyebrow raised. When Cai passed out after the surgery, she shooed everyone but me from the room.

Rill continues staring at Cai deep in thought.

I startle again when something moves in his shirt pocket and can't believe my eyes when a tiny white mouse pokes its head out to look at me, its whiskers quirking back and forth. Rill scoops it out absently and moves it to his shoulder.

"When I was a wean, used to give me a terrible fright when my mam and da fought. They were the only family I had, ye see, and the idea that my world could fracture, well that was brock, ye know? But really, they got along most of the time. I think they really loved each other. They said it often…to me, to one another. I know it's not like that for everyone, but that was how it was for me, for us, livin' here in this God-forsaken place."

"You've lived here your whole life?"

"Aye, born and raised and remainin'. Alone for a good while, but then I got some company, as ye see." He motioned to Lucy.

"There's something I've been meaning to ask you." I hesitate, not sure the time is right to ask about Robb's odd reaction to seeing all of us.

"Go on then, lass."

"It's just, well, during the rescue, Robb seemed surprised or…upset, even, to see so many of us in the plane. 'There are six of them,' he said. Why is that a problem?"

Rill doesn't look away, but I notice that Lucy has gone completely still at the counter. A tense moment passes before Rill nods and answers.

"Where to begin?" he asks himself.

Lucy looks over her shoulder. "The beginning is usually a good place."

"Aye, well it goes all the way back to my childhood really. It was Jam—uh, Dr. Jameson Murphy, who started the project. Jam was of the same generation as my parents, but he was raised in New Juneau, like ye all, instead of the Farms. My folk and his knew each other from way back during the emigration from Ireland. He was a good friend to my mam and da, and one hell of an engineer. Never knew another sapiens who could see so well into the future, not prescient like ye lot, but smart, ye ken?"

I nod, wondering where this story is going, but willing to hear him out.

"Jam was convinced that survivin' here meant leavin' here. He started workin' on plans to escape the station and taught me everythin' I know. He passed years ago now, my da and mam too."

"I'm so sorry."

"Thank ye. It was up to me then. Course, there's only so much one eejit can do by himself, and it wasn't until Robb and Po arrived that the project got any new life. We've an experimental aircraft, ye see, that we've been workin' on forever, but Vengi, well, he knew ye were comin' and that ye'd have some of the tech we lack."

When he stops and glances at Lucy, I realize I'm holding my breath. "Well, that's great, right? We have the tech from Cai's plane and, I mean, if anyone can solve technical problems it's my brother, and May's not bad either."

"I'm sure ye're right. I'm sure." He pats my hand.

"So what's the problem?"

"Well, the ship can only hold eight people, ye see. So finding six of ye was a big surprise."

I bite my lip, then shake my head. "We'll figure it out. There has to be a way around that. When can we get everyone together to go over your plan?" I move to stand, but Rill waves me back.

"In good time. We'll wait 'til everyone's had a long rem, and then we'll walk ye through it. But I want ye to know, if some have to stay behind, we'll make our peace with it and depend on ye all to find a way to come back for us. It's not like we're not used to bein' alone here."

Based on the way he holds his posture proudly, I can see that right now isn't the time to argue. I consider his words and make a promise to myself to find a way to get all of them—this old man especially—out of this prison.

"I'm so sorry you were alone here for so long. It seems impossible to believe that anyone gave up on this place, knowing there were people here."

"If ye understood the great storm better, ye'd understand why they must've believed we were lost. I don't suppose anyone's studying the storm anymore. I, on the other hand, have had a lotta years to become an expert, as ye say, but that doesn't matter, as it goes. Couvies started fallin' outta the sky, oh, I guess 'tis over two decades now." He shrugs. "Somebody's gotta scoop 'em up and look after 'em, and since God drops them right on top of me, I guess that someone's me. But what about ye? Where're ye from? Who're yer people? I get the feelin' that this lad is new to ye all."

"You're right, he is. So is May, or…relatively…to some of us anyway. TJ's my twin, May's his bride. Mercy and Van have been our friends since childhood. We're the children of diplomats— thrown together since the crib. We've been a family to each other ever since."

"Did ye live together then?"

"No, just TJ and I. Mercy and Van had normal families. But my parents were…*are,* a little like yours, I guess. In love, I mean. Sometimes I looked at them—the way that they seemed in orbit around one another—and I got the feeling that they'd forgotten us. Like someone adding more mass to their universe would have switched all the orbits, so they made a choice.…"

Rill shifts and I'm embarrassed to have said such a thing. I want to explain them…my parents, but I'm not sure I even understand them myself.

"My mother almost died during our birth. Whenever she talks about it, my father becomes almost desperate. Not outwardly, of course, but inside. Even as children, TJ and I could sense it. I would try to soothe my father, to make the terror in his thoughts go away, but it was TJ who always succeeded in bringing my parents back to reality. He did it through fantastic acts of disobedience." I laugh, thinking about where we currently are. "In fact, he's still doing it. Only this time, the stakes are higher than just my father's melancholy."

"There's a war." Rill lifts his chin.

I shouldn't be able to, but I think I feel a wash of frustration from him. "Yes, potentially. My parents on one side, against the parents of the others. You see, my mother is Pèlerine Reine LeRoux, Fleet Admiral of SciCorps."

"*Pilgrim Queen.*" Rill's voice is a whisper.

"You know your French."

He waves a hand. "Live with Couvies and it becomes a survival skill."

We laugh, and both of us are quiet for a moment.

"Yer da?"

I smirk. "Admiral Yuri LeRoux. A force in his own right, but give him a mission from my mother, and he's a machine. Driven, clever, far-sighted. They both saw my path to Gran Bozan well before I did. Like a chess move…. Do you play?"

Rill shrugs. "Some. Tell me about yer path…this *Gran Bozan* thing."

"Oh, it's…a spiritual leader? Like president of the Legion. They're selected by their predecessor, not elected, but it's worked for generations. There's a sash, and this whole council role and everything."

"Now I've met ye, I can see it. The weight of world…*and* yer resistance to it. Ye must be mighty close to the Almighty then?"

I nod, but I can't look in his eyes. I'm ashamed of my indecision.

"So, the last Gran Bozan…she passed, did she?"

I close my eyes and take a deep breath, surprised by how much it still hurts. "Yes."

"Recent like, I see." Rill lifts a wrinkled hand to my shoulder, and the mouse scurries down his arm and onto mine. "This is Sweets."

I gently lift the mouse off my shoulder and raise him to eye level. "Hello, Sweets." I smile at his twitching little nose before moving him back to Rill.

"And now you're what? Running away?"

"No!" I blurt, my voice is louder than I intended, earning me a sharp look and shush from Lucy. I shake my head. "Sorry, no. We're on a mission, and I'm…thinking things through. We're on our way to help Cai's people in Chileru, a group we only recently became aware of."

"And after that?"

"After that, I have to decide."

Rill nods. "I've learned a few things, even livin' here on my own. Sometimes all the Creator asks is that ye take the next breath, the next step, the next task. Faith. If ye can't stand to look at the long haul, ye just need to focus on where to put yer boot next."

I smile at his wisdom. "Sound advice."

"Well, lass, it's what I ken. It's what I've done. For me it's led to a long life and friendships as deep as the storm is strong. I've seen a great many things in the people I've met, and in ye I see a leader. But tell me, what does yer future role as Gran Bozan have to do with a war? And how does this lad and his secret people change the picture?"

I have a choice now…make the excuse of needing my rem or take the time to tell this old man what I know about the world.

"Well…what do you know about the prophecy of the Culmination?"

Sweets squeaks and scurries back into the safety of Rill's pocket.

I smirk, wondering if that's what I'm doing by choosing to go to Terra Faire. Maybe Cai's home is a pocket large enough for even a Gran Bozan to hide in.

Vengeance Forge

Current year: 2701
Thursday, 2:00 AM
Subterranean Severe Weather Research Station 21A, North America

Vengi peeks around the corner in the hall to watch his mother and his sister where they talk, foreheads touching, huddled close at the tiny kitchen table. They hold hands and have tangled up their arms into a pretzel of shared limbs on the table's surface. Their faces are wet, and he can't tell if they're crying or laughing. Maybe both. May's dog, Piper, sleeps in a ball of white fur at her feet.

"I remember him well enough that I miss him in specific ways, you know?" May says to his mother. "It's not vague missing. I mean, it's not just general. I miss the sound of his laugh, the way his beard scratched my face when he kissed me good night, and how his hand felt so huge and rough when I held it, which I guess sounds silly since I'm grown up now."

"It's not silly," his mother answers. "I miss little things like that all the time. And more. Sometimes Vengi does something so like your father that I can barely stand the ache—"

"Did you never…" His sister stops talking and shakes her head.

"What?"

"Nothing. Never mind."

"What?" His mother shakes their intertwined arms. "You can ask me anything, Mayhem. We've missed too much time with each other to hold back now."

His sister's quiet for a moment, and Vengi almost steps through to join them.

"Did you never consider the *aeterna sui rituali*? I mean, I always remember you wishing for more children—siblings for me—you must have wanted the same for Vengi."

"A clone? Here?" His mother smiles, but it's a sad smile. "I might have considered it once, but even if we could devise the nutrients and the ritual setting, it was soon clear that this place was going to be hard enough to keep going without more mouths to feed. And Vengi…well, he's turned out to be more than I could possibly have hoped for. For me, for all of us—"

Vengi clears his throat and steps around the corner, heat flaring across his face. He fiddles with the tools in his toolbelt to give his hands something to do.

"And there he is." His mother wipes her face and smiles. Her tears have cleaned the dust where they tracked along her facial scar, making it even more prominent. "Come here, Vengi. Sit with us."

"Okay…you wanted something, *Maman*?"

"No…well, yes, I guess. Sit down."

Vengi avoids looking at his sister. It's not as hard as looking at the other two women, but it's not easy. These new women are nothing like his mother at all. They're young and unpredictable and they talk a lot—asking loads of questions—well, when they're not sleeping. So far, they've done a lot of sleeping.

Vengi walks around the table to an empty chair—it's one of the seats they seldom use, since it's just the two of them, or it *was*, and he has to squeeze along the wall to get to it. His knee bangs the table and the dishes clatter, making Piper whine.

"Sorry." He stretches awkwardly in the tiny space between the wall and table, trying to keep his ribs from riding on the table's edge. He's lanky, and he can't figure out where to put his arms. He wants to shrink away from their stares. Two people in this small kitchen is easy, but three? Three is a little much.

His mother squeezes his hand. "Listen, Vengi, I really need to get back to the infirmary, so I was hoping you could show May around?"

"Um, yeah, okay."

May sits back. "It's fine…*we're* fine." She looks at Vengi then, appraising. "It'll give us a chance to get to know each other a little. Go take care of King Cai, and I'll see you later."

His mother smiles. "I like the sound of that— 'see you later.' I missed you so much, Mayhem."

"I know, *Maman*. I missed you, too."

Vengi tries to swallow past the pressure in his throat as he watches his mother and his sister exchange a long hug. He looks away and finds the emotions almost bearable. Almost.

"Be good," his mother warns with one of her meaningful looks, and then she's gone and he's alone with his mythical sister and her quiet dog.

They sit in silence for a moment, and Vengi can feel his sister's eyes on him as he stares down at his hands and fiddles with the handle of his ball-peen hammer.

"I like your toolbelt," his sister says. "It looks very handy."

"Uh, thanks. It used to be Old Rill's."

His sister smiles and looks around the kitchen.

"I knew you were coming!" He's immediately embarrassed for blurting it out like that. His face burns as he tries to explain. "I mean, I didn't know *you* were coming, just that *someone* was coming. I'm prescient, like you. I mean, *Maman* told me that you're prescient, too. From when you were little, I guess you still are, I mean…" He blows out his breath.

"Yeah." May leans back in her chair and looks at him. "Only about big things, though. And not consistently. Is it the same for you?"

"Yeah. When I was really little, I didn't understand that there were things that only I knew—I thought everyone understood what was going to happen. When I was three, Old Rill fell into one of the reservoirs and almost drowned. Po saved him. But a while before that I'd started calling him 'Fishy Rill.' My *maman* sort of figured it out then—*our maman*, I mean. She's your mother, too, of course. But you know that." Vengi hangs his head as his cheeks heat again.

May chuckles.

Vengi narrows his eyes at her.

"Oh!" She holds up her hand, "I'm not laughing *at* you. It's okay, Vengeance, really. I'm nervous, too. I didn't even know I had a brother. At least you've known about me, even if you didn't think you'd ever meet me."

Vengi cocks his head to the side. "I think I *did* know that I'd meet you, one day. *Maman* told me everything about you, and you were the star in most of my favorite bedtime stories.… Divine grace, this is weird."

"That's not weird, but you know, I was little when she and Papa were lost. I don't know how much you can really know about me." May tosses her coils of amber hair over her shoulder. A few tight braids that Vengi hadn't noticed before separate from the rolled coils.

"I know how you got your rolled hairstyle."

May stares at him.

"I do! You started rolling it yourself when you were four. You did it as a nervous habit—*Maman* thinks you were already becoming aware that they'd be lost one day and it troubled you. She couldn't comb them out, and you hated when she tried. One day you hid all the combs and refused to tell anyone where they were until she agreed to roll and braid the rest of your hair and stop combing it."

Vengi looks up to see a tear rolling down May's face. She wipes it away. "Yeah…she was right, I think. I can't remember exactly what I knew, but I tried to convince them to give up scavenging. For a long time, I was frantic when they left on a trip. Did she tell you that?"

Vengi nods.

May sniffs. "So, what else?"

"Um…I know that you wanted our parents to have another baby and you wanted them to name it Ramirez because that was Grandma Dixie's birth surname. That's my middle name, by the way. So, in a way, you helped name me."

May makes a strangled noise. "Okay, yeah. That's good," she whispers.

Vengi rushes on, uncomfortable with the emotions threatening to overwhelm him. "I know that your favorite color is blue, you can run really fast, you love animals, you're an amplifier—I felt that when I touched your hands back in the plane—and that you're vegetarian. We're mostly pescatarians here—we farm a few varieties of fish. We have a few hens for egg laying too, but they're like pets. And we have one dairy cow left. Matilda, but she's getting pretty old."

"Well, that's a lot then. You know me, I guess." May smiles sadly and slaps her hands on her thighs.

Vengi squirms in his chair. "I guess we missed a lot."

"Yeah, some." May shakes her head. "I can't believe I'm feeling sad about this—I mean, I should only feel happy, right?"

Vengi shrugs. He feels sad now, too. "It's like being robbed, I think. All the things we should've shared, all the things we missed—they don't belong to us and there's no getting them back."

May reaches over, and Vengi thinks she's going to hold his hand, but instead she traces one of his rings with the tip of her finger. "I remember these."

"They were my papa's—I mean, *our* papa's."

"Do you remember him?" May's voice is quiet and hopeful.

"Just a little…I remember his voice, his face. I remember riding on his lap in his wheelchair, from before he had to stay in bed. I remember him in the infirmary…." Vengi looks down at his cherished Couvie rings. "I guess these should be yours, too." When he moves to pull one off his finger, May raises a hand.

"No, you keep them. I don't have any more fingers." She holds up her hands to show her sparkling Couvie and comm rings. "So, how about you tell me about you?"

"How about I show you instead? We can walk and talk. I'll show you all of my projects and give you a tour of the station. We can get Piper a treat."

The word is like magic. Piper gives a little yip and crawls out from under the table to look up expectantly at Vengi. Her fur is soft as he pets her head and scratches her ears. "I would've loved to have a dog growing up here."

May pushes back her chair. "Well, Piper has enough love for everyone. We can share her. Besides, now that she knows you have T-R-E-A-T-S, you'll probably have a hard time getting rid of her. Let's go."

Outside in the hall, Vengi chooses an electric scooter that will fit them both. "I'm finished with my chores for today, but tomorrow you can go with me, and I'll show you the greenhouses and the aquifer. *Maman* says to wait on the Tumbler; they want to show everyone at once. Climb on." He scooches forward and May steps onto the board behind him, grabbing his waist for balance. They take off down the long hallway with Piper trotting at their side.

"What's a tumbler? Hey, you're almost as tall as me."

"Yeah, *Maman* says I'll probably grow ten more centimeters. She says Papa was above average for a praenex, like TJ is. I'll never be truly tall like Van Elder, though."

May laughs. "No one's as tall as Van Elder, trust me. Even among sapiens, he's enormous. So where are we going?"

"I have something really great to show you. But first tell me, if you could visit any place on Old Earth, where would it be?"

"Anywhere?"

"Yeah, anywhere."

"Well…I've always dreamed of homesteading—of going someplace completely new and untamed, and making a life there. I think it'd be the ultimate adventure."

"I guess there're lots of places in Old Earth history where that happened. I like history. So, how should we pick?"

"If you like history, you should talk to Cricket."

"Who?"

"Oh, Mercy Adams. She's a historian. When she gets going on any topic, she'll chatter on forever. That's why we call her 'cricket'."

"We don't have crickets here, but I know what they sound like from the vids. I've got it! Why don't I show you what *this place* looked like about a millennia ago, when settlers first came here?"

"This place?" May waves a hand at the industrial corridor in which they travel.

"No, I mean, before this. They used to call this land 'Oklahoma,' and they were famous for homesteading when this continent was first conquered by the Europeans." Vengi stops the scooter outside the Holographic Lab. "And I can show you one of my hobbies, too."

Inside, Vengi starts the process of powering up the equipment. He finds a protein ration and throws it to Piper, who catches it mid-air and scampers off to eat.

"Friend for life now." May smirks. "So, it's a Virtual Reality

Theatre?"

"Sort of." Vengi hands May an interlink device. "It was designed for research, I think, but it's recreation for us. The imaging box is simple. Scientists built it as an upgrade after they started staying here for longer and longer periods and venturing outside became more dangerous, but I added these." He holds up the small device, and then turns his head to show May how to wear it just behind her ear.

"What do they do?"

"They extend the visual and auditory experience inside the box to include thermal, olfactory, and tactile sensations."

May turns the device over in her palm, studying the intricate wiring and pulsing lights. "You fabricated this from a model?"

"No, I built it."

"From a schematic?" May carefully pulls back her hair and presses the device to her skin.

"Well, yeah...*my* schematic." When she turns to stare, he throws up his hands.

"What? Don't Couvies invent things anymore?"

"Sure, we invent things." She wiggles an upraised hand. "Our tiny weapons have come a long way since our dad first put on those rings, for example, and we've got some good, engineered grains— actually, those came from Alberta Farms. Anyway, this is a big deal. You invent stuff?"

"All the time. Or I take stuff someone else invented and make it better. Sorry, that sounds conceited...I make it *different*, and *more*. My *maman* says—sorry, *Maman* says it's one of my gifts. But it doesn't feel like a gift, it just feels like me, you know?"

May nods and signals Piper to stay. "Okay, let's see this Oklahoma."

They step into the box. Vengi waves to a chair next to his. "Computer, begin program Oklahoma alpha three. Did you know, you're the sixth person I've ever met?"

"Wow."

"Yeah." He inhales deeply and smells the wild scents of animals, flowers, and rusty earth. As the walls around them transform into a sweeping prairie of tall grasses and scrubby, wind-swept trees, Vengi hears the nicker of a nearby stallion.

May turns to him, her smile as bright as the noonday sun overhead. "Horses?"

Vengi just nods, afraid to try to speak over the lump that's grown in his throat again. He's sitting here, in real life, with his *sister,* magical May.

May laughs—a genuine, loud, and unrestrained sound—so much like Vengi's mother that he has to grip his armrests to keep from choking out a sob.

"I love horses," she says, and reaches over to squeeze his hand. "Thanks, bro."

"You're welcome…sis."

They smile at each other, hands entwined, and then tilt their heads back to take in the warmth of the sun against their skin.

15
Cai

Current year: 2701
Thursday, 7:25 AM
Subterranean Severe Weather Research Station 21A, North America

Waking up is the first thing that makes me uneasy. It wasn't yet time for my rem.

"You're alright, doctor." Lucy is busy at my bedside. "You blacked out during the MRT extraction, but the device turned itself off and detached, so I didn't see any reason to wake you. Your vitals look good. You probably feel a bit groggy, as I gave you a mild sedative along with some muscle relaxant. How does the knee feel?"

I move my leg slightly and feel a twinge of pain, but nothing like earlier. "Better. How long was I out?"

"About twenty hours. The images look good." She turns the display so that I can see them, and she's right, the wound is healing well. "I think we should support it for another day or two, then we'll start some PT, if you agree."

Twenty hours. A day or two. I'm beginning to doubt we're ever leaving this place. I rub my gem and try to remember that it isn't Lucy's fault. "Thank you. Where are the others?"

"Seeing to chores, or asleep, like that one—" She points over my shoulder and for the first time I notice Eddie, slouched onto the bed just behind my head, fast asleep with her left hand still resting on my shoulder.

My chest squeezes again, but not as painfully as before.

"She fought and fought to stay awake, but finally fell into rem a couple hours ago. I think she thought if she took her eyes off you, you'd disappear again." Lucy smiles at Eddie's sleeping form. "She gives off an image of the ice queen, but she's really all heart, isn't she?"

I smile in agreement and touch Eddie's hand. She doesn't look very comfortable.

The movement makes me realize that I'm not very comfortable either. I need to get out of bed. Hell, I need to get out of this station. "I'd like to wrap the knee and then get up and move around, if that's acceptable?"

Lucy snaps her comm rings and asks Po to join us. When he arrives, we work together to wrap my knee and get me dressed in simple medical scrubs. Lucy offers me a choice of crutches or a cane. I take the crutches, knowing it's too soon to put much weight on my knee. "What about Eddie? Can she sleep here? I hate to wake her."

"Yes, that's fine." Lucy and Po half lift, half roll Eddie onto my cot and I help cover her with a soft blanket. What I wouldn't give to lay down beside her and let the medicine lull me back to sleep.

With a rush the image of waking at Giza's bedside fills my

mind. I grit my teeth and push down my impatience. I have healing to do and no way to rush it. As unnatural as it feels, I have to put my faith in these people and wait for the right time to advance my agenda.

I turn away and we dim the lights.

The hall is plain and dirty-white, but not sterile—everything is too dusty to feel sterile. I follow Lucy as she leads me along, past closed doors and a few windows, inside shades drawn.

"I'm sorry about the dust. We weren't expecting company."

I smile at her joke as we maneuver slowly around a cylindrical robot vacuuming a section of wall. Its dented head swivels toward us to reveal a faded cartoon face drawn in a childlike hand. The scrunched metal forehead and dull facial features give it a weary expression, but its pincers guide a vacuum smoothly across the wall's surface.

"You have robots."

"Well, just the two, Rosy and Tinker. We had more, but Vengi can't seem to keep more than these two serviceable."

"Vengi? He repairs them?"

"Yes." Her chin lifts in pride as we come to a junction and turn down another long corridor. "My son's gift—he can fix anything."

"I imagine that's quite helpful." I try to move a little faster, but a spike of pain slows me down again and I lean hard into my crutches until it passes.

She waits patiently for me. "How's the knee?"

I grimace. "Doing fine, thank you."

"I suspect that's enough walking for now. Luckily, we're here." She pushes open a door and steps back to allow me to enter first. I hobble in.

The room is a large, comfortable dining hall. Like the corridor, everything is an aged white. Stacks of chairs line the wall. Dust trails on the floor show some recent disturbance, which I suppose is from the setup of the extra, empty table and chairs. It's tucked in beside a table that's cluttered with bins of condiments, linens, and utensils. Po and Robb sit along one side, and the old man, Rill, sits at the head. I get the impression they've spent a lot of time here, each in the same space. Their conversation, spoken in an easy French, stops as we approach.

"Won't you sit down?" Lucy pulls out the other end chair and offers me her arm.

"I can manage, thank you."

She waits until I gracelessly fall into the chair before taking a seat to my left. I lean my crutches against the table's edge and try to catch my breath.

"Well, how're ye feelin' now? Ye look like ye're wired to the moon, but that's probably the drugs." Rill's voice is rough, but not unkind. In fact, these people are all quite transparent and relaxed. I sense that they're patient and content by practice, which I guess they'd have to be to stay sane in this forgotten place.

"I'm feeling quite well, thank you. And, uh…" It has suddenly occurred to me that I owe this group of strangers my life. "I want to thank you for coming for my team…for coming back for me—"

"Don't mention it." Rill leans forward. "And I do mean, don't mention it. We're all well pleased to be of use and right glad to have ye find us." He slaps a hand on the table as if to close the subject. "So now, let's get through the formal introductions and bring ye up to speed, as they say, on what we have here. I'm Rill Ban O'Brien, and this lively place is the Subterranean Severe Weather Research Station 21A."

"The SS Worse," Po adds.

Robb smiles. "Cuz if you thought it was bad before, things can always get worse." The men chuckle and I notice for the first time how much they look alike, down to the rough pale squares of their gems. Couvies.

"Ha, ha. That's craic." Rill waves a hand. "Make yer jokes, but this place saved yer miserable selves, sure as dust is dry."

"How long has this place been here?" I ask.

"The military built it in the 1950s in what history calls the Cold War. They refitted it for scientific purposes in 2090 as part of the Halocarbon Reform Bill. The UCA kept it up, and then the praenex took over 'til 2631. Best we can tell, they lost contact with the scientists here and assumed we were lost to the storm. My folks were young scientists from the Farms then—Alberta Farms, as ye say. They signed on for a five-year mission and ended up spendin' the rest of their days once the communication systems gave out."

"The government never sent anyone to check?"

He shrugged. "I haven't a baldy notion. No one that survived, I guess. The storm grew pretty swift back then. Anyway, there were but twenty scientists left then, my folks among them. They're all deceased now, God rest their souls, and I was the only wean born here, until Vengi, that is."

I look questioningly at the men.

"You've met our original castaways now." Rill indicates the

men. "Poacher and Robbery—two witless Couvie brothers scavenging so far east that they stumbled into one of my lateral turbine shafts. I haven't been able to shake 'em yet."

Po laughs, and smiles at the old man with deep affection. "How could we ever leave this paradise?"

"And if we did, how would you live ten minutes without us?" his brother jokes.

"Sure as I'd do just fine—"

"Gentlemen," Lucy interrupts. She turns to me. "Po and Robb have been here for nearly twenty years. Aside from being fine mechanics, they keep the weather instrumentation working and help Rill with the heavy lifting in the greenhouse and maintenance systems." She leans back in her chair and seems reluctant to go on.

"And you? How is it you ended up here?"

She blows out a breath. "Much like these two, I guess. My husband and I grew up in the Verge. After we married, we took on work as scavies. It was good work. Adventurous, and it could be very rewarding. We were on a long run into the Albuquerque ruins, but we stayed too long. A storm hit and we had some engine trouble midflight, which turned into worse trouble when a twister snagged us up and pulled us far enough east for the great storm to get its grip on us. Dumped us right at Rill's doorstep. Most of the crew were killed in the crash. Two more, including my husband, died later of complications. I got off easy." She traces the scar that runs down her face and gives me a sad smile.

"I'm sorry for your loss."

Rill gets up from the table and brings over a pot of tea. Passing a cup to Lucy, he pours one for me and brings it around. "The day

Jealousy crashed at my front door was the luckiest day of my life—saved me from an eternity doomed with these two eejits!" He points at Po and Robb.

"Jealousy?"

"Jealousy Meadow Forge, that's me." Lucy shifts her eyes to the ceiling. "God help us Couvies and our sins-of-man names." She smiles at me. "I prefer Lucy, for short."

"Our *savior*, Lucy!" Rill says. "Luckiest day of my life. And the day she gave birth to Vengeance was the second now."

She laughs and swats him. "Stop!" Her eyes express the same kind of adoration that the brothers show toward the old man.

"It's true. I never had seen a lady other than my mam in real life, and I was a dumbstruck pup the moment I set eyes on her." He chuckles and shuffles back to his chair. "Your husband was a lucky man, and I wish with all my heart that he were still here with us, but he gave us a gift in that lad."

The group is silent for a moment. I can feel their old sorrows and long regrets as they think about the people they've lost. "Did he meet Vengi?"

She looks up at me and grins. "Yes. Vengi was just learning to walk when my husband passed. They shared a few precious months together. We didn't know I was pregnant until after the crash. It'd been so many years since Mayhem was born, she was seven when we… We were so lucky, so blessed."

In the quiet contented silence that follows this story, I begin to relax. The tea is bitter and hot. It warms me from the inside out. My knee is pain-free if I keep still, and I begin to focus on other feelings when my stomach growls embarrassingly.

"Excuse me."

Lucy smiles as she reaches across the table to unwrap a tray of bread and cheese that she offers me.

"Cheese?" I don't see how they can have something so fresh.

"We have one remaining dairy cow, almost as old as Rill," Po tells me.

"Oh, that's craic now." The old man makes a sarcastic, noisy laugh, but I can tell he's not offended. "That heifer'll outlive you two eejits."

The cheese is smooth and mild. The bread, heavy and slightly warm. I send a prayer of thanks heavenward as I savor the flavors. I drop my guard and let the pleasure of a full stomach fill me. It's then, with my mind relaxing, my barriers dropped, that I sense a faint, but insistent thread of eagerness in the minds around me. These people are practiced at keeping an even temperament, but as I probe their feelings, I start to understand that they're excited, too.

Trying not to be obvious, I carefully push my plate away and look around. They're all staring at me. I raise an eyebrow and they seem to remember themselves. They look away and fidget in their seats.

"Don't mind us," Lucy offers. "We're just not used to new people. We'll give you some time to relax a little and get your bearings."

Robb, who has said very little, looks sharply at her. "What?"

She glares at him. "He's been through a lot in the last few days. We can give him a few minutes before the briefing—"

"Looks okay to me." Po pulls the plate of cheese and bread toward him.

"What briefing?" I ask.

She huffs out a breath and ignores me. "Really, Po. He's crashed his beautiful plane—that signal you followed was from my crashed heli by the way—he's been tossed and lost in a dune storm, performed surgery on himself, and been drugged into sleep."

"That was then, this is now." Po points with his butter knife. "Seems fine now, *d'accord?*"

"Really, Po—"

"What briefing?" I repeat.

"Briefing that's waiting on you," Po answers.

Lucy gestures at the dishes. "It's a cup of tea and some cheese. Five minutes—"

Rill raises both hands and silences them. I meet his eyes and see behind them a keen mind and protective instincts. I know the moment he decides. "Aye, he seems sturdy 'nuff to me. Maybe one meetin' won't kill 'im then."

Lucy's brow is furrowed in frustration, but when I probe harder, I realize she's actually shielding her thoughts from me. What I first saw as transparency was actually trained control.

I push harder, not so much as an invasion, but certainly beyond the manners of privacy I usually adhere to. Her shield is easy to breach, now that I can sense its shape, feel its mental edges. With a rush of excitement I begin to understand. These people have secrets.

Vengeance Forge

Current year: 2701
Thursday, 8:20 AM
Subterranean Severe Weather Research Station 21A, North America

The unexpected bark of a dog makes Vengi drop his tools with a clatter. "Whoa there!" He bends to give Cousteau a welcoming rub.

"You're not supposed to let him jump all over you like that." TJ joins him at the workbench. "You have to *be the human*."

Vengi loves the way his brother-in-law's dog—he has a brother-in-law! —licks his face and pokes his wet nose into his hand for attention. "I don't mind it. I never had a dog. He's so…happy." Vengi smiles and looks up. He's immediately embarrassed by how childish he must look, hunkered down on the floor playing with the dog. He straightens to stand as tall as possible and brushes his hands across his clothes to shed some of the dog hair. He doesn't want TJ to think of him as a kid.

At TJ's signal, Cousteau sits back and waits obediently. "I thought I'd come down early for this mysterious briefing, but what's all this?" TJ motions to the workspace Vengi set up in the shop.

"I'm working on a completely new robot."

"It's small."

Vengi lifts the central component to show him. It fits in the palm of one hand. "It's specialized for the greenhouses. I'm trying to make a picker that's smart enough to judge the ripeness of various fruits and vegetables with the same accuracy as a human."

TJ picks up two of the detached, articulated legs. "How many of these are you going to use?"

"Eight."

"Eight? Like a spider?"

Vengi grins, but realizing how giddy he must look, rolls his shoulders and tries to speak with more dignified control. "Exactly like a spider. Mother Nature is the queen of design, don't you think?"

"I do, yes."

"Spiders are extremely adaptable. They can climb, run, and jump, but they're graceful, too. I'm trying to create a picker that can travel through the fields and into trees without damaging anything, and with the tactile and sensory capabilities to pick the right food. They'll also be linked to our supply chain network, to know exactly what we need in the kitchen and when."

"That seems like a lot of work for something humans can easily do." TJ leans a hip against the table and examines the lines of code scrolling across Vengi's screen. "It looks like you're almost done."

"Two prototypes are already working. I'd like to get one more going this week."

"It's a lot of work for a little labor savings. I know enough about this briefing to know that you've all been working on some kind of escape vessel. We'll be leaving soon."

Vengi shrugs. "Better safe than sorry, *Maman* always says. And our big robots spend almost all of their time just removing the dust and sand. I'm sure you've noticed it's everywhere."

"Yeah, including on me. I showered before my rem, but I still woke up gritty."

"My *maman* says it's good for the skin, but I can tell you it's hard on electronics. That's something else I need your help with." Vengi moves over to another table covered with a tarp, motioning TJ to follow. "I need your help installing this." He pulls off the tarp to reveal the power converter they took from Cai Varela's plane.

TJ smirks and starts fiddling with the converter. "I was wondering when we'd get around to this. So where are we installing it? Can I get a preview before the briefing?"

"Um…" Vengi looks down at the floor and scuffs his foot back and forth in the dust. "Hey, you're a pilot, right?" He looks up to see TJ's serious face. "I don't know if I should, but…" He activates the virtual display behind him and brings up the schematics he's looking for. "I can show you the design. It's a few years old, but it's finished."

"Huh." TJ reads the display and begins flipping through different sections of the orthographic projection. "It's…unusual, I'll give you that."

"You boys aren't talking schematics without me, are ya?" May holds the door open as Piper trots into the shop.

"Of course not!" Vengi feels a flush of embarrassment heat his cheeks before he realizes she's kidding.

TJ wraps an arm around May. "We were just getting to the good part."

Vengi nods, giddy again. He flips to the plan view. "It's a vortex flyer, capable of navigating in conditions up to level four on the Fujita scale. It interprets constantly changing environmental conditions to plot a general course through a storm, allowing the aircraft to preserve power and avoid damage while generally heading in the direction programmed into the computer without fighting against the storm's elements."

May switches to the top view, zooming in and out on the detail sections of the bizarre looking craft. "This doesn't look compatible with Cai's power converter, but I bet we can fix it."

"Yeah, I hope so. We've been stuck on this for a while—"

"This is amazing." TJ flips back to the elevation view and just stares. "It could just work, but I'd have to see the software. And the retrofit could take a few days. How long have you been working on the aircraft?"

"We estimated about three years, but it only took us just over two and half." Vengi proudly flips back to the top view. "The jet wings were the most difficult part—"

Vengi's comm alarm beeps. "Oh, okay, I have to go now and pick up Van and the others. It's too bad Eddie is sleeping. *Maman* really wanted her to be here when you all find out about Rill, Po, and Robb." Vengi slides off his stool.

"Wait a minute." TJ wraps a cool hand around Vengi's forearm. "What do you mean when we find out about them? Find out what?"

"Well, that they volunteered to stay behind, of course."

TJ stares at him blankly. "Why would we leave them behind?"

"Cuz there's only room for eight people? Hey, I gotta go."

May pulls TJ's hand from Vengi's arm. "Yeah, you better go."

Vengi scurries to the door.

"It *is* too bad Eddie won't be awake to hear that," May shouts after him.

"Oh, she already knows. Rill told her yesterday," Vengi calls over his shoulder.

He hears TJ's groan as the door swings shut behind him.

16
Cai

Current year: 2701
Thursday, 9:00 AM
Subterranean Severe Weather Research Station 21A, North America

Lights illuminate only the corridor in the area where we stand, but I can sense that the hall stretches far and deep to the right. I clench my hands on my crutches and grit my teeth in sudden panic at the idea of walking to wherever it is we're going.

"Want a ride?" Vengi is grinning ear to ear as he stops the small open-top vehicle in front of us. It was so quiet, I didn't hear its approach. Van jumps down from the passenger seat and holds out a hand to shake Rill's.

"Well, sure is some place ye've got here, Rill." Van's enthusiasm eases some of the tension throughout the group.

I relax just a little as Lucy climbs nimbly into the second row of seats, leaving the front seat for Rill.

Po points to the rear facing seat at the back. "This should work for you. You can sit sideways and rest your leg straight along the seat."

Van holds out a hand so I have something to grab, and after a couple of failed attempts at getting up the step, I finally make it up to sit on the bench.

Van grabs hold of the overhead bar and stands on the bumper step. "Ready to roll!"

Vengi doesn't hesitate and soon we're descending into a strange, dark space. The ceiling gets higher and the walls get farther apart. The entrance where we started narrows into a distant speck behind us. Gone is the dusty white-on-white theme of the living spaces; this section of the compound is entirely concrete gray. The motion-activated lights along the ceilings and walls blink out as we pass, and in a few short minutes I've lost sight of our starting point.

We arrive in a hangar-like space. Lights flicker to life around us, revealing an eclectic mix of vehicles, from sleds I recognize from the rescue, to Jeeps, trailers, small construction vehicles, and even a dilapidated helicopter. Another area holds dismembered aircraft parts, several fuselages, wings, and jet engine housings, gutted and empty.

"This is the shop." Vengi jumps out ahead of the others, the tools in his toolbelt rattling like a chime. "We've got a bit of everything. No boats, though." He smiles, a boy showing off his most prized treasures.

"Over there's the maintenance area." He points to an enclosed space to one side.

I wave to TJ and May where they stand inside near a disassembled robot. "Your mother tells me you like to fix things. Is that your shop?"

He smiles proudly. "Nothing here is mine. Nothing here is

theirs." He points to the others. "The only way this place works is that *everything* is *ours*. Our food, our fun. Our troubles and our work. Our Creator and our survival."

"Aye, a smart approach, to be sure," Van says.

"It's Rill's way, and he taught us."

I nod. "A wise man."

"The wisest—"

Rill shuffles over to us. "Alright, then let's get to the point so these people can learn what they need to, and then this man can get some rest and heal."

"We're here." TJ says as he and May join us. "We're leaving the dogs in there to keep them out of the way."

"Where's Mercy?" May asks.

"Still with those old crew logs stored in the station." Van shakes his head and laughs. "It'll be hours before I can pull her outta those records now. History no one else knows? It's like her birthday."

"On we go then." Rill points to a panel down the wall and Po jogs over to it. "Once ye see the Tumbler, it'll be least an hour before we can pull ye out again."

"Tumbler?" Van raises an eyebrow at me.

I shrug. Even reading their thoughts I couldn't get a clear grasp on what exactly this aircraft is.

A short whine sounds, then a hiss, and I follow the sound to the opposite side of the shop where the corridor seems to abruptly end at a metal wall. As I watch, the wall divides in the center and two massive wings of steel roll inward on rubber rollers. The ingress leads into a black space beyond.

Vengi races toward the opening and I have a second of panic

when it looks like he'll fall over the edge into darkness, but as he pivots to walk backward—his arms thrown wide, his violet eyes alight—he activates the lights to reveal the strangest looking craft I've ever seen.

He turns toward the ship, his arms spread wide like entering an embrace and stands with his head thrown back so his voice echoes against the walls. "This is the Tumbler."

"That's just what we call her," Lucy explains as we walk together toward the craft. "But her real name's the Berylhenge." Lucy points to the ball-like, transparent compartments at the ends of the ship's four arms. "Four identical cockpits with full redundancies attached by jet arms to the central fuel hub and computer core."

"Jet arms?" I glance at Van.

Vengi grins. "I named it for the four pods, like Beryllium protons. See?" He points to the four cockpits. "Plus the way the jet arms turned out like webbing reminded me of a lattice diagram. That's how I got to thinking of Beryllium. And then Henge because I love them. I visit three in the VRT, and I always feel close to the Creator there. Henges were important to ancient people. They were a symbol of man's understanding and respect for nature, you know?"

TJ gives him a dumbfounded look.

"Anyway," Vengi continues awkwardly, "Berylhenge is a kinda long name, so we just call her the Tumbler."

Van gasps next to me. His mouth has fallen open and he has one hand resting on the top of his head, like he's holding in his brain.

I blink hard and turn back to the ship.

I'm a grown man. A doctor, a teacher, and a leader of a whole society of people. I've seen and heard just about everything imaginable in our broken and segregated world. I've talked my way out of and into situations my whole life. Convinced others to see my way of thinking and follow my direction even when their instincts lead them elsewhere. My words convinced the leaders of Scorch to entrust me with this invaluable group, my team, but I am beyond speechless as I look at this bizarre aircraft. I don't even know where to start.

"It's Vengi's design, but we've all had a part in building her. Some of the engine components were designed by Rill's old crew." Lucy nudges my arm. "We'll show you the schematics later, but how about a look inside to start?"

My crutches seem to automatically swing forward to follow as the group moves toward the first…*ball*, I want to call it. It's only about three meters off the ground—Van can reach the undercarriage and I watch as he stretches up to run a hand along the pitted silver surface of the composite skin. Inside the sphere, two seats are arranged to face the controls running in a ring around the inside of the dome. Behind them is a short hall and aisle. The ball is only slightly larger than the cockpit. It's attached to the "jet arm" via a lattice of the same pitted silver metal that covered the undercarriage. Another expanse stretches left and right connecting to the neighboring spheres like a web.

Vengi scurries past us and then up a step ladder set near the back of the first sphere. He reaches up to pull down a recessed flight of accordion stairs set into the back of the cockpit.

"Each chamber is accessed individually." Vengi waves for Van to take the stairs. "Just press the lever and the door will fold in. I'm afraid it's going to be a little tight for you, Van."

Van smacks his head on the top edge of the hatch. "Holly mother of God!" He swears and rubs his forehead briefly before ducking into the cockpit.

"Sorry!" Vengi laughs. "The Creator told me to make it big enough for sapiens, but he didn't tell me to make it for *giants*."

I can't help but smile. As I get closer to the fuselage, it's apparent that each little pit in the skin, about the size of my thumbprint, is a camera lens. I look down the length of the jet arm to the disc-like central hub and realize there must be thousands of them.

As if reading my thoughts, May points to the surface of the ship. "The cameras are part of the sensory network that guides navigation and allows the computer to calculate the necessary adjustments to fly through a vortex filled with debris."

I stare at her, wondering how she knows so much.

She shrugs. "We got here early. I had a few minutes to look at the specs."

"Did you say fly through a vortex?"

"Well, *tumble* really, not fly."

My face must show my horror because she laughs.

"Think of it like a philosophy," Lucy explains. "Instead of swimming against the current, the Tumbler goes with the flow. You don't set a flight path so much as a final destination, and the computer will get you there by the path of least resistance. You have to ride the storm, not fight against it."

Vengi steps up beside us. "In theory, anyway. Come take a look inside, you'll see better how it works."

I open my mouth to ask a question, but I still don't know where to start. I shake my head, set down my crutches, and start the near impossible task of climbing the stairs without bending one knee. Thankfully my leg can take a little weight now. When I finally reach the hatch, I'm surprised by the gap between the skin of the craft and the inside chamber. From the door I can see what I couldn't from the ground; the ball is a sphere within a sphere. I stick my hand into the open space between the two spheres.

"It's designed so that the inner sphere can always orient to the horizontal plane." Vengi sticks his hand in too. "Regardless of how much the ship is tumbling, the passengers will always be right-side up."

"Brilliant." Slowly I step into the short corridor, pulling my bad leg behind me. It's tight, but tall, and I stand upright easily. On my left, I recognize familiar storage compartments for food stuff, kits, and baggage. I push the little door on my right and am surprised to find an efficient little latrine. I glance into the cockpit at Van's broad shoulders and shake my head, trying to suppress a laugh.

"Yeah," Vengi says, "that's going to be interesting for him."

As I move into the cockpit, the area opens up. To my left and behind one of the pilot seats is a low narrow bench that curves slightly around the rim of the sphere. It's just long enough for your average praenex to sleep. Based on the tidy folded blanket and pillow strapped under the safety harness, I guess that's just what it's for. The rest of the cockpit is familiar, but more open than the aerodynamic shape of airplane cockpits. Some of the instrumentation is a mystery, and the number of controls is impressive, but when I look straight up, I can't help but gasp.

Through the clear bubble of the chamber's roof above us, the inside of a massive silo rises seemingly forever into a void. "Where are we?"

"Missile silo." The pleasure in Vengi's voice is unmistakable. He's enjoying all our surprises.

"No kidding?" Van has both hands pressed against the glass roof and gleefully looses a string of curses and exclamations, some that I've never even heard before.

"Missile silo?" I ask.

"Yes. The people who retrofitted this place removed the missiles, but the aperture still works, or, well, it does now because Po and Robb fixed it."

"I'd like to go back out and take a closer look."

"Me, too." Van tries to step past me, but there's not enough room. "Okay, yer Highness, after ye."

He waves me forward and I follow Vengi to the hatch.

"Well now, what's this supposed to be?" The latrine door squeaks. "Look, Cai, it's a piss pot with a door."

I turn around to start the tricky process of getting down the ladder without bending my knee and see Van's look of disbelief as he tries various ways of fitting inside the latrine.

"Try backing in." I call and watch as he does, but his shoulders won't fit unless he angles them. "Maybe you can hold it."

"Hold it? Was that a joke? Ye don't *make* jokes, yer Highness!"

I'm trying not to laugh as I continue backing down the ladder.

It's more like a controlled fall, really. "Let's go, Captain. We've got a missile silo to explore."

Lucy helps me down the last step and hands me my crutches. "The original builders stripped the silo, but when Vengi finished the design for the Tumbler, we added a modified magRail system."

She leads me over to the wall and I realize for the first time that the four stripes disappearing up the wall are magRails. "We're at the bottom of the silo. It's about eighty meters to the top. The Tumbler attaches to the magRail by these arms." She points to a long extension arm tucked along the floor and attached at one end to the magRail.

Van bends to examine the arm and Vengi continues the explanation. "The arms propel the Tumbler up the silo and then boost her under power into the sky. In theory."

"Boost her?"

Vengi smiles and nods.

TJ scoffs. "You mean you just fling the ship into the sky?"

"Under power, of course," Lucy adds.

"In theory," Vengi says again.

"The launch will have to have enough power to gain altitude sufficient to counter any immediate downward force the storm might push against it." Lucy uses her hands to demonstrate, punching her fist into the air, and then swirling it up and down like a corkscrew.

Van laughs. "Better make sure the roof is open!"

Vengi chuckles. "The roof is brilliant. Instead of simple doors that lift up, the architects built it on a spinning platform. The disk uses centrifugal force and huge blowers to clear the debris before the doors slide into giant pockets. Then we just shoot the Tumbler out."

I look at his eager youthful face. "In theory?"

He nods vigorously.

"Wait." Van holds up a hand. "Why do ye keep saying that? Haven't ye ever tried this out?"

"Oh sure. We've run the whole thing through a bunch of sims."

"Sims?" Van and I ask in unison.

"Sure."

Lucy touches my arm to get my attention. "It's taken us nearly three years to build all of—"

"Just over two and a half, actually," Vengi blurts out.

Lucy points a warning finger at him for the interruption and he grins. "Anyway, we don't have the resources to test things out, so it's a one-shot deal."

I can't believe what I'm hearing. "You mean you've never actually flown the Tumbler?"

She shakes her head.

"How do you know it will work?"

She opens her mouth to answer but Vengi beats her to it. "God told me it would work," he says matter of factly.

I'm praenex. I know the Creator's voice. I have a deep and abiding faith. But even I believe in a test drive. My incredulity must be clear on my face because Lucy is shaking her head and tugging on my sleeve.

"Wait! Don't get discouraged." She grabs ahold of Van's sleeve now, too. "Let me show you why we're so sure. Why we've known almost since the moment you crashed that this is all Divine design."

Van's still staring in shock at Vengi. As a sapiens, he can't hear the Creator's voice like a praenex. In that way, his faith in all our ideas is probably the most remarkable thing of all. Half the time we must sound insane to him.

Lucy smiles and waves us back over to the Tumbler, past the ball-shaped cockpit and engine arm to the central hub. Vengi races around us to open the instrumentation panels. The belly of the craft sits lower here, like a giant bowl, and Van has to duck slightly to see inside. I move around him to get a better look.

"Ta da!" Vengi spreads his arms toward a gaping hole in the engine.

"What am I looking at?"

Vengi's smile falters. "This is where we'll mount your power converter—the one we took from the Agulha. It'll be perfect."

I shake my head. "That's—"

"It'll take a couple days to redesign the connections," May says.

"Maybe less if we skip rems, but I also need to update the software," TJ adds.

May nods. "We should try to apply Cai's cloaking technology."

I shake my head again. "Wait. We don't have time—"

"You have cloaking technology?" Vengi interrupts. "Like Klingons?"

The reins I hold on my patience don't just slip, they snap. "Stop! Everyone, listen to me."

They look at me like I've grown another head.

I take a deep breath. "I can tell just by looking at the space that it's too small. The component from my ship is at least twenty centimeters wider and quite a bit taller. We're going to have to peel back the surrounding hull and figure out how to make it fit."

They all look from me to the gap in the hull. A few seconds tick by and then they're right back in triage mode.

"Three days," TJ insists. "We can do it in three. I've skipped a rem before. These relays just need to be rerouted—"

"I'm not flyin' in something ye fixed instead of sleepin'," Van says.

"You're talking about step 257 when we're still on step four," May scolds them. Their technical chatter fades into the background as I take in the whole of what I've learned. I close my eyes and reach out in prayer to feel a warm, glowing peace deep within my mind. When I next look, I see with new eyes. I see our way out of this underground prison and back to Terra Faire. I see us safely home, but then my brain catches up with my heart and I see what I'd been ignoring.

"Lucy?"

She stops talking and turns to me.

"Is there passenger space in the central hub?"

Her smile fades. "No. Only emergency access tubes. Minimal life support."

I exhale heavily. "Then there's only room for eight people."

"Wait, what?" Van's brow creases. "Eight?"

I focus on Lucy. "Who are we leaving behind?"

Rill O'Brien

In the past…
February 11, 2698, three years ago
Subterranean Severe Weather Research Station 21A, North America

Rill heard the door slide open behind him. The light quick footfalls warned him to brace for the onslaught of youthful enthusiasm that always followed.

"It's lashing outside!" Vengi, Lucy's nine-year-old son, skidded to a graceless stop at Rill's elbow. "*Maman* says the basins will be full by morning."

"Uh huh." Rill kept his focus on the AI component he was repairing, preferring to let the boy run off some steam before stopping to see what he wanted.

"She's still down in hydro-G, checking on aquifer levels, but she said the drought is over."

"Aye."

"So maybe we could try my boat again. I mean, when you have time…. Doesn't have to be now. *Maman* will be here in a minute; she said I could come ahead." The boy leaned in to see Rill's project. "What're you doing?"

"Just some wee repairs."

"Want help?" Vengi tossed a tablet onto the counter and climbed onto the tall stool next to Rill, his gangly limbs sticking out like a spider moving up a thread.

Rill had never seen a young praenex before Vengi was born—all the others he'd known had been fully grown. He was constantly amazed by how quickly the boy grew, and by the intelligence that seemed to grow at an even keener pace. The only thing that grew faster was his own love for the child. Helping to raise him had made Rill feel like he had family, real family, for the first time in a long while.

"Naw, thank ye, lad. What did ye want to talk to me about, then? Hmmm? The boat? Or some other such thing?"

Vengi was an inventor. His appetite for new tech was insatiable. He was always designing things, building them, or modifying something they already had. They'd all learned to keep a watchful eye on him or suffer the potential consequences. Normally his tinkering was harmless, sometimes it was entertaining, and sometimes downright useful. But Rill had learned that he sometimes had to wait to see which way an invention would go before deciding.

He'd been angry—they all had—when they discovered the noisy modifications the boy had secretly made to the snowmobiles they used outside. The change seemed frivolous, and even annoying, when Vengi sheepishly explained that he'd ridden a real snowmobile in a sim in the VRT and wanted to make them more authentic. It wasn't until later, when they'd had to make a two-man emergency repair outside, that they'd realized the huge advantage of a noisy sled out in the storm. It gave them another way to keep track of one another and could even save a life if someone got separated or had a computer failure.

Rill took off his loupe and rubbed his eyes before reaching toward his shoulder to scoop up Sweets and lift him over to Vengi's waiting hand. "So? What have ye got, lad?"

Vengi smiled at Sweets and pet the tiny mouse before setting him down and reaching for the tablet.

The door whooshed open again. "Did you show him?" asked Lucy, wiping dust and sweat from her face.

"Not yet." Vengi raced to his mother's side, dragging her over to the counter. "I wanted to wait for you."

Lucy smiled. "Divine grace with you, Rill. How's your day going?" She squeezed his shoulder.

"Oh, it's a quare day, thank ye. I'm a wee bit curious now, knowing whatever it is our boy here has to show me requires his mam's help."

Instead of looking down in shyness as Rill thought *he* would have done as a child, Vengi grinned hugely. He tapped a command into the tablet and shoved it at Rill. "People are coming."

Rill straightened and looked at Lucy. She nodded and raised her hand in caution. "Not today, not even this year, but sometime. I've dreamt it, too. We didn't want to tell you until we were sure."

"Well now, what's made ye sure?"

Before she could answer, Po arrived, striding quickly across the lab, wiping his hands on a greasy rag he brought with him from the garage.

"Oh, that's craic." Rill put one foot on the floor and came half off his stool. "Surely this is somethin' bigger than I thought if it takes three of ye to tell me."

Vengi snorted. "Robb would be here, too, if he weren't in rem."

"Vengi." His mother shook her head.

"What? He would. He's been having lots of dreams, just like you."

Po raised his hand. "Easy now, Rill. This is news, but the good kind." He reached across Rill to lay an inviting hand palm-side up on the counter next to the mouse. *"Bonjour, Sweets. Ça va?"* When Sweets climbed into his hand, he brought the mouse up close to his face so the little creature could touch noses with him, and then he gently slipped the mouse into Rill's pocket. "We're going to have some company, it's true, but first we have a big project to prepare."

Rill's heart was beating hard. He looked at the eager but serious faces around him. Only Vengi seemed unconcerned about how the news would affect him. "Jesus, Mary, and Joseph, ye're givin' me a spell! One of ye want to start at the beginnin'."

"I think we should start at the end!" Vengi typed in a few more commands on the tablet, and then cast the information onto the large monitors on the walls above the counter. "We're finally building the aircraft!"

Rill cocked his head to the side, trying to make sense of the odd schematics and drawings flashing across the screens. "Saints alive. How?" He shook his head. "Nothing can fly through the storm."

Po blew out a breath. "That's what I thought, too, but we've been studying Vengi's drawings and the design is sound. It's wildly unusual, but possibly has just the creativity our other designs lacked."

"I think it can work," Lucy added. "It's going to take a long time—probably three years—and more materials than we've got, we'll probably need to up-cycle some metals and salvage materials around the station, but I think we can do it."

"*Two* years!" Vengi bounced on his seat. "I think we can do it in two."

"We'll see." Lucy slung an arm around her son's shoulders and squeezed him.

Rill looked back at the diagrams, and then tapped on one display to zoom in. "This looks like it's built for…eight people?"

"*Oui!* That's how we know for sure that people are coming. God wouldn't fill my head with these pictures if they weren't coming, too."

Rill went very still. His pulse jumped, and then slowly evened out as he focused on his breath. "Alright then, alright. Let me have a juke at these plans."

He shuffled through the screens. "Well now, it's a smart design, but I still don't see how this can work. It's so small. I don't see how it takes off. Am I missin' somethin'?"

"It's an ingenious design." Po pointed to the schematic. "Lightweight and brilliant for high winds—"

"It will go like this." Vengi picked up a nearby rubber band, fit it between his stretched fingers and let it fly straight up to the ceiling. They all watched it bounce off the cement. "See? The ship will catapult up the silo, through the retracted roof, and soar up into the storm to reach a faraway land." He grinned at Rill. "All you have to do is design the catapult while we get to work on the ship."

"Well," Po made a slowdown motion with his hands. "We'll need new simulation software, and we might need to do live tests with the catapult."

Lucy nodded. "Robb thinks we can use the hangar space for component construction and then assemble in the silo base. But there's really no way to do a full functional test before the launch, only sims."

"It's a one-shot deal," Po agreed.

Vengi bounced on his toes. "One good shot is all we need, right Rill?"

The boy stared at him with such absolute confidence that Rill realized he had little choice. "Well now, sure. I suppose I could work on a…catapult, did ye say?"

Vengi nodded wildly.

Rill took another breath and reached up to stroke Sweet's tiny head. "And ye're all sure that the sims are good enough?"

Lucy grimaced.

Po scrunched up his face, then nodded. "We'll know if they aren't and make adjustments. I think it's worth a try."

Rill sat forward with both hands on his knees. "Alright. When do we start?"

17
Eddie

Current year: 2701
Thursday, 8:00 PM
Subterranean Severe Weather Research Station 21A, North America

The acoustics of the silo's cold cement walls turn my tiny piccolo into an eerie orchestra all by itself. The slow cadence of the notes flutter upward and ping around the deep space before fading into the blackness overhead. Sitting on the floor of the dark, cavernous space, with only a task light to illuminate a circle around me, my back against the wall grows cold. My fingers itch for the strings of my violin, but when the song ends and I close my eyes, the peace stays with me.

Difficult decisions are coming, and difficult tasks too. My hand strays to my pocket and I rub the edge of the red sash hidden there. How did Gran Bozan Li manage the uncertainty of leadership? She must have been through times like this when so many moving parts depended on faith—faith in the Creator, yes, but also faith in the people available to help.

I turn my head toward a scritch of sound. Mercy slips into my dark cave through the huge bay door, causing a beam of bright light to cut a ribbon across the floor in front of me.

"TJ said I'd find you here." She hesitates, then sits cross-legged across from me. "Are you alright?"

I force a smile. "Of course. Just taking a minute for myself." I hold up my piccolo.

She nods, then looks up and around. "Your violin would be amazing in here."

I sigh. "You know me so well."

Her eyes meet mine; her worry and sympathy are all wound up together in tight lines radiating from their corners. She holds up a hand to me.

I press my palm to hers and thread my fingers down. Somewhere deep within me, confidence rises. I squeeze her hand and push the emotion out through my gem to wash over us. "We're going to be fine. Everyone's going to be fine."

"I know." She squeezes my fingers back, then peels our hands apart. "But now we have to talk with the others. They're waiting, and then we have another training exercise."

I rise and stow my instrument in its case. Dusting the grit from my skirts, I follow my friend out of the darkness and into the light.

The overheads in the shop turn it into a fishbowl. Through the windows, TJ, May, Van and Cai are all waiting for us, but none of our new friends are here.

"Where are the others?" I ask Mercy.

"In the garage, I think. The one near the entrance with the sleds. They said something about maintaining the tunnel."

I follow her inside. All chatter stops as the team focuses on us.

"Divine grace," I greet them.

It's an awkward delay before May answers, "And with you. We're sorry to interrupt your playing—"

"We need to go through the plan, make sure everyone's clear on priorities." Cai yanks back a stool, motioning for me to join them at the table.

"Aye, but if we can do it with a wee bit more courtesy, I'd thank ye." Van wraps an arm around Mercy and snuggles her into the space between his knees where he sits on another stool.

She blows out her breath. "Why is everyone so angry today?"

"Lack of rem, primarily," May says.

"You keep saying that, but I'm fine. I've managed on a lot less sleep before," TJ growls.

Van laughs. "Sure ye have, but that doesn't explain why I had to stop ye from throwin' that screwdriver drill across the shop a few minutes ago."

TJ throws his hands in the air. "One stupid screw! It wouldn't go in."

"Aye, cuz ye had the drill in reverse. I've said it before, I'll say again, I'm not flyin' in somethin' ye built instead of sleepin'."

"Enough!" I close my eyes and take a deep breath. "Let's just go over the plan and get ready for training. Cai, do you have an agenda?"

"No, but I have a list. TJ's working on the software updates. May's working out the compatibility issues. I'm working with Vengi—when he's not doing chores—on expanding the physical space in the engine to accommodate the tech from my plane—"

"And I'm workin' on the weight issue," Van cuts in, "and I

have to tell ye, it doesn't look good. I'll keep goin' on the math, but I don't see how we're gonna fit Old Rill into the plan, let alone the two brothers."

I rest a hand on the table. "That's a priority for me, for us."

"It's unlikely we can accommodate that much variance from design." Cai shakes his head. "We need to focus on getting the ship operational. It would be better for Van to work with Mercy on the cloaking tech, but we'll need to abandon even that if it's not ready when the engine is finished. Plus, we have more training."

"We can add a few more days, a week—"

"No!" Cai bangs his fist on the table, making the scattering of tools and tablets bounce.

We wait in stunned silence as he visibly wrestles his temper under control.

He takes a deep breath, then looks around at us. "I'm sorry, but we don't have time. There are…urgent events unwinding out in the world while we're stuck here. We have to get back, fast."

"At what cost?" My question is cut off by a station alarm. "What's that?"

"Checking." TJ taps a system display hanging in the air over the table. "Proximity alert."

"Proximity alert?" I stand with everyone else.

We rush out of the shop and jump into the waiting golf cart. It's more humans than machine by the time we all find a place. May throws it into gear and we hold on for dear life as she speeds down the corridor, lights blinking on with our movement and off again behind us like we're a ball of light careening through a tube.

I try my comm ring, but no one answers on the local network.

"Can you reach Lucy?"

TJ shakes his head. "No, but if they're in the garage, they'll know what's going on. The radar showed an object right near the base of the tunnel."

"That's gotta be near Lucy's crashed heli," Van shouts.

My eyes go wide. "Near the beacon, you mean."

"Aye."

"Hold on!" May shouts. She takes a ninety degree turn at speed. We all instinctively lean to the right as the cart heaves into the turn.

The fire doors to the garage are straight ahead. May slams on the brakes and we scramble down and into the garage.

Lucy and Rill don't even glance our way. They're huddled over the video unit watching the image on the screen intently. We close in around them.

"Do *not* damage that blower, do you copy?" Lucy shouts into her mic.

"Copy that. Easing by the blower." Po's voice is tinny and distant as we watch on the screen as he, Vengi and Robb maneuver their sled through the tunnel towing a trailer. Atop the trailer sits a dusty black hunk of metal.

"What's going on?" I ask.

Rill straightens. "Drone. Crashed right by the tunnel exit. Boys are bringing it in. Come on." He waves us toward the staging area.

The sled's roar is getting closer now. "Did that look like one of the drones we saw headed to Terra Faire?" I ask TJ.

"No, those were armed strategic drones. From what I saw on the screen this looks like a standard surveillance model."

"Here they come!" Lucy pushes ahead of us. "Keep clear."

The sled eases through the dust curtain and stops a few meters away. We help the men with their gear, and TJ and Van push the sled further into the garage.

We gather around the simple black drone strapped to the trailer.

"What is it?" Vengi asks.

"Let's see." TJ brushes sand from a clear panel, flips open the casing and taps a few keys. The drone's fuselage peels open to reveal a simple communication board. Lights flash and a life-size hologram forms in the air over the drone.

I blow out the breath I was holding. "Hello, Mother."

The holographic image flashes and then the recording begins.

"My name is Fleet Admiral Pèlerine Reine LeRoux, leader of SciCorps."

My mother's image looms over us, her expression severe. She's garbed in full ceremonial dress—the black-on-black severity of her suit's offset only by the sparkling onyx stones decorating the clasp that holds her one-shouldered cape. She looks taller with the cape artfully cascading down her side and through her bent arm. As I follow the flow of fabric where it tucks into a loop at her waist to fall fluidly down to her booted ankle, I'm struck by a memory of giggling in her arms with my legs and the cape flying out around us as we twirled.

"Jesus, Mary and Joseph." Rill's mumbled exclamation startles me back to the present.

The holographic message continues. "This drone was sent in search of a vessel carrying my two offspring and four other citizens." My mother's jaw clenches and she goes on, her voice struggling to cover her emotions. "These people are…precious to us and we will not stop until we find them. Within this drone we've placed technology capable of sending a recorded message back to a network we've installed throughout your area. Any one of those devices can transmit along a relay to technology outside the Great Storm. We ask that you please share with us any information that you have regarding our lost citizens. We stand ready to launch manned rescue operations in two days' time if we do not hear a response. Thank you for your assistance, and may the Creator bless you."

Silence falls around us as the hologram shuts down, then chaos ensues. Everyone talks at once. Cai and TJ argue over the drone, poking into the fuselage in search of the tech. Po and Robb noisily shed their environmental suits while shouting commands at Van to get him to move the sled. Mercy, Vengi and Lucy all talk to me at once.

"Beep, beep, beep!" The horn pierces the air.

I throw my hands over my ears and swivel to face Rill where he stands by the sled's controls.

"Do I have yer attention, or do I need to honk it again?"

"No!" we chorus.

"Alright then, settle down. Seein' as this message came from a LeRoux, seems only fit one of ye two should decide what's next." He motions between TJ and me.

My brother turns to me. "I'll work with whoever wants to help with the tech, but you should record the message."

I nod. "We need to get it out quickly; we don't want any other people trying to reach the station. It's too dangerous. Vengi, can you help me with the recording?"

Vengi straightens. "I was hoping you'd ask."

Cai steps between us. "We don't have time for a lot of fanfare. Just record a quick message now, and let's get back to work."

I hold his gaze for a moment while I think of what to say. "Did you see all that my mother just said?"

"*See* what she said?"

"Yes. Full title, ceremonial dress. She's sending a message from the commander of Scorch." I run a hand across my hair and shake off the dust. "Here we may be focused on the tasks at hand, but out there," I point up the tunnel, "out there, a civil war is brewing. We're still on a mission—a TAC mission backed by the Legion. Any message I send is likely to rebroadcast on an endless loop throughout our settlements. I will not miss this opportunity to present a strong and capable resistance to SciCorps for simple lack of soap. We have a training exercise, and then I need a smidge of time, Ambassador."

"Aye, and ye have it," Van says, moving his bulk into the space at my side.

Cai stares at me. "I hope you know what you're doing. Time is not a resource we have in abundance just now."

I nod. "I agree. Let's all get back to work then. This adds one more thing to do before we can launch."

"Alright, everyone listen up."

Lucy uses her drill-sergeant voice to get our attention. Up until now, most of our drills have been seated behind pilot controls. Grueling mentally and even emotionally, but physically dull. I get the feeling that's about to end.

Lucy raises a hand for emphasis. "This drill is an evacuation from one pod to another. It's going to be physically demanding and spatially stressful. You need to concentrate on each step."

I shake my head to clear my fatigue and try to focus.

"You're the flight crew, and right now you're exhausted." She looks at each one of us before continuing. "And that's good. It'll make this drill even more realistic, because in my experience, things don't go wrong when everyone's happy and rested and enjoying brunch. Things go wrong when everything is already a mess and everyone's at their wit's end. So line up with your pod mate and let's give it a try."

Vengi and I step into position at the front of the ladder to pod 1. Behind me, Van, Mercy, Cai, May, and TJ shuffle into line.

Lucy moves down the line and stops next to me. "Your skirts are going to be a problem."

"Not today." I unhook one end of the decorative cord looped around my waist, flick it behind me and bend to reach between my legs to pull it through to the front. Like I practiced in my room, I gather my skirts into layered folds and stretch the cord back up to my belt, fastening it to hold my skirts in the shape of baggy pants. My leggings-clad calves stick out like pale twigs.

Mercy giggles and claps. "Perfect!"

Lucy smiles. "That should do."

My satisfaction lasts only a second until Lucy turns to Van.

"Van Elder, step out of line please."

"What's wrong with Van?" Mercy asks.

"Where to start?" TJ jokes.

Lucy narrows her eyes at my brother before huffing out a breath. "He's too big."

Van's shoulders slump. "This again?"

"I'm sorry, Van." Lucy pats his massive bicep. "We remeasured, and you simply won't fit through the evac tunnel. You can help us observe and suggest any corrections to the plan, agreed?"

"Aye, I can do that."

"Good man." Lucy waves an arm to Vengi and he turns to face us.

"I'm going to explain the process out here," Vengi says. "There's not enough space inside the Tumbler for everyone to watch." He points to the ship where the pod connects to the jet arm. "The hatch is at the back of the pod. When you open it, if the lights are working, they'll automatically turn on. You'll pull yourself with your back oriented to the outside using handholds embedded in the tunnel surface until you get to here." He points to the junction of the jet arm and ship's core.

"Why does orientation matter?" I ask.

"Good question." Lucy moves under the jet arm. "These jets are hot. The surface inside the tunnel won't burn your skin instantly, but it's not going to be comfortable to touch. You'll want your back to the heat, and your hands on the coolest rungs possible."

Vengi nods. "Same thing is true of the engine core, so at the junction, you'll have to open the hatch and roll quickly to reposition your body so your back is toward the inside. Use your foot to press the 'close' button on the inside near the hatch. You'll continue to pull along the hull and keep going until you reach your destination pod. Then you open the hatch," he points to the next jet arm, "crawl through the tunnel and enter the safe pod."

"Any questions?" Lucy asks.

Mercy steps out of line and threads her hand through Van's arm. "What'll happen to Van if he can't escape?"

"Come on now, lass." He tips her chin up and kisses her lightly. "Nothin's goin' to happen to me."

I'm touched by his gentleness, but a small part of me doubts Van's words. We've known each other for a long time and he's always the one getting hurt. Mercy must have the same thought because she reaches up and runs her thumb along the new scar on his forehead.

"You always say that, and you always get hurt," she whispers.

Van pulls her into a half hug and turns back to Lucy. "Let's get goin' now. Time's a wastin'."

Lucy nods to Vengi and we follow him up the ladder and into the pod. Without waiting, he opens the hatch and crawls inside the tiny passageway.

"I'm closing the hatch!" he shouts back to me. "Everyone needs to enter and exit like they're the only survivor."

I shudder at the morbid implication of *that* training concept, but stay clear as the hatch clinks shut. I listen a moment for the sound of the hatch opening and closing on the other end, then open the hatch again and climb inside.

It's small, but not tight for me. I think I could probably crawl on my belly. "Why don't I just crawl through?" I shout.

"Gravity!" Lucy shouts back. "The Tumbler will orient to the external conditions. You need to hold on."

"Fine," I mumble under my breath, hit the close button and flip onto my back. I find the embedded rungs along the ceiling of the tunnel and pull myself along. I'm strong like any praenex, but this is basically pull-ups one after another all the way to the end. I'm sweating as I reach the hatch. *Core* is written in reflective letters on the back. I open it and it clicks in place magnetically to the inside of the tunnel. I twist around and belly through before using my toe to hit the button to release the hatch magnet. It thumps shut. Squirming into position, I'm more thankful for my yoga practice than I ever imagined I would be.

Inside the core tunnel, it's more of the same, only in a constant backbend as I traverse the circular chamber that holds the engine. I takes a lot longer to reach the hatch to pod 2. As I open it, I hear a noise behind me. I have just enough room to look under my arm and watch Mercy effortlessly scamper rung to rung behind me. Her head knocks into my foot before she realizes I'm still here.

"Oh! Sorry." She grins. "This is kind of fun."

"Yeah, sure."

Her face falls. "But they're right; Van would never fit."

I sigh. "I'm going through. Stay clear of the hatch and I'll see you on the other side."

I continue without waiting for a reply. Sweat runs down my face as I push open the catch and tumble gracelessly onto the floor of pod 2.

Lucy bends to haul me up. "Are you alright?"

I wipe my face with my sleeve and grimace at my body odor. "Yeah. Glad I'm not last."

"I'm last," she says, smiling. "When you're all through, I go. Then we repeat until it's muscle memory."

"What?"

She points down the ladder where Vengi stands drinking from a long flask of water. "Take a break and get ready for another go."

I nod and let gravity do most of the work as I slide down the ladder to the silo floor.

"Want some water?" Vengi offers me a drink.

I chug from his container, pleased to find the water ice cold.

"Pretty fun, huh?" Vengi nudges my elbow.

"I really hope we don't need to do this for real."

"Me too. With the engine running and the jets firing, we estimate a tunnel temperature of 38 to 42 degrees Celsius."

I swivel to see if he's joking. He's not. "That's—"

"Hot. Yep." He grins.

Mercy hops off the ladder nearby. Van strides over to her with a water container. She drinks and hands it back to him. He lifts her hand, twirls her once and they join us.

Vengi waves toward the Tumbler. "Of course we can't run the drill with the engine running and jets firing—too many risks, but I've figured out a way to drill in similar conditions."

"What conditions?" Mercy asks.

"Hot," I reply.

"Ooh! It'll be like hot yoga!" She bounces on her toes. "That'll be fun."

I grimace at her. Straightening, I face Vengi. "I hope you're joking."

Cai joins our circle, breathing hard. He braces his hands on his knees. "Someone's joking?"

"Nope. No joke." Vengi rocks back and forth on his heels. "Tomorrow, we'll be ready with a course simulation in the west turbine shaft. Gets plenty warm in there. It'll be just the thing."

May steps heavily off the ladder and takes a fresh water from the bin nearby. "No grown person should have to do that," she says before gulping water.

"I agree." I pat her shoulder. "So, what do you know about muscle memory?"

Vengeance Forge

Current year: 2701
Friday, 12:20 AM
Subterranean Severe Weather Research Station 21A, North America

Vengi adjusts the simple video image framing Eddie's face where she sits at the table in the Holographic lab. He sighs.

"What's wrong?" His sister asks.

Vengi shrugs over the small drone that SciCorps sent them. "The technology is too simple. I don't understand why they didn't include more capabilities—geographic readings, schematics, tactical information."

May rests her hand on his shoulder. "I guess they were in a hurry and focused on the most important thing, the people."

He shrugs. When she squeezes his shoulder, a surge of energy rushes up his arm.

"Are we ready?" Eddie asks.

Vengi looks down at the video image, rather than the live woman sitting across from him. He'd thought it was silly, maybe even a little vain, when she'd insisted on showering and changing clothes before they recorded. But now he understands. He thought he was getting used to being around females, but this is something else.

She's intensely beautiful—so striking in her paleness that he can't look directly at her. She's done something elaborate with her hair; it's piled on top of her head like a swirling white tower, making her lavender eyes huge. Her fitted white vest exposes straight shoulders and muscled arms.

But what really captures his attention is the calm authority in her posture and expression. He *feels* her presence. At this moment, he's pretty sure she could assign him a week's dust duty and he'd do it without a blink.

"Eddie, you do know that your mind control won't work through the camera, don't you?" his sister asks.

Eddie slouches slightly and waves her hand. "I'm sorry. It's just not easy to fake."

"Wait, what? Mind control?" Vengi asks his sister.

She cocks her head to the side. "Can you handle her gift a little longer, bro?"

"Um…" Vengi glances at Eddie, the real one this time, and she seems softer, less frighteningly perfect. "Uh, sure. I guess."

Eddie smiles at him, further breaking the spell. "Thanks. Now let's get this done."

When she straightens and angles her chin, it's like standing too close to a candle when the match first flares and the wick sparks to life. All at once Vengi's caught again by Eddie the Bozan. He shakes his head to try to clear it and shifts his gaze to the video image on his screen. "Okay, recording in three, two, one…"

"This is Bozan Edelweiss Renee LeRoux, reporting to you from the Subterranean Severe Weather Research Station 21A at coordinates…"

18
Cai

Current year: 2701
Sunday, 8:00 PM
Subterranean Severe Weather Research Station21A, North
America

Two days! Two. Days. Two more days have passed and there are moments I think we will never leave. No one's getting much rem and everyone's overworked. Today has already been a very long day…. I dread what comes next.

Eddie's tour of the progress with the Tumbler is winding down. She jokes with Van as they walk toward the shop, skirting around the mound of debris we've stripped from the Tumbler—doors, covers, carpet, latches, cushions, panels—you name it. We've removed anything without an essential function in order to carry more weight.

When they enter the shop, her relief is a tangible thing.

She may be euphoric, but *my* stress is growing in proportion to her glee. We are running out of time and I can predict more arguments ahead.

"He told you to *back in*? That's hilarious." She's laughing when she turns to me. "You might have a sense of humor after all, Ambassador."

She pulls out a chair across from me at the conference table in the lab. Joy flows from her in waves. I watch it lift up the people around us like foam on the tide. Do they know just how easily her emotions could carry them all away? A laugh dies in her throat when she catches my expression.

"What?" Her voice remains light even as a sense the weariness cuts through her high spirits. "What's wrong with Cai?" she asks Van when I don't answer.

"Ah…" He scratches his head and swings a chair around backward before he straddles the seat. "Cai has a problem with the math. We all do."

She looks back and forth between us. "What do you mean? What's wrong with the math?"

"There's nothing wrong with the math!" Vengi throws his hands in the air. "It's exactly what the Creator told me to build. We all agreed!"

Eddie tips her head to the side. "What do you mean, 'you all agreed?' Could somebody tell me what's going on?"

"Eddie…" Van shakes his head but doesn't say anything else.

I don't know how to explain it to her either. "Sometimes the game is longer than it seems."

"What game? What're you talking about? Lucy, please tell me what's going on."

Lucy rests a hand on Eddie's shoulder. "Believe me, I wish things were different, but sometimes even the Creator has to leave people behind."

"Leave people behind?" Eddie stands abruptly. "What're you—" She pushes away from Lucy and rushes across the room to the computer we've been using to recalculate the Tumbler's maximum takeoff weight. TJ and May are still there, talking quietly to each other.

I stand to follow, but Van steps in my way. "Well now, just ye let her be for a minute. Let her have a chance to catch up with the rest of us, without ye shovin' it in her face."

What a strange accusation. "Shoving it in her face? What're you talking about?"

"I'm talkin' about you, King Cai, and how ye always have to be in control of everythin'. So does she, so ye let her catch up with us, fair and square, before ye go telling her how it's goin' to be."

"I—"

"I think that's a good idea," Lucy agrees.

I shake my head. "She feels responsible—"

"As do you, I understand." Lucy steers me back to my chair and I let her. "Leaders are the hardest people to lead. It doesn't take being a GB or an Ambassador to know that."

"Best let the lass work it out for herself." Old Rill leans back in his chair. I almost forgot he was there. "I'll talk to her myself. She's less likely to skin me alive than you." He chuckles. "Just give her a minute."

"I can hear you," Eddie calls over her shoulder. She gasps, whispers something to TJ and the three of them come back to us.

Eddie stands with her hands on her hips looking around the room, her fingers drumming against her skirts making waves in the fabric. For a minute it looks like she's trying to pick a target. We all hold our breath. "Van, it can't be right. Look at all the stuff you pulled out." She motions to the pile of debris from inside the Tumbler.

"Aye, I'm sorry, lass. As I'm the problem, I'm willing to stay behind—"

"You are not staying behind!" Mercy pokes him in the chest.

He throws his arms wide. "Look at me, will ye? I'm sixteen stone! We can fit two men and both—"

"No, no, no!" Mercy marches away.

Van follows her. We all try not to hear their urgent whispers.

Eddie huffs out a breath and drops back into her chair. "Who's—" She fights to level out her breathing. "Who's staying behind?"

For a moment, no one says anything. Her frustration fills the room.

I roll my shoulders. "Rill, Po, and Robb are staying at the station along with—"

"No!" She drops a fist on the table and turns to the old man. "No, Rill. You've had enough, it's your time to leave, to see more of the world before…before…"

"Oh, now." Rill rests a hand over hers. Age has wrinkled and spotted his skin, making hers look childlike in comparison. "Ye're a good lass to be worryin' 'bout me, but I've always known this is my place. No trick of fate is goin' to get me out of it."

"But—"

"I love Rill too," Vengi interrupts, "and Po and Robb, but the Creator has a plan. I just followed the plan. At least they'll have the dogs to keep them company."

I sigh and rub a hand across my gem. The boy has no tact.

"The dogs?" She spins to look at TJ and May.

May covers her mouth with a hand, her eyes filling with tears. She rushes from the room.

I watch her go and work to reinforce my mental shields. The sorrow in this room is stifling.

"TJ?" Eddie reaches for her brother.

He shakes his head. "There's no other choice."

Van pulls Mercy back over to us. "There's *my* choice. I can stay and Rill and one of the brothers can go along with both dogs."

Po kicks the empty stool next to him sending it clattering across the floor. We all startle at his aggressive act.

I lean forward, ready for action, but aside from that outburst, he appears completely calm.

"No way I'm leaving my brother," he says, "and no way he's leaving me. Van is welcome to stay, but it seems an awful thing to separate two people so newly wed."

"Eddie—" I lift a hand.

"Don't you 'Eddie' me! This is *not* happening, even if you're fine with it."

"I'm not fine with it, but it's what is. We don't have time for more deliberation. We need to prepare to launch."

"Van?" She pulls her hand from under Rill's and I'm struck again by how childlike it is.

"I'm not a child!" She shouts at me and stands.

I raise both hands in surrender. "Not what I meant, and you know it."

"What're they talking about now, lad?" Rill asks Van.

"Telepath stuff, my guess." He shrugs.

"If Van stays, I stay too." Mercy plants her feet and glares at her husband.

"Ye can't stay, Cricket. They need ye for all this Culmination stuff."

"Me and May, then." TJ suggests. "You'll come back for us."

Eddie straightens. "That could work—"

"No." I shake my head. "You can't separate May from her mother and brother after all this time. That's just cruel—"

"Oh, perfect!" She throws her hands in the air and turns on me. "Now I'm cruel *and* a child?"

"Here we go," Van sighs. "We're getting the full diva now."

"Shut up!" she shouts at Van.

Mercy steps between them. "Look, everyone just take a breath. We're all tired—"

"Stating the obvious," TJ says.

Eddie points a finger at her brother. "Now don't *you* start!"

"Eddie—" I plead.

"Stop saying my name like that! Like you know me. You don't know me! You don't know what I feel for these people."

"I know, because I feel it too."

"Ha! How could you? Two Couvies and an elderly sapiens, a couple of dogs, how could they possibly factor into your world, Ambassador? Huh?"

"They do. You do. Eddie—"

"Stop!"

The force of her anger buffets me like a blow. I push back my chair and stand with the others. "Stop this now."

"What's goin' on?" Rill asks, shakily rising to his feet with the rest of us.

Eddie just shakes her head and scrubs her fingers into her hair. Her eyes glisten with unshed tears and my throat constricts.

"Eddie, dear." Lucy steps toward her, a hand outstretched.

"No." She shrinks away from Lucy's touch as tears run down her face.

Mercy's crying too now. Van pulls her into a hug.

I strengthen my mental shields even more and hold up both hands in surrender. "I think Mercy's right, we're all just too tired to handle this right now. Let's talk about the launch—"

"Oh!" Eddie covers her face with both hands, anger roiling in the air around her.

"Oh, now, lass." Rill takes a step toward her.

It seems so brave, but then I remember that he's sapiens; Eddie's anger isn't pounding him like heart blows.

She sniffs and raises her teary eyes to him. "Please Rill, just…"

"Here now." He wraps an arm around her shoulder as another garbled sob escapes her throat.

My heart squeezes and I reach for her. "*Minha flor*—"

She shakes her head. "No! Leave me alone!"

I stagger back under the cadence of her command. The instinct to walk away…no, run *away*, is so strong that I've taken a few more steps before I catch myself. It's *her* will, not mine, that has my feet moving. The shock of it—of bending to her mind control—is enough to give me strength. I raise my mental walls higher and prepare to fight off her influence.

"Stop this!" My voice has the command of my station, but it's nothing compared with what she can do.

"Seems ye have the power to stop it yerself, lad." Rill makes a shooing motion toward the door. "Ye don't have to win this one. Go on now."

I look around and see that the others are already filing out the door, too easily influenced by her command to resist. They cast woeful glances my way.

Van shrugs, also unaffected. He bundles Mercy toward the door, stopping in the doorframe. "That's fine, princess. I'm goin' too. But when ye're finished with this tantrum, we're goin' to talk this out. Ye're not the only one with a stake here. We all get a say." He shifts his eyes to me. "Good luck, King Cai. Remember, we're with *her* to the end, tantrums and all. Ye're just along for the ride."

"Yeah, thanks, Van." I can't keep the sarcasm from my voice.

When I look back at Eddie, she's raised her chin, but I sense her remorse. She's already regretting her outburst.

"I can help you learn to control that better."

She casts her eyes down to the floor. She seems to be debating something with herself. "Ha!" She laughs and shakes her head, pulling away from Rill to slide into her chair. "Now you want to *teach* me something?"

"I…"

Rill takes a step behind Eddie's chair. This is awkward, even more than usual.

Eddie sighs. "Listen, Cai, I understand that your role as ambassador comes with responsibility and power over your people. But I don't think you can really understand what's expected of me…what it means to be GB to the people of Scorch. So how about you give me a break here? I want to talk to Rill."

It's all I can do to keep from telling her everything then…to tell her I'm president, to tell her my best friend is dying. To tell her how I feel about her. But now's not the time. I sense the truth of it in my reluctance to talk about myself at all, about what I know, and what I really am. "You heard what Vengi said. This is the Creator's will."

She huffs out a breath. "He dreamt it when he was nine years old."

I lift my shoulder. "Spherans start professions near to that age."

She narrows her eyes at me. "Then *I'll* stay. I'll stay here with Po and Robb and the dogs. Rill can have my seat." She glances up at the old man standing behind her, then they both look at me.

A tendril of ice slithers up my spine. It's a bluff. It has to be.

But what if it's not? Could anyone really force her to leave here? If she stayed…my plans are nothing without her. The certainty of it makes me shudder. I know she sees it; I know she feels my terror at the idea of leaving her behind. The sheer impossibility of it.

At first, she only stares back at me, and then her shoulders relax. "But as tempting as that sounds, I know I can't stay here. That doesn't mean I give up. There has to be a way, we just need to find it."

I sigh. "We only have two days until the next lull, the next launch window."

"What's the difference?" She squeezes Rill's hand. "We can wait another cycle, there's no rush."

"No, lass." Rill shakes his head.

I nod. "There *is* a rush. Think about it…. Think about who

you are, who your friends are, and yes, who I am too. Right now, three societies are in hysterics thinking they could still lose us. The Verge, the Legion, Terra Faire. Your message may keep them at bay temporarily, but eventually they'll send a mission to save us."

"He's right, as annoyin' as it may be." Rill shuffles back to sit in the chair next to her and waves a hand at me. "And that's not the end of it."

I nod. "Think about your parents. How long will *they* wait before they send rescuers into the storm after us? Hmmm? How many lives will your indecision cost?"

"Aye." Rill patted her arm on the table. "The people I loved gave their lives to save me, to keep this place goin' for me. It's not a debt I'd wish on anyone else."

I know I have to push her. We must leave soon, of this I am certain. I spread my feet and get ready. "Who will you risk for the chance to resist the Creator's design? One of Van's siblings? Your own father? *Mercy's* father? They'll all want to search."

"Agh! Stop!"

Her anger lashes out at me, but I'm ready this time. I push back hard with my mind. The effort makes my own anger rise. I take a few steps toward the door before I give voice to my frustration. "Two days. Deal with your emotions as you must, but in two days we say goodbye to those men."

19
Eddie

Current year: 2701
Monday, 2:00 AM
Subterranean Severe Weather Research Station 21A, North America

Music fills my mind with life and longing. The sound takes over my senses.

The lilt of a violin; the light of the morning sun.

The tremor of a drum; my pulse, a liquid energy tied to the rhythm.

The tangy scent of friction on steel strings, of spit on wooden reeds; the shush of lavish gowns drifting through a dance.

Layers of sensation build as I sink into Igor Stravinsky's 1925 American debut conducting the New York Philharmonic at Carnegie Hall in New York City. This moment in the VRT is just for me—the next moments will be for *us*.

"Eddie?"

When I open my eyes, Mercy is smiling down at me.

"Oh, sorry. Computer, end simulation." I untangle my yoga pose as gracefully as possible, but still feel clumsy as I straighten and greet my friends. "Divine grace with you both."

"Well now, this better be good." Van's mass nearly fills the box. He slouches under the transparent roof and I realize it's too short for him to fully stand. He grimaces. "I was just about to go to bed when you called."

"I—"

"What's going on?" TJ's the last one to arrive at the holographic lab, shifting Mercy out of the way so he can shut the door. We all scooch together to sit on the blanket I spread on the floor.

"I was just about to explain. Um, thanks for coming."

I'm nervous, an odd and unfamiliar emotion. This is a role-reversal for me. *I'm* usually the one that people come to with problems, not the other way around. I hedge. "Where's Cousteau?"

"He's keeping watch over May's rem. Thank the Creator we all have time to get some sleep before the launch window opens." My twin cocks his head to the side. His questions press on my mind. For Van and Mercy's sake, he speaks aloud. "So, what's going on now?"

"First, let me activate the simulation. Vengi taught me how to run the VRT and I've had some time to search through the sims. Everyone put one of these on." I hand around the interlinks. "Computer, play simulation DC delta three. Close your eyes!"

They do. I watch as the images form and tighten around us. The hot wind kisses my cheek as the noise of the crowd swells. "Okay, open them."

"Whoa!" Van's head is on swivel. "What is this?"

"Mercy, any guesses?"

She looks at all the happy people around us, the food and toys spread around them, and then her gaze sharpens on buildings in the distance—a grand Neoclassical building of white stone at one end of the massive lawn, and an incredibly tall Egyptian-style obelisk at the other. "I know this. It's the National Mall! The grounds in the center of the former United States capital city. This is amazing."

TJ watches a couple of dogs race after a ball. "What's with all the people? I've never seen such a big crowd."

"This is a recording from the end of the 20th century, before the coronavirus pandemic," I explain. "This year the crowd drew over 400,000 people for the Independence Day fireworks."

"Four hundred thousand!" Mercy stands to get a better look. "That's more than all the people on Scorch!"

"That's nothing though. I read that when this country celebrated their bicentennial, one million people filled this mall."

"It's a lot of sapiens." My brother looks unimpressed.

"Obviously, but…okay, close your eyes again. Mercy, sit back down and try this. Close your eyes."

"Do we really have time for this?" TJ sniffs. "Mercy and I just got up, but Van should probably sleep before tomorrow."

"What am I, a baby? Come on." Van spreads his muscled arms wide.

"You were just complaining about going to bed," Mercy says.

"I dunno what ye're talkin' about."

"Fine." TJ closes his eyes.

"Close your eyes and tell me what you hear." I watch them.

Mercy giggles. "I hear children…children everywhere.

They're…laughing and arguing and talking over each other."

"What else?"

"Okay…" Van squeezes his eyes shut in concentration. "I hear the breeze in the trees. A dog barkin', and birds…sparrows, maybe a crow or two…lots of pigeons."

"I can *smell* the pigeons," TJ complains. "Which is surprisingly good tech. Who invented this interface?"

"Don't get distracted. Come on, play along, bro."

"Fine." He sighs. We wait. He cocks his head to the side, and then his eyes flash open and he stares at me. "I hear languages…English, obviously."

"Obviously."

"Shh!" He wrinkles his brow. He's in it now. He never can resist language games. "Spanish, Hindi…some Bengali. Chinese…French! I hear a Frenchman! Is that…Portuguese? Yes, I've been practicing for Terra Faire."

"What else?" Mercy leans in, encouraging him.

"Afrikaans, and a couple of others I'd place in the same continent, but I don't know what they're called. And also…Japanese. Korean, I think. Russian, Polish—"

"Alright!" I laugh. "You get my point. Now, open your eyes and tell me what you *don't* see."

"What don't we see?" Van leans back on his hands. "I don't see praenex."

We all give him the same look.

"What? It's comfortin'." He shrugs.

"I don't see soldiers," TJ adds.

"I don't see anger," Mercy whispers.

"Exactly. There are 400,000 people sharing the lawn, and no one is fighting. Men. Women. Young and old. English-speakers, and a few dozen other tongues. Skin of every shade. Orientations and identifications of all varieties. Faiths of every kind, and none at all. These people are all here in one place for one purpose to celebrate one thing they all enjoy together…freedom." Despite my best efforts, my emotions are soaring now. I know I'm projecting, but I trust my friends to accept it, to accept me, even after yesterday's outburst.

"Computer, mute simulation." TJ grabs my hand as the noise fades. "Enough. What's going on?"

I try to pull my hand free, but he squeezes harder. I have to yank it away. "While you were in rem, I checked the math—"

"Nah, not this again!" Van leans away and moves as if to get up.

"Wait!" I motion with both hands. "Just wait, please. What I was going to say is that it's indisputable. I asked everyone to make it a priority, to figure out a way to get all of us out of here, but we can't." I swallow. "I'm sorry for my tantrum. I shouldn't have laid any of that on you. You all had enough going on."

They're silent. My stomach drops as I look at their blank faces. What if they don't forgive me for my outburst yesterday?

"Huh." TJ's jaw hangs open. "Did you just admit to being wrong?"

Van shakes his head. "Sounded like but can't be."

Mercy smacks both of their knees. "Stop it you two! Eddie, you were right to keep trying. We don't hold that against you. We all wanted everyone to be able to escape."

"I know, it's just…I think I kind of suck at this leadership thing most of the time. Look at how our missions have gone so far. We tried to rescue your parents, we got *one* of them back. Fifty percent. Then we try to fly to Terra Faire—a simple flight! —and we end up lost in the desert."

"Technically, we're not lost," my brother says, then grimaces when he sees the look I give him. "Sorry, go on."

I sigh. "Now we have to leave three people and both dogs in this place."

"There's nothing you can do about that, nothing any of us can do, except help the Terrans rescue them." TJ says. "And you don't have to worry about the dogs. There's no way May and I will leave them here forever if the Terrans can't get them. We'll be back for Cousteau and Piper."

"I believe that! But…"

"But what?"

"Why is everything going wrong?" I throw my hands in the air. "This is only our second official mission as adults. We're bungling adulthood."

"Oh, I don't know if I'd go that far," Mercy says.

"We crashed the plane, and it's totally gone now. Our escape is going to be risky at best, we may not survive. And we're leaving people behind."

Van sits forward. "We did the right thing comin' here…followin' the beacon. We did the right thing."

"I know, it's just…"

"Eddie," TJ squeezes his eyes shut for a second. "Just what? Tell us what this is all about."

"It's about Rill, okay! It's about leaving someone behind. Someone who's never had any of the freedom we enjoy. He's never *been* in a crowd. He's never even seen the sunshine, for divine grace. How can I leave him behind?" I rock back and forth, trying not to cry.

My brother reaches out and pulls me forward so our foreheads meet, gem to gem. His hand behind my head is gentle, but firm. "Those people in that sim weren't just celebrating freedom, they were celebrating free will. Rill accepts that he has to stay, and so do Robb and Po."

Mercy wraps her arms around us and leans her head in. Van does the same so that we're in a huddle now. Me, my brother, and our two best friends. "Let's pray for a moment," she whispers.

I try to quiet my anxieties and focus on my connection with the Creator, to find that point of light within me that makes me more than muscle and bone, which makes me part of something bigger, part of the Divine. As my mind reaches out, I find an inner strength. My mind conjures the image of a blazing path ahead of me, and I realize I need only take one step to start the journey. Just like Rill said.

Mercy sighs. "Things are going to turn out better in Terra Faire. I feel it. The mission might look clumsy right now, but I think we were meant to be here. I think Lucy and Vengi have a part to play."

"I sense the same," my brother agrees. "I think even the ambassador knows it, although he's too proud to admit it."

Van snorts. "Aye. It's goin' to be worth it just to watch how King Cai responds to bein' a passenger in a ship whose whole design is basically out of control—to tumble through the storm instead of piercin' it in his fine Agulha 3."

"Still, he'll control what he can," TJ says.

"What do you mean?" I sit up and we pull apart.

TJ shakes his head. "Cai took the liberty of working with Lucy on the pod assignments. He's got our departure all planned."

"See! That's it. He has to control everything! All the time."

Mercy shrugs. "It's okay if you're mad at him, but I think you should give the others a break."

"I'm not really mad at them, how could I be?" I take a deep breath and pinch the bridge of my nose. Suddenly I'm more tired than I can ever remember. My head hurts. It's the constantly surging emotions, I know it.

"Well, what now?" Van asks.

"Now I'm getting my rem. When I wake up, with divine help, I hope to know how to handle our departure." I look around at the muted images of the crowd at the National Mall. "All these different sapiens, and they all managed to agree…"

"In that moment, at that place," TJ adds. "It's not your job to make everyone happy."

I look at him and raise one eyebrow.

"Well, okay, maybe that *is* sort of your job as GB, but not tomorrow, and not next week."

"And we'll be here to help you," Mercy adds. "Even when you're scary angry and make people scatter—"

"And it looks like that vein in yer forehead is gonna explode," Van adds, pointing a finger at my temple.

I drop my head into my hands. I wondered how long it would

take for them to start teasing me. I'm so embarrassed. "Was it that bad?"

They're silent.

My brother holds up his hand. "I didn't feel anything."

"Me either." Van shrugs. "Well now, what were you saying about that rem?" He stands and hauls me up as the others stand and make their way out of the box.

"Computer, end simulation. One more thing…" I pull the interlink from behind my ear and place it in the tray with the others. "Our pins." I rub a finger over the neutral insignia that's become an ordinary part of my routine these last months. "We're going to Chileru with different viewpoints, each of us. But there, I think we need to be a team, even more united than before."

"You think we should remove our pins?" Mercy asks.

"I dunno." Van looks at the pilgrim insignia TJ wears on his shirt. "Isn't it important for them to see that we can disagree and still cooperate?"

"No, I think she's right." Mercy nods as she removes her pin. "It's a distraction. Let them get to know us first before they're confronted with our civil divisions."

TJ holds up his pin, already removed. "Will you hold them for us, sis?"

I open my palm to reveal my pin, inviting them to add theirs.

Van is the last to comply. He looks me in the eye as he drops his Terran pin into my palm. "I hope ye're right about this, Eddie. And about everythin' else, too." He turns to follow the others out of the lab.

"Van?" I catch his sleeve as I shut off the lights. "Was it really that bad?"

"Huh?"

"My…*outburst*, in the workshop. I'm so sorry if it hurt anyone."

"Oh…well, let's just say that everyone has a better appreciation for the strength of yer…*gifts*."

"Ugh, no. I'm a monster. They must despise me."

"No ye're not and no they don't. Now, don't worry. I'm sure it's nothin' a good sleep and a bit of space can't mend."

I sigh. "Thanks, Van."

"Don't mention it, princess."

He holds my elbow as we follow the others down the hall toward our quarters. I remember then how disappointed he looked staring at me from the doorframe, preparing to help all those people struggling with my mind control. It couldn't have been easy to cover for me then. "You're always helping everyone, and I made it harder. Do you forgive me?"

"Oh, aye. Forgiveness is easy when I know how to even the score."

I stop and he drops my arm. "Even the score?"

He smiles and shouts at Mercy. "Hey, Cricket, Eddie wants to know how ye're doin' on that presentation on the history of aeroponic farmin'?"

"I what?"

"Oh!" Mercy spins a circle and bounces on her toes. "I'm almost done! By the time you finish your rem, I should have about 10,000 words, plus the cross-reference and statistical tables. Don't worry! I'll be ready to brief you over breakfast. I'm on it." Mercy salutes me, and then turns back around and skips the rest of the way to her room.

I turn to Van. "You're diabolical, you know that?"

He smiles and shoves his hands in his pockets, leaning back on his heels in his signature shrug. "I dunno what ye mean. Good night now, princess. See ye at the launch."

Rill O'Brien

In the past…
February 02, 2699, two years ago
Subterranean Severe Weather Research Station 21A, North America

"Tis well and truly banjaxed!" Rill pounded a fist on the magRail control panel.

Vengi shifted at his side. "Can we abort the test?"

"I already tried that, didn't work." Rill snapped his comm rings. "Robb, we got a problem. We need ye in the silo ASAP."

"Roger that," Robb answered. "ETA four minutes."

Rill and Vengi stood alongside the silo wall, gazing nine meters above them at the robot struggling to dislodge its pincer from the active magRail track. The long catapult arm buzzed and strained against the obstruction. All around the silo, the other magRail arms yanked against the weight of the ballast hanging in the carriage at the center of the silo. They were testing the catapult with a partial load—a giant bag of sand—to see if they could launch it through the roof.

"We shoulda waited for Po." Rill smacked his toolbelt.

Vengi mirrored his gesture, setting the tools in his own belt jangling. "Yep."

With an ear-piercing screech, the magRail arm inched upward. The robot doubled its efforts to pull free. "Warning. Malfunction. Assistance required," it said.

"I have an idea!" Vengi dashed over to the silo wall and scampered up the recessed ladder before Rill could grab him and hold him back.

"Now wait, lad! No!"

"I can do it!" Vengi shouted back.

Rill watched as he approached the area opposite the robot. "Yer mam'll have my hide if ye get hurt, lad. Ye come on down and let Robb handle it."

"Robb's not here and Rosy needs my help."

Vengi shifted his grip on the ladder so that he could reach for a handhold near the magRail track with his left hand. Rill held his breath as Vengi missed the handhold and swung out from the ladder before regaining his grip.

"Stop now, lad. 'Tis too dangerous."

"I'm fine." Vengi pulled a small crowbar from his toolbelt, held it in his left hand and reached again, this time grabbing the handhold easily. "Don't worry, Rosy. I'll get your hand free."

"It's not a hand—it's a robotic pincer. Rosy's a robot, ye silly twit. It don't need savin'. Now come on down with ye."

Rill could see what the boy had in mind. He'd positioned himself a foot above the jammed robot and intended to pry its pincer free. What Vengi couldn't know was how fast that catapult arm was going to move once it was free.

"Ye won't be able to move outta the way in time, youngster.

Stop that now and come on down here. I mean it!"

"Just cuz I'm young doesn't mean I don't know things."

"Aww, that's not the point I was tryin' to make—"

"Agh!" Vengi screamed and let go of the handhold.

This time as he swung back toward the ladder, Rill noticed that the lower part of the catapult arm had snagged Vengi's shirttail and was slowly winding it in toward the laboring gear.

"No!" Rill shouted.

"Help! It's got my shirt!" Vengi tugged at the fabric. A loud tearing sound joined the noise of straining gears.

Rill didn't know what to do. He started toward the ladder just as a rain of sand fell on his head. Coughing and covering his head, he dove back along the wall. The giant bag of sand had started to leak. The whole thing could come down on his head at any moment if he didn't stay clear.

"Robb, where are ye, man?" Rill shouted into his comm. "Vengi's in trouble. Hurry!"

"Vengi? I'm almost there," Robb answered.

"Just hold on, lad!"

A metallic pop rang through the hollow space above him. Rill watched in horror as the catapult arm gained a few more inches, dragging Vengi's belly closer to the articulated track.

"Bloody hell! Rosy, Vengi's in danger. Stop that arm from movin'!"

Far above him, the robot's head swiveled down toward Rill. Lights flashed on its control panel and lightning-fast, it jammed its other pincer into the track above the arm.

Rill held his breath. "Stop struggling, just hold on!"

Vengi's body was stretched awkwardly now with two feet and his right hand on the ladder and his torso elongated toward the magRail. His back arched while his belly curved toward the track. "Help, Rill! I'm falling."

With another loud groan, the magRail jerked upward.

"Agh!" Vengi lost his left handhold as his shirt pulled further into the mechanism.

"Rosy, do somethin'!"

"Evaluating." The robot's lights flashed briefly, and then, in time with the next mighty screech of the catapult arm, it smashed its head into the gap above the jam, temporarily stalling the mechanism's perilous progress.

"Aye, good thinking, robot!"

"I'm here!" Robb shouted.

Rill watched Robb race past him. Robb didn't pause before scrambling up the ladder after Vengi, moving as fast as his bad knee would allow.

"Hurry!" Rill shouted.

"I'm falling!" With a horrendous rip, the gear consumed Vengi's shirt, stripping it right off him.

"Agh!" The sudden loss of support wrenched Vengi's right hand off the ladder and he fell.

"No!" Robb shouted and jumped, already six meters from the ground.

Rill watched in horror as his friend collided with the falling boy. They landed in a heap. Robb's left leg broke with a gut-wrenching crack; his skull smacked the concrete and he went completely still. Vengi landed on top of him, his right arm snapping against the hard floor.

Rill raced over to them. At the same time, the catapult broke free of Rosy's obstructions and the carriage rocketed up the silo. Rosy clattered to the ground a meter away.

"Computer!" Rill shouted. "Sound the emergency alarm. Get everyone here, now. Medical emergency."

Lights flashed, a siren wailed.

A loud whoosh sounded overhead. Rill looked up the silo in time to see the bag of sand flung out the aperture into the storm. Their catapult worked, but he had no time to celebrate.

"Are ye alright, lad?" Rill took a second to run his hands over Vengi's head and shoulders as the boy slid off Robb and sat up.

Vengi clutched his arm to his chest. "Yeah, but I think I broke my arm. Again."

Rill nodded and quickly checked the pulse at Robb's neck. The man was unconscious. "Robb!" He found a strong pulse and moved down Robb's body, checking for obvious injuries as he went. By the time he got to Robb's leg, a red stain of blood spread along Robb's pantleg where his shin twisted at an odd angle.

"I think he broke his leg," Vengi murmured.

"Aye." Rill carefully examined a tear in the fabric and saw bone glinting in the pool of blood beneath. "An open fracture. Yer mam's goin' to have her work cut out for her. I just hope he didn't crack his skull, the damned hero of a man."

Robb's eyes fluttered open. He turned his head to look at Vengi. "Safe?"

Rill scurried back up to his friend's head. "Oh, aye, the eejit's safe. Don't move now, ye had a bad fall. Yer leg's broken, don't try movin' it! And ye hit yer head mighty hard when ye landed. Helps comin'."

"Head's hard, you always tell me—" Robb winced and held his breath.

"Aye, that it is."

"Hey," Robb stared calmly up the silo, clearly in shock. "It worked."

Rill and Vengi followed his gaze. High above, the sky swirled stormy brown. The loose arms of the catapult dangled with the carriage netting whipping in the wind between them.

Rill nodded. "Aye, but at what cost we've yet to see."

"Will be worth it to get out of here." Robb swung his head toward Vengi before looking back at Rill. "Gotta get this boy out of here, old man. Gotta—" He broke off as a wave of pain hit him.

"Aye, we will. Just hang on now, don't try to talk."

Rill patted Robb's shoulder and looked over at the brilliant young praenex he loved like his own child. They were so different, he and Vengi—they weren't even the same subspecies—but they had one thing in common: they were both boys born in a godforsaken prison. He'd be damned if he let them both die there too. "We'll get ye outta here, lad. I swear it."

Vengi hung his head. When he looked back at Rill, his eyes were filled with tears. "At what cost, Rill?"

Rill opened his mouth to answer and found he didn't like the answer. He let the question ping around in his brain for a minute as they waited for help. He thought of all the people from his past who'd persevered for the sole purpose of trying to get *him* out of the station. In the end he decided his instinctive response was correct. No other boy was going to live his whole life down here like Rill had—without seeing the sun, without swimming in the ocean, without finding someone to love.

"At any cost, lad," he finally answered. "At any cost."

20
Eddie

Current year: 2701
Tuesday, 3:00 PM
Subterranean Severe Weather Research Station 21A, North America

When I wake from my rem in this strange underground station, I'm momentarily surprised to be alone. In all of my travels I've shared a room with Mercy, until recently. Even when our rems are on different cycles, I'm used to waking to see her books and tidy piles of clothing and papers in our room. But now she's married, and I'm alone away from home too.

I slide my feet onto the cool cement floor and tiptoe as fast as I can to the small rug in front of the bathroom sink. I'm not used to being cold, and the chill of this underground place has begun to seep into my bones like a quiet thief, stealing away my warmth and leaving me with a perpetual shiver. It's exhausting, and I'm starting to feel the strain on my temper.

My reflection in the mirror doesn't help. I had a long martial arts workout yesterday and went straight from the shower to bed. Wet hair didn't seem like a problem then, but now it's a wild white disaster. Towering cowlicks line each side of my part, making my albino face appear narrower. My lilac eyes are startling in the expanse of white. I'm used to looking icy, but this is something more—a skin tone closer to blue than translucent.

I've been arguing with pretty much everyone for the last few days, since I learned that Rill, Po, and Robb plan to stay behind. Vengi insisted it's divine will. Rill insisted they've reconciled themselves with staying, that the only thing they care about is getting Vengi out of here so he can experience a normal life.

And Cai…Cai kept pressing *their* freedom to choose and *our* need to be going. I'm not sure which was more important to him, but he matched my every argument with an arrogance that suggests he's been deferred to most of his life. He wouldn't let me succeed in even this little flex of my leadership muscle—my need to save these people—and the tension has been nearly unbearable.

For my part, I'm done arguing. I had little success in changing their minds. A rather rude French expression kept running through my mind. *Pisser dans un violon.* Pissing into the wind. I was wasting my efforts.

I'm past it, and I should be relieved, but the frustration and the sadness remain. By the time I'm finished dressing and fighting with my hair, I'm anxious and angry and starving. The edge of a migraine has me slightly off balance and I yearn for strong tea. With a sigh, I slip on my boots and listen to voices outside in the corridor as they pass my room. Van, TJ, and the two Couvie men, Po and Robb, move down the hallway, their voices loud and eager, but not angry. A soft knock sounds.

"Come in."

Vengi pokes his head in the door as I stand and straighten my skirts.

"Divine grace."

"Peace with you," I answer. The light coming in from the hall is too bright and I look away, shading my eyes, as Vengi steps inside.

"My *maman* thought you might want breakfast before it's put away? And Ambassador Varela is asking for you."

My annoyance that Cai is sending for me now overpowers my joy at the thought of food. "Fine." Stealing myself against a wave of nausea, I step past him, pull the door open and head toward the kitchen.

Vengi trots alongside, easily matching my long angry strides. "Are you all packed?"

"Yes."

His silence makes me realize I'm snapping at him, and it's not his fault I'm in this mood.

"And you? Are you ready to go?"

"Oh, yeah. I've been ready a while now."

"You're excited then, about leaving?"

We turn a corner and the comforting scent of toast and eggs warms me a little.

"Oh, not about *leaving* really. I'm excited to go to Terra Faire, though. I've got a lot to do."

"You do? I'm confused…you have a lot to do in Terra Faire?"

"*Oui.*"

He's such a curious praenex, this brother of May's. "Well, what is it?"

"I don't know yet." He opens the door to the cafeteria and steps back so I can enter. "But I know it's going to be important."

I look into his lavender eyes and see his sincerity. For a moment, I forget my own anger and smile back at him, but then I look around and see that everyone is waiting for us—for me, and the irritation returns. I haven't seen most of them since my tantrum in the shop, so there's some embarrassment mixed in too.

"Good day." Lucy pushes out the chair next to hers and hands me a clean plate. "Everything's arranged on the counter, just help yourself."

I give the dogs a cursory greeting, scratching behind Piper's ears while Cousteau rubs against my ankles. Dusting off my hands, I take the plate and nod to the others as I pass to the counter. My stomach growls at the sight of food. I avoid looking at Cai, but I can feel him tracking my movements as I fill my plate. If he tried to penetrate my mind now, I wonder if I'd notice it around the headache? Would it be worse?

When I sit at the table, Piper crawls underneath to lay on my feet. Even through the fabric of my boots, the warmth of her body seeps into my toes. I take my first bite and savor the food. I exhale deeply, propping my head on my hand as I shade my eyes from the overhead fluorescents. My elbow is cold on the table as I slowly chew. Cousteau whines behind me, and it's then that I notice the tension I had so carefully ignored. Everyone has stopped talking. They're clearly waiting for me to start.

I'm working up the strength to apologize for my recent outburst when Cai clears his throat.

"The group has come to an agreement."

I lift my gaze and feel a stab of hope. Maybe they figured out a way for Rill to come with us. But when I look around only TJ meets my eyes. I squint against the glare of the overhead lights—they're too much. I lean back into my hand as I take another bite.

Cai clears his throat again and it's like sandpaper on my brain. He doesn't know that I've reconciled to the fact that we have to leave people behind, but I already feel like he's rubbing it in—that he was right and I was wrong. The constant thread of anger I so carefully suppress jumps to life. I let my fork drop noisily to my plate.

"Are you ill, Ambassador?" I force myself to ignore the lights and look directly at him.

A small crease of confusion appears on his forehead, making his gem look like an exclamation point. "What?"

"Your throat. You're constantly clearing it. Are you ill? Do you need a lozenge perhaps?"

"Eddie…" Mercy's voice has a pleading quality that reminds me I'm not alone with this man who's pushed me to the knife's edge of my temper.

I sit up straighter and face him. "Excuse me. What has the group agreed to then?" I think I can guess, but he doesn't need to know that.

"When we leave, we'll take the research data and their briefing logs, and arrange with the powers that be to send another team to rendezvous here as soon as can be arranged. It's the best we can do."

"I see." I turn to Rill. His expression is firm, but not angry. "And you understand, sir, that it may be impossible to reach here again? That you may be trapped here until…" I don't know how to finish. My temper, as so often happens, has pushed me into a corner.

"Until I die?" Rill chuckles. "Lass, I appreciate yer concern, I truly do, but I've spent my entire life here. 'Tis my home. Like I've already told ye, if it's God's will that I should leave it in the hands of others, well then so be it, but I won't leave it untended."

I turn to look at Po and Robb where they sit flanking the old man.

"We're not leaving Old Rill." Po nods to his brother and lifts his hand to the back of Rill's chair. "We'll be here to train a new group if they decide to keep this place running. If not, well, we'll see it through, either way."

They're so brave, so proud. I know I have to honor that, but it's still so hard. Defeat drains through me like sand through a sieve. It exfoliates my hope, sloughs it away and replaces it with dread. We're leaving these men behind, but we're also putting ourselves in terrible risk. Leaving them here could be saving them—it's possible that none of us will reach Terra Faire.

The migraine sinks its teeth one bite deeper and I wonder if this is what it would be like to be GB. Did Gran Bozan Li face this kind of defeat, this kind of risk? What would she have done in my place? What would a leader do? Everyone's waiting for an answer.

I push back my chair and stand, sending the dogs into a fit of activity. I'm humiliated to find that I need to grip Lucy's chairback to steady myself against a wave of vertigo before summoning the strength to face Rill. "In that case, allow me to honor your bravery and thank you again for the shelter you've given us…for the family you kept safe for us." I smile weakly at Lucy. "If you'll excuse me."

I'm not running, I'm really not. My pace as I leave this room is my normal fast stride—the dogs keep up just fine. It would be ridiculous to run. It's also ridiculous to feel like I'm leaving those men behind, like I'm risking all of our lives. Ridiculous. They're adults, much older than *I* am actually, and my friends are willing to take the risk of an untried aircraft, a theoretical escape.

I've got to keep this in perspective. I'm not their Gran Bozan. They're not my lost flock.

I have to find a way to push down this panic. Panic about leaving them. Panic about killing all of my friends. I've work to do. We leave in only a few hours, and I need to shed this fear along with this headache. As I reach my room, I shoo away the dogs and shut the door hastily behind me. My hands are trembling. My legs, too.

I brace my hands on my knees and fight a wave of nausea.

"Don't throw up. Don't throw up."

I run to the bathroom and throw up.

When my stomach is empty, I brush my teeth and wash my face with a cold rag, leaving it pressed to the back of my neck for a minute. The cement floor is ice under my feet and somehow, I'm freezing and burning up all at the same time.

I toss the rag into the sink, disgusted with my own weakness, and go back into the bedroom. My satchel sits open on the other bed. I cross the room quickly and pull out the narrow black box that Sibling Rumesa gave me before I left. I've had so little time for music here. As I hold the case across my palms, I try to breathe.

In and out.

Breathe.

The piccolo is like a soft kiss against my lip as I begin to play. The song chooses me, as it often does, and I blow all my frustration and energy and worry into the shrill, sometimes fierce, quick notes. And as the music changes, the ballad winds its way into forgiveness. The strength of my fingers replaces the shakiness, the sureness of my soul replaces the uncertainty of having lost an argument, and I know the peace of letting go. All of it replaces the dull ache of my migraine. The last note hangs in the air like birdsong when a knock sounds at my door.

Stab, stab, stab! The staccato rap hits my temple with surprising precision.

"Come!" I shout before they can knock again and make it worse.

I squint into the harsh light as the door swings in. Cai stands in the opening holding a tray, his form silhouetted to a fuzzy gray shadow in the bright light. I wave him in and hurry across to hastily push the door closed behind him.

"I thought you might like to finish your breakfast. Why is it so dark in here?" He limps a few steps and sets the tray on the nearby desk.

It's not just my plate, but a longed-for cup of dark, steaming tea. My stomach growls noisily in the silence. I press a hand against it, and another to my eyes as I summon my calm. "Thank you." The air is thick with tension. I don't know what to say to him. "Your knee…it's better?"

He's quiet for a minute, cautious. Then he bends and rubs his knee. "Getting there. No more cane. Thank you for asking." A few seconds pass, and then he takes a small step toward me. "I want to talk to you before we leave—it's a long flight and I'd rather we reach some kind of peace between us before…"

He stops and tilts his head to one side. The crease reappears on his forehead and he raises a hand as if to touch me. "What's wrong?"

I sidestep before he can reach me, slide into the chair at the desk, and begin eating. "Nothing. Just hungry."

He's quiet again, then moves to lean against the wall next to the desk. I don't like the way he's watching me, but at least I can focus on my plate rather than look at him.

"Alright, well, as I was saying, I want to talk about the situation."

"You mean that you want to try *again* to convince me that it's fine. That my repeated failure at every mission is not a big deal. That it's *success* to leave those men behind." My tone is sharper than I mean it to be, so I take another bite to avoid saying more.

"It's the Creator's will."

I drop my fork again and lean into my hand, pressing hard on my eyes to keep them from exploding. "Well, maybe in this case, the Creator is…"

"What?"

"Nothing."

"Come on…it's just you and me here, and the Creator already knows what you were going to say. What is it?"

I blow out a long unsteady breath. I'm pretty sure a GB should not have these thoughts, these doubts. I look up at Cai and see that he sincerely wants to know. "Maybe in this case the Creator's wrong." I wait for a breath, but nothing dire happens. I'm not struck down for questioning the Almighty.

Cai exhales. "I know how you feel."

I look away. "You do?"

"Of course. I don't have a perfect record. Other people's choices have derailed more than one of my missions in the last few years, but that's how it goes. Free will is one of God's greatest gifts, yet sometimes, because of it, we find ourselves not completely aligned with what others do, with what we know the Divine wants, how we should behave. Gran Bozan Li knew this."

"How do you know that?"

He waits a few heartbeats before answering me, and I can feel the slight pressure of his mind gently probing at the edge of mine. "I was with her in her last moments of life. She shared with me, one leader to another. I understand what you're up against, perhaps better than you do."

This cuts. I grimace against the wave of jealousy. As my barely suppressed thread of anger surfaces, a new spike of pain hits my temple. I gasp and reach for my tea. It's cooled enough that I can take a deep drink. It's so delicious that I'm distracted and I let my mental shield slide just enough that some of my pain leaks out.

"Good God!" Cai straightens. "You're in pain! Physical pain!"

Before I can stop him, his hands have cradled my head from behind in a warm, firm grip. His fingers press lightly on my temples, cheeks and jaw.

"It's just a headache." I struggle awkwardly against his grip and the alarming sensations his touch creates.

"It's unnecessary, is what it is. Why didn't you tell me?"

"It's nothing."

"Did you hit your head? Are you injured?"

"What? No! It's just a migraine. If you'd leave me alone—"

"Shhh…"

At first, it's just the tactile strength of his warm hands wrapped around my head. His thumbs trace up and down the back of my skull causing ripples of sensation up my spine and down to my toes. Slowly, the pain folds back and I can feel him in my mind now, hunting out the hurts, soothing away the spurs of pain like a sculptor wielding a tool. My pain recedes and my emotions rise, melding with his until I can't tell where my feelings end and his begin. It's euphoric. I rise from my chair, like I'm pulled by strings, and turn into him.

His grip on my head loosens, allowing me to swivel around.

I want the warmth. I want more of that smooth, mellow pleasure. When I look up, his eyes are still closed in concentration—his breathing even, but loud from exertion. My body hovers as the blissful feeling of relief—and something more— courses through my body to settle in my core. I lean in and when my front presses lightly against his, his eyes shoot open.

Their violet depths swirl in tune with my emotions and I rise on my toes to press my lips gently to his.

I count one breath.

His lips are warm and soft.

Two breaths.

The warmth of his breath stirs against my skin.

Three breaths.

Cai is motionless—he's not returning my kiss. I pull back and realize that my body is leaning into his. His heat thrums through me, trembling against my skin. It's a pleasure I never imagined, not at all like hugging a friend. I could purr.

And then, just as quickly, the warmth is gone.

Cai steps back, not slowly with a parting caress of lips and gentle hands, but abruptly and entirely. Cool air buffets the sudden space between us—that cold and quiet thief again. For the briefest moment, we stare at each other, the only sound is the crashing huff of our breaths.

Then Cai clears his throat and limps to the door. He speaks over his shoulder without looking back at me. "I'm glad we…talked. I'll see you at the hangar."

I fall into my chair. As I lift the tea to my lips, they tingle in little pricks of sensation as my blood pressure begins to even out.

I kissed him…. What now?

I kissed him…and he didn't kiss me back.

Embarrassment stings my cheeks as I take another sip of tea. The drink slides easily down my throat, and for the first time I notice that my migraine is gone.

I set down my cup with a clack and take stock. Nausea…none. Dizziness…I stand and move to the opposite wall…gone. I flick on the overhead light…not a bit of sensitivity.

"Huh." I relax my shoulders and let out the first deep, pain-free sigh I've had all day.

Cai took my pain away.

As the realization settles into relief, a niggling new question comes to mind. Why? Is this yet another assertion of control, a trade for something he wants? Is it kindness, goodness? A new debt?

Or could it be something else entirely?

21
Cai

Current year: 2701
Tuesday, 11:00 PM
Subterranean Severe Weather Research Station 21A, North America

As I approach the central hub of the ship, TJ and May are already at the power converter, heads bent together in deep discussion. I'm confused for a moment when I listen to their voices and it takes me a second to figure out why. They're speaking Portuguese…fluently. It's surreal to hear voices that conjure images of home here in this cold gray place, a place so devoid of life.

"*Hallo?*"

"*Bom dia,*" they both reply.

"*Seu Português é excelente.*"

May looks at TJ before responding. "*Obrigado.* It's a hobby of ours, languages."

"An interesting hobby in a world with so few."

She smiles and her mental shields slam shut. "True, but sometimes it's handy to know something others don't. For example, we can share a private word within a crowd of people."

"Or understand the private words of others who don't know you speak their language," I counter.

TJ shifts. "We like to be prepared—"

"In any case," May interrupts him, "it's a lovely language, and knowing it has been helpful in some of the diagnostics on this power converter. Not everything was in English."

"Ah, yes, I was just coming to check. I've finished my other preparations."

"You mean your conversation with my sister?" TJ asks.

I raise an eyebrow and before I can respond, his mind pushes on mine, not at all gentle or hesitant. I block him easily.

"TJ." May tugs his sleeve.

TJ takes a step toward me. "You know I was grateful last week that you gave her the space to decide on this mission on her own, and that hasn't changed. I get it. I know you could be more…*persuasive* if you wanted to, and I when I saw her a little while ago, I got the impression that maybe something else had happened during your *preparations*."

I stare into his eyes for a minute and appreciate his fierce protectiveness. I want to protect her, too. "She had a headache…a migraine. I healed it."

"And what did that entail?"

I blow out a breath. "You've seen my healing powers before. My hands and my mind together were able to relieve her pain. Sometimes that kind of connection…well, it can be difficult for the patient to separate their relief from the gratitude they feel toward the healer—"

"Is that what happened? She showed you her gratitude?"

May wraps a hand around his bicep.

How can I explain? "I was still in my healing meditation, not really aware, when she…"

TJ strains against May's hand holding him back. "You kissed her."

"I didn't! But…she *did* kiss *me*. It was innocent, automatic—"

"So now you're saying she can't control herself? She's what…falling in love with you, but it's just gratitude? Do you even know her?" He takes another step toward me. "My sister doesn't just kiss anyone. She's—"

"TJ!" May steps between us. "I think Po could use some help with the dogs. Can you take care of it?"

I watch as they exchange meaningful looks. Finally, TJ's shoulders slump. "Yeah, right. This conversation is *not* over," he says to me.

May and I watch him go.

"Thank you."

She chuckles. "Oh, you thought I was getting you out of it?" She laughs again and shakes her head. "I've spent my whole life as an orphan. In the last week I've gained a sister *and* a brother. Can you imagine that there's anything I won't do for either of them?"

I look into her serious eyes. "I'm not a danger to her."

"Because you love her too?"

"Love? I…"

May cocks her head to the side and I get the odd impression that she can read my heart the way that I read minds.

"Do you have any idea what it must be like for her, given who she is, given the course of her life, to kiss a man who doesn't return her feelings?"

"It's not my intention to embarrass her. It wouldn't be right…." I stop myself before I reveal any more. We launch in minutes. Now is not the time to tell them about…oh, God, Giza! Giza could be dying right now. I clench my teeth to keep from groaning.

May's eyes narrow. "Whatever it is you're hiding from her, from us, you need to think long and hard about the tipping point."

"The tipping point?"

"The point where the damage caused by keeping a secret outweighs the benefit. The tipping point. These are good people, but they know about deceit and betrayal. Firsthand. They're forgiving, sure, but there's a big difference between forgiving an outsider and welcoming him in. You have to decide where you want to be."

"I want to be, and I am, in the heart of this mission. It's everything to me."

"Well, if that's true, then you're lucky to be in the pod with my *maman,* because if there's one thing being in love is going to teach you, it's that the mission isn't everything. There's a whole lot more you're going to have to carve out room for."

With that, she strides away and leaves me staring at the power converter. I'd like to think she's wrong, but somewhere deep in my heart I know she's right. I didn't set out to do more than save my people, conduct this mission. But now that I know Eddie, I don't see how I can separate the woman from the goal. If her blood can save an entire society, what can her love do?

Vengeance Forge

Current year: 2701
Tuesday, 11:30 PM
Subterranean Severe Weather Research Station 21A, North America

Vengi can't stop reaching out to his friends; he squeezes their shoulders, clasps their hands and holds their forearms when they pull him close and kiss the top of his head.

Goodbyes, he decides, are terrible things.

His *maman's* laugh, thick with tears, rumbles through Po's room. They're assembled here, his family, his crew, to help settle the dogs in their new home and to say their farewells. His throat feels bruised from long minutes of holding back tears. His eyes can't stop scanning the room for details to file away about his friends, as if he truly never will see them again. The thought sends a new pang of misery through his heart.

"Here now, lad." Old Rill swings his arm behind Vengi and squeezes his shoulders. "Ye've gotta focus on the adventure, on all the new things yc'll ken, not on what we'll be doin' here."

"I know."

"Aye, I know ye do, so let's see a smile now, and give yer mam a bit of peace from worryin' 'bout ye."

"Okay." He reaches behind his back and unfastens the hook that holds his toolbelt in place. He holds it out to Old Rill. "Here. Will you hold on to this for me? I don't have any extra ounces in my personal allowance."

Old Rill fingers the worn fabric. "Of course. Let's see a brave lad now, right?"

"I'll expect it back, once you're rescued."

Old Rill takes a deep breath. Everyone is listening to them now. "Aye, ye'll get it back, not to worry."

Vengi nods and wipes his face with the hem of his shirt. "Don't forget that filter on the east side of the aquifer, the sensor's still out and—"

"Sure, we'll remember," Old Rill assures him.

Po rubs Vengi's shoulder. "I've got that, son. That and all the other little things you've been doing for us." He grins and leans back to get a better look at Vengi's face. "In fact, I want to thank you. We had no idea just how much you did for us without being asked. Robb's downright vexed by all the new chores on my list, as he knows it'll cut into my cooking time."

Robb humphs. "Ha! Your cooking's not all that, brother. Everybody knows it's Lucy that keeps us from starving to death." Robb lets go of Vengi's *maman's* hand and eases down into a chair, careful not to put too much weight on his bad leg.

Vengi sits on the chair's arms. "I'm so sorry, Robb." He gestures to his friend's injured leg. "I wish I'd listened to Rill. I wish I'd listened to all of you better, then maybe—"

"Eh, now." Robb waves off Vengi's words. "That's forgiven.

From the time you could pick up a spanner, we've all known you're not the type of praenex to be held back from exploring how things work and how to fix them."

Po sighs. "And that's what it's all about. We're depending on you, Vengeance. We're depending on you to go out there and make your mark, change the world, even if it's only by being part of it."

Vengi bites his lip as fresh tears run down his face. When Piper rests her head gently on his knee, he strokes her soft fur. "I'm glad you'll have the dogs. I mean, if they have to stay behind, I'm glad you'll have them."

"So are we, lad. So are we." Old Rill shuffles over to hug Vengi's *maman* one more time, just as a knock sounds at the door.

Po opens it, and Vengi isn't surprised to see his sister's face already red from crying.

TJ clears his throat next to her. "Divine grace with you all. We wanted to say one last goodbye to the dogs before—" TJ's words stop abruptly and Vengi watches his Adam's apple bob furiously on his neck.

"We understand." Vengi's *maman* moves toward the door. "Come on guys. Let's give them some privacy."

When the others file out of Po's room, Vengi hesitates.

His sister wipes her eyes and looks at him. "You want to stay?"

All he can do is nod.

"Okay." She squeezes his hand before sinking to the floor.

Vengi read about dogs and their place in human society, sure, but he'd never really believed that the bond between human and canine could be all that strong until now.

May and TJ sit cross-legged on the floor, each of the dogs

climbing into their laps in turn, as if they know they're saying goodbye. It's all Vengi can do to keep from sobbing out loud when TJ lifts Cousteau's paws to his shoulders and bends his head to rest on Cousteau's forehead—a gesture most praenex reserve for family and the closest of friends.

May repeats the gesture with Piper, Piper's bright pink tongue lapping out to kiss the tears from May's smiling face.

Vengi waits, relieved when they all break apart and he has the chance to give each dog a final rub before helping secure them in their crates.

TJ holds the door. The dogs whine. May curls into Vengi's hug as he bundles her out the door.

In the hall, he looks into TJ's face as he transfers his sister into her husband's arms. "I had no idea. I'm sorry. Maybe we should wait a few hours—"

"No." TJ shakes his head. "It won't get any easier, and we need to get going."

"If it's so painful to leave them, then why…" Vengi cringes at the awkwardness of his statement. "I'm sorry. That's a stupid thing to think."

His sister sniffs and turns to him. "No, it's okay. It's like everything worthwhile. You gain so much more than you risk. Our friendships with other people, with our animals, with the world around us…it's what ties us together, it's what binds us to the Almighty. The Creator made all of us. We honor all of that when we trust enough to love each other and the world. Don't be sorry—be happy that love runs this deep and spreads this wide."

Vengi rolls his shoulders. "Okay, I'll try."

She smiles. "It'll be fine."

TJ waves up the corridor. "Let's go. We've got a lot to do before launch, and there are other people who are going to need May's strength before we lift off.

Excitement replaces some of his sadness as Vengi hops aboard his hover bike for the last time. He follows his sister and her husband down the dusty white halls, wondering what the greater world will share with him and what he'll be able to give. He knows one thing for sure—he's going to really listen to his friends from now on, and he's going make the most of it.

22
Eddie

"It's basically a huge catapult." I tip my head back to look up the old silo. "Simple really, but I'm glad we had a chance to help with this, since we're the ones taking advantage of it."

Mercy stands next to me gazing at the arms attached to four junction points on the Berylhenge. The launch deck is a flurry of activity, unlike the dimmed and quiet corridors down which we came. The whole station has been on minimal power for several hours as the system stores up the reserves needed to launch us through the roof and into the storm.

"I agree that it's exciting, but I'm a little scared too." Mercy worries a fingernail in her teeth, then continues. "Catapults are ancient, you know. The Greek inventor, Dionysius, created the first form around 400 B.C. Since then, they've evolved and were used extensively by navies, including the UCAs, which used them to launch planes off flight decks at sea, very much like this application. Very safe. Proven and effective. In 2105—"

"Cricket." I take her hand to slow her down. When she finally turns to me, her eyes are rounded, brows pinched in fear. "It really *is* going to be okay. Isn't that right, Vengi?"

"What?" Vengi stops short as he hears me say his name. He's been running back and forth, giving instructions and moving loads.

"I said it's perfectly safe." I gesture toward the aircraft.

"Oh, sure." He turns and takes a short look at the ship before shrugging his shoulders. "In theory. Say, you two better check in with Old Rill. We're T-minus 15."

I look at Mercy. She looks at me. We both swallow hard. "Come on."

I drag her over to where Rill is standing with several others from our group. He has an old-fashioned computer tablet in one hand and seems to be checking things off a list. We join the group and share a general greeting. I wish I had the courage to look Cai in the eye, but after that kiss—or half-kiss—it's much easier to keep my gaze anywhere else.

"Okay then. All passengers accounted for." Rill taps his tablet. "Let's go over the plan one more time with the rest of ye…."

I only half listen as Rill runs through the flight plan—5,600 kilometers, duration ranging eight to eleven hours depending on storm impact, course corrections, emergency procedures…. Over the past days I've run through the training, the simulations and studied the controls like the rest of them. I hope I won't have to use any of that training—I'm no pilot—but if we get into trouble, at least I can help.

Vengi nudges my elbow and lifts his eyebrows up and down. "Ready to fly, roomie?" His enthusiasm is contagious, if a little immature.

I smile. "Ready as I'll ever be." Vengi and I'll be flying in pod 1, with Cai and Lucy taking pod 4. It made the most sense for Vengi and Lucy to split up since they're both experts on the aircraft. I'm grateful for the chance to spend time away from Cai before we get to Terra Faire. Every day I'm more certain he's keeping something important from us, but even with May's skill amplifying mine, I can't get a handle on what.

The others return and gather to us. A hush falls over the group.

Rill turns to me. "Bozan, will ye lead us in prayer?"

I nod and kneel, resting back on my heels. I wait for the others to kneel and then reach out my hands. I watch as we make the connections, one by one around this circle of 11 souls, and when May connects the circle by joining hands with TJ on one side and her mother on the other, the now familiar surge of power ripples through the circle. Most take it in silence, some can't help but make a small gasp, but Cai is searching again for its source.

I reach out to him with my mind and immediately connect. The *click* of our joined thoughts comes faster now, more naturally, and more unnervingly. When his eyes meet mine, I send him the same thought that Mayor Dixie sent to me back in the Verge. *Let be.*

He's reluctant, and for a moment I wonder if we're right to keep him out of the circle of those who know about May's gift. There's still something that holds us back from trusting him like one of our own. I'm not the only one who wants to see Terra Faire before making up my mind about Spheran society and its ambassador. Perhaps he senses this too, because he nods and relaxes enough to show me that he's done as I asked.

The group quiets and a sense of calm concentration fills the air. I take a deep breath and reach for the right words.

"Blessed Creator; it is because of power, perception, and purpose that we pray to you today. We thank you for the power you provide us to live, to create, to share…to forgive and to love. We thank you for the perception you grant us to support one another, to do the hard things, to celebrate the good, and to keep our faith. We thank you for guiding our hands and filling our lives with purpose…to heal hurts, to build a future for our world. We ask for your blessing on this station, this crew, and this ship. Help us to feel your hand in ours as we embark upon this journey, and to hear your voice tell us the way. It is not our will, but yours be done, through your divine grace eternal. Amen."

A chorus of amens follows as we climb to our feet and make our goodbyes.

"*Allons-y! Allons-y!*" Vengi bounces with excitement, grabbing on to anyone who hovers too long, or fails to move toward the Tumbler.

I step over to Rill and shake his hand. "May your soul feel the glory, Rill Ban O'Brien."

"Divine grace with ye, lass." His eyes sparkle with unshed tears as he watches Vengi gathering our group.

"We left something for you in the holographic lab—something I hope will make it easier here."

"Oh, that's right kind of ye, but it's me who should be

thanking *ye*. That lad has great potential. I couldn't be happier to see him off to fulfill it…and ye, too. Whatever ye decide about yer title and all that, well…an ocean's an ocean whether ye're a captain or a fish. Go be what ye will, and divine blessing on ye."

I smile. "Thank you."

I touch hands with my friends before climbing aboard pod 1. Rill's eyes are on me all the way up the ladder. Onboard, I fasten my safety harness and fit my head into the restraint attached to the chair. Through the windshield, I watch the tearful goodbye between Lucy, Vengi, and the men who stay behind. I swallow past a lump in my throat as they separate, and seconds later Vengi drops into the seat beside me.

Grinning and bouncing with energy, he opens the communication channel between the pods and the command center. "We are ready to rock and roll! T-minus four minutes on my mark. Now!"

Down on the launch pad, Rill gives one last wave as the giant doors fold shut on the launch pad. What happens next is a series of checks and signals before the motors thrum to life.

"It's time to snug into your flight seats, ladies and gentlemen." Vengi's voice is filled with glee, like he's the host of the greatest entertainment on Scorch. He reaches over and points to the button on my harness's chest plate. "Look straight ahead, take a deep breath and hold it, and then press the button on your chest." I breathe like he says and he presses the button for me. The harness and headgear adjust to a tightness that's just shy of panic-inducing. "Breathe normally now. I promise, you'll appreciate the tight fit once we're tumbling through the air. This button is a toggle; when we reach calmer air, you can press it again to loosen it."

Vengi adjusts his own harness and with a quiet rumble, the ship begins to vibrate to life. I watch as the sling arms move slowly up the tracks in the silo's walls and feel the sudden weightlessness as the aircraft lifts free of its supports.

"Adjusting spheres for forward-facing velocity…hold on, folks." With Vengi's warning, I'm expecting it, but I'm still startled when the inner sphere tips us onto our backs. Now we're staring up the long barrel of the silo to a pinpoint of light that slowly widens as the launch doors open to the swirling brown night sky.

"Good God!" Mercy exclaims from pod 3.

"This is going to be great!" TJ adds.

"Enough chatter now." Lucy's voice is serious and commanding. "All teams report in."

"Pod 3, ready." Van starts, and one by one everyone signals in.

Vengi confirms. "Command, this is Berylhenge, ready for launch."

"Acknowledged, Tumbler. Ready for launch in ten, nine, eight…"

As the countdown continues, I pray for our safety. I pray for those we leave behind. I think about the machine to which we've strapped our bodies—to the structure we're now a part of. Within the walls of the silo, the restraining mechanisms will soon release the powerful magnets whose fall will catapult us into the sky. The storm swirls above us and I have the fleeting thought that maybe it's not too late to get out, to change my mind…

"…two, one, and liftoff."

My body slams back into my seat. The skin of my face pulls

tight as the force propels us upward. The world outside the pod is a blur of gray walls and piercing light. Voices squeal in joy, in fear, in fun, and in terror. Before I can take a breath, we're sailing through a sky filled with dust and wind and speed.

Vengi gives a hoot next to me. "Yeah! Command, this is the Tumbler. We are clear of the silo and ascending to 160 meters. Acceleration is on target and looks good."

"Roger, Tumbler. Radar contact. God speed to Terra Faire."

Cheering voices burst through the microphone before the tower disconnects.

This isn't so bad. We're flying fairly steady from what I can tell. A full moon illuminates the dust and clouds around us. I'm just getting used to the speed and odd sense of openness when the storm catches us. I shriek as the world begins to tumble. This is nothing like the simulations! I clench my teeth and grip my armrest.

"This is nothing like the simulations!" Cai shouts over the comm. A large animal carcass passes through the open space between us and the next sphere. The plane lurches just in time to avoid a collision.

"It's normal." Vengi somehow manages to act like the world isn't spinning ferociously outside our pod. "Relax and focus on the horizontal plane. Remember, you're always upright, only the ship is tumbling."

I close my eyes and breathe. Without my sight confusing me, it feels much like any bumpy airplane ride—like moderate turbulence.

Over the comm, it's clear that Mercy's arguing with Van.

"I'm going to be sick!"

"You should have taken the medicine like I did," Van tells her.

"I don't get motion sickness. But this is terrible."

"Now you know," Van replies.

"I'm going to throw up!"

"Don't! Just—"

The sound of vomiting makes me cringe.

"Oh, now. Well, I'm glad ye found the bag." Van's voice is softer now. "Try to relax, Cricket."

"Mercy!" I can help her if she'll listen to me.

"Yuck! Ugh. How can I relax? The ship is literally tumbling—" Her argument is cut off by a scream as the plane lurches upward and then slams to the right.

"Don't puke again!" Van's voice is more sympathetic now.

"Mercy!" I try again to reach her. "Mercy Adams!"

"What, for divine grace?"

The anger in her voice makes me smile—well, probably grimace actually, since the aircraft is moving violently again. "Close your eyes…all of you! Close your eyes and focus on my voice. You are on an airplane. You're safe. It's only turbulence. Take a deep breath. Can you feel the power of the aircraft? Can you hear the sound of the jet engines, the whine of the machine? You're safe."

I open my eyes and stare straight ahead at the horizon. It takes a moment for me to make it out in the moonlight, to ignore the distraction of the Tumbler constantly reorienting around me, but finally I have it in focus and my head and stomach settle. "Better?"

"Yes," Mercy answers.

"It's better," May agrees.

"In a moment you're going to open your eyes and look straight ahead. Remember, the ship will reorient with the storm, but the pod will always face forward and always stay upright. If you feel sick again, just close your eyes. Ready…and…open your eyes."

"Oh! So much better!" Mercy giggles and Van grunts in relief.

"This is terrific. So much better than the Agulha 3—" There's a smacking noise and TJ mumbles something before May comes on the line.

"Thank you, Eddie. The prayer was nice, but that trick was even better. Pod 2, signing off comm. Happy travels, everyone. Listen, flyboy—"

I grin, knowing that the rest of May's words probably set my brother in his place.

"Thank the Creator," Vengi says next to me.

"What?"

His cheeks redden and his smile is almost contrite. "I'm just so glad it worked." He waves a hand around the cabin. "Not just theory anymore."

I roll my eyes and am quickly reminded that that's probably not a good idea while tumbling through a storm in an experimental ship. "Me too."

"Next stop, Terra Faire." Cai's voice is calm. He's chatting with Lucy before they too shut off their comm.

"So, want to play a car game?" Vengi grins again and props his feet on the console. "This thing flies itself."

"In theory," it's my turn to say.

"Ha ha, but yeah, I get it. Still, we're out of the storm's reach so it should be smooth sailing now."

My jaw drops as I swing my head toward him. "God's grace! I can't believe you said that!"

"What?" His face is completely blank as he stares back at me.

"Don't you know anything about tempting fate?"

"Tempting fate?" His head cocks to the side, as if the gears will turn better that way. "You mean because I said 'smooth sailing'?"

"Uh, yeah."

"You don't really believe that do you? I mean, you're like a priestess or something right? Surely you know it's not fate, but nature, or our wills and the Creator's that bring about events, right?"

I narrow my eyes at him. "Here's what I know, Vengeance Forge: if something happens to us now, it's on your head." I slump back in my seat and wait for the other shoe to drop.

Rill O'Brien

"What is it?" Rill turned the silver sphere in one hand, examining the rigid steel exoskeleton. Sweets nearly fell out of his pocket trying to sniff it, so Rill held it closer so the mouse could get his fill.

"Only one way to find out." Po held up the tablet that the flight crew had left in the VRT. "Computer, play program Rescue alpha one," he read from the tablet.

An image of Vengi, TJ, and Eddie materialized in front of them. The image spread around the box and the men found themselves in a simulation of the holographic lab.

"Divine grace," the recording of Eddie said. "We wanted to say thank you for all you've done to make today's launch possible—"

"We don't actually know that they'll watch it *today*," TJ interrupted.

"Yes, we do!" Vengi insisted. "They'll be too curious to wait. '*We left you something in the holo lab*.' Please. They'll go straight to the lab before the aperture closes."

Rill looked at his friends; they all had similar smirks on their faces. "Lad knows us well."

"If you two don't mind," the recording of Eddie said, "I'd like to finish this recording before the Tumbler leaves without us. As I was saying, we couldn't have done this without your faith and dedication. We'll never forget it, but we don't want to leave *your* rescue to fate. If something were to happen to us—"

"She means if we die," Vengi said to TJ.

"Yes, I got that." TJ nodded.

"We're not going to die," Vengi sulked. "The design is perfect."

"Vengi?" Eddie waved to the screens behind them.

Vengi stepped back. "Oh yeah. The sphere we left you is a one-way, single-use communication device." He pulled up the schematics. "You'll find all the specs here, so that you can make more. And in this file…you'll find the design for the cannon—"

"It's a launch tube," TJ corrected him.

"I know, but cannon sounds so much better."

"It's scientifically inaccurate. A cannon requires detonation. The launch tube isn't a gun—"

"Guys!" Eddie shook her head and stepped forward. "You'll find everything you need to build this in the lab. We designed the sphere to reach the correct altitude above the storm and broadcast all the information our Scorch scientists need to devise a mission here. We've included some ideas for a ground rescue that Van and May drew up. You can refresh the local data as quickly as you can build a new sphere."

"With any luck," TJ continued, "by the time you're ready to

launch the first sphere, we'll have provided our teams back home with all the information they'll need about what we learned here…about the SS Worse and all of you."

Eddie nodded. "They'll be waiting to hear from you. So, good luck and divine grace with you, Rill, Poacher, and Robbery. We'll keep you in our prayers."

The recording ended, and Rill sat down heavily in Vengi's old chair. "Jesus, Mary and Joseph, when did they have time to do all this?"

Po shook his head. "If Eddie told them to do it, well…"

"Aye, she's convincing, that lass." Rill wrapped both hands over his cane and rested his chin on top. "They weren't here long, but I'm gonna miss 'em."

"It won't be the same without Lucy and Vengi," Robb agreed, "but I think we've had all the time we can spare to dwell on it. This place won't run itself, so we best get back to work."

"Besides, it looks like we're starting a new project. Right, Rill?" Po asked.

"Oh, that's for certain." He stood and stretched his back. "Don't know how long I can last here anymore with just you two eejits and a couple of dogs for company. The sooner we get started, the sooner we can hand this place over and I can get outta here and get me some of that 'life' ye all keep goin' on about."

Robb chuckled. "So much for *this is my place,*' huh?"

"Don't be a melter, lad. I only said that to help them along—wasn't any way we could have fit on that crazy excuse for an airplane. So if ye're done pondering who said what and why, let's get down to the lab so I can start on the bill of materials for the cannon."

"It's a cannon, then?" Po asked, holding the VRT door for Rill.

"Aye. It'll be no small miracle if they hear from us, so it's a cannon blast that'll make it happen. The lad always did have a way with namin' things."

23
Cai

Current year: 2701
Wednesday, 2:00 PM
Somewhere over the South American continent

I've spent nearly two months among these Scorch citizens now. I've been to New Juneau, the Legion's Enclave, the Tether Base, SciCorps's Hub and SATO Science Station—though as a prisoner only—and Vancouver Colony, the Verge. And then somewhere few of them have seen—the lost subterranean weather station. The only significant location I failed to see firsthand was Alberta Farms, but the briefing I received from General Elder was so complete, I could draw a map, or maybe plant a row of cabbages.

With all I've seen, and all I've experienced, I can say with some degree of certainty that Scorch is a very *sapiens* place. The praenex may not realize it, but many parts of their customs and culture are uniquely sapiens. Aside from the things that make the praenex different—their speed to maturity, their novus gifts, their diminutive size and high intelligence—they've adopted a sapiens culture so strongly influenced by their sapiens ancestors, I fear that Terra Faire is going to seem shockingly alien to them. I regret not being there with my colleagues, as the transports arrived almost two weeks ago. I'm sure they've had their share of challenges, and I wasn't there to help.

The external communications light begins to flash on the panel in front of me.

"Thank the Creator!" Lucy types in a command and nods to me.

I take a deep breath. "This is the Berylhenge, calling to any station within communication range. Do you read me?"

"Affirmative…*Berylhenge*. We're unfamiliar with your aircraft, please identify yourself."

"This is Ambassador Cairo Varela onboard a new 'Tumbler' class craft, the Berylhenge, clearance code Pi 314, do you copy?" I stare at Lucy during the short silence that follows. "They're checking my code."

"It's Terra Faire then?"

I nod.

"Roger, uh, *Ambassador*. This is Terra Faire Tower. We're happy to hear your voice, sir." In the background, we can hear cheering and exclamations. "We're notifying Secretary Ilorin now and I'm sure she'll be online in a few seconds."

"Thank you. Please send immediate communication to Scorch leaders in Terra Faire, Vancouver Colony, and the Enclave informing them that all of my crew is alive and well. We also recovered two Verge citizens, Jealousy Meadow Forge and her son, Vengeance Ramirez Forge. I'm sending the full report now." With a wave from me, Lucy sends the prerecorded log each of us made for this purpose. "Please inform those governments they can reach my fellow travelers on this channel when we terminate our comm.

Please send word directly to Sheriff Arson Forge that his sister and nephew are on route to him in Terra Faire."

"Yes, sir. As instructed in case you contacted us, I'm pleased to inform you that Citizen Giza Sall is awaiting your contact. Secretary Ilorin is ready for you now, sir."

Giza! My eyes pinch as I force down the wave of emotion that crashes through me when I hear that she's still alive. It takes all my will to hold back the questions and focus on the moment. "Please inform Secretary Ilorin that *Ambassador* Varela is ready and patch her through."

Lucy raises an eyebrow at me, and I know she caught my emphasis on *ambassador.*

The smiling image of my good friend and colleague, Ilorin Orlov, appears on my view screen. "Cai! Peace with you, *Ambassador.* I'm so glad you're not dead!" she laughs. "We heard Bozan LeRoux's response, but then the days lagged on."

"By divine grace, I live to serve another day, Ilorin. Apologies for the delay."

"Are you well? How are the others?"

"The others are fine. I had a leg injury, but it's nearly healed."

"What happened?"

"We strayed off course to follow an SOS and happened upon some old friends. It took time to arrange our departure. Apologies for worrying everyone."

Ilorin shakes her head and laughs. "What a relief. Speaking of which, allow me a moment to call off the search parties. They've been at it for days, and the missions are getting more and more dangerous." She speaks to someone off screen and I take a second to focus on Lucy. She seems anxious.

"Are you alright?"

She passes a hand over her mouth. "I think I'm in shock. I mean, I knew we'd reach them soon, but I guess I didn't really believe it would be so easy. I'm going to see my brother…today!" She chokes on a laugh.

"Ambassador?"

I look back at Ilorin. "Yes?"

"What happened to the Agulha 3?"

"She crashed, unrecoverable. The people we met invented this aircraft."

"Very good. Can you share your ETA please? Our citizens will want to greet you, as they've been very concerned."

"What about Giza? Any change?"

"I'm sorry, no. She's the same, but bravely persevering."

"Okay. Um, our current ETA is 4:45 PM, give or take 10 minutes—" There's a commotion on Ilorin's end and her attention is diverted.

"Oh," she says. "Yes, 30 seconds, please…Ambassador. Sheriff Arson has reached a communication hub and is demanding to speak with his sister. Do you have anything else to report at this time?"

"No, Ilorin. All the details are in my encrypted report. I'll see you soon."

"God speed, Ambassador."

"Peace with you, Ilorin."

She disconnects and the screen flickers.

"I'll reroute here," Lucy says, nervously toggling the comm to her own view screen. She leans in just as Arson's face appears.

"Lucy? My God, I can't believe it. When they told me…"

The painful joy in his voice causes a lump to rise in my throat.

"Arson!"

They laugh together and I watch the tears stream down both their faces. I blow out a breath and wipe away a few tears of my own. For what seems like an eternity, they just cry and stare at each other.

Lucy reaches down to touch the screen. "You got so old!"

Arson's laugh is strangled in a sob. He fights for control as he tries again to speak. "And you look exactly the same. Prettiest sister ever!"

"Always the charmer." I watch as she unconsciously covers the long scar on her face.

"Aro?" Arson asks.

Lucy shakes her head. "I'm sorry," she whispers hoarsely. "I can't…I…" She turns to me and squeezes my arm. Shaking her head, I know she can't speak the words. I pat her hand before toggling the view screen to a larger, virtual display over both of our seats.

"Sheriff Arson, greetings."

"Ambassador. My niece is safe?"

"She is. I've had an opportunity to talk at length with your sister here. She explained to us that her husband passed 11 years ago due to complications from their crash near the subterranean station where they took shelter this last decade."

Arson nods, his Adam's apple moving wildly as he fights for control. "And I have a nephew?"

I look at Lucy and she mouths *thank you* to me before clearing her throat. "You do! Vengeance…Vengi. I can't wait for you to meet him. He's…I just can't wait for you to meet."

I shrink the screen back to Lucy's side of the cockpit and get up out of my harness. I need a break, and they need some privacy. When I move to stretch along the cushioned bench at the back of the cockpit, I find nothing but a blank space and a neatly folded thermal sheet. I remember now that we stripped out the bench to reduce our mass. I shrug and lie down on the floor, pulling the thermal sheet all the way up over my head. It crinkles into place. I can still hear Lucy and Arson's voices, but the darkness brings a kind of solitude.

I have only a few short hours before this group of stubborn, perceptive, and curious leaders land in my home city.

Before my control of what they learn about my people is out of my hands.

Before many of the truths I've withheld become glaringly obvious.

Before they judge for themselves.

Before Eddie decides for *herself*.

Van was right when he said that when someone sends out an SOS, you don't run away, you run toward it. It's very close to the time they'll realize what they've been running toward, because I *am* the SOS sent by Terra Faire. I *am* the flare burning bright over Chileru. I am the SOS and I sent myself.

"Penny for your thoughts." Lucy smiles over at me, breaking me out of my daydreams. She's been quiet too, after talking to her brother. I wish I could have given them more privacy, for themselves, but also for me. The overflow of emotions—the tears, the stretches of gasping silence as each of them tried to control their feelings—was a test of my strongest mental shields, and they didn't hold completely. I'm happy for her, and for Vengi. Their reunion with the world will be a joyous event.

"Excuse me?"

"I said 'penny for your thoughts.' It's an old Earth saying. It means, what are you thinking about?"

"Oh, well…" I blow out a breath and thank God this Couvie woman is not a strong telepath. For that reason, I'm safe thinking freely around her, but also because she's mature compared to the rest. Wise, in her own way.

"You don't have to tell me if you don't want to. Besides, I can probably guess some of it."

This surprises me. "You can?"

She laughs, and points to the comm switch set to private mode. "No one can hear us right now, and I'm guessing even Bozan LeRoux can't read your thoughts with all the other distractions of this flight. I'm a good listener, whether you want my opinion or just want to vent. Something tells me that once we reach Terra Faire, you'll have less opportunity to gain advice from an older, shall we say 'seasoned' set of ears."

"That's surprisingly perceptive, and absolutely true." We sit in silence for a few moments as I deliberate what to say. "Soon we'll arrive in a world so very different from the settlements you know on Scorch, that it may seem alien to you and the others. The way our society evolved—its origins, its history, its sociology—is so unlike what occurred in other places. Also…let's just say I have some information that I've withheld that will quickly become known."

"You're worried they'll hold that against you."

"Wouldn't you? This group, this…team, is young, but basically trusting in nature. There's little they've withheld from me. Won't they resent it, that I kept my secrets?" "Why did you? Keep secrets, I mean?"

I close my eyes and reflect on my choices. "This group of Eddie's…they're easily distracted, unfocused, and undisciplined. They allow so many things to get in the way of their objectives…it threatens their goals. I guess I wanted them to stay focused on the most important thing with which we need their help—curing the Trade before my people become extinct. Everything else seems, I don't know, trivial."

"But it won't seem trivial to them when they learn more for themselves. They'll think you lied by omission."

"Yes. I see that now. I'm their opposite, I suppose. I've created a risk through intense focus on my goals, my own purpose."

"Well…" Lucy stretches her arms out in front of her and groans. "This is a long time to sit. Anyway, I don't think this is all on you, and I don't think you're the only one keeping secrets."

"What do you mean?"

She gives me a serious look. "Really? With all of your abilities, you haven't noticed the awkward silences, the covert looks?"

I shake my head, but then I wonder, *have* I noticed it? Have I noticed and simply chosen to ignore it so that I can keep *myself* focused on what's ahead, not what's right here? "I…maybe you're right."

"In any case, I'd spend less time worrying about what they might learn and more time considering what they need to hear from you. You still have time to share with them; we're a captive audience." She gestures to the pod. "On that note…" She flips the comm switch to open a channel to the other pods. "This is pod 4. If anyone wants to stretch, this is a good time to do so. I'll remind you of the training. Please identify the green band of light running along your ceiling. This band is also present along the wall of the latrine. As long as it's green, you're safe to move around. When it changes to yellow, you have about one minute to get back in your harness. If it turns orange, there's a good chance you'll need to snug in. Red will automatically snug any harnesses that aren't already set."

"Acknowledged, pod 4," Van answers, "and thank ye."

Rustling sounds come through the comm as the others move around. Lucy stands and places a hand on my shoulder as she passes by. When I look up, her eyes portray a wealth of understanding. Her wrinkles crease deeper as she smiles and pats my arm. "Think about what you want to share. They're ready to hear you."

In my position, public speaking's been a frequent and easy task for me. It's routine. Simple. Nothing to cause anxiety. In fact, I sometimes enjoy the research and reflection of reading historical speeches and using them as a basis for my own. I've done just that for our arrival in Terra Faire—drawing on a famous speech of Franklin Delano Roosevelt as the foundation from which to assure my fellow Spherans that our isolation is essential to our survival. For formal occasions, I still compose notes ahead of time, but normally I'm comfortable speaking to an audience without much preparation. After all, when speaking to an audience of telepaths, like I do back home, half of what I say is read in my thoughts and not only my words. They can sense my intention where words might confuse an issue.

I'm surprised to realize that the idea of opening the comm and speaking to my team has me terrified. My palms are sweaty. I rub them on my knees, then run a hand down my face, pausing as my fingertips brush the rough texture of my gem. It's a quick reminder of the importance of my mission—a reminder of the number of gems fading to gray in Terra Faire even now. How many of my people has the Trade claimed in my absence?

I blow out a breath and press the comm button to open a channel between our pods. Rustling noises immediately come from the pods that left their channel open, then the light flashes to show that all the pods are listening. When I open my mouth to speak, there's nothing there. No welcoming comments. No gracious greeting. I don't know where to start.

Lucy reaches over and squeezes my arm. Someone clears their throat. I look at Lucy and she smiles and nods.

"Good afternoon." My words hang in the air a moment before we hear more rustling.

"Divine grace with you," replies Mercy Adams, the little diplomat.

"Peace with you, Dr. Adams." *Dr. Adams?* Why am I being so formal? Five words in and I'm already blowing it.

"Hello everyone," May says, before whispering something to TJ.

"Greetings, Ambassador." The ice in Eddie's voice has me swallowing hard. "Is there something you wished to discuss?"

I clear my throat. I'm struck by a random memory of how peaceful she looked on the cot in the infirmary, worn out and comatose after caring for me straight into her rem. And then the fleeting memory of the soft, warm touch of her lips on mine, so unexpected. "I…Yes, I'd like to share some information with you all in hopes that it will make your introduction to Spheran society a little easier."

"Oh, wonderful—" Mercy's exclamation is cut short by a muffled comment from Van.

"Splendid." TJ's voice is dry sarcasm. "It's been ages since we've heard one of your lectures. By all means, instruct us."

Lucy waves a hand in dismissal. She reaches over and mutes our pod. "Ignore them. Just get it out." She clicks the audio back on.

A long sigh comes over the channel, and I know it's Eddie's. "Alright, Ambassador, let's hear it."

"Well…as you know, the biosphere is an artificial environment. We have approximately 16,000 residents, all praenex. When we land, we can expect a large crowd at the airfield, possibly as many as 10,000 will greet us. The shielded zone contains the airfield, masked by the same technology that hides our city.

"The biosphere and airfield comprise a large portion of Terra Faire, but outside these boundaries we also have a small crop farm composed of organized planting, wild crops and a few groves. We have a small dairy and raise fowl for eggs, not meat. Most Spherans are vegetarians."

The audio from Van's pod reconnects. "Much like our settlements then…I have a million questions about yer farm."

"I'll see that you get a full tour. You can observe the workers if you like."

"Well now, I'm not much for *observin'*, but show me what work needs doin' and I'm happy to help yer folk."

"Of course. Thank you. So…the city contains many warehouses of goods, preserved from the-time-that-was, but we also have a small waste management facility and recycling center outside the city walls. It's connected to a simple foundry and fabrication lab and supplies the parts and products we can't get from our warehouses."

"It sounds well thought out," Eddie comments, "Well planned…I'd like to know more about the city—how it was built, what powers it, how it is organized?"

I relax into the telling now. "Our founders built the city in the 22nd century at the base of a volcano. El Misti's side vents provide a structure for the foundation of the city, which is a rough circle in shape with an inverted conical elevation. Builders made the structures and streets from the local volcanic silica stone stable enough to withstand seismic activity that still occurs. The government offices are at the highest elevation in the center of the city, with streets and buildings spiraling out and down to the curtain wall and gates."

"Interesting design," TJ mumbles.

"*Now* you're listening," May remarks.

"Now it's something worth listening to. Power source?"

"Thermal and solar," I reply. "The volcano is not highly active, but it still generates a lot of heat. Also our roofs are solar, but we have an external solar source as well—solar umbrellas of different sizes. They're a unique design made to blend in with the natural surroundings, since shielding isn't practical."

"Tell us more about your people," Mercy adds. "How is your society structured? How are vocations assigned? Who are your leaders?"

Here things are going to get more complex. "I could probably talk for hours about my people—"

"Please do not— Ouch!" TJ is quiet again.

"Please go on, Cai," May suggests.

"Terra Faire is a peaceful place, but also somewhat…sullen, I suppose you'd say, as younger and younger citizens fall ill with the Trade. We have an excellent hospital and thankfully, our children mature quickly—around eight or nine years—so they help us focus on the positives. Familial groups share the responsibility of raising children. It's not uncommon for multi-generational families to share a group of apartments—most of our housing is urban and we have common recreational spaces. Most citizens prefer using our canteens for meals, rather than cooking at home. Vocations are assigned based on interests, talent, and the needs of our society.

"One thing I believe you'll find unique is our use of robots. They're much more common than what I've seen in your settlements. They do a large portion of the manual labor required to run the city—everything from laundry processing, to farming, to building maintenance."

"Individual units or central processing?" TJ's keen interest isn't surprising. He and Vengi are the technicians of the group.

"The robots share a central data repository but they encode the information to identify its source, thereby creating a memory or experience uniquely tied to a specific unit. Individual bots are adapted for special functions as well—for example, specialized tools suited for a specific task. In this way, they all share the knowledge, but they aren't interchangeable."

"AI?"

"Yes, they learn and adapt. Some of their instruction is self-determined—if they see a problem, they fix it. They design their own tools and have a degree of autonomy, but you won't find them to be emotional, or humanized. For one thing, they don't look like humans, and while some have been personalized, and given names, they are, for the most part, subservient to their tasks and our citizens."

"I'd like to know more about your social structure," Eddie says. "Can you tell us about your government, and who we'll meet when we arrive, who's in charge?"

Here I have a choice to make…I look at Lucy. She's staring back at me with an open and encouraging expression. Her eyebrows jump, and I know I'm stalling.

"We are a simple electoral democracy, with electorates structured by age group into eight, five-year increments, rather than geography. We allow citizens to vote starting at age five, however the weight of their vote is half that of citizens 15 to 25 years old, and one-third the weight of those 30 years and older.

The top tier is 40-plus."

"Everyone over 40 is in the same tier? That doesn't seem fair to yer elderly," Van comments.

I close my eyes and reach for calm. "Sadly, we don't have enough citizens older than that to warrant additional segments. If we did segment further, it would give a small few too much power."

Silence follows this explanation. A wave of pity comes at me from Lucy even as I tighten my shields—I don't mind their pity, but it's their understanding that I want.

I take a breath and continue. "The top two citizens in terms of electoral votes are President and Vice President, each for a six-year term. It's customary for them to select their seven-seat cabinet from the highest popular vote totals. Unlike your society, we don't have a spiritual branch; there's no Legion in Terra Faire. Instead we have one government with seven departments including—"

"Ambassador," Eddie interrupts me, "thank you for the civics lesson, but I believe you've missed a key point. *Who* is in charge?"

Damn perceptive woman! I look again at Lucy, and she makes a twirling motion with her finger.

I clear my throat. "I am…I'm in charge."

24
Eddie

Current year: 2701
Wednesday, 2:30 PM
Somewhere over the South American continent

I am more than the gray matter inside my skull. I am a bright light, a little piece of the Divine, and I am not defined by the acts of others. I reach for the Creator. I reach and reach, but I can't settle into reaching. There's a persistent buzzing in my brain. Cai isn't just Ambassador Varela, or Dr. Varela, he's *President* Varela.

"Son of a bitch!" Van's cursing matches so succinctly with my own reaction, I'm tempted to give it a try. Mercy shushes him before their pod disconnects from audio.

TJ laughs. "'King Cai' wasn't so far off, then." My brother's temper is as sharp as my own. Knowing I can't do it myself, a small part of me *wants* him to rip into Cai over the open comm. "Of all the low-handed—" TJ growls before his comm disconnects as well.

My new sister-in-law is turning out to be quite assertive. Good for her. He needs a strong hand to rein in his impulses.

I rub the back of my neck, but the buzzing only gets louder. When I try to focus on the sound, I realize it's Cai's voice talking frantically over the open comm, trying to defend himself.

"…so small," he's saying, "more like a mayor than president, really." … "I realize I lied by omission, but…" "Only the best of intentions…" "You have to understand my mission…"

Anger is simmering through me with such force that my legs are trembling. The pod's comfortable 21 degrees feels suddenly icy as prickles of adrenaline flood my system. I retreat into my mind, searching first for a thread of calm to suppress the anger, and then reaching further for a melody to soothe.

When I have the notes firmly in mind, I remember the feel of my violin's strings—the bite against the fingers of my left hand, the gentle-but-commanding grip on my bow—and in my mind I play. The music—only my violin at first, and then building to a full orchestra—changes me. It stretches me out, sloughs away the weight of anger, of resentment, until a spark like a warm ember spreads pleasant heat through my body. I let my soul emote through the bow, through the rise and fall of chords until I reach the crescendo and descend into a state of peace. And in that fleeting moment, the Creator's hand is on my shoulder, and I know that everything is going to work out.

I am a bright light, a little piece of the Divine. I take a deep breath, holding close that last fading moment, before opening my eyes and looking around the pod.

"Wow." Vengi's eyes are wide. "Where did you go?"

"Hmmm?"

Cai's voice continues over the comm at a frantic, almost panicked pace.

"You, like, left the pod…left the planet, I think. Where'd you go?"

"Oh, that." I reach over and press the button to disconnect us from the others. The sudden silence is like a punch to my ears. "I was just…do you play a musical instrument?"

"Clarinet, but it's been a while. It broke and I didn't have time to fix it. I like to *listen* to music too. I've seen all kinds of concerts in the VRT. One of my favorites…"

I let Vengi's story ease me into a dozing, floating kind of meditation. I'm awake, and replying easily, but part of my mind is adrift—circling around my feelings, examining them, dissecting them—as we get closer and closer to Terra Faire.

Blip, blip, blip! A light starts flashing on the panel in front of me.

"There's another call coming in, Vengi."

He presses a few buttons. "Huh…not for me, though. This one's addressed to you."

"I already spoke to everyone back home—"

"Holy sands! They're not waiting for an answer…they're hacking into my system!"

"What? They can do that?" I lean forward, watching as his hands fly across the controls.

"No way! Whoever they are, they're good. I can't…oh, okay…and they're in."

The video feed on the console comes to life, and at first, I don't know what I'm seeing—the screen is a sheet of blue fabric, and an occasional flash of skin.

"What do you mean, you got it?" a woman's voice says. "Well, where is it?"

I know that voice…it can't be…

A jumbled male voice answers.

"What? Oh!" The fabric recedes and my mother comes into view as she sits gracefully in the chair in front of the camera. "Oh, hello, Edelweiss."

I don't know what to say. All of my messages to my parents before we left went unanswered. I haven't spoken to her in months, yet here she is, apparently off duty in jeans and a dark tee. Her black hair falls in long glossy waves down the front of her shirt and her face is free of the makeup she usually wears, making her look so, so young. And, of course, I recognize myself in so many of her features, it's like looking at my doppelganger.

Why is she calling me?

"Mother."

"Well, what a relief." She tucks her hair behind both ears, and for a moment, she actually smiles as she stares at me. Then she seems to remember herself and waves a hand in the air. "You know I don't like to pry, but when we heard nothing more after your reply to my message…well, I can see you're fine."

"I am."

"And your brother? How is Tern?"

"He's fine, too."

"Ah, good. Good. Well—"

"As is May, his wife."

"Ah, yes, of course. His…wife…the…*girl*…from Vancouver Colony."

"Were you going to say 'null', Mother?"

"Of course not. Such a vulgar expression. I understand you're on your way south." She relaxes back in the chair and crosses her legs. Her manicured fingers drum the arm rests. "Don't forget to protect your skin, Edelweiss. Wear a hat. You don't want to get wrinkles, and with your fair skin, it really could be harmful."

"It's not a vacation, Mother. I'm not going to the seaside. It's a mission."

"Oh, right. I'm sure. Well, I expect to hear all about it when you return."

"Speaking of returns, you need to release Mercy's mother right away. Like, this minute."

My mother sits up straighter, and her casual, concerned-mother persona transforms into Fleet Admiral Pèlerine Reine LeRoux, the most powerful person on the planet. "Release her?" She looks off-camera at someone else in the room and gives a sharp nod, before turning back to me. "You've been misinformed. Dr. Coral Adams is our honored guest and fellow scientist. She's far too busy with her collaboration on a number of projects to return home now. I suggest you keep your attention focused on your new *friends* in Terra Faire. I'll bet they've never met a Bozan before. You're going to be quite popular. As for the rest of it, it's far too complex for your concern."

"Too complex!"

"Remember that hat, Edelweiss. Goodbye now."

"Wait!"

The video cuts out.

I slouch back in my seat. "Unbelievable!"

"Wow—"

"Not a word, Vengi! Not a word."

He makes a zipping motion across his lips and tosses an imaginary key over his shoulder.

Instead of a nap, I get to ponder my toxic parental relationships. I really didn't expect her to call. What does it mean? Was she really worried?

When I peel away all the condescension and small talk, one truth remains: my mother has no intention of releasing Mercy's mother any time soon.

Vengi's hands fly over the controls. He flips the switch that connects us to the other pods. "Okay, friends. We'll be starting our decent in about—"

Beep, beep, beep. Several warning lights flash on the console.

"Proximity alarm!" Vengi shouts.

"Again?" I can't believe this is happening again.

"I jinxed it; you were right!"

"Confirmed." My brother's voice is all business. "It's one of those drones."

"Visual contact," Van says. "It must have been waiting for us. It's matched our course and speed, but it's not coming any closer."

Cai's and Lucy's voices mumble incoherently before Cai clears his throat. "If we allow it to follow us to Terra Faire, SciCorps will know precisely where our airfield is. We have to stop it."

"Aye, but ye know as well as we do that the Tumbler doesn't have any weapons."

I shake my head. "Can we lead it away?"

"To where?" TJ asks. "We can't fly around forever; more drones will eventually arrive."

"Think!" May says. "We have to disable the drone and we have to do it fast. How?"

Vengi twists back and forth in his seat. "It's true we don't have any weapons, but.... I have an idea." He looks at me with round eyes. "But I don't think you're going to like it."

"What is it, Vengi?" His mother is first to ask.

"We designed the Tumbler to *avoid* obstacles, but with a few lines of code, I could reverse that programming—"

"I love it!" TJ speaks quickly, already following a plan. "We'll have to sacrifice one of the pods—"

"What are we planning exactly?" A shiver races up my spine.

Vengi's hands are flying over the controls again. "We're going to use our pod as a battering ram. It'll be destroyed, but so will the drone."

"Wait a minute—" I hold up a hand.

"He's right," TJ agrees. "It has to be your pod. Van can't evac so he'll have to remain. Evacuating the opposite pod should give us the best chance; we'll use Van's pod as counterweight."

"Exactly." Vengi nods. "Eddie, you need to go to pod 4 now, join my *maman* and President Varela. I'm almost done with the software update, then I'll go to pod 2 and we'll control the Tumbler from there."

"Aye, and Mercy can join either pod now too. Go Cricket."

"I'm not leaving you alone," Mercy argues.

"It'll be safer in one of the other pods, Mercy," I agree. "I'll meet you in pod 4."

"No. No way. I'm staying right here with Van."

I can picture her in my mind as I unfasten my safety harness and head toward the escape hatch. Her arms are folded over her chest and her chin is raised. I've seen that look before.

"Please, wife—"

"I'm staying."

"Enough!" Cai's impatient as always. "Everybody get ready."

I quickly tie up my skirts again and hustle into the escape tunnel. "Good luck," I shout back to Vengi as I reach for the first rung. Muscle memory kicks in, just like Lucy said it would, and my foot has closed the hatch and I'm halfway to pod 4 before I hear it open again. I know Vengi is faster than me, so I double my efforts. My heart is pounding in my chest when I push open the hatch to pod 4. I reach for the floor, but a strong hand grabs mine. Cai pulls me through and we stand, nose to nose, in the small space at the back of the pod.

His eyes search mine. I expected anger to fill me at our next meeting—anger at his deceit, anger at his lack of trust—but the wave of regret and desperation that assaults me when I meet his eyes breaks down my temper. He wants so much for everyone to be safe, to forgive him, to survive.

I inhale slowly. "We'll talk later, but for now, we need to focus. Agreed?"

He lifts his chin. "Agreed. Come on."

I reluctantly allow him to pull me by the hand, but I dig in my heels when he drops into his seat and pulls me toward him.

"Wait. What?" I tug my hand away.

"Hi, Eddie." Lucy smiles up at me. She press the button to

snug into her harness, worry creasing the corners of her eyes.

"Divine grace," I greet her absently before focusing back on Cai.

His arms are spread wide. "You can't sit with Lucy—you'd crush her—and we don't have any other safety harness. Come on." His fingers curl, beckoning me to sit on his lap so we can share his seat and safety restraint.

"I really—"

"Ready!" Vengi's voice startles me. I momentarily forgot that the whole ship could hear us.

"Pod 3 ready," Mercy says.

"That leaves us." Cai raises an eyebrow. In any other situation, I think he'd be smirking, but he must see on my face that I don't find this at all amusing.

"Hurry, please." My brother's not happy either, but he's right. "We're getting too close to Terra Faire."

I gingerly slip onto Cai's lap, marveling at the strong muscles that shift under my thighs as he maneuvers the harness to hold us both. Heat rises in my cheeks as the belt snugs into place, smashing our bodies together. I have only a few seconds to fight the electrifying sensations surging through me before the danger of our next move refocuses my mind.

"Aligning pod 1 with the drone," Vengi says. The Tumbler swivels so that the now-empty pod 1 is lined up with the drone. "Targeting drone," Vengi says. "Everyone prepare for impact."

"I'll count down," TJ offers. "Van, Mercy—hold on. You're in for a wild swing. Three, two, one."

Pod 1 disappears from view, moving like a slingshot toward the drone. Nothing happens.

"Dust it!" Vengi growls. "I missed."

"Confirmed," TJ says. "Realigning. Let me give it a try."

"Okay," Vengi sounds defeated. Pod 1 reappears. "In three, two, one." Pod 1 rockets back again, and still nothing happens.

"Agh! This is gettin' to be more than my stomach can handle," Van complains.

"Huh." My brother sounds surprised that he missed too. "That drone has an operator."

"They probably saw the first maneuver and anticipated it," May says.

"We don't have time for this!" Cai grumbles behind me. I feel him tensing up. "We're almost to Terra Faire."

"Agreed," May says. "Time to end this. My turn. Taking control. Hold on, Van. Time to try something different." Pod 1 reappears.

"What do you have in mind?" TJ asks.

"A simple feint."

"That could work. Realigned and ready," TJ says. "Three—"

Pod 1 jolts backward, then bounces right back. The Tumbler shifts slightly, then pod 1 rockets back again. I'm jarred to the side as a crash reverberates through the aircraft.

"It's a hit!" TJ shouts, just before a second collision knocks us sideways. "What was that?"

"Something struck pod 3," May answers. "Van!"

"We're hit!" Van shouts. "The drone hit our pod!"

"Is it down? Did it work?" Cai asks, his breath hot on the side of my neck.

"Aye! It's plummeting. No way it'll recover from that."

"Confirmed," TJ agrees. "The drone is destroyed. What's the condition of your pod, Van?"

Van doesn't respond. My heart lurches. "Van? Mercy?"

"Hold on!" Mercy responds. We hear scrapes and bumps coming from their pod. "Our windshield is cracked."

"Resuming course to Terra Faire," Lucy says. The Tumbler spins so that our pod is out front. We accelerate, pressing me back into Cai again.

"Cabin pressure decreasing in pod 3," TJ announces. "Status?...Van?"

"Oh no," Mercy's voice is laced with fear. "Van's passed out."

Lucy scans her controls. "Oxygen levels in pod 3 are falling; they won't be safe for Van's sapiens biology for much longer. Accelerating to maximum speed. We should be in Spheran airspace in—"

"Berylhenge," a voice comes through the comm, "this is Terra Faire Tower, monitoring your descent. Advise you decrease speed and prepare for approach. Over."

"Roger, Tower," Cai replies, "Code 7700. We have damage to two sections of the aircraft; we've lost cabin pressure and have one passenger in need of emergency medical attention. Over."

"Roger, Berylhenge. Emergency crews notified. What is the status of your landing gear? Over."

"I think we're okay!" Vengi shouts. "I'm not reading any damage to the jet arms or landing gear."

"Roger, Berylhenge," the controller answers. "We've cleared the airfield, we'll confirm landing gear status when we have a visual…"

With my heart in my throat and my head filled with prayer, we start our descent into what looks like a vast desert. Reddish brown earth stretches in three directions, with a massive volcano dominating the north. To the west a jagged dark stripe narrows toward the distant horizon—the ocean perhaps, though from here it's just a gray line fading into blue sky. After a moment, the stripe changes into a rushing river cleaved into the land stretching west. I can't see a city or any sign of habitation. We continue our descent, the ground getting rapidly closer.

"Uh, Tower?" Lucy's voice quavers. "I can't see the airfield. Over."

Cai shifts behind me, like he wants to take the controls. "It's okay, Lucy, it's just the cloak. "Tower," he says, "we're ready to clear the shield in three, two, one…"

Light flickers and a crackle of static fills the pod before the land below us transforms. The world outside is wild, majestic and just a little other-worldly. The desert is gone, replaced by dappled color. Beyond what must be the airfield, the sphere—a half sphere, actually—rises out of a craggy hill, shimmering with glass and steel. On one side, I discern a deep cliff edge and remember seeing it from high above. It must be a dramatic drop from the cliff to the water below. On the land, the sphere nestles in the ridged arms of the massive, towering volcano. El Misti embraces the city in a protective hug. *Protected from whom?*

A large crowd has gathered on the periphery of the landing area, pushed back into a protected rim of airport buildings and frontage roads. Numerous colorful umbrellas shield them from the heat of the sun. I see their many shapes like a stipple painting—a fabric of round canopies and upturned faces—some old, but mostly young—against a ground surface awash with color and dappled texture that I can't understand.

"God's grace!" Mercy's exclamation echoes my reaction. "There must be thousands of people down there."

"I'd estimate close to 10,000," May says. "Look up the avenues, they stretch as far as you can see."

"Well, let's see if we can do this gracefully then. No pressure." Lucy's hands fly across the controls. "Switching to landing mode."

Our forward motion slows and just like that we're hovering over the colorful pavement.

"Tower to Berylhenge, visual confirmed," the air traffic controller says. "Uh, we see significant damage to, well, um… That's an unusual aircraft. One of the connecting segments appears to be damaged."

"Roger, Tower." Cai's voice reverberates through my body. "We had a run-in with a drone. Stand by for landing. Over."

"Controls indicate pod 1 is askew." Lucy strains to see around us. "I think it's going to touch down first before the landing struts."

"Confirmed," TJ says. "I have a visual. The canopy is damaged. The fuselage is bent at the joint with the jet arm, and I can see that the strut is not long enough to reach the ground first."

"Does it look like the structure will hold?" Lucy asks.

I listen as TJ and Vengi debate what they see from pod 2. We're getting closer to the ground now, descending in a hover like a helicopter. The images outside my windshield sharpen and for a moment I feel like I'm sinking into the mouth of a strange and nebulous creature. Colorful shapes flicker on the tarmac. Tiny specs move in the breeze like something alive. What is this?

"Uh, I think the structure will hold, yes," Vengi answers. "I recommend we set down slowly with pod 3 strut first, and ease into the rest."

"Please hurry," Mercy says. "Van is coming around, but I think we still need a medic."

"I can land us, if you want me to," TJ offers.

Lucy glances at Cai. I feel his body shift as he shakes his head. She flashes us a grin, then, brow creasing in concentration, turns back to her controls. "Appreciate the offer, but I have her. Okay, everyone. Here we go."

Our descent continues slowly. Just when it really does feel like we might be dropping into a hole, the first strut taps down with a gentle thump. The Tumbler hovers one more moment, and then a screech of metal fills the air as the damaged pod reaches the pavement.

"Okay, just a little more." Lucy waggles her hand in the air. "Gravity will decide for us."

Clunk! We land, leaning slightly aft on pod 2's strut so that our pod's strut doesn't quite reach the ground.

"Nice work," Cai says. His arm hugs around my middle for one charged moment before I realize he's searching for the harness release.

I press it quickly and struggle to stand in the unlevel pod.

"Ha! We did it." Vengi's joy is infectious. "I'm heading to you!"

"Nice work, Lucy." I brush out my skirts and scooch away from

Cai. "Thank you for getting us here safely."

Lucy nods. "Tower, this is Berylhenge, powering down and preparing to receive emergency personnel."

"Roger, Berylhenge. Welcome to Terra Faire."

The hatch at the back of the pod thumps open, and Vengi tumbles in. He stands with one hand braced on the ceiling and grins at us. "I'm so glad we didn't die."

"Me too." I laugh and ruffle his hair.

25
Eddie

Current year: 2701
Wednesday, 5:15 PM
Terra Faire, Chileru, South America

After all that drama, I'm finally ready to make my entrance into this strange world of Cai's, if for no other reason than a keen desire to put my feet on the ground.

"*Allons-y!*" I wave toward the hatch. "Let's go."

Vengi pushes open the pod door and activates the ladder. "Ready?" He waves his arm for me to go first, but Cai squeezes my elbow.

"Let me." He steps around me. "It'll be a short jump to reach the ground. I'll help you all down."

I watch him back out of the pod and follow, running a hand along my hair. This is it.

Climbing down to the color-washed tarmac, I'm distracted from examining the strange surface when the warm wind caresses my neck, tousles through my hair. It's gentle. Inviting. With a deep breath of fresh, foreign air, I find I can smile and mean it. When my feet touch the last rung, I send a prayer of thanks out into the world. We're safe. With a little hop, I'm caught in Cai's arms and gently settled on my feet. Lucy is right behind me, so there's no time to dwell on the awkward rush of heat that spreads through me again at Cai's touch.

Mercy reaches the ground from her ladder at pod 3. A group of medics rush up the ladder into the pod.

"Eh!" Van's shout is loud from inside. "Hands to yerself. I'm fine, just need to catch my breath."

The medics come pouring out of the pod. From their expressions, I'm guessing they haven't seen a sapiens Van's size among the people that arrived here two weeks ago. I cover my mouth to hide my smirk.

Van climbs down the ladder and agrees to sit on the tailgate of the small ambulance. Once he has an oxygen mask on his face and a swarm of EMTs poking him, Mercy looks my way and I wave her over. Cai passes by her on his way to check on Van.

She twirls as she rushes toward me, staring at the color palette beneath her feet. "Bless the Creator!" She huffs as she grabs my head, and with a giggle I find contagious, we touch foreheads. Filled with relief, we slide into a quick and easy heartfelt hug.

"We survived!" She grins. "Van's going to be fine, I can tell, but Cai will make sure."

"He sounds good—all that complaining. I'm so relieved. That was really something."

"And now we're finally here." She turns another slow revolution. "And we've landed in some kind of fairyland!" We both gaze down at the painted ground around us. A vibrant mural of exotic botanicals covers all the concrete we can see. Fresh flower petals swirl along its surface, dancing in the wind and dappled with light making it look alive.

For just a second my confidence wavers—I must look so strange against this backdrop with my albino skin and white hair and clothing. Like snow…or ice. "Do you think they did this just for us?"

"I'm sure of it." Mercy stills and takes my hand. "Listen, Eddie, about Cai's big secret—being president and all—"

She's cut off when Cai himself ducks under the nearby engine arm and approaches us with a beaming Lucy by his side.

His face is serious and closed as he signals a nearby group of Spherans to wait.

Vengi, TJ, and May join us. Cai gathers us in under the shade of our pod. When he turns to me, I meet his gaze squarely.

"Your prayer worked, and I'm thankful to be safely home." I guess he's done begging for forgiveness; he's not looking for my approval now.

I nod, keeping my thoughts closed to him.

When he sees I won't reply, he turns to the group and continues. "Van is fine. He'll be with us in a moment. Vengi, Lucy, thank you for your excellent piloting."

"Of course," Lucy says.

"I helped," TJ interrupts. May elbows him. "Well, I *did*."

"And I thank you," Cai continues. "Allow me to welcome you all to Terra Faire. What follows now is a bit of diplomacy—" he glances around at the decorated concrete and dusting of flower petals tickling his boots "—and pageantry, apparently, but I promise to keep it short. I'm sure you're all eager to get settled after the flight. Please, follow me."

The small group of people that have been waiting nearby greets him eagerly, exchanging touches and hugs that mark them clearly as close friends. I stay back with the others to give him a moment. He's been away for a long time, and though he's only been out of contact for two weeks, they're bound to want to look him in the eye and see that he's okay.

The short delay provides me with an opportunity to notice how impeccably dressed these people are—just like all the Spherans we've met. A quick glance confirms it's not just Cai's friends; even the children wear fancy clothes. Cai waves us forward, and we follow him toward a small, shaded platform that's been erected for the occasion. Tiny children race toward us to scamper ahead, tossing more flower petals at our feet. A sweet fragrance rises as we crush the petals with every step.

"Let me through, dammit!" Arson's voice rises above the wall of silently waiting Spherans.

Half of my group detours toward his voice. The crowd parts and Arson crashes through, rushing into the waiting arms of his sister, Lucy. Arson lifts her up and twirls her once around. When they stop, Vengi grabs ahold, and Arson sways under the weight— and joy. May joins in, reaching around to try to hug the whole group at once, and they sink to their knees, laughing and crying. Lucy stretches out and grabs TJ's arm. I can't stifle my laughter as I watch my stiff, disciplined brother give up and fall into this group of untamed, ecstatic Couvies.

I'm so wrapped up in the reunion that I don't notice the noise until it's rising like a song. The crowd has surged forward from the periphery of the airfield. Sighs and tears spread through the mass of Spherans inching toward us. Beneath their umbrellas, they touch their heads with their neighbors. The smallest among them clamor to be picked up and held, giggles of joy escaping them. They reach out to one another to touch hands, exchange words. Among telepaths, joy is contagious.

Cai breaks the spell by striding over to the Couvies, and with a few whispered words, they stand and break apart. Lucy doesn't let go of her brother, and he has Vengi's elbow linked through his own. Like a human chain, May tows the group along after Cai, and onto the platform with us.

As I wipe my own tears and look out into the faces of the people gathered to greet us, I'm struck by the change. Their stillness has returned, but now it's soft and open, like they're waiting to listen. Praenex crowds back home are patient, but this is something else. I notice too how few adults I can see, and then remind myself that Spherans mature earlier and many here likely *are* adults.

Mercy slips her hand into mine as we wait for Cai to greet a few people. One of them clips a small microphone to his shirt and hands him an old-fashioned tablet. He reads it quickly, nods and then moves to the center of the platform.

"This is very strange," Mercy whispers to me. "Eerie, almost. Their demeanor changes like the wind."

A few people at the front of the crowd exchange looks and glance around. Several others, including the two women Cai just spoke with, look directly at us.

Telepaths.

I catch myself just before I roll my eyes. "Telepaths, Cricket."

I nudge her with my elbow and whisper sotto voce, "For all we know, they could be cheering wildly."

She curls her lips over her teeth to suppress a giggle.

"Greetings, my friends. Blessings on you all." Cai's voice booms out over the crowd.

While he speaks, I watch the people. Their focus is precise and concentrated.

"Please join me in welcoming new friends to Terra Faire." Cai waves his arm to encompass our group and the strangest thing happens. The entire crowd bends their elbows and begins to snap their fingers. The clicking of 20,000 fingers fills the silent airfield with a strange wave of clattering noise. The wind catches the sound and tosses it about like the flower petals, lifting and falling in surges before finally settling back to silence.

I glance at my friends and know that my own face mirrors their astonishment.

"Divine grace!" I laugh, unable to help myself.

Some in the crowd laugh too. And this is how I arrive in Terra Faire—laughing, crying, awed, and equally confused.

Some minutes later, I've come to understand that "keeping it short" means something entirely different to President Cairo Varela than it does to me. My attention has wandered to the people around me. As Cai consults his tablet and launches into a new topic—this one appears to be the state of Spheran independence and separation—I notice a group of people in the crowd who look just a bit different than the rest.

While most of the Spherans appear meticulously clean and well groomed, this group appears a tiny bit on the wild side. Some wear their hair long and loose, though a few have braids which are common among the other Spherans. Several of them have beards, the only ones I see in the crowd, and a few of the children are barefoot. Their clothes look worn and ill-fitting compared with the meticulously styled people in the bigger Spheran group. What's more, the rest of the Spherans, though not overtly separating themselves, seem to give this group more space, as if a subtle boundary exists between them. A narrow perimeter of open space circles the group.

There's a sudden jab of thought—someone focusing intently on me—and I zero in on its source. A woman, standing at the center of this unusual group, stares back at me with fierce violet eyes set in a stunning dark face. They're small like Mercy, but with broad, muscled shoulders emerging from a snug fitting vest that hugs an athletic torso. Their features are compelling—large round eyes with heavy lashes, a long bony nose and high cheek bones that at first distract from the whole, but then seem to map their face so that you see it all at once. The intensity of their beauty is punctuated by an elaborate crest of dark braids that wind around their head and down both sides of their neck before joining again above their left breast like an off-center, knit collar. The thick rope of hair flows all the way down their front to dangle just above their knee. I've never seen anything like it.

As if my scrutiny annoys them, they jab a hand toward the ground. I lock my eyes back on theirs and wait for what I know will come. I don't have to wait long.

Welcome to Chileru, Tesouro Branco. Bozan LeRoux, my people greet you.

I notice then that they are all looking at me now, this group on the fringe. Their expressions are closed, but not unfriendly, as if they are waiting to make judgement.

Divine grace with you.

Thank you. In the next weeks, you will see many things here. It's our hope that the Creator will bless you so that you can look with clear eyes and see…that you will listen with ears that hear, and that your voice will ask the questions that need to be asked.

Who are you?

Cai's voice rises, and we all look at him. I see he's done it on purpose, to get our attention back as his speech continues.

"It is with great heart that I find my voice an echo of wisdom from a great leader who lived nearly 700 years ago. Today, I share his message with you, adapted for what we now experience in our own lives.

"The political situation in the north causes grave concern and anxiety to all Spherans who wish to live in peace and amity. SciCorps' greed for power and supremacy is devoid of any sense of justice and humane considerations.

"On my trip across the world and back, I have seen much evidence of a new cooperation between the Terrans of Scorch against the Pilgrim tyranny. I see their material and spiritual well-being making great strides forward as a means to defend their views against the SciCorps policies they so despise. We support their efforts to heal our planet and we will lend our knowledge and energy to that goal."

In the crowd, small movements occur. So slight, I can't be sure I truly saw them until a movement in the corner of my eye catches my attention. I look to the odd group of Spherans who greeted me earlier and see that all of them, except the woman, have turned their bodies at a right angle to the stage. As I watch, the woman smirks at me and jauntily swivels their body to match their people's posture.

Cai continues without missing a beat. "…I know the security and peace that covers our Sphere, our home. Almost inevitably I have been compelled to contrast our peace with very different scenes in other parts of the world. Those who cherish their freedom and recognize and respect the equal rights of their neighbors to be free and live in peace, must work together for the triumph of principles in order that peace may prevail. There must be a return to a belief in a pledged world, and so the Terrans will help us with the Trade, and we will help them with the Loom.

"The majority of people in the world want to live in peace. They want to exert themselves in technology, in agriculture, and in science, so that they may show their faithfulness to the Creator. To increase their worth through healing each other and the world, rather than engaging in military conflicts that destroy human lives and useful property. There is an interdependence about the new world, both technically and morally, which makes it impossible for us to completely isolate ourselves. But they do not need us to be what we are not, what we do not recognize of ourselves. They do not need an army."

A wave of motion happens now. Those who previously turned away, turn further—their backs to the stage. Numerous others turn at a right angle to us, like the others had before. Still others snap their fingers in the Spheran version of applause.

Mercy stirs at my side. "What is *happening*?"

"I have no idea."

Cai pauses, then hurriedly continues. "…How happy we are that circumstances permit us to put our energy into cures, reforestation, the conservation of our genetic health, and many other kinds of useful works rather than into armies and implements of war. Surely the 90 percent who want to live in peace in accordance with moral standards that have received almost universal acceptance through the centuries since the Call, can and must find some way to make their will prevail.

"It is true that the moral consciousness of the world must recognize the importance of removing well-founded grievances; but at the same time, it must honor the sanctity of separation—"

More people turn their backs, others who previously faced forward turn at angle. Cai hesitates, then forges on. "Of respecting the rights and liberties of Spherans and of putting an end to acts of international aggression. No society ever loses its dignity by conciliating its differences, and by exercising great patience with, and consideration for, the rights of others."

There's more finger snapping in the crowd, but it dies quickly.

"War is a contagion. It can engulf people remote from the original scene of hostilities. We are determined to keep out of war. We are adopting such measures as will minimize our risk of involvement, but if our civilization is to survive, cooperation with the Terrans must be achieved.

"Most important of all, the will for peace must express itself even though it may tempt SciCorps to violate the rights of others who will desist from such a course. There must be positive endeavors to preserve peace.

"Spherans hate war. Spherans hope for peace. Therefore, Terra Faire actively engages in the search for peace."

I catch movement in the corner of my eye again. A youth skirts out in front of the crowd to reach the woman in the strange group. They do not speak, but an intense look passes between them. Both of them immediately separate from the crowd and rush away.

I'm still wondering what's going on when I realize Cai has also stopped talking. Another youth has approached him, and the same kind of silent communication is happening. I quickly try to reach out with my mind, but it's too late. I can't read their thoughts. The youth throws me a surprised and somewhat disapproving look before stepping back. Heat rushes to my cheeks.

"I'm sorry, I must leave you," Cai says to the crowd. "Thank you again for the warm welcome and for the beautiful art you prepared for us today." He motions to the mural painted on the concrete before stepping back from the podium. The crowd snaps politely and begins to disperse.

Cai turns to us. "I'm sorry, urgent business takes me away. This is Ilorin Orlov, *pronoms fem,* my Secretary of State." Cai motions to a young woman waiting quietly behind the platform. She's small like the others and her face is obstructed by a pair of large, dark sunglasses. "She'll take you to the city and see that you get settled."

He turns to me then. "I don't know how long I'll be away, but I hope to see you all for dinner." He gives me a short bow and leaves, his steps fast and sure.

"Okay." I turn to my friends and realize Van has joined us.

"What in God's name just happened?" Van asks. "Were those people turnin' 'round, or do I have a brain injury from passin' out? What's with the snappin'?"

I touch his arm. "I'm glad you're alright. As to this," I shrug, "more polite than clapping, I guess."

"I found it quite interesting." Mercy laces her arm through Van's and smiles. "That was FDR, you know. A famous American isolationist. They called that the Quarantine Speech."

TJ waves a hand. "I found the rhetoric heavy handed."

Arson lets out a loud breath. "Lines up right with the general feeling I've gotten from the folks in charge here—not the common folks, mind you, they're nice enough—but the team running this place has made it fairly clear…*we* are a necessary evil."

There's a strong presence from behind me before someone speaks—high and light like a child. "That evil is *ever* necessary is, of course, of great debate."

"Oh, I'm so sorry. We're being terribly rude."

Secretary Ilorin smiles. "I don't mind. It's entertaining really, to know how strange we appear to you, how alien, in fact. And yes, Major LeRoux, you look just as strange to us, as you wondered."

"Telepaths," TJ murmurs.

Van laughs and punches TJ lightly on the shoulder. "You'll have to keep that internal sarcasm in check, my friend."

Ilorin smiles, but behind her sunglasses I sense she's keeping a secret.

What? I ask her telepathically.

She turns toward me, and then seems to make up her mind. "Several sapiens arrived here last week with the crew from Alberta Farms. We were all very interested to see if we could read their minds, like the first generation praenex could, especially after learning that our young friends who spent so much time with you in the last months could not."

"What?" Van's mouth hangs openly slightly as he stares at Ilorin.

"Oh, yes. About half of us can read you, though it's very different than telepathy between praenex. It's more like another kind of gift we didn't know that we had…because there were no sapiens here." She turns toward Van. "No, please. You don't have to stop cursing in your mind, too. We find it rather…colorful."

I nudge Van. "See? Not to worry, they find it *colorful*."

"Well I'll be—"

"How are our young friends?" I ask as I take Ilorin's offered arm. "Nairobi and Fez were with us at the beginning of this whole thing, but I haven't spoken with them in weeks."

We turn and walk toward a long open-top tram. Ilorin's graceful—her steps measured and almost careful—and I find her a little peculiar, a bit haughty, almost like a cleric in my order back home. I'd like to see the eyes behind those sunglasses. I listen as she tells me about Fez and Nairobi, about the reports they've provided, and that they plan to stay in the Verge to continue their ambassadorships.

As we walk, she keeps one hand gently resting on a handle protruding from the side of a round robot that's keeping pace with us.

"This is Shepherd." Ilorin tilts her head toward the spherical robot. "It's my visual assistant and all-around companion. "Say hello, Shepherd."

The robot trills a cheerful noise.

If their AI can't speak, then they're way behind our tech.

"Stop joking!" Ilorin bonks the robot lightly on the side.

"Hello," it says.

"Ah! That's the same voice as our AI. I can't believe it. And you said it made a joke? Like, of its own?"

"It's old tech at the core, and not very funny." Ilorin reaches over to search for the handle again.

"Wait a minute…you're blind!" Vengi blurts.

I cringe.

"That's amazing!"

"Vengi!" Lucy scolds him.

"It's alright." Ilorin waves a hand. "It's true, and yes, as unusual here as in your settlements."

"They can't cure you?" I immediately wish I hadn't said it, but Ilorin just laughs.

"There's nothing to cure. I see in other ways. In fact, I was nearly six months old before they realized I couldn't see like you do. Here we are."

The robot has led us to the tram and May's family climbs aboard, absorbed again in their reunion. Porters load our bags on the trailer connected to the passenger car. My fingers itch at the thought of my instruments. I would love to take one back to the center of this exotic, artistic concrete world of wind and flower petals and fill it with song, but I know that's not to be.

"Perhaps you can come back another day," Ilorin suggests. "I'm sorry, I wasn't trying to pry, but your desire is very strong."

"No, I'm the one who should apologize. Cai—I mean, President Varela—he's right, I can't stay focused."

She laughs. "Is that what he says?" She smiles and holds out an arm for me to get in before she does. "Well, *Tesouro Branco*, he's not always right."

I'm wondering at that strange expression again, and also how well she knows Cai. I look up at the towering city beyond the roofs of the airport concourse. The modern buildings at city center rise in an elegant silhouette against the backdrop of the majestic volcano. Silent citizens dressed in all their pageantry stream between the airport buildings in efficient lines, with more robots like Shepherd quietly rolling along with them. The colorful concrete mural continues even here, and I wonder how far into the city we'll be chased by stray flower petals.

A child catches my eye. They've stopped a few meters from our tram and are staring intently at me. Their curly hair is neatly trimmed around a face of light brown skin and purple eyes, much like Cai's. I open my mouth to speak, but suddenly an adult is there, quietly admonishing the youth and reaching for their hand. The two are nearly identical—the child is an *aeternus*, a clone, almost certainly. Even their fancy clothing matches, just different in size. So odd. The child smiles broadly at me and shyly waves, before allowing their parent to move them on.

Ilorin laughs next to me.

I look at her from the corner of my eye. "What's so funny?"

"Oh, I'm sorry. Vengi has a song stuck in his head."

I twist to look at him. "Care to share?"

He grins. "I just keep singing, *we're off to see the wizard.*"

I raise one eyebrow in question.

"You don't know that one? Okay, adding it to the list of vids you have to watch."

"Ready?" Ilorin asks.

I nod and watch as Shepherd rolls around to the front of the tram, reverses into a slot between the wheels, and pulls us away.

"The robot is also a car!" Vengi laughs. "This place is going to be amazing!"

Epilogue
Cai

Current year: 2701
Friday, 5:40 PM
Terra Faire, Chileru, South America

My mind is too consumed with fear for me to notice much about my beloved city as my vehicle races through the streets toward the hospital. One of the powerful transportation robots pulls my sleek, closed rickshaw up the wide avenues that have been cleared ahead of us for swift passage. We're traveling very fast, but it's not fast enough. Time is running out.

We park at the rear of the tall building, right next to the express elevators that will take us directly to the floor I need. My aide struggles to keep up, but I'm not waiting. They squeeze through the elevator doors just before they close.

"Come on, come on. Why is this thing so slow?" I press the button again, as if that will make the car go faster.

The aide clears their throat. "The nurse informs me that they just administered a dose of pain medication and it's likely the patient will be asleep when we arrive."

"They couldn't wait five minutes?"

"Um, *they* could wait, but the patient…"

I squeeze my temples. *What am I saying?* "I'm sorry, please forgive me, that was rude. Of course they'll do whatever is best for the patient."

The elevator doors open and I stride down the hallway. I nod at the nurse working at the nearby station.

"Good evening, I'm here to see—"

"Yes, Mr. President, I know. She's there." The nurse points to the room directly behind us. "We wanted to keep her close. If you hurry, you may still catch her before the medication puts her to sleep. Her last visitor let us know you'd be here soon."

"Thank you. Divine grace with you."

"The Creator's hand in yours, Mr. President."

I nod and step over to tap lightly on the door. When I peek inside, I'm confused by how they could have sent me to the wrong room, but then I realize they haven't. No amount of internal prepping, no information from the personal briefings, no reports could have prepared me for this.

The woman lying in the bed is Giza, but not. The last time I visited her in the hospital before I left for New Juneau, she was sitting in a chair in the corner, upright, rosy-cheeked and smiling, so it was easy to ignore the tubes running out from her sleeve and the monitor taped to her hand. Her voice, as she encouraged me to keep an open mind, to trust the people I was about to meet, had been the soft but firm voice I had known all of my life—my best friend, my former partner.

To see her now is to see her one foot already dangling in the grave. I inhale a quick breath and steel myself to sit next to her bed.

She's sleeping, and I'm thankful to have the moment to build up my defenses, to hide what I'm feeling—the guilt and remorse, and anger—before she senses me here and wakes, as I know she will. I stare at her face, knowing the gentle features—her tiny nose and brown freckles—as well, if not better, than my own. I know that when her eyes open, their clear, almost startling purple will pull my attention away from the chalky whiteness of her dying gem.

How could I have left her to this? The constriction in my throat is painful and without realizing it, I grip her hand as a counterpoint. She stirs.

"Cairo," she whispers my name as her lashes flutter open.

The wet heat of tears stings my eyes as I bring her hand to my lips. She'll give me a moment, I know she will, but I can't fathom how I'll ever accept this. I'm losing her. This is the fate of all of my people if we can't find a cure.

I lay her hand back on the sheet and bend my head to kiss it again, my tears dropping onto her pale, bruised skin.

"Shhhh," she shushes me. "Don't cry, darling. Don't cry."

Her free hand strokes my hair as an uncontrollable sob escapes my throat. Time is running out.

Flare Characters

Main Characters

- **Ambassador Cairo (CAI) Varela (he/him), Doctor, President of Chileru, age early twenties**

  Cai is a medical doctor, and ambassador from Terra Faire, the secret society in Chileru. He is a praenex of Brazilian decent. He's on a mission to save his people from extinction at the hands of the Trade disease. His praenex gifts include telepathy and the power to heal.

- **Edelweiss (EDDIE) Renee LeRoux (she/her), Omag Gran, Scorch Legion, age 18**

  Eddie is the leader-elect of the Legion, a religious order. She's a praenex of French descent. Her parents are the leaders of SciCorps. She is TJ's twin sister. Eddie is the first albino praenex, and her blood carries a cure for the Trade disease. Her gifts are many, including telepathy and mind control. She is a musical prodigy and multi-instrumentalist.

- **Mayhem (MAY) Rose Forge (she/her), Vancouver Colony Police Deputy, age 19**

  May works in law enforcement and her family leads Vancouver Colony, the Verge. She is a praenex of Mexican-Scandinavian descent and is TJ LeRoux's wife. Her praenex gifts include prescience, linguistics, and amplification—she enhances the gifts of other praenex.

- MERCY Abigail Adams (she/her), Doctor of Philosophy in History, age 16

  Mercy is a history scholar and a praenex of Chinese-European descent from New Juneau, Alaska. She's the daughter of two prominent leaders and the best friend of Eddie LeRoux. She's married to Van Elder. Mercy's praenex gift is precognition—she sees the future in brief visions.

- Tern Journey (TJ) LeRoux (he/him), Lt. Commander, SciCorps, age 18

  TJ is a pilot and officer in SciCorps, the militarized scientific and space exploration branch of Scorch government. He's a praenex of French descent. His parents are the leaders of SciCorps. He is Eddie's twin brother, Van Elder's best friend, and husband of May Forge. TJ is a technically savvy polyglot, gifted in linguistics and interspecies communication.

- Sylvan (VAN) Cré Elder (he/him), First Lieutenant, Terran Army Corps, age 18

  Van Elder is a soldier and farmer. He's a traditional human or sapiens of African-Irish descent from Alberta Farms, an Irish resettlement. Van's father is a popular general and he is the best friend of TJ LeRoux. He's married to Mercy Adams. Van stands out among praenex because of his large size.

Supporting Characters

- **ADMIRAL Yuri LeRoux** (he/him) (praenex) – A leader of SciCorps and father of Eddie and TJ. Husband to Fleet Admiral Pèlerine Reine LeRoux.

- **Sheriff Arson Henderson** (he/him) (praenex) –Terran Army officer and MP from The Verge, May Forge's uncle, and Dixie Henderson's son.

- **Bozan Rumesa Kahinu** (they/them) (praenex) – Eddie's mentor, Legion cleric.

- **COUSTEAU** – TJ's dog.

- **General Addiction (Dixie) Ramirez Henderson** (she/her) (praenex) – Terran Army officer, Mayor of The Verge, May Forge's grandmother, and Arson's mother.

- **FLEET Admiral Pèlerine Reine leRoux** (she/her) (praenex) – The supreme leader of SciCorps and mother to Eddie and TJ. Wife to Admiral Yuri LeRoux.

- **Gran Bozan Li** (she/her) (praenex) – Former spiritual leader of Scorch, deceased.

- **ILORIN Orlov** (she/her) (praenex) – Terra Faire Secretary of State, and Cai's friend and advisor.

- **Jealousy (LUCY) Meadow Forge** (she/her) (praenex) – Long lost mother of May Forge; rescued by Rill, she gave birth to Vengi while living in the SSWRS. Sister to Arson Forge, and daughter of General Dixie Henderson.

- **Lt. Caesar Naveen** (they/them) (praenex) – SciCorps soldier and the group's Pilgrim rival.

- **Lady PIPER** – May's dog.

- **RILL Ban O'Brien** (he/him) (sapiens) – Caretaker of the SSWRS, an engineer, and leader of the station.

- **Robbery (ROBB) and Poacher (PO)** (he/his) (praenex) – Two resourceful Couvie brothers who were rescued by Rill and live in the SSWRS.

- **Vengeance (VENGI) Ramirez Forge** (he/him) (praenex) – 12-year-old brother of May Forge, son of Lucy Forge. An inventor born and raised in the SSWRS, Vengi is prescient.

Other Titles by Sandra Macek

If you enjoyed FLARE, be sure to catch the beginning of the saga with

available at Amazon.

Coming in 2025:

MAGMA

Book 3 of the Scorched Earth Series

The biosphere in Chileru feels like a dream for Eddie LeRoux, full of music, intriguing new friends, and important scientific work to defeat a killer disease. The war back home seems a million miles away—until bombs start falling on her head.

Acknowledgements

A second book is all about momentum. My greatest thanks to my family—Steve, Parker, and Rebecca—for continuing to believe in me and providing me with the freedom to continue writing about Scorch. To them, Mom's writing time has become a new normal, but I recognize it for what is—their belief that my writing is essential to my happiness. Thanks so much, my awesome family!

The Society for Children's Book Writers and Illustrators (SCBWI) has always been my writing home. I continue to appreciate the camaraderie of my local chapter members and the resources of my Illinois and Wisconsin organizations.

Flare would not be in your hands without Dorothy Dreyer, Lyssa Chiavari and the Snowy Wings Publishing team. My thanks for all their hard work that went into the publishing process.

And it wouldn't be so pretty without the clever cover design of Sarah Hansen of Okay Creations. I loved the Kindling cover, but this one takes my breath away. Thank you, Sarah, for capturing Scorch in vibrant color and flaring light.

My editor, Laurel Garver, challenged me to let you inside Cairo Varela's mind and heart. Laurel, thank you for helping me improve this story in ways that I couldn't have imagined. Your collaboration and insight went so much further than three vs. four dot ellipses! I'm grateful for your big ideas and small corrections alike. Additional thanks to my friends, Amy Sekili and Michele Moras, for providing additional proofreading in both English and French.

Merci!

Finally, thank you to the teachers, librarians and readers who share indie author titles like Kindling and Flare. There's no greater joy for a writer than knowing that readers enjoyed their story and recommended it to others. I hope also that you read some Seamus Heaney poems after Rill's terrible moment. Poetry inspires me almost as much as science fiction and I love to share it.

About the Author

Photo by Michael Delott

Sandra Macek is the author of the young adult sci-fi series Scorched Earth, which includes the novels Kindling, Flare, Magma, and Firestorm. After graduating with a degree in rhetoric, she dreamed of becoming a novelist; instead she got a job so she could eat. Now she's an IT professional by day and a writer by night—surviving suburbia on a continuous diet of science fiction. Given the chance to be anyone else, she'd be Buffy, Bella, or any woman in Paris.

You can find her online at SandraMacek.com